I0788455

THE MAKING
OF AN
ASSASSIN
ATLANTA

By

JIM WEST

My special thanks go to my longer than time itself friend, John Fleenor, whose satirical wit keeps me straight. Thank you, John.

ISBN
Hardcover: 978-1-964289-36-6
Paperback: 978-1-964289-21-2

Other Books by Jim West

DNAlien

DNAlien II

DNAlien III

Genocide by GMO

To the memory of my father, a man who could say more with just a glance than any man I've ever known. Speaking little and never raising his voice, he taught me with his actions, not his words.

Although there were times I never realized what valuable lessons I was learning through the many years I watched my father working on the farm and interacting with all the neighbors, now I look back and see the value of everything that he imparted to me during those critical years.

His acceptance of my mistakes and his insistence on me assuming responsibility for each of my numerous errors in judgment laid the foundation for the way I am today.

From complete honesty to keeping your word, even when it wasn't in your best interest, he gave me the rules of life for any man. The shake of a hand meant more than the signature on any piece of paper a thousand lawyers wrote. When you lose your honor, you lose everything that has meaning among honest men.

Regardless of the punishment he dispensed, he never stopped loving me and accepting me as the person I was then and became in later years.

My greatest hope is that I may be half the man as the hero of my youth.

ACKNOWLEDGMENTS

I would like to express my appreciation for all the people who helped me complete this novel.

First and most importantly, I'd like to thank all the members of the United States military. Regardless of the branch of service, I've got the deepest respect for each and every single one of you. Although I served in both the Navy and the Air Force, I've dealt closely with the other branches and have many friends and family who served from WWII through today's conflicts in the Middle East.

Throughout the book, I've used various forms of writing the rank of officers, sometimes abbreviated, sometimes not. Lieutenants are Lt., regardless of whether a 2nd or 1st and called *Lieutenant*. Captains are Capt. Lieutenant Colonels are written as Lt. Col. but called *Colonel* when addressed. Colonels are Col. and called *Colonel*. Generals are addressed as *General*, regardless of the number of stars.

I'd specifically like to thank the following individuals for their stories, mildly chastising me for my mistakes, and efforts to ensure accuracy where required:

Col. Matt Campbell, USMC, 1970–1996

Capt. Ray Barber, USMC, 1957–1965

S. Sgt. Eugene C. Lashley, USMC, 1966–1970

Dr. Fred Allison, USMC Historical Division, Marine Corps Base, Quantico, Virginia

Annette Amerman, USMC Historical Division (Research), Marine Corps Base, Quantico, Virginia

And as always, I want to thank my very good friend John Fleenor and my cousin Kay Pratka. I'm never sure just how much they can put up with my efforts to write. But regardless of my errors in wording, punctuation, verbiage, spelling, or continuity of thought, they help provide at least a semiliterate result.

To these people and the countless others who provided their stories or experiences, thanks.

PROLOGUE

They were heading slightly east of due south as the sun continued its relentless slide toward the horizon in the west. American Airlines flight 387 was cruising at flight level 330 (FL 330) or 33,000 feet above sea level at a speed of .82 Mach, just a little over 639 miles per hour. For those true aficionados, it's about 525 nautical miles (nm) per hour (knots or kts). With the jet stream running almost perpendicular to their southerly flight path as was typical across the Northern United States during the winter months, their ground speed was roughly the same as the airspeed.

The flight originated at Chicago's O'Hare International Airport (ORD) and headed for Hartsfield-Jackson Atlanta International Airport (ATL). The distance of 527 nm was scheduled to take just over one and a half hours, including taxi time out of ORD and into ATL. They would arrive two and a half hours after the departure because of the one-hour time difference. The takeoff at 5:35 p.m. was just before sunset, and for the majority of the flight, the copilot, First Officer Jim Lashley, had been enjoying the prolonged setting sun, watching the beautiful pink, blue, and orange colors slowly fade as it sank below the horizon.

The first half of the flight had been very smooth, with little to no miscellaneous vectors from either O'Hare departure or Chicago Center Air Traffic Control (ATC). Jim had flown the inbound leg from New York, and now Capt. Randy Johnson was handling the flight to Atlanta. The number one Flight Attendant, Amber Bell, had brought their dinner just after level off, and they were waiting for her to finish serving the first-class passengers before she checked on them again. The now-empty trays were sitting on the open cockpit jump seat of the McDonald Super 80 as Randy monitored the autopilot and Jim monitored the radios.

"Any plans for Atlanta?" Randy asked as he adjusted his seat to recline slightly more.

"Not really," Jim answered as he switched the radio to the new frequency Chicago ATC had just given him. "I'll probably just hit the room and check my e-mail to see if anything exciting has happened."

"Indy Center, American 387 at 330," Jim spoke into his microphone that rested just against his lips.

The single earpiece in his right ear received the acknowledgment as well as the overhead speaker that was currently turned on. "Good evening, American 387, Indy Center. How's the ride?"

"Smooth so far," Jim replied. "Any reports further south?"

"Some light chop around Louisville from a United about forty-five minutes in front of you," a voice from Indianapolis Center told him.

"Thanks," Jim answered, taking his hand from the microphone switch on the control yoke.

"I'll let the Flight Attendants know," Randy said as he unhooked the telephone handle just behind the center console.

After advising Amber of the probability of rougher air and hearing that most of the service was concluding, Randy replaced the handset, lowered his armrest, and relaxed in his seat.

"What about you?" Jim asked. "Any plans for the night?"

"Park the bird, ride the bus, sign in at the front desk, find the room, change clothes, hit the bar, and hit the bed," Randy told him. "Standard layover, another night in another hotel."

"Yep," Jim said, nodding. "Three days, six legs, two hotels, and no time to sightsee."

"Not to mention that it's been so late every night when we get to the hotel," Randy told him. "But at least it's not one of those 3:00 a.m. wake-ups in New York. Hell, that's two o'clock on my body. That's about when I go to bed back home in Fort Worth."

"Small blessing," Jim said as he emptied the last of his Dr Pepper into the Styrofoam cup now half filled with melting ice. Draining the last few drops, he turned and placed the empty can on the finished dinner trays.

"What's this been?" Randy asked as he turned to look at Jim. "It's got to be the fourth time we've made this trip this month."

"Sounds about right," Jim said. "Probably get the exact same rooms as last time."

"Probably so," Randy acknowledged. "It'd be simpler if we just left our civvies in the rooms."

"I've thought about that," Jim told him. "But there're at least four more crews that use the same rooms when we're not there."

"I can solve that," Randy said, smiling. "Every crew

member keeps his clothes in a hang-up bag. Then, after the last trip, they take them home."

Jim frowned and said, "Might be rather smelly after a month of hanging in a closet with all those other sweaty things, don't you think?"

"No problem," Randy said, shaking his head. "We just take a couple of those urinal cakes and drop them in the bottoms of the bags."

"I just hope you get fresh ones," Jim answered, laughing. "But knowing how cheap you can be on a layover, you'd probably get yours from the men's room in the restaurant."

"Of course not," Randy said with a pained expression on his face. "I'm not really cheap. I just have three ex-wives that get the majority of my pay."

"So I've heard, so I've heard," Jim said, shaking his head. "Ever thought of marrying someone that's not a Flight Attendant? Maybe they wouldn't know all the ways to catch you screwing around and take your pay."

"Tried that with number 2," Randy replied. "She just found a lawyer that had handled other airline divorces. Same result."

"How about not screwing around?" Jim asked.

"It's about to get to that," Randy acknowledged. "Mostly hags and fags now anyway since they removed all those very, *very* necessary restrictions on who can be Flight Attendants."

"How about switching sides, taking one of the sweet boys?" Jim joked. "If you'd pick the right one, you could double your wardrobe, and he wouldn't worry about you with other women."

"Nope," Randy told him emphatically. "Think I'll stay with the team I've got. Though there may be a lot of problems dealing with them, women are the most delightful beings in the world."

"I'll go along with that," Jim said as he watched a shooting star cross the darkening horizon miles to the west of them.

Jim leaned back and began to run through everything he needed to do once he'd checked into the hotel. Contrary to what he'd told Randy, his plans tonight would hopefully conclude all the effort he'd taken on the previous three nights in Atlanta and leave the next morning with his mission accomplished and no possible trace of him having fulfilled his first contract with Muddy Water.

Page Blank Intentionally

CHAPTER 1

Before American Airlines, Jim Lashley had been a typical kid growing up in rural America. And as a typical kid, he got into typical troubles as he tried to find his way into adulthood. The biggest difference between Jim's early life and today was the Vietnam War. Having lost his college exemption because of some errant behavior, he decided to join the Marines instead of being drafted into the Army.

And like so many young men during that time, Jim had previously never even considered taking another human life. But the Drill Sergeants and instructors at his numerous training assignments taught him the basics and assured him that he'd do the right thing for his country when the time came.

And the time finally came. Almost nine months into his second tour in Vietnam, Jim found himself, along with his 11-man reconnaissance team, on a small hill watching a group of about 100 or so Viet Cong (VC) crossing the valley below. Suddenly, the men below broke into groups of 10 to 15 men and began fanning out toward where Jim and his team were hiding.

When it became evident that they had been spotted, and after Jim radioed for help, they began to crawl back down the hill, hoping to be gone before the enemy got to them. As they neared the bottom and headed to the nearest tree line, the first shots rang out. Another group of VCs was waiting as they fled.

Returning fire as they raced for cover, their only hope for salvation would be if the fighter aircraft and the rescue helicopters could get there before they were slaughtered by the overwhelming enemy forces.

In what seemed like hours but were only minutes, most of Jim's teammates were either dead or badly wounded. When a flight of F-4s finally arrived and began strafing the ground between Jim and the VC, Jim grabbed a wounded teammate and carried him to a small clearing where the chopper could land and get them out of the death trap. Laying the dying man on the ground, Jim made nine more trips to bring the rest of his team to the clearing.

On board the chopper and heading back to their base, Jim held the only other survivor as he watched the blood leaking from his friend soak his clothes as the life seeped out of him. Now the only man left alive from his team, Jim finally learned the lesson his Sergeants had told him would happen—life was cheap. And it was better to take it than have it taken from you.

Jim's actions that day didn't go unnoticed. The pilot in the lead aircraft who had been responsible for driving the VC back so the rescue could take place was, in fact, the Commanding General of the division. As soon as Jim's wounds had been tended to, he was directed to report to the Commander, General Gene Barker.

During the meeting, he learned that this was the second

time a recon team had lost their lives on that particular hill. Jim's reward for his actions in getting every single body, alive or dead, off the hill was to be assigned to his choice of base upon return to the United States.

The biggest surprise was when he was offered the chance to become a Marine pilot. The shortage of pilots was well-known but generally required a college degree; however, General Barker explained that a little-known program called MARCAD (Marine Cadet Aviation Program) would make it possible for Jim to receive his commission as a Lieutenant in the Marine Corps and attend flight training with only two years of college or its equivalent.

After returning to the United States and visiting his family, Jim was flying to San Diego (SAN) when he happened to meet a cute little redheaded Flight Attendant whose name tag simply read "Jewell." The obvious chemistry between them started the minute Jim walked aboard the airplane.

Stopping Jim as he stepped on the plane, Jewell asked, "May I see your ticket, Sergeant?"

Handing her his ticket, Jim asked, "Is there something wrong, Miss?"

"There certainly is," Jewell smiled. "Your ticket says you have a seat in coach on this flight. But I'm sure that's a mistake."

"What do you mean?" Jim asked.

"I mean that you'll have to sit up here in first class so I can keep an eye on you," Jewell said as she pointed to two empty seats.

During the flight, Jim was provided all the comforts of first class, numerous drinks, and an occasional visit when Jewell would come to sit and visit. The almost four-hour flight seemed to fly by.

Jewell asked Jim to wait until all the other passengers had gotten off before he left. Finally, alone after all passengers and the rest of the crew had gone, Jewell sat in the seat beside Jim and asked, "What are your plans for the next few weeks, Sergeant?"

"Not really sure," Jim answered. "I'm reporting to Camp Pendleton for duty. Not sure exactly how long I'll be there."

"How far is that from San Diego?" Jewell asked as she cocked her head and looked at Jim.

"Not exactly sure," Jim told her. "I think it's 40 or 50 miles north. Why?"

With a mischievous smile, Jewell answered, "Because I'll have three or four layovers here this month. And I just thought that maybe you could find your way back down to San Diego for a night or two."

Stunned, Jim could only say, "I'd like that. I can't make any promises, but if you give me the name of the hotel and the nights you'll be here, I'll do my best."

"I think I'll like your best, Sergeant," Jewell said as she handed Jim a note she had already prepared. "I also added my home number, just in case."

At Pendleton, Jim was immediately taken to the headquarters, where he was presented with his second Purple Heart and the Silver Star for his actions in bringing all his team back from the failed mission. Also, he was given a transcript with 60 hours of credits from Palomar, the college located on the base. That entitled him to become a Cadet in the MARCAD program at Pensacola Naval Air Station. His orders for transfer, along with the airline tickets to get there, were handed to him in an envelope as he was dismissed.

Realizing that his orders meant flying to Florida the

following morning, Jim wondered if he'd ever run into Jewell again.

The next day after arriving at SAN, Jim presented his ticket for the flight to Florida. Noting that it had a change of planes at Dallas-Fort Worth (DFW), his hopes were optimistic that he'd see her again.

When the flight crew arrived at the gate, Jim looked anxiously at the Flight Attendants, just hoping she'd be there. But when the boarding began, Jewell wasn't to be seen. Somewhat let down, Jim took his seat toward the rear of the plane and waited for the flight to depart.

Just before the door was shut, and as the last passenger was coming down the aisle, Jim saw Jewell walking toward him. As she reached his seat, she said, "There are a couple of open seats in first class if you're interested. But there's an entire row toward the back that we can share if you'd like some company back to Texas."

"I'd like that," Jim said with a huge smile on his face.

"I figured you would," Jewell said as she led the way to the rear of the plane. "I'll bet the service back here will be better than up in first class."

"I can hardly wait," Jim replied as he slid into one of the seats. "Don't you have to work?" Jim asked as she sat in the seat beside him.

"Nope," Jewell answered as she put her hand on Jim's leg. "I was supposed to be on a later flight, but they rescheduled me to go back to DFW on this one. Then I fly to Chicago this afternoon. And I thought you were supposed to be stationed here anyway. Why are you going back so soon?"

"Change of orders," Jim said as the plane started pushing back from the gate.

"Guess I'm lucky to be on this flight," she told him.

"Otherwise, we might have missed each other."

"Maybe some things are just meant to be," Jim said as he put his hand over hers.

"Maybe so," Jewell said as Jim squeezed her hand. "Maybe so."

CHAPTER 2

After landing at DFW, Jim traded his ticket to Pensacola (PNS) for a ticket to Amarillo and called home to get his dad to come get him. He had a couple of extra days before his class was supposed to start, and he really wanted to take his car.

After spending the night at home, Jim tossed his bag and some extra clothes in the trunk of his old Corvette told his folks goodbye once again, and headed for Florida.

Finally arriving at Pensacola late in the evening, Jim stopped at the gate and showed the guard his ID and orders.

"Welcome, Sergeant," the Corporal said. "You need to check in at the headquarters building. It's just down the road where you see the flag."

"Thanks," Jim said, taking his ID back. "See you around."

After checking in, he was assigned a room in the MARCAD barracks, where he would share a room with three other Cadets. He selected one of the four empty beds and put his bag on top, signaling that the bed was taken. With nothing else to do, he decided to head into town to see if there was somewhere to get a burger.

Stopping at the gate, he asked the guard where he could find someplace good to eat, and he recommended a small burger joint just short of downtown, telling Jim they had a really cute little waitress there.

A few minutes later, Jim parked in the almost empty lot, took a seat, and waited for the waitress to arrive.

When the young lady wearing an apron came to his table, Jim smiled at her and ordered a medium rare cheeseburger with mustard, mayonnaise, and all the fixings, french fries, and a Dr Pepper. Scribbling his order on the ticket, she told him she would be right back with his drink and turned away.

Glancing out the window, Jim sat waiting and watched the cars passing on the road outside. He could see the reflections of a couple of other people in the glass and overheard much of their conversation. Having noticed their short haircuts, he assumed that they were attached to the base, but their conversations gave him no clue as to what they did there.

Waiting for his meal, Jim reopened the packet he had been given at the gate and started reading. The first thing he determined was that there was no flying here at Pensacola for at least three months. The curriculum included classes on aerodynamics, the Uniform Code of Military Justice (UCMJ), math, physics, engineering, physical training, and leadership.

Jim had no problems with the UCMJ or physical fitness classes; he had almost three years of daily application of these most rudimentary Marine requirements. There might be some problems with physics and engineering, though. His test scores when he graduated from high school indicated an aptitude for math and engineering, but his performance in college hadn't been much to brag about. But then, he hadn't really applied himself. Chuckling to himself, he remembered the days he slept through most of the classes, having spent the night before pursuing either beer, women, or both—usually both.

As the waitress approached with his Dr Pepper, Jim thanked her and continued thinking about the academic program. Although he had a lot of time flying around Texas in the little airplanes his father had owned, his only knowledge of aerodynamics was that if you went fast enough, you would fly. If you slowed down enough, you would land. Wondering just what they would expect him to learn past that, he could only imagine. *It couldn't be too tough, though,* he thought. *Some of the dumbest people he had ever met could fly an airplane.*

He was just beginning to read the part of the curriculum that covered the actual flying when his burger arrived. Sliding the material back into the packet, Jim thanked the waitress as she placed the plate in front of him. Pouring a copious amount of ketchup on the fries, augmenting the mustard and mayo on the burger as well, Jim was pleased to see the meat wasn't overcooked.

The first bite of the burger was perfect; the juice from the patty oozed down his chin, mixed with the excess ketchup and other condiments. Pulling a handful of napkins from the holder, Jim wiped his face and knew he had found the closest thing to a What-a-burger he could expect around here. This would definitely be where he would eat every chance he got.

Finally finished with his meal, Jim picked up his packet and ticket. Leaving a good tip, he walked to the counter, where the cash register and waitress were. "That was about the best hamburger I've ever had," he said as he handed her a twenty.

"Thanks," the waitress replied as she took his ticket and rang up the sale. "You from the base?"

"Just got here," Jim answered as she counted his change back to him. "You'll probably see a lot more of me in the months to come."

"Oh," she said, looking at him, smiling. "Is it for the burger or for the atmosphere?"

Recognizing the flirtation, Jim grinned back and answered, "Probably both, Ma'am. I haven't had a chance to see much around here, but I doubt there's much to beat what's right here."

Blushing, the waitress told him, "Well, you just hurry back any chance you get. By the way, my name is Jennifer, and my Mom and Dad own this little place."

"Nice to meet you, Jennifer. My name's Jim, and I'll certainly do just that," Jim replied as he turned for the door. "I'll *definitely* keep that in mind. You have a nice day."

Poor Marines around here better watch out, Jim thought as he opened the door to the 'Vette. *Bet I'm not the first Jarhead that little lady has tried to snare just to get a ticket out of here.*

The trip back to the base went quickly, and the gate guard was standing beside the booth as he drove up. Slowing to show the Corporal his ID, Jim was waved through without completely stopping. Knowing that the Marine probably remembered him or his car from his previous entry and exit within the last hour or so, Jim just waved and headed for his quarters.

Several more cars now littered the parking lot when he pulled in. As soon as he approached his room, he noticed the door open and a guy wearing slacks and a short-sleeved knit shirt opening a suitcase on one of the other beds.

Tapping on the door as he entered, Jim said, "Hey, guess I've got my first roommate. I'm Jim Lashley."

The other man turned and answered, "Hi, Jim, I'm Ray Sproc."

Jim shook Ray's hand and replied, "Good to meet you, Ray. Where'd you come in from?"

"Philadelphia," Ray answered. "How about you?"

Jim pulled one of the chairs around the table out and sat, saying, "Well, I'm originally from a small town in West Texas, but it's been a few years since I really lived there."

Ray continued unpacking his suitcase and said, "I see from your bag on the bed that you're already a Marine. I guess this is all old hat for you."

"Not really," Jim answered as he watched Ray. "Some of this is familiar, but this program is different in a lot of ways from what I've done before."

"Really?" Ray asked as he slid his empty suitcase under his bed. "What'd you do before you came here?"

Jim leaned back, crossing his legs beneath the table, and said, "Oh, I guess you'd say I was just another grunt slogging through the mud, doing whatever I was told."

Ray took a chair opposite Jim and asked, "You have to go to Vietnam?"

"Yeah, I went," Jim answered. "Twice. Did a lot of slogging through the mud and jungle over there. That's what Marines do."

Ray mulled it over and told him, "I never really thought about being a Marine, but I was pretty sure I didn't want to stay in Philly. I guess the thing that swayed me was the chance to fly one of those fast planes I saw on the news. I'm not sure I want to do much work in the mud, and I know I don't want to spend any time in the jungle."

"Well," Jim answered, "I don't know exactly how this

MARCAD program works, but generally, a Marine is a Marine. If they need you to be a mud grunt, you're a mud grunt. This may be different, but I wouldn't count on it in the long term."

"Well," Ray responded, "the recruiter that signed me up for this program told me that I'd be a pilot and not have to go through all the other stuff."

Jim just smiled and said, "Maybe you're right. I'm sure that your recruiter knows more about this program than I do. Either way, it looks like we've got a few months to determine exactly what we've gotten into."

Jim got up and started putting his clothes in one of the lockers. As he finished hanging his uniforms in the closet, he said, "I'm gonna take a shower and do a little more reading about what they expect from us for the next few weeks. I'd bet that come Monday, we learn a lot more about things than what's written in the pamphlets they've given us."

Jim grabbed his shave kit and headed for the showers with a towel wrapped around his waist. The flip-flops on his feet made their customary noise as he walked down the hall. He smiled to himself, wondering how this young Philly boy was going to fare in the coming weeks and how he would do with the academics as well as putting up with some of the civilians he was sure to meet either tomorrow or Monday.

CHAPTER 3

The next morning, Jim rose early and quietly headed for the showers, trying not to wake Ray, knowing that once their class officially started, sleeping in was going to be a luxury. As he entered the "head," the Marine terminology for the bathroom, Jim encountered several other men showering, shaving, or using the other facilities. Nodding a good morning to them, he sat his shave kit beside one of the sinks and removed the items he would need to prepare for the day.

Although most of the men had the standard Marine haircut, there were a couple who still had long hair. It wasn't hippie length, but it was a far cry from regulation. Even officers kept their hair strictly within the narrow guidelines, although a few of them who weren't in the field had the *high and tight* close-cropped coif that the enlisted men usually had.

Once finished with his morning rituals, Jim headed back down the hall to his room. Easing the door open, Jim saw Ray sitting on the edge of his bed, scratching his scalp. "Morning," Jim said as he hung his wet towel on the end of his bed.

"Good morning," Ray responded. "What's on your schedule today?"

"Not much," Jim answered as he took his Wranglers out of the closet. "Thought I'd ask around to see where most of the guys eat here on base. After breakfast, I'll probably drive around a little and scout out the terrain. What about you?" Jim continued as he pulled on a clean T-shirt and sat on the edge of his bed. "Got anything planned?"

"No, guess not," Ray answered. "From what I've read, things don't get started until tomorrow when we meet our class leader. Maybe I'll see if there's someplace to get a few things I forgot."

"That's great," Jim told him as he pulled his boots on. "We can go to the Exchange for whatever you need. Since you don't have an ID yet, I'll be glad to buy it for you."

"What's an Exchange?" Ray asked.

"Sort of like a large department store," Jim explained. "They've got just about everything you'd need from the bottom of your feet to the top of your head."

"Sounds good," Ray responded as he took his shaving kit from beneath the bed. "I'll get ready as fast as I can."

"No rush," Jim told him as he made his bed and put all his things away. "I'll be downstairs in the common room getting a little 'intel' before we start our recon."

Ray nodded and headed toward the showers. Jim followed him out the door and advised him, "Just a suggestion. You might want to make sure your bed is made, and all your things are squared away before you leave the room."

Ray stopped and asked, "Squared away?"

"Put away," Jim explained. "Clothes in the closet, personal items in the chest of drawers, bed made, kind of like your mother probably made you do."

"Squared away," Ray murmured, shaking his head. "Guess I've got to learn a new language along with the rest of this."

"You'll catch on," Jim answered as he headed toward the stairs. "The Marines have their own unique way of saying things. Much of it comes from the Navy, but the Marines bring their own jargon to the table. See you in a few."

Downstairs, Jim saw several men in neatly pressed khaki pants and shirts sitting around. Noticing the unique emblem on the epaulets, he surmised it represented the rank of the Cadet versus those of commissioned officers. There were some who had the Navy anchor and others who sported the Marine globe and anchor on their hats. Additionally, there was a set of wings that resembled the old Army Air Corps affixed to their collars.

Approaching one of the men with the Marine emblem, Jim introduced himself, "Good morning. I'm Jim Lashley."

"Nice to meet you. I'm Mark Barber," he said. "You just get in?"

"Yesterday," Jim answered. "How about you?"

"I've been here a little over two months," Mark told him. "I'd guess that you're about to start with the new class tomorrow."

"That's correct," Jim said. "Mind if I ask you a few questions?"

"Not at all," Mark answered. "What'd you need to know?"

"First, is there a specific chow hall for us? Or do we use the Enlisted or Officers' Clubs?" Jim asked.

"We have our own club called ACRAC. I think that stands for Aviation Cadet Recreational Club, but it's only open on Friday and Saturday nights," Mark told him. "And you don't get to go there until you've been here about eight weeks."

"Once everybody in my class arrives, we'll march to the mess hall that's reserved for the base staff and us for breakfast," he continued. "Then it's on to the religious services. After that, we pretty much have the rest of the day to ourselves. Since your class hasn't started, I'd guess that you can wander around as you wish."

"Any problem with wearing civvies?" Jim questioned.

"Not for now," Mark responded. "Most of your class is probably just out of college, and you won't get your uniforms until tomorrow. Until then, wear what you got."

"What about you?" Mark continued. "Did you just get out of college? I'd guess from your haircut, you're previously enlisted."

"I guess you can say both," Jim explained. "I'm about a year from the end of my enlistment, and I also just completed the credits to qualify for MARCAD."

"Welcome," Mark said. "I'm sure you'll find this place is a lot like boot camp at the start, but that shouldn't be a problem for you. Once you get through the indoctrination week, it's more like college until you finish the preflight phase."

"What's the preflight phase like?" Jim asked.

"Well, like I said, the first week is indoc, which is mostly getting your uniforms, haircuts, and learning the basic rules. Then you'll have classes all day and lots of PT," Mark told him. "It's not too bad, but it's sort of like trying to take a drink from a fire hose."

"Wow," Jim said. "Sounds like it's going to be some serious studying. When do we get to start flying?"

"After you pass all the academics, swimming, and PT

tests," Mark answered. "That takes another two months or so. Then you'll move up to Saufley Field for the initial flight training."

"What about going off base?" Jim asked.

"You'll be given weekend liberty once you get to Saufley," Mark explained. "You can go off base from Friday afternoon until 1600 Sunday, but you have to wear your uniform until you solo the T-34."

"Well," Jim responded, shaking his head, "it certainly does sound a lot like boot camp. At least there isn't a Drill Instructor here."

"Oh, but there is," Mark laughed. "The DIs will march you everywhere and teach you the Marine way until you finish preflight. The First Lieutenant that's assigned as your class leader is only there if you have problems. No, sir, the DIs are your mother until you get out of preflight."

"And I thought I'd left that behind three years ago," Jim mused. "I never anticipated having a hard-assed DI hovering over me again."

"Hey," Mark said, "it's still the Marines, and most of us guys are straight out of college. How'd you expect to learn everything? I guess they figured that what worked on the new enlisted troops works just as well on us." Mark finished, "Anyway, my class is all here, and we've got to get into formation and march to chow. Take care, and I'll see you around during the next couple of months."

"You too," Jim replied. "Good to meet you, and thanks for the info."

Jim watched as Mark's class fell into formation, and the razor-sharp Marine DI ordered them forward. Remembering his days back at boot camp, Jim wondered how many days it would take to bring the bunch of college kids up to speed on the Marine way of doing things and how many would fall by the wayside during training.

CHAPTER 4

Jim was standing in the common room when Ray came down the stairs. "Learn anything?" Ray asked as he looked around the room.

"A little," Jim answered. "Looks like we better take advantage of today if we want to get off the base. It's gonna be a couple of months before we get to go again."

"Two months?" Ray asked incredulously. "What are we supposed to do for two months? Just sit around here?"

"Two months is nothing," Jim told him. "That's about like going to boot camp, but you don't need to worry about sitting around. There's plenty of stuff to keep you from being bored. You're in for a whole new world here, and it ain't gonna be like college where you can hang out with your friends and chase the girls."

"When do we get to go off base?" Ray asked, resigned to the fact that his life was no longer in his control.

"When we finish preflight," Jim told him as he headed for the door. "Don't even think about going to town until that's done. Just concentrate on the job at hand and take it one day at a time. You'll be surprised at how fast the time passes. Now let's hit the Exchange, and then we'll go to a little hamburger joint I found yesterday."

At the car, they climbed in, and Jim started shaking his head as he contemplated his decision to become a Marine pilot instead of finishing his enlisted time and going home. More basic training wasn't exactly what he wanted at this point.

Once at the Exchange, Jim told Ray to follow him into the store and pick up whatever he thought he'd need. "Just keep it to the basics," Jim told him as they entered. "Deodorant, toothpaste, soap, just personal items."

"What about socks, underwear, T-shirts?" Ray asked as he put several items into the basket he was carrying.

"Didn't you bring enough to last a week or so?" Jim asked, wondering just how someone could come here without an adequate supply of basic needs.

"I guess," Ray responded. "I just don't know how much of everything I'll need before I get to wash clothes. I'd rather have too many than have to wear them more than a day or so."

"I'd say that if you can go a week without having to wash clothes, that'd be enough," Jim answered. "But you make your own decision. It may be one of the last decisions you get to make for yourself over the next year or so."

"What does that mean?" Ray asked as he finished loading his basket.

"It means that there'll be someone making most of your decisions as to what to wear, when to eat, where to go, just about every aspect of your daily life," Jim told him knowingly.

"Crap," Ray said as they approached the cashier. "I wonder if it's too late to tell them that I've changed my mind and just go back home and finish college."

Jim stopped quickly and turned to Ray, saying, "Now listen, my friend. You can quit anytime you want. But if you think the Marines are going to spend half of a million dollars training you and let you play with their multimillion-dollar airplanes without making sure you can handle every aspect of being a Marine, then you better reconsider where your priorities lie."

Ray stood still as Jim continued, "Being a Marine is one of the most demanding things you'll ever attempt. And being a Marine pilot is something that most people can only dream about. You've been given a chance that very few can only imagine. Yes, it's going to be tough for the next year and a half. But the reward is something that will last for the rest of your life. Even with giving it everything you've got, we'll probably lose half of our class before it's over. This isn't a game, Ray. Not only are you signing up to learn to fly, but you're also placing yourself at the tip of the spear when you're sent to fight."

Jim looked Ray square in the eyes and told him, "I've been through worse programs than this, and I've seen what happens to those who are in the fight. If there's any doubt in your mind, put that crap back on the shelves, pack your bag, and go home to mommy."

Jim waited for a response and then said, "If you really want to be a Marine pilot, I'll do my best to help you in any way I can. Being a Marine is more like being a brother to every other Marine. We stand together and help one another in every way possible. But you've got to earn their trust and respect as well as carry your share of the load."

Ray stood quietly listening to Jim and finally answered, "I guess it's just happening so fast, and I'm maybe a little unsure of myself right now."

Jim put his hand on Ray's shoulder and said, "I know,

believe me, I know just how you feel right now. I remember the first day at boot camp, having the DI screaming at us, being told how worthless we were, and watching everything I thought I knew being reduced to nothing. But if you just hang tough for a couple of months, you'll find the best friends you'll ever know for the rest of your life."

Pausing for just a second, Jim told Ray, "Now let's pay for this shit and enjoy our last day of freedom for the next couple of months."

Jim took Ray's basket and showed his ID card as the cashier rang up the total. After paying, Jim took the bags and headed out the door, with Ray solemnly following.

Once back in the car, they sped toward the gate as Ray tried to come to grips with his new future. Through the gate, they headed straight to the burger shop, and Jim wondered if Ray would be one of the many who just couldn't handle the pressure and demands that would be required over the next 18 months.

Pulling into the parking lot, Jim said, "There's a pretty cute girl that waited on me yesterday. Maybe she'll be here today. I must admit, I'd rather be served by a tiny hiney than most of those grain-fed heifers that work at most of the fast-food places."

As they walked into the diner, Jim noticed the same waitress and went to the booth where he had sat just yesterday, hoping that she would serve them this time.

"Well, hello again, Jim," Jennifer smiled as she placed two menus in front of them. "Back to see me or just for the food?"

"A little of both," Jim told her, returning her smile. "This is my new friend and roommate, Ray. Ray, this is Jennifer."

"Hello, Ray," she said, barely glancing his way. "What

would you gentlemen like to drink?"

"Dr Pepper, please," Jim said. "Also, I'd like another of your mighty fine burgers, medium rare, and with everything on it and an order of tater tots."

"You got it, honey," she answered. Turning to Ray, she asked, "What for you, sir?"

"I guess I'll have the same thing," Ray said, handing his menu back to her.

Turning back to Jim, she grinned and told them, "I'll be right back with your drinks, and the burgers will follow as quickly as I can get them."

Ray watched her walk away and asked, "Just how well did you get to know her yesterday?"

"Just chitchat while I was here," Jim responded as he watched her also.

"Well," Ray said, "You seem to have made an impression on her. I think she may even have a small crush on you. Did you notice that she barely acknowledged my presence?"

"Yeah, I noticed," Jim told him. "That's another thing you will probably learn while you're here. There are a lot of these young girls who are just waiting for the right man to walk through that door and take them away from here. If you think they don't know that they're in demand to the lonely Marines at the base, you would be wrong, oh so very, very wrong. And by right man, I mean *anyone* that will take them away."

"Are you trying to tell me that there are obstacles to worry about besides the training?" Ray smiled.

"Oh yes," Jim answered. "And don't forget that you can't get married until you finish all the training, and that's about 18 months down the road, not to mention that you'll change bases at least three times before you're done. Hell, by the time we get to come back here again, she'll probably have found another prospect."

When Jennifer returned with their drinks, she sat them on the table and put her hand on Jim's shoulder, saying, "Your burgers will be right out. If there's anything else you want, just let me know."

Jim shook his head as she walked away, saying, "I'm sure you know all about what happens when you put little boys and little girls together. Sooner or later, they'll take their clothes off and start playing. Just remember that you probably won't be the first Marine to jump into that foxhole, and always, *always,* dress your little soldier before you send him into battle."

"That's an interesting way of putting it," Ray acknowledged. "Pretty much the same back in college. If I learned one thing back there, it was to dress properly for the dance."

"Well, it's even more important here," Jim told him. "Some of the Marines have been overseas and might have brought back some *unwelcome friends* to attend the dance. Not to say that all of us have had to visit the Medic on occasion, but some of those bugs from Southeast Asia are pretty nasty and hard to get rid of."

As soon as the burgers arrived, Jim thanked Jennifer, and they ate silently as thoughts of what tomorrow would bring occupied their minds. Once finished, Jim waved for the check.

"Anything else?" she asked, putting the check in the middle of the table.

"Reckon not," Jim answered as he took the check. "Still one of the best burgers I've ever had, but it'll probably be a couple of months before I get to come back."

"Oh," she responded. "Nothing wrong, I hope."

"No," Jim told her as he stood. "We're just starting class tomorrow and can't leave the base for the first part. But don't worry, I'm sure both of us will be back as soon as they let us out the front gate again." Jim put a tip on the table and smiled. "Just keep making burgers like these, and you couldn't keep us away."

She walked with Jim to the register and took the money to pay the bill and retorted, "Well, if it's just burgers you come for, I'm sure they'll always be here."

"It's more than the burgers," Jim told her. "It's also the wonderful service and friendly atmosphere."

Smiling as she handed Jim his change, she replied, "I'm glad you think so, and I hope to see you again when they let you come back."

"I'm sure you will," Jim told her. "But for now, Ray and I have to get back on base. Thanks again."

"Nice to have met you," Ray said as he followed Jim toward the door.

"You too," she said as she returned to the table to start cleaning it.

Walking to the car, Ray said, "Well, I guess if I hope to get her attention, I'll have to come without you."

"Not a problem with me," Jim told him as they got into the car. "I wish you the best of luck with that one."

Back at the base, Jim parked the car, made sure the windows were up, and locked the doors, saying, "Don't guess I'll need this thing for a couple of months either."

"Probably not," Ray acknowledged as he waited for Jim to finish.

Once back in their room, Jim noticed suitcases sitting on the two remaining beds. "Looks like everybody's here. I'm going downstairs to make a phone call, and I'll see you later."

Again, trying to reach Jewell, Jim listened to the unanswered ringing until he was sure she wasn't home. Giving up, he returned to his room and met the two new members of his class. After normal greetings, Jim told them that he'd like to hit the sack early tonight since tomorrow would start pretty early.

After a few minutes of watching the new guys put their things in their closets and dressers, Jim finished filling out the forms from his packet, undressed, and crawled into bed, asking the last man to turn out the lights. As soon as everyone was in bed and the lights were out, Jim lay quietly, thinking about tomorrow's activities, until he finally fell asleep.

CHAPTER 5

At six o'clock the next morning, Jim had just returned from taking a shower and was quietly dressing when someone pounded on their door, shouting, "Rise and shine, my lovelies! Fall in downstairs in thirty minutes! *Let's go, let's go!*"

As the other three sprang upright in their beds, Jim told them, "Well, ladies, welcome to the Marine Corps. Today we get to meet our friendly advisor, the Drill Instructor. A word of advice, don't be late, or he'll ride your ass for the rest of your time here."

Jim finished lacing up his boots as the others quickly began either dressing or heading for the latrine. Shaking his head knowingly, Jim headed out the door with his completed forms so he would be waiting in the common room when the rest of his class arrived. Remembering boot camp, he knew to be ready when the DI got to the room where the pamphlets had said the initial formation would be. He also knew not to make himself conspicuous; his previous training would become evident soon enough.

Sitting in one of the chairs, reviewing his forms, Jim

watched as a few more men he hadn't seen before walked into the room. Shortly after that, Ray and several others arrived and took seats around the room. Noticing that none of them had brought their documents, Jim slightly smiled to himself, knowing that the DI would take this opportunity to let them know how unprepared this group of misfits were for the rigors of Marine training. *Well,* he thought, *let the fun begin!*

The DI marched into the room at precisely six thirty and barked, "On your feet, ladies! I want two straight lines facing me! Now fall in!"

Jim waited until approximately half of the class was standing beside one another, facing the DI, and then rose and walked to stand behind a man about his own size one-third of the way from the right end.

The minute the last man was barely standing, the DI shouted, "All right, ladies, when I tell you to fall in, I mean for you to *fall in* at attention! I want your heels together, your shoulders square, your thumbs touching the seams of your trousers, your head erect, facing forward, and your eyes looking straight ahead! Now before you bunch of pussies really piss me off, FALL THE FUCK IN!"

Knowing better than to smile right now, Jim snapped to attention and waited for the DI to address and correct each man in the front row. Words of disappointment spewed from the DI's mouth as he inspected every single man. Jim remained perfectly still until the DI finally reached him.

Staring directly into Jim's eyes, the DI said, "Finally, someone who at least has a vague concept of what standing at attention means. What's your name, Cadet?"

"Jim Lashley," Jim said without moving his eyes.

"Cadet Lashley, you mean, don't you?" the DI queried.

"Yes, Sergeant," Jim answered again, knowing not to

"sir" the DI.

The DI stood looking at Jim for another second and proceeded down the rear line until he finished correcting each man's stance. Finally, though, he marched to the front and turned to face them.

"My name is Staff Sergeant Wheeler," the DI told them. "You may call me Sergeant when I give you permission to speak. You are all now Cadets, and you will call each other Cadet when not in your rooms. Is that clear enough, or do some of you need me to explain it to you personally?"

Pausing barely a second, the DI loudly asked again, "Is that clear? Do none of you understand how to answer a basic question in English? Didn't your parents teach you to answer when asked a question?"

Not quite in unison, the men all said, "Yes, Sergeant."

"That's close," the DI said. "Now, do you Cadets know why you're here?"

"Yes, Sergeant," they replied almost together.

"I really, *reallllly* doubt that," the DI told them. "You think you are here to become Marine pilots, don't you?"

Before anyone could respond, he continued. "That is *not* correct. You are here to become Marines. Should any one of you fail to meet the high standards to become a Marine pilot, you will fulfill your obligation to the Marines in another fashion. My job is to make sure you will become Marines, and I don't give a rat's ass whether or not you become pilots. And you will become a Marine before I'm done with you. Are there any questions now?"

"No, Sergeant," came the unified voice of the class.

The DI continued, "All right, I want you to take your right hand and hold the forms you were directed to fill out waist-high in front of you for me to take. NOW!"

Having done this countless times before and knowing there would be no action, the DI scorned, "I can't believe it, I just can't believe it. A simple request for you to arrive with the completed forms, and you can't seem to handle it. You did read the instruction letter, didn't you?"

Standing with his hands on his hips, the DI looked at each man standing at attention before him and said, "We aren't off to a good start, are we, ladies? All right, when I give you the order to fall out, I want each and every one of you to be back in your exact position within five minutes with the completed forms. Do you think you can handle that?"

"Yes, Sergeant," the now concerned Cadets answered.

"Good," the DI said. "*Fall out!*"

The group almost stampeded, heading out of the door, leaving Jim standing alone. The DI walked directly to him and asked, "What are you waiting for, Cadet?"

No longer at attention, Jim reached behind his back and pulled the completed forms from where he had stuck them into the top of his trousers. Coming to attention, he handed them to the DI, saying, "I have mine with me, Sergeant."

Taking the forms, the DI said, "I expected you to, Cadet Lashley. I reviewed each application for this class and knew that a certain Staff Sergeant Lashley was going to be here. Don't think that cuts you any slack, Cadet. Do you understand that?"

Still at attention, Jim answered, "Yes, Sergeant."

"Good," the DI said as the rest of the class started arriving.

As the DI walked back to his original position, Jim relaxed and waited for the rest of them to fall into formation. As the last one arrived, the DI announced, "Class, TEN HUT!"

For the next couple of hours, the DI tried to teach the class the basics of marching as they gathered their new coveralls and other clothing items, had their heads shaved, fed, and returned so the cadets could put everything away and change out of their civilian clothes.

CHAPTER 6

Once the cadets were reformed in their coveralls, the DI brought them back to attention and told them, "Cadets, we are waiting for your class leader. First Lieutenant (1st Lt) Tim Bailey has been saddled with your sorry asses for administrative purposes until you either graduate or leave. He's a Marine officer, and you will speak only when directly spoken to. You'll remain at attention when he's speaking to you unless given permission otherwise. While in formation, I'll salute the Lieutenant and speak for you. You *will* answer any question he asks with only 'Yes, sir' and nothing more. I'm sure that's perfectly clear to you, ladies."

Almost immediately, a dull green Chevrolet staff car pulled to the curb and stopped, and an impeccably uniformed Marine with silver bars on his blouse stepped from the car. The DI snapped to attention and saluted crisply as the Lieutenant drew near and said, "Sir, Cadet Class 67-22 is standing by for your orders."

Returning the DI's salute, Lieutenant Bailey ordered, "At ease, Sergeant. Wheeler." He started, "Gentlemen, I'm your class leader and am responsible for each and every one of you until you either leave on your own volition, are discharged, or complete the program and receive your gold bars as a Second Lieutenant in the Marine Corps as well as the gold wings denoting you as a Marine pilot."

Continuing, he said, "It's my duty to train each of you to the high standards we Marines hold sacred and get the most of the dollars spent on your training. Having said that, I fully expect to lose at least half of you before the end. Personally, I couldn't give a shit about which ones can't hack the program because of your lack of initiative, personal toughness, intelligence, or any other reason. I *will* demand that you strictly adhere to every order Sergeant Wheeler gives you, follow every rule in both letter and spirit and give the Corps your very best."

Pausing for merely a moment, he said, "Now, as I said, I'm here basically for administrative purposes. If an emergency arises or you decide to 'self-eliminate,' you'll advise the DI of your situation, and he'll either solve the problem or obtain permission for you to see me. It's my greatest desire that I do not see any of you until graduation, nor do I want to hear your names, except when you receive your gold bars and wings."

Lieutenant Bailey continued, "I know this is going to be a demanding course, and there'll be times when you think you can't handle it anymore. That's exactly what we're looking for: the point where you just can't hack it. Whether it be a physical limitation or a mental one, I *will not* allow a single Cadet to complete this program unless you're willing to give Sergeant Wheeler, myself, and the Corps everything you have to give."

Lieutenant Bailey finished by saying, "Now I know you have questions, but I don't want to hear them. Sergeant Wheeler is here to guide, train, and direct your every move for the next couple of months, and he'll be the one to answer you. Is that perfectly clear?"

"Yes, sir," came the response from the class.

Lieutenant Bailey turned to Sergeant Wheeler, who had come to ramrod-straight attention, having participated in this well-orchestrated routine numerous times, and said, "They're all yours, Sergeant. Carry on."

The DI snapped his salute and waited for the Lieutenant's return of the time-honored show of mutual respect. "Thank you, sir," the DI said as the Lieutenant saluted and headed for his car.

Turning to the Cadets, he said, "Cadet Lashley, fall out and report before me."

Jim took one step to his rear, pivoted, and marched around the formation, stopping three feet in front of Sergeant Wheeler. "Yes, Sergeant?" he asked.

"Cadet Lashley," the DI told him, "I'm appointing you as the guidon bearer for this ragtag group. Your job will be to ensure that the formation will be ready for my inspection every morning, to be available to answer any question regarding my fine Marine Corps, and to be my point man for any instructions I may have for the class when you are not performing physical training or any of the academic studies."

Jim stood at attention and simply said, "Yes, Sergeant."

The DI turned to the formation and explained, "There'll be times after class or meals that I'm not available to wipe your sorry asses. That now falls to Cadet Lashley. You're to follow his orders just as if they had come from God through the Lieutenant and through me. Cadet Lashley has previous experience as a Marine Sergeant and will be your best source of information that just may help you endure this program. He's not your mother or father, nor is he anything but a conduit from me to you. He can also explain what Boot Camp is like should you not finish here. Are there any questions?"

"No, Sergeant," came the response.

"Very well," the DI said. "Cadet Lashley, you will fall in the rear line in the rightmost end and remain in the guidon's position until relieved of your duties."

"Yes, Sergeant," Jim said before pivoting and joining the rest of the cadets where he had been ordered.

"Class 67-22," the DI said, "we're going to march to where your first class will be held. Once there, you'll fall out on command and enter the building in an orderly fashion. This will provide you with the material you'll need to learn about military formalities, tradition, and proper behavior. You'll be provided with other study material for additional classes as you progress through the program.

"Tomorrow, you'll have the first of many such classes designed to teach you how the military operates, customs, rules and regulations, and everything else we have taught thousands of Marines before you. You're about to begin understanding what a special group you're trying to join, the United States Marine Corps."

Sergeant Wheeler then marched the class to a large brick building before stopping them. After issuing the command to halt, he ordered a left face and said, "Fall OUT!"

After entering the building, the Cadets were directed to a classroom where they were told to take a seat at any of the tables. Upon each table, there was a stack of books and a class syllabus in front of each chair.

Once each Cadet had the syllabus opened, the DI told them, "Cadets, this is your road map to becoming a Marine pilot. You'll notice that each hour of each day is accounted for over the next two months or so. Along with the listed activities, there's a guide as to the level to which you're expected to be performing. If you fail to attain these proficiencies, you *will* be removed from this class. If it's the decision of Lieutenant Bailey, you may be reassigned to the next following class to complete the section in which you are failing to attain the required level of performance."

The DI ordered, "Now, Cadets, you'll gather your material, place it beneath your left arm, leaving your right hand unencumbered so as to be able to render a salute if so required and form up outside. Cadet Lashley, you'll bring the formation to attention as I approach. Now fall out!"

Again outside, the DI marched the class back to the barracks, ordered them to place their books in their rooms, and returned within five minutes. As they fell back into formation, he then marched them to the dining hall for lunch.

Given the standard 30 minutes to eat and reform, Sergeant Wheeler then marched the formation back to the barracks and instructed them to return to their rooms, change into their PT (physical training) gear, and be back in formation in 20 minutes.

So it begins, Jim mused as he headed for his room. Having watched his fellow classmates since this morning, he wondered just how many of them would be around when the wings were finally pinned to his chest.

CHAPTER 7

For the rest of the week, there were classes on math, physics, aerodynamics, and engineering, as well as daily PT and swimming. When Friday night finally arrived, most of the class sat around in the common room, wishing they were back in college, where Friday night meant beer, girls, and parties. Here, it meant nothing.

Already, two of the initial Cadets had requested SIE (self-initiated elimination) and left the program. Both had asked Jim what it'd be like to attend Boot Camp and be an enlisted Marine. Jim explained as well as he could that the physical demands of Boot Camp would be more rigorous than what they were experiencing here at MARCAD, with more emphasis on rifle training, obstacle courses, and military formations. Another major difference was that Marine pilots needed to know more about the subjects they'd been studying, while enlisted Marines needed to know how to maneuver on the ground instead of in the air. In other words, be a mud grunt.

The main issue to these two seemed to be that by eliminating themselves from this program, they'd only have a four-year commitment to the Marines instead of the almost five required after finishing MARCAD. When Jim tried to explain the dangers that faced the enlisted Marines in Vietnam, their counter was the death rate of Marine helicopter pilots. Although not all MARCAD pilots were destined for helicopters, that was the pressing need currently.

Finally, Jim just told them that it was their decision, and regardless of how they served, the fact that they'd become Marines at the end of their training would be something that they'd always be proud of.

Starting the second week of training, the remaining cadets received their new uniforms, khaki trousers, shirts, blouses, hats (called covers), and dress shoes. From this point on, they'd wear the uniform everywhere they went.

The PT classes were a cinch for Jim, and he easily outperformed every other Cadet. This was to be expected since he'd spent almost three years maintaining his physical conditioning. Another area of excellence was concerning the history of the Marines and other subjects he'd learned in boot camp or during his years of enlisted service.

Math came particularly easy for Jim as well, but physics turned out to be a very difficult subject. Fortunately, there was a little thing called a gouge that listed almost every question from over the last years of tests along with the answers. If you had a basic knowledge of the subject, this would get you through the tests. But most Cadets would intentionally miss a question or two, believing that it'd prove they hadn't "cheated" on the exam. Most of the instructors were well aware of the "gouge" and knew it was widely used. They never mentioned it as long as the Cadets knew the basics when asked questions in class.

Aerodynamics came relatively easy for Jim as well. Although he'd never known the names of the forces that came into play with an airplane, he understood their importance and quickly learned how each acted upon the wings, tail, flaps, and rudder. Learning about cambered airfoils, dihedral, wing shapes, and the changes that moved the airplane about its axis was basically learning the names of all the things his father had taught him about flying.

As difficult as physics was, engineering was his major problem. The mandatory two-hour study period was more than enough for the other subjects, but engineering was eating his lunch. Fortunately, the study materials were well-written, and the instructor was more than willing to spend a little extra time with Jim. Everyone involved with the MARCAD program knew by now about his previous service and recognized that along with the Silver Star and the two Purple Heart medals, Jim had performed his service well above and beyond what most Marines had ever attained.

The medals and ribbons were just a minor part of why every instructor gave Jim a little "extra" credit and offered any assistance in passing the courses. The major factor was Jim's attitude. The biggest difference was that Jim never gave up, nor did he ever make excuses for his mistakes. If he erred, he acknowledged it and tried twice as hard to master each subject. His attitude alone would have gotten him extra help.

With no other previous enlisted Cadets in his class, Jim found he had little in common with his classmates. Even though he was only a couple of years older than most of them, he found them to be as juvenile as his friends from back home. It was still early in the program, but Jim could almost tell which Cadets would be missing by the end.

Fortunately for Jim, Ray seemed to have developed a serious attitude about becoming a Marine pilot. Although Ray didn't have the drive to excel that Jim had, he nevertheless took his studies seriously. During PT, Jim would push him as hard as he thought he could to get just a little more out of Ray.

Ray seemed to accept Jim as his mentor and slowly pulled ahead of the rest of the Cadets. Maybe the short talk back at the Exchange had done some good. Or maybe hearing some of Jim's stories about enlisted training impressed him to do better. Jim didn't care, which was the reason; he'd developed a liking for Ray and wanted to see him do well.

After the evening meal on Fridays, the Cadets marched back to their rooms and were dismissed until Saturday morning, when the DI would march them to breakfast. It was tough to watch the more senior classes heading to the ACRAC, where they could enjoy beer and pizza. The base also allowed local ladies access to the club on Friday nights.

As Jim watched the other classes heading to the ACRAC, he wondered if Jennifer was there. True, he still wanted to see where things went with Jewell, but he certainly wouldn't mind spending a little time with Jennifer, not necessarily for anything romantic, just a chance to talk to a female, especially a cute one. Maybe dance, maybe just hold hands and talk about their feelings. *Riiiight!*

On Sundays, they were marched to the base chapel for religious services. It didn't matter what your religion was; you went. That's unless you hid in your closet, which several of the Cadets did. Jim had no strong religious convictions and almost resented the time he had to spend listening to the various sermons that seemed to be more about what the pastor thought than what he had learned growing up as a Baptist in a small Texas town. Even those long-ago lessons didn't seem to fit the world as Jim now saw it.

The next seven weeks passed at a snail's pace, but

when the Cadets were finally allowed to go to the ACRAC, Jim made sure that he looked his best. It had been almost two months since he had any contact with anyone other than the Cadets, and he was looking forward to the beer and pizza. Maybe he was looking forward to seeing Jennifer again, you know, just to talk to a female, maybe dance.

Still another eight weeks before they could touch an airplane, the Cadets at least had an opportunity to relax outside their barracks on the weekend. However, the continued pressure from the academics and PT seemed to increase as they neared the end of this phase. Every week another Cadet would be removed from their class, either to join the following class to try to complete one of the courses they were having problems with or be eliminated from the program.

Jim continued to push himself and Ray to excel, and by the end of the preflight phase, Jim was easily the number 1 in his class and Ray a somewhat distant number 2. Once that phase was complete, they moved to Saufley Field and prepared for the first flying phase of their training. Now, they could at least go off base on weekends. From the end of the day on Friday at 1600 (4:00 p.m.), they could go to town and enjoy their freedom until Sunday at 1600. The only restriction was that they wore their uniforms.

Jim had continually tried to contact Jewell, but with limited time to make calls and no number for her to reach him, there had been nothing for almost two months. Now that he could go off base, he hoped that he would finally reach her, and she might come down for the weekend.

On their first day off base, Jim and Ray returned to the diner for a hamburger. Jim had met with Jennifer at ACRAC a couple of times, and they'd danced a little and talked over beer and pizza. The more he was around her, the more he liked her, but Jewell never left his mind.

Sure enough, as they walked in, Jennifer saw them and smiled. Taking the same seat they'd always taken, Jennifer was there before they'd completely sat down. "Well, look who's here," Jennifer said as she placed the menus on the table. Looking pointedly at Jim, she asked, "What would you like today, the same old hamburger? Or are you interested in something else?"

Smiling, Jim answered, "For now, the same old hamburger. We'll have to see if anything else comes to mind later."

Turning slightly to Ray, she asked, "And how about you?"

Shaking his head, Ray replied, "Looks like I better just ask for the hamburger again."

As Jennifer walked away, Ray said, "I don't know how you do it, but she barely knows I'm here when she sees you."

Jim just smiled and said, "That's because she knows I'm a nice guy and not trying to pull her panties down the first chance I get. Women seem to be able to read men with just a glance, and maybe you give off the wrong signal."

"I don't think so," Ray answered. "I think she's just made her mind up that she wants *you* to pull her panties down and couldn't care less what I think or want."

"Well, I guess she may be in for a disappointment," Jim said. "But in life, you never know what the future may bring. I'm in no rush to get involved with a girl like her."

"You're telling me that you'd turn that down?" Ray asked incredulously.

"I didn't say that," Jim answered, shaking his head. "I just said I'm in no rush. I also said that you can never tell what the future may bring. We've still got over a year before this thing is over, and I'm not making any decisions that I may regret later, especially since we'll be moving away from here after we finish the first couple of phases of flight training. I'll just say that I'm keeping my options open for now."

Once they'd finished their meals and the casual flirting, Jim and Ray headed into town to drive around looking at the local restaurants and nightclubs. After a couple of hours, Jim wanted to get back to the base and study a little before they met their instructors. If there was a single phase of this program where Jim wanted to excel, it was the actual flying. Not only did he want to be the first to solo, but he also wanted to demonstrate that he was the best student they'd ever had.

CHAPTER 8

With preflight behind them, the remaining 25 Cadets began training and flying the T-34B, basically a Beechcraft single-engine, two-seat airplane. The classes were geared to learning everything about the airplane and the maneuvers they were to perform. Although Jim had seldom flown an aircraft with a stick instead of a wheel for the ailerons and elevator, it took almost no time for him to be completely comfortable with the new controls.

After his solo flight and the obligatory ceremony, Jim returned to his room and began packing his bags for T-2A training. While packing, Ray came in and thanked Jim for his help in getting this far through the program.

"No problem," Jim said. "Just remember that all it takes from here on is to study and apply yourself. If you manage to get jets, maybe I'll see you in Meridian."

"What about Jennifer?" Ray asked as he watched Jim. "Are you going to tell her where you're going?"

"Probably," Jim answered, knowing he would. "I'll at least let her know that I'll be gone for the next eight or nine weeks. I really doubt if she'll want to wait around for me anyway.”

“I don’t know,” Ray told him. “She sure seems to be stuck on you.”

“For now, but as soon as I’m gone, she’ll get stuck on someone else,” Jim answered. “Maybe you should try again after I leave tomorrow.”

“Hell, she hasn’t seemed too interested in me so far,” Ray answered. “I doubt if that’s changed.”

“You never know,” Jim said as he placed the last of his personal items in his seabag. “As soon as I go get my orders for Meridian NAS, why don’t we go pay her a visit?”

“Sure,” Ray said as he began to change from his flight suit into jeans. “I can’t wait to see her reaction when you tell her you’re leaving.”

“All right,” Jim replied as he walked toward the door, “I’ll come back and get you in a few minutes, and we’ll head over there.

After getting his orders and advance travel allotment, Jim came back to Saufley and waited for Ray to come down to the car. Heading toward Pensacola and their favorite burger place, they discussed what would happen to each of them over the next few months.

Knowing that Ray would probably end up in helicopters, Jim tried to encourage him to strive to prove that he could handle any assignment. Not wanting to tell Ray about his true feelings about the differences between “Rotor Heads” and “Jet Jockeys,” Jim stressed the accomplishments of completing a very demanding program that few ever had a chance to enter.

As they walked into the diner, Jennifer spotted them and almost beat them with two Dr Peppers to the table where they always sat. “Afternoon, gentlemen,” she said as she looked at Jim. “What’ll it be this time?”

Jim smiled and said, "Well, I guess I'll have the same old thing. When you find something you like, stick with it."

"So, you've found something you like?" Jennifer teased. "What about you, Ray?"

"Same for me," he answered. "Looks like I'll have to order on my own after today."

Jennifer looked at Ray for the first time and asked, "What do you mean?"

Jim put his hand on Jennifer's arm and told her, "I'm leaving for Mississippi in the morning. I've finished here for a couple of months, and I'm going to fly jets up at Meridian."

"You'll be coming back, won't you?" Jennifer asked with disappointment clearly on her face.

"Yes," Jim told her, "but for just a few weeks. Then, if everything goes well, I'll head to Texas for about five months, and then I hope to get orders for the F-4. That'll mean going to California for another six months."

"Well, at least I'll get to see you again," Jennifer said as she turned and headed for the cooking area. "I'll have your burgers and fries out as quick as I can."

Ray leaned over and lowered his voice as he said, "I don't think that went too well."

"About as well as could be expected," Jim answered. "I don't know what she expected, and I've never made any promises that I'd be around forever or take her with me, not to mention that I've never done anything except dance with her and flirt a little. Besides, I really doubt if this is her first experience with departing Marines."

"Maybe not," Ray said. "But I don't think she's any happier about it. And I bet she keeps some hope alive that you'll want to take her with you when you head for Texas."

"Hope springs eternal," Jim smiled. "Maybe she'll find another Cadet at the ACRAC in the meantime. Since she already knows you, you just might be the lucky guy."

In a few minutes, Jennifer returned with their burgers. "Here you are, guys. Hope they're good enough to bring you back again," she said pointedly at Jim.

"Don't worry," Jim told her as he sipped his Dr Pepper. "You can expect to see me again in a couple of months. I haven't had anything this good anywhere else."

As Jennifer walked away, Ray again softly said, "Don't you think you're leading her on?"

Jim sat a moment and then said quietly, "Never lock any door that you may have to use later. She's a big girl, and I never said anything about coming back for her, just the burger."

"Right," Ray said, starting to eat his burger. "But you know damn well that she thinks you're referring to her."

"I know," Jim smiled. "But I can't help what she thinks, and I may have a change of heart in a couple of months. Regardless, she knows I'm leaving and have a year or so left in the program. What she does from here on is entirely up to her."

Jennifer returned after seeing that they were through eating and laid the check on the table, asking, "Anything else?"

Jim stood and took the check, saying, "Nope, not for now anyway. You take care of Ray while I'm gone. He needs close supervision."

As they walked toward the door, Jennifer called out, "You just be safe, and I'll have something hot waiting for you when you get back."

Jim smiled and waved as he left and got in the car. "We'll see, we'll see," he said as they backed out of the parking lot.

CHAPTER 9

Jim rose early the next morning, showered, and dressed in his jeans and boots. Although it was just slightly over 190 miles and would take about three and a half hours, he wanted to be there by noon and get checked into the base. His roommates were all up and getting ready to head to the flight line when Jim carried his bags down to the car.

Ray followed him and finally said, "Well, this may be goodbye for quite a while. I'll be gone when you come back, and if I don't get jets, I doubt if we'll ever see each other again."

Jim tossed his bags into the trunk and said, "It could be a while for sure, but Marine pilots are a small group and have very few bases. I'm sure we'll see each other again."

Shaking Ray's hand, Jim restated, "You just keep at it, and you'll do fine. Always give it everything you've got, and never settle for anything other than striving to be the best. The rest of it'll work out."

"If there's one thing that you've taught me here, it's that nothing worthwhile is ever easy," Ray said, releasing Jim's hand. "I don't know if I'd have gotten this far without your constant bitching at me. Keep in touch."

"That I will," Jim smiled as he got in the car. "Regardless of where you go, just remember that you're a Marine pilot. Semper Fi."

As he headed for the gate, Jim watched Ray in the rearview mirror and waved as he left his only real friend here behind.

After leaving the base, he joined I-10 to Mobile and then US 45 North toward Meridian. Approaching Waynesboro, Mississippi, he exited and looked for a place to refill the gas and eat. Seeing a sign for the Sonic Drive-In, he followed the access road a couple of blocks off 45 and pulled into a gas station across the road from the Sonic. Once the tank was filled, Jim paid for the gas and crossed the road to the Sonic.

Pulling into one of the slots, Jim killed the engine and looked at the menu. *This certainly isn't like the burger joint back at Pensacola,* Jim thought. *And I'll bet the waitress isn't as cute, either.*

After deciding what he wanted, Jim called in an order of a hamburger, fries, and Dr Pepper. As he sat waiting, he watched the girls on roller skates delivering meals to the other cars parked around him. Most of the cars had teenage boys and girls talking about whatever teenagers talk about. Very few even glanced his way except to look at his car.

When the roller-skating girl arrived, Jim paid her, told her to keep the change, and opened the wrapper around his burger. Having not eaten since the previous evening, Jim quickly finished the burger and most of the fries. Holding his drink between his legs, he started the car and backed out of the slot.

Once back on the highway, Jim munched on the remaining fries as he continued north toward Meridian.

Watching the countryside pass, he was anxious to get to the base and get ready for the next phase.

Just under two hours later, he pulled up to the main gate and showed the guard his orders and ID. After getting directions to where the Duty Officer was, he drove the short distance and parked.

Again, with his orders in his hand, he went inside the Administration Building and was assigned a room and a pamphlet describing the course and where to report the following morning.

After putting his bags in his room, Jim drove down to the flight line and asked the first officer he saw if he could look around at the airplanes parked just a few yards from the building.

"You here for training?" the Lieutenant asked.

"Yes, sir," Jim answered. "I just finished down at Pensacola and wanted to get a look at the planes before I report back tomorrow morning."

"I'm Lt. Jerry Nelson," Jerry said, sticking out his hand to shake. "I'm one of the instrument instructors here for the T-2A."

"Nice to meet you," Jim said, shaking his hand. "I'm Cadet Jim Lashley."

"Navy or Marine?" Jerry asked.

"Marine," Jim replied.

"What college did you come from?" Jerry asked.

"That's kind of a long story," Jim told him. "I was at West Texas State University until I joined the Marines. Then I got the rest of my credit hours from a little school out in California."

"I guess that means you were enlisted," Jerry said.

"Yes, sir," Jim answered. "I was actually on my way to be a DI at Parris Island before I was accepted into the

MARCAD program."

"Well," Jerry said as he turned and started walking. "Follow me, and I'll get you your flight gear and some study material. Then we'll go out, and I'll show you the airplane you'll be in for instruments."

Jim followed Jerry around the area for a few minutes, carrying everything he was given. As soon he had all the material, Jim said, "I'm going to toss these in my car. I'll be right back."

Returning to where he had left Jerry, Jim said, "Sir, I appreciate you taking the time to show me the planes."

When they got to the closest plane, Jerry told him, "This is the T-2A. It's our instrument trainer. Go ahead and climb up and look around."

Jim climbed the ladder hanging from the forward cockpit, looked at the instrument panel, and asked, "Do you instruct instruments?"

"Yep," Jerry answered. "I also teach formation and acrobatics. I'll probably fly with you a few times during your two months here."

Jim spent a few minutes familiarizing himself with the numerous gauges and climbed down, saying, "I've never flown a jet before, and it looks like I've got a lot of things to learn."

"Most of our students haven't, but it comes pretty quick," Jerry said. "The books will give you the method. I just teach technique. Not to say mine's the best. Everyone has a different style. But the basics are all the same."

"While we're here," Jerry continued, "let's take a look at the T-2C. That's our formation and acrobatic plane."

The first thing Jim noticed was that the *C* model had two jet engines, while the *A* only had one. "I guess I've got twice as much to learn here with two engines," he said as they approached.

"Not really," Jerry told him. "Just another set of gauges to watch, but you'll like the way this plane flies. It has lots more power and is very responsive. That's why we use it for acrobatics and formation."

Jim spent a few minutes looking in the cockpit and climbed down, saying, "Well, I was planning on relaxing this evening. Now I think I better hit the books."

Jerry laughed and told him, "Don't worry too much about it. The ground instructors will make sure you learn everything you need to know. If I were you, I'd enjoy the evening. Starting tomorrow, you won't have a lot of time to relax."

Jim thanked him and headed back to his room. He decided that he'd still spend the rest of the day trying to learn the airplanes and have some advantage over the rest of the Cadets tomorrow.

For the next several weeks, the instructors worked with the Cadets, teaching them everything they needed to know about this phase of the training.

Six weeks after arriving at Meridian, Jim headed back to Pensacola.

CHAPTER 10

As soon as Jim got close to the base, he knew that he'd stop for a burger. He wondered whether Jennifer was still there or she was still what he preferred to think of as available. *Maybe Ray ran off with her,* he thought as he saw the diner just ahead.

Pulling into the parking lot, Jim killed the engine and walked to the front door. Upon entering, he saw Jennifer looking at him with a big smile on her face.

"Well," she said as she walked up to him, "look who's finally back. May I take your order, sir?"

"Yes, you certainly may," Jim answered, smiling. "Do I need reservations, or may I take any open seat?"

"You can take anything you want," Jennifer teased. "I'd be more than happy to take care of *anything* you need."

"Good to know, very good to know," Jim teased back as he took the same seat where he always sat. "Shall I tell you what I want, or do you remember?"

"I remember," Jennifer replied. "I wasn't sure if you remembered."

"I do. But I might be interested in seeing what the *menu* has to offer in case there is anything new," Jim said, grinning.

"The menu hasn't changed," Jennifer told him. "There's pretty much the same thing available that there was when you left. You only need to order it."

"Well, for now, I'll just have the same thing," Jim said, looking at Jennifer. "Maybe another time I'll try something different."

"Your choice," Jennifer replied as she headed away to turn in his order. "I'll be right back with your Dr Pepper."

Jim watched her walk away and wondered what it would be like to get involved with her. His attempts either to contact Jewell or to arrange a meeting had thus far failed miserably. It has always been said that absence makes the heart grow fonder, but in this case, it also makes the mind wander.

Jennifer came back with his drink and asked, "Mind if I sit with you while you wait for your burger?"

"Not at all," Jim replied. "Please sit down."

"Thanks," Jennifer said. "I'll be right back with my drink and join you."

Returning with her drink, she took the seat opposite Jim and asked, "How long are you going to be here this time?"

"Only a month or so," Jim answered. "Then I'll head for Beeville, Texas."

"Where's that?" Jennifer asked.

"It's just a few miles north of Corpus Christi," Jim told her. "And Corpus Christi is about halfway between the east edge and the west edge of Texas, almost on the Gulf of Mexico."

"How long will you be there?" she asked.

"Probably about five months or so," Jim answered. "That's where I'll take advanced jet training."

"Are you coming back here after that?" Jennifer asked, hoping that the answer would be yes.

"Probably not right away," Jim replied. "After Beeville, I hope to go to California for F-4 training."

Hearing the cook announce that Jim's order was ready, Jennifer rose from her seat and said, "I'll be right back. Do you mind if I still sit here while you eat? There's nobody else here right now, and I'm bored."

"Not a problem," Jim told her. "I'm always happy to have a pretty lady around me regardless of what I'm doing."

When Jennifer came back and placed Jim's tray on the table, she sat and asked, "How long do you think you'll be in California?"

"About six months," Jim answered as he poured some ketchup on his fries. "Once I complete the training in Beeville, I'll be commissioned as a Second Lieutenant in the Marines. After that, the Marines own me, and anything can happen."

"That means that you'll be gone for almost a year," Jennifer said disappointedly. "I was really hoping that you might end up around here."

Jim took another bite of his burger before answering, "It may not be as bad as it sounds. We have to fly several cross-country flights, and we try to go to different bases. So, I might be able to get back here a few times during training."

"That sounds better," Jennifer said, staring at the table. "I don't know. I guess I made myself believe that you'd be back here longer this time and that there was a chance you'd get stationed here after your training."

Jim sat his burger back on the plate and looked at Jennifer for a few seconds before he explained, "You know I enjoy being around you, Jennifer, but I've got this opportunity to do something that few men ever get the chance to do. I've never made any promises to you. I've done my best never to lead you on, and regardless of what I want at this point, the Marines still own me."

"Can't you ask to be assigned here?" Jennifer hopefully asked.

"I can't," Jim told her. "I've got to finish this program before I get commissioned, or I'll end up going to Parris Island for the rest of my time."

Picking his drink up, he continued, "There have been too many people helping me get this far, and I can't disappoint them. Besides, regardless of whether or not I finish this program, I seriously doubt that I'll ever get stationed back here."

He reached across the table and put his hand on hers, saying, "Let's not talk about what happens in the future. I'm here for a couple of months, so let's just enjoy what time I have here and see what happens later." Looking her in the eye, he softly said, "Do you think you can do that? Or would you rather me not come around here again?"

"No," Jennifer told him. "I still enjoy being around you. Could we maybe go dancing or something once in a while?"

Smiling, Jim nodded and said, "Sure, there's nothing I'd like better than to pick up where we left off. That is if you haven't found something better while I was away."

Jennifer grinned and replied, "Of course not. I think Ray really wanted to get something started, but I've always thought of him as just a friend. I did meet him at the base once or twice, but I've kind of been waiting for you to get back."

"Now you'll make me blush," Jim said, picking up a french fry. "I'm sure there're plenty of eligible men out at the base. And any number of them would love to take you out."

"Oh, there've been offers," Jennifer admitted. "But most of them seem so immature. Besides, most of them have the same problem that you have. They can't do anything until they finish training, and they all leave sooner or later."

"Well," Jim answered, "you can always find one of the local boys."

"*Riiight*," Jennifer sarcastically replied. "That's what every girl wants, somebody without the brains or ambition to leave this place. The ones that had any of those traits left for college and found wives there. No thanks, I have higher standards than that."

"Well, I guess you're stuck with me for the next few weeks," Jim told her as he dipped the edge of his burger in the ketchup on his plate.

"That's fine with me," Jennifer answered, looking at him. "I guess we'll just be stuck with each other for a while. Think you can handle that?"

"I'm pretty sure I can put up with you for a few weeks," Jim grinned. "After Marine Boot Camp, I can do just about anything for short periods."

"Oh, so now I'm being compared to Boot Camp?" Jennifer teased.

"No, not exactly," Jim retorted. "I just mean that I can endure most unpleasant things for a long period."

Taking a fry from Jim's plate, Jennifer threw it at him and said, "You're such an ass sometimes, Mr. Marine."

"You know I'm joking," Jim said. "Being around you is nothing like Boot Camp. That was actually easy compared to figuring out what to do with you. At least there, the DI told you what to do and how to do it."

Taking a fry from his plate and dipping it in the ketchup, he continued, "You are something that I've got to figure out on my own. And, my dear, that makes the decision much harder."

Finishing his burger, Jim placed enough money on the table to cover his bill and a generous tip, saying, "I've got to get out to the base and check-in, but I'll be back tomorrow, and we'll talk about that dancing stuff you seem to be interested in."

Jennifer rose as Jim did and followed him to the door. "How about coming back tonight after I get off work? Maybe we can just go down to the beach and talk?"

"That sounds all right with me," Jim answered as he opened the door. "What time do you finish today?"

"I'll be ready to go about seven o'clock," Jennifer told him. "If it's okay with you, we can swing by my apartment, and I'll change into something more appropriate and drop off my car."

"Sure," Jim said, nodding. "Just what do you consider more appropriate?"

With a devious smile on her face, she replied, "Well, I guess you'll just have to wait and see. Now you go do your little boy stuff at the base, and I'll think up something you might enjoy later this evening."

Shaking his head, Jim smiled, saying, "I hope I'm not being led down a path I'll later regret. But I'm sure you wouldn't lead me anywhere. I don't want to go anyway."

Jim climbed into the Corvette and backed out, waving as Jennifer stood at the door watching.

CHAPTER 11

Jim drove to Pensacola NAS and stopped at the gate once again to show his ID and orders. After a quick chat with the guard, he proceeded toward where he'd be staying for the next few weeks.

Arriving at his barracks, Jim checked to make sure he was heading for the correct room. Satisfied that he knew where he would be, he went to the room and selected his bed from the two that appeared to be unused. Then he returned to his car and began to carry in his bags.

Everything properly stowed and hanging neatly in his closet, Jim removed his Wranglers, boots, and shirt. Wanting to get to the flight line and possibly get some study material, he pulled on his flight overalls and rubbed his chin to see if he needed to shave before meeting any of the instructors he might run into.

Satisfied that he wouldn't be embarrassed by his appearance, Jim left the room and headed back to the car. The route to the flight line had been memorized when he had been here before, so it was a quick trip to the parking area beside the hangars and the flight line.

Once parked, Jim placed his flight cap squarely on his head and walked onto the ramp where all the aircraft were parked.

As he headed for the operations center, Jim saw one of the instructors he had flown with right before he soloed the T-34. Walking directly up to him, Jim saluted and said, "Good afternoon, sir."

Returning his salute, Capt. Mike Knox replied, "Good afternoon, Cadet Lashley. Looks like you made it through acro and formation. I guess you're back here for the gunnery school and carrier qualification."

"Yes, sir," Jim answered. "I was hoping I could get some study material and spend a little time getting ready for my first class."

"I remember that about you," Mike said. "You were always prepared for each class or flight. I just wish everyone else had your drive. Now, let's head in and see if I can get you started."

Entering one of the classrooms, Mike walked to a table at the front of the room and selected four manuals from the stacks. Handing them to Jim, he said, "Here are the manuals for the T-2 B and C, gunnery, and carrier operations. I imagine you'll have them memorized by tomorrow, won't you?"

Smiling as he took the manuals, Jim told him, "I wish! Unfortunately, I need more time than the average man to get information into my brain. That's why I wanted to get an early start."

"You forget," Mike replied, "I flew with you before. And you may not believe this, but we instructors discuss you Cadets when you're not around."

"I'm sure you do, sir," Jim said, placing the manuals under his left arm. "I just hope that a poor old dumb-ass country boy like me can ever get to fly the F-4 and maybe get one tour back in Vietnam.”

“I’ve no doubt that you’ll get what you want, Cadet,” Mike said. “But if I were you, I wouldn’t wish for a tour over in ’Nam. Let’s just hope that you never have to risk your life over there again. From what I’ve heard about you, you’ve done your share for that little skirmish. Now, unless you have anything else for me, I’ve got work to do.”

“No, sir,” Jim said, coming to attention and saluting. “I appreciate your help and will remember your advice.”

After Mike returned the salute, Jim headed back for his car and smiled to himself, thinking that regardless of what Mike had said, he really wanted to do a tour back in ’Nam in the F-4. Remembering how that particular airplane had played a major part in his safe recovery from the death trap into which he’d been placed, he wanted to be back there to maybe provide the same service for the next group of Marines who found themselves in a like situation.

Back in his room, Jim started looking through the manuals, trying to determine which areas he’d need to concentrate on. After almost two hours of reading, he closed the books and sat back, wondering just how he was going to learn all this in the short time allowed.

Looking at his watch, Jim realized that he had scant time to shower and get ready to meet Jennifer at the café. Putting all the manuals neatly on his dresser, he grabbed his shave kit and headed for the showers.

Once shaved and dressed, he headed for the ’Vette, wondering just what Jennifer had in mind for this evening. Memories of the few times he had seen Jewell or had talked to her found their way into his mind as he drove off the base.

Certainly, he had special feelings for Jewell, but the lack of communication and inability to see her was a major stumbling block to developing any long-term relationship. The same may be true with Jennifer, but at least he could see her, touch her, and spend time enjoying having someone with him.

The last few months of being around Jennifer off and on made Jim realize that he'd never endure a long-distance or sporadic relationship. Even with Jennifer, it'd never work until some stability came into his life. And that was probably years in the future. True, once he finished the MARCAD course in Beeville, Texas, he would be free to marry. But for now, not only couldn't he do that, but he also really didn't want to.

What he really wanted was to finish this program, be commissioned as a Second Lieutenant in the Marine Corps, go to F-4 training, and do a tour back in Vietnam. Knowing that it would take at least two more years to accomplish that, Jim was, for now, just trying to enjoy the company of someone he liked. And Jennifer certainly fits that.

It was almost seven o'clock when he pulled into the parking lot. Sitting there in the car, Jim watched Jennifer finish her work. *Yes,* he thought, *she's someone that I'll enjoy being around for the next few weeks.*

Jennifer looked out of the window and waved when she saw Jim sitting in his car. Holding up five fingers to signal that she would be ready in five minutes, she smiled and turned away.

Sure enough, a few minutes later, Jim saw her hang her apron up and wave to the cook as she headed for the door. Once outside, she walked to where Jim had parked and said, "Well, are you ready to follow me back to my house?"

"Sure," Jim replied. "Have you figured out what we'll do tonight?"

"I have a pretty good idea," she smiled. "But you'll just

have to wait until I've showered and cleaned up a little. That's unless you like the smell of hamburgers, onions, and pickles on a lady."

"Well," Jim said, grinning, "those are some of my favorite smells, but I think I'd prefer to only smell them when I'm eating."

"Okay then," Jennifer said, turning away. "Just follow me, and keep thinking about what might be in store for you later."

"When will I know if I'm right?" Jim asked.

Jennifer turned slightly and said, "Oh, I'm pretty sure you'll find out rather soon. By the way, what beer would you like? I've got Budweiser at the house. If you want something else, we'll have to make a quick stop."

Grinning devilishly, Jim told her, "I just may want something else, but for beer, Budweiser will do just fine."

"Never ask for something you don't want," Jennifer said, heading for her car. "You might just get it."

CHAPTER 12

Jim followed Jennifer as soon as she got in her car and headed away from the café. Not sure exactly where she lived, he stayed close and hoped she'd at least use her turn signals to give him a little notice before making any quick turns.

Five minutes later, he followed her into an apartment complex and waited until she parked before he found an empty slot. Standing there waiting for him, she was smiling as Jim locked his car and walked toward her.

"Thought of anything?" she smiled as they walked toward her apartment.

"Lots of things," Jim said as she unlocked the door.

"Got a favorite?" she asked, opening the door and walking inside with Jim close behind her.

"For now," Jim said as he looked around at the sparsely furnished living room, "I'll just take a beer."

Jennifer sat her purse on an end table and motioned for Jim to follow her into the kitchen. Opening the refrigerator, she took a bottle of Budweiser from the shelf and handed it to Jim.

"There's plenty more if you finish this one before I

finish my shower," Jennifer said, smiling as she softly held his hand around the bottle.

"I think I probably better not get too far ahead of you," Jim said, letting her hand rest on his. "I'll just take it slow and wait."

Sliding her hand up his arm as she removed it, Jennifer said, "Slow is always good. Now, let's turn on the TV for you while you wait."

Jim followed her back into the living room and sat on the couch while Jennifer turned the set on and asked, "Anything in particular you want to watch?"

"Oh, I can think of several. But for now, just put on the news," Jim teased.

Jennifer switched the channels and said, "You just sit here and wait like a good little boy. I won't be too long."

Jim watched her walk away, wondering just where this night was going. As she left the room, he took a sip of the beer and turned his attention to the news. Pretty much the same as always—more footage of Vietnam, protests at the colleges, a little local news, and endless commercials.

Jim had been watching for maybe ten minutes when he heard Jennifer call from another room, "Hey, Jim, can you come back here and give me a hand with something?"

Jim sat his beer on the table and rose to follow the sound of her voice. Leaving the living room, he walked down a short hall to what appeared to be the only bedroom. As he entered, he saw the door open to the bathroom, heard the shower running, and heard Jennifer's voice urging him to come in.

Jim walked in, saw the shower curtain closed, and asked, "Need a towel or something?"

Jennifer peeked around the curtain, smiling, and told him, "What I need is for somebody to wash my back. Think you could help a damsel-in-distress?"

Looking at her head and shoulder exposed, Jim answered, "Be glad to assist, but how do you think I can do that without getting wet?"

"Oh, I think you'll have to get wet," Jennifer said as she pulled the curtain away from her body. "But I think you need to take your clothes off so *they* don't."

Seeing her standing in the tub with soap bubbles slowly running across her breasts, Jim quickly removed his boots. Never taking his eyes off her, he slipped his T-shirt off and unbuckled his belt. As he let his jeans slip down around his ankles, he watched Jennifer's eyes travel down his body.

Removing his socks and underwear, Jim stepped over to the tub and asked, "I guess you thought I needed another shower?"

Grinning, Jennifer reached out, took Jim's hand, pointedly looked down at Jim's obvious excitement, and helped him in beside her, saying, "No, but I think you need something else. At least that's the way it looks to me."

As soon as Jim was beside her, Jennifer pulled the curtain closed and put her arms around his waist. As she pulled him against her, she tilted her face up and met his lips with hers. Standing there with the warm water hitting his back, Jim slid his hands around Jennifer and felt the firm, supple muscles in her back. Sliding his hands down, he caressed the smoothness of her behind and felt her push her body against his.

Feeling, more than hearing, the soft moan that escaped Jennifer's mouth, Jim ran his hands up her back and pressed her against his chest. Feeling her breasts against him, Jim slid his lips down and gently sucked on the side of her neck.

Jennifer leaned her head back and moaned, "Oh god, yes. That feels so good."

His hand on her waist, Jim leaned down and ran his tongue down across her breast and took her nipple into his mouth. Gently sucking on it, he felt her hand slip from around his back until she held his erection. Now, it was very evident that she was having the desired effect on him.

As Jim raised his head and looked into Jennifer's eyes, he said, "Do we need to wash any more, or should we come back later and finish the shower?"

Jennifer turned the shower off and answered, "I think we may need to come back later. There are two towels hanging right beside the tub. If you'll grab them, I'll dry you while you dry me."

Jim pulled the curtain aside, took both towels, and handed one to Jennifer, saying, "Just be careful how long you dry me, or we may need another shower quicker than you think."

Laughing, Jennifer told him, "I'll be very quick and avoid any *sensitive* areas for now. And you don't need to spend any extra time with your towel either."

Wiping the water from her back, Jim stepped back a little and rubbed the towel down across her breasts and stomach. Now admiring the fullness and firmness of her ample breasts, Jim lingered there for a second before sliding his towel down across her thighs. Bending down, he ran his tongue down her stomach as he wiped her calves.

As soon as he rose, Jennifer ran her towel across Jim's shoulders and down his back and lingered on his butt. Then she pulled the towel back to the front and slid it down across his chest and stomach, much as he had done to her.

Kneeling in front of him, Jennifer slid the towel down between Jim's legs and softly took his erection in her mouth as she finished his legs. Jim's head tilted back, and he told her, "I've warned you about what could happen if you aren't careful.”

Jennifer smiled up at him as she rose and answered, “I don’t expect it will take too long before we’re back here anyway. But just to be safe, let’s get to bed.”

Both dropped their towels, and Jennifer took Jim’s hand as she walked to the bed. Throwing the covers back, Jennifer pulled Jim down on the bed with her arms around him. Lying half on and off her, one of his legs across hers, Jim’s lips sought and found Jennifer’s as she reached behind him and slid her hand up his back. Their lips together, Jim’s hand went to her stiff nipple and down her side to her hip.

Sliding on top of her, Jim’s lips moved from hers to her neck and began to slide down to her nipples. His hands softly squeezed her breasts; Jim moved his body further down, her legs around his as he listened to her breath gasp with each move of his lips, fingers, and tongue.

Jennifer put her hands behind Jim’s neck as he slid further down and ran his tongue across her stomach. Hearing her moans, Jim slid down a little more until his face was between her now open legs. Feeling her hips raise, Jim softly moved his tongue down until he heard her gasp. Lingering, he ran his tongue up and down her and slipped his fingers into her. Continuing until he felt the urgency of her body, Jim relished the effect he was having on her as well as himself.

Feeling her hands now pulling him up, Jim ran his tongue back up her stomach and breasts. Finally, now back to her lips, Jennifer reached down and took Jim in her hand and slipped him into her. Slowly at first, Jim cautiously slid in and back out, making sure she was ready for him. As she indicated her acceptance, Jim made a quick thrust, burying the entire shaft.

Jennifer moved with him until she could stand it no

longer. Reaching around Jim's back, she pulled him roughly against her and felt him deep within her. She arched her back and gasped as the first wave of the orgasm hit her. Squeezing her legs, she pushed hard against him as another one shook her body. Unable to speak, Jennifer just buried her head against Jim's neck and felt a final orgasm throughout her body.

Feeling her tense over and over, Jim finally made another quick thrust and felt the release that had been building since they had left the shower. Drained, Jim lay almost breathless on Jennifer's now wet body and whispered, "Wow, that was certainly wonderful."

Rubbing Jim's back with her hands, Jennifer murmured, "I've been waiting for you for a long time now. And it was certainly worth the wait."

They lay there in each other's arms quietly, each softly stroking the other as they tried to regain their strength. Jim slipped off until just one leg lay across hers and caressed her stomach without saying anything as she ran her hand down his arm that lay across her belly.

Several minutes passed before either spoke another word. Finally, Jennifer opened her eyes and whispered, "Is there anything else you'd like to do this evening?"

Jim looked at her and said, "I can't think of anything better than to just lie here with you."

Smiling as she softly ran her fingertips along Jim's neck, she asked, "Maybe I can talk you into something besides just lying here?"

A slight smile slid across Jim's lips as he answered, "Baby, I think right now you can talk me into just about anything. But I may need another couple of minutes to recuperate."

Jennifer pushed Jim's leg off, sat up, and said, "I'll

give you a couple of minutes, but not much more. Now if you'll let me up, I'll go get a couple of fresh beers while we wait for your battery to recharge."

Jim sat up as Jennifer got out of bed and watched her walk out of the room. Admiring the view from behind, he smiled to himself and thought, *I think I'll enjoy the next couple of months. But I'm still leaving alone when I finish this diversion. But maybe, just maybe, I'll find some way to get back here a little more often than I'd originally planned.*

Jennifer came back carrying two beers and a small plate with cheese and crackers. "Think that'll satisfy you?" she asked, getting back into the bed.

Taking a beer, Jim replied, "This may recharge the batteries but might not satisfy everything."

Jennifer sat the plate on the bed between them and asked, "Just what needs won't this satisfy?"

Smiling, Jim replied, "To start with, the major *need* has been partially taken care of. As to being food, it's a start. Now I'm going to suggest something, and you let me know what your preferences are."

"Okay," Jennifer answered. "I can honestly tell you that I prefer anything that keeps you here in bed as long as possible. So, what else can there be?"

Jim took a long swallow of the beer and said, "First, would you rather go out and eat or order something to eat here?"

"Eat here," Jennifer said, taking a cracker from the plate.

"Okay," Jim told her. "Next question, do you think we can take a quick shower, start round 2, and then get something to eat?"

"Oh, no question about that one either. Shower, round 2, shower, round 3, shower, food—in that order," Jennifer joked.

"All right let's start with the shower, round 2, and then reevaluate the order of the rest of it," Jim said, finishing his beer. "I'll head for the shower, and you can either wait or join me, your choice."

As Jim climbed out of bed, Jennifer sat her half-finished beer on the table beside the bed and told him, "You get the water running, and I'll be there. I'm not going to waste a single minute we've got together."

About thirty minutes after their shower and enjoying each other again, Jim and Jennifer lay together quietly until she asked, "Are you going to spend the night?"

Jim looked into her eyes and answered, "As much as I'd like that, I can't. I've still got some studying to do tonight, and I want to be the first one at the flight line tomorrow morning."

"I promise I'll get you up at whatever time you need," Jennifer begged.

"I really can't do it," Jim told her. "Maybe later on when the routine is more established, but for now, I'm staying on base and doing everything I can to complete this course as quickly as possible."

Jennifer drew back from him and, obviously disappointed, said, "I was hoping that you could at least stay with me until you had to leave for Texas."

"I'm sorry, baby," Jim said, sitting up. "You know that I've got to do this. The best I can tell you is that I'll spend as much time with you as I can, but this school has to come first."

"Crap," Jennifer told him. "I guess I'll have to take whatever time you can spare, but I don't have to like it."

"No," Jim acknowledged. "I wish things were different, but you've known my plans ever since we met, and they haven't changed. Now, should we get cleaned up and get something to eat?"

"You go ahead and shower," Jennifer told him. "I'll be there in a minute or two."

Jim got up and headed for the bathroom, knowing that she wouldn't be joining him this time in the shower. Taking just a couple of minutes to rinse off, he was almost done drying when Jennifer came in.

"Finished?" Jennifer asked as she entered.

"Yep," Jim answered, hanging up the towel. "I'll get dressed, and we can figure out what we want to eat when you're done."

"Okay, I'll be out in a couple of minutes," Jennifer said, stepping into the tub.

Jim picked up his clothes from where he had dropped them only an hour or so ago and headed for the bedroom. Dressing quickly, he took his empty bottle and went to the kitchen. Getting another beer from the refrigerator, he sat on the couch and waited for Jennifer to dress and join him.

Ten minutes later, Jennifer came out wearing a pair of jeans and a T-shirt with nothing beneath it. Staring at what was barely hidden by the shirt, Jim thought, *I guess I could stay just one night. But if I do, she'll expect me to stay every night. I just can't do that, and there's no sense in letting her think I will.*

"Ready?" Jennifer asked as she picked her purse up.

"I reckon," Jim said, finishing his beer. "Where are we going?"

"Thought we would get a pizza and come back here if that's all right with you," she answered.

"Sounds good to me," Jim said, standing. "Want me to drive?"

"Sure." Jennifer smiled.

As they walked to the car, Jim followed her and, for the umpteenth time, admired the way she looked from behind. *Callipygian,* Jim thought, watching her. *Now, I truly understand the meaning of that word.*

After a quick trip for the pizza, they returned and spent the next couple of hours eating and talking. Jennifer knew better than to press Jim on the issue and decided to accept him for what he was, at least for now.

It was later than Jim wanted when they finished eating, but he tried not to appear in a hurry to leave. Finally, he told her, "Baby, I've got to get back to the base. But I'll try to stop by tomorrow, and I'll know better about my schedule. Maybe I can spend the night here at least on weekends if you want me to."

"I understand," Jennifer reluctantly replied. "I know you've got to do what you think best, but my offer stands. I would love to see you whenever you get a chance. If that means only weekends, then at least I'll have that much."

"Thanks for understanding," Jim said, standing. "I really do want to spend as much time with you as I can, and maybe I can work out something other than just the weekends."

Jennifer stood and put her arms around his waist, saying, "You go on back to the base and get your ass in the books. I want you to do well and get this program over. We can always discuss things later."

Jim bent down and took her face in his hands, kissing her. "Thanks," he said as he straightened up. "I'll be by tomorrow as soon as I can."

Jennifer walked to the door and opened it, saying, "I look forward to seeing you then. I've enjoyed today and hope we can do it again soon."

"Me too," Jim said as he left her apartment. "I'll let you

know tomorrow how much time I have off this week. And like I said, I hope to at least have the weekends off to spend with you."

With a final kiss goodbye, Jim walked to his car and got in. As he left, Jennifer was still standing in the doorway, waving. Jim waved and headed back to the base. Tomorrow was going to be a busy day, and he hoped he could keep his promise to see her later in the afternoon.

CHAPTER 13

The next morning, Jim rose early and headed to the flight line. He'd already spent several hours studying the material and felt ready for whatever the instructors had to ask. At least he knew enough to participate in any discussion and, more importantly, knew what questions he needed to ask about the material he hadn't quite understood.

Seeing Captain Knox standing at the front of the room, Jim walked directly to him and stopped at attention. When Mike turned to him, Jim said, "Good morning, sir. Cadet Lashley, reporting for training."

"Good morning, Cadet," Mike responded. "Let's get you a locker and see if we can find a spot for you at one of the desks. I see you've got your manuals and assume that you've spent a little time memorizing each detail."

"I've tried to get as much information as I could," Jim replied. "But I know there's a lot that isn't in the books, not to mention that I'm not smart enough to memorize everything. I just hope that I know enough not to look too stupid while you try to teach me."

"Don't try to bullshit me, Cadet," Mike told him,

smiling. "Now, let's go over a few basics and see exactly how much you've managed to learn on your own."

For the next hour or so, Mike quizzed Jim and discussed the curriculum for the next few weeks. Satisfied that Jim was certainly more prepared than most students, they signed out an aircraft and headed for the flight line. With their helmets and parachutes placed in the plane, Mike followed Jim as he performed the preflight inspection.

As they climbed into their seats, the ground crew prepared the airplane for engine start and stood by, awaiting the signal from the pilots. Once started, Jim signaled the crew chief to pull the chocks and held the brakes until the chief was back in front of the plane.

Getting clearance to taxi, Jim signaled that he was ready, and the crew chief motioned him forward and saluted as they pulled out onto the taxiway. Returning the salute, Jim listened to Mike give him instructions on the route they would take from the ramp area to the runway. Remembering most of it from before, Jim had no difficulty in getting to the runway and waited for the tower to clear them for takeoff.

The flight went smoothly, and Mike showed him the landmarks that would keep them in the assigned areas and basic instructions on the protocol for entering the gunnery range and how to get clearance to approach the simulated carrier deck.

Slightly over an hour later, they returned and landed. Taxiing back to the ramp, Mike sat quietly in the back and offered no instruction.

"Not bad for a first try," Mike told him as they entered the classroom, and he pulled out a folder that held all of Jim's flying history. "Do you have any questions?"

"Yes, sir," Jim answered, "I'm sure I do, but I need some time to figure out what I want to ask."

"That's normal," Mike said. "First, let's review the flight from start to finish and see if that brings to mind any questions."

Jim listened intently as Mike covered each aspect of the flight and suggested techniques that might prove beneficial. Taking notes in his binder, Jim asked occasional questions and, after about thirty minutes, felt that he had learned a lot for the first flight.

Finally, Mike stood and said, "If you have no further questions, I suggest you grab some lunch and be back here in an hour for your next flight."

"Yes, sir," Jim said, coming to attention. "Who'll I be flying with?"

"Me," Mike said, picking up the folder that had his notes from the previous flight. "I don't want to punish any of the other instructors for now. Maybe I can teach you enough that you won't be risking their lives every time you touch an airplane." Smiling, Mike continued. "See you in an hour, Cadet."

"Yes, sir," Jim said, knowing that the sarcasm was standard behavior when things had gone well.

Jim slipped off his flight overalls, hung them in his locker, and headed for the parking lot. Starting the 'Vette, he headed for the main gate and shortly arrived at Mom and Pop Burgers, where he knew Jennifer would be working.

Pulling into the parking lot, he saw her waiting on one of the tables where a couple of enlisted Marines were sitting. Smiling to himself, Jim walked in and took his customary seat that thankfully wasn't occupied.

Jennifer gave him a quick smile as she turned in the order she had just taken and waited a minute longer than necessary to come to his table. "What'll it be today, sir?" she asked with a slight smile.

"I was thinking pizza and beer," Jim grinned back.

"I don't think that's on the menu," Jennifer retorted. "I might be able to suggest where you could get that, but here, we specialize in burgers."

"Okay," Jim said, nodding. "I guess I'll have a burger, medium rare, fries, and a Dr Pepper."

"I'll see if I can get the cook to do that," she told him, having already written his order before he'd asked. "I'll be right back with your drink."

Jim watched as she headed for the counter, noticing that there was a little extra hip movement as she walked. *What a tease,* Jim thought as he noticed the two Marines were also watching closely.

When Jennifer returned with his drink, she asked, "How'd it go today?"

"Fine," Jim told her, "but I've got another flight this afternoon. I'll feel better when I finish that one."

"When will you be done today?" she asked, standing beside the table with her arms crossed.

"The flight will be over in a couple of hours. Probably finish the debrief an hour later, then get ready for tomorrow's flight," Jim answered, taking a drink.

"Think you'll be done by seven this evening?" Jennifer asked hopefully.

"I think so," Jim answered. "Anything in particular you want to do?"

"Nothing I think you'd object to," she teased. "Want to come over after I get off work?"

"I'd love to," Jim said. "But I still can't spend the night and can't stay too long. I've got a lot of studying to do, but I'll come over. Maybe we can go somewhere for dinner?"

Jennifer laughed and said, "If you insist, but I'd rather just have you alone at home for the few hours I get to spend with you."

"I guess I can manage that," Jim told her. "I'll just grab something to eat and bring it with some beer."

"That'll be just fine," Jennifer replied as she turned to walk away. "I'll be right back with your food. If you're still here when the others leave, I'll come sit with you."

There were still other customers arriving and eating when Jim finished his meal. Leaving the money for the tab and tip, he headed for the door, saying, "Thanks, Miss. I'll see you later."

"Thank you, sir," she responded. "Be careful out there."

Jim returned to the base and parked by the flight line almost thirty minutes before he was supposed to meet Mike. Slipping his flight overalls back on, he went to the same desk they'd used before and resumed studying the manuals and reviewing his notes from the previous flight.

Mike arrived right on time and said, "Let's brief this and get going. I've got another new student after we get back."

For the next half hour, they covered what they'd be doing, where they'd be going, and what Mike expected of Jim on the flight. Finally finished, they walked to the flight line, inspected the airplane as before, and climbed in. Ten minutes later, they were taxiing to the runway, and Jim was fully confident that this flight would go better than the first one.

After landing, Mike told him, "That was good, Cadet. I really don't have anything to tell you that we didn't cover in flight, so if you have no questions, I'll fill out your report and see you tomorrow."

"No questions, sir," Jim said. "Will I be flying with you tomorrow?"

"No," Mike answered. "I've already got a full schedule, so you'll be with another instructor. Don't worry; he'll review your flights, and I'll brief him on what I think you should concentrate on for your flight."

Putting his flight gear back in his locker, Jim carried his notes and manuals back to the car and returned to his room. For the next hour, he sat with the manuals in front of him, mentally flying each maneuver until he had each procedure down pat. Now, the only thing left to do was actually fly them.

It was almost seven when Jim put the books away and headed for the shower. Remembering the shower from Jennifer's house, he smiled to himself and quickly dressed.

Stopping for a pizza and a six-pack of beer, Jim arrived at Jennifer's just before seven-thirty. Seeing her car, he parked in the same slot as yesterday and carried the beer and pizza to her door. Knocking, he said, "Pizza man!"

Jennifer must have seen him pull in and open the door almost before he finished speaking. "Come in, pizza man," she said. "Just put it on the table, and I'll take care of the bill in a minute or two."

"It's going to take more than a minute or two to settle this bill," Jim joked as he put the beer in the refrigerator and the pizza on the counter. "And I hope the tip will be substantial after all the effort to get this here on time."

"I'm sure you'll like the tip," she joked back. "Want to eat now or later?"

"Definitely later," Jim said, turning to her. "What do you suggest while we wait for the beer to chill?"

Jennifer reached for his hand and replied, "I may need some help with something back here. If you'll just follow me, I think you're just the man to take care of it."

"Always ready to serve." Jim smiled as he let her lead

him to her bedroom. Knowing that every encounter with Jennifer was going to make it more difficult when he ultimately left, Jim reasoned that she was a grown woman and could make her own decisions as to when this should end or continue.

Besides, after all his attempts to contact Jewell, he'd only had two brief conversations with her. And it didn't appear that between the MARCAD program and her flight schedule, they'd get to spend any time together for the next year or so. Maybe after Beeville. Maybe never.

CHAPTER 14

For the next four weeks, Jim flew as often as he could be scheduled and visited Jennifer almost every evening. On weekends, he would spend the night with her, but he reminded her that some of that time would be devoted to studying. Happy to have him there, Jennifer gave him as much space as possible just to ensure that he would continue to give her those two days each week.

Finally finished with this phase of the program, Jim packed his few belongings and left the base for probably the last time. Having promised Jennifer that he would spend a couple of days with her before he left, Jim stayed with her since she had taken those days off work. Most of the day, they would spend time on the beach or one of the parks, where they could be alone and talk about what was about to happen to them.

Finally, the day arrived when he had to leave and drive to Beeville for advanced jet training. This five-month program would be the longest time that Jim wouldn't be around Jennifer, and he knew that she was unhappy about his leaving. Although he'd always been completely honest in his relationship with her, he also knew that she'd hoped that things would turn out differently.

Several times, she'd hinted that she'd go with him to Texas since the rules didn't prohibit any relationship except marriage. Knowing what the answer would be, Jennifer never came out and said that she'd gladly go with him. But Jim knew what she wanted and never broached the subject since he knew it'd disappoint her. Sometimes, it's better to leave the question unasked if you don't want to hear the answer.

The trip to Beeville was a little over seven hundred miles, and Jim planned to take two days to drive it. He'd decided that, although it was a relatively easy trip on I-10 and could be made in one long day, he'd spend the night in Lafayette, Louisiana. That should make it two five- or six-hour days, and Jim was in no great hurry to get there. Not that he wasn't as motivated as before, but an extra day to sort out his personal feelings and take a break with no demands on him seemed well-advised.

It was almost four in the afternoon when he pulled off I-10 and took I-49 South into Lafayette. Jim pulled into the first reasonable-looking motel and put his clothes bag in his room. It was no luxury, but it was much better than the barracks at Pensacola or Saufley.

That taken care of, he locked the room and got in the car to look for someplace to eat. Finding another small burger shop near the motel, Jim walked in and took a seat. Looking at the waitress as she approached, Jim thought, *That's certainly no Jennifer!*

After eating his standard burger, Jim went back to the motel and tried again to call Jewell to at least tell her he was heading for Texas on the off chance that he'd even reach her or that she might be somewhere close enough that he could see her. As usual, no answer.

The next morning, Jim rose early and loaded his bags in the 'Vette. After paying his bill, he headed back north on I-49 and then rejoined I-10 westbound. The only part of the remainder of the trip that worried him was going through Houston and taking US 59 on toward Beeville. The rest of the road pretty much bypassed the small towns, and other than a couple of stops for gas, Jim estimated that he would reach Beeville shortly after noon. That'd leave plenty of time to get his room, find the flight line, hopefully, get the manual for the F-9 he'd be flying, and study a little before he hit the sack.

There was not much traffic as Jim sped westward, and soon, he had passed Lake Charles, Louisiana, and shortly afterward crossed the Texas state line just north of Orange, Texas. Remembering all the small towns with strange names around where he had grown up, Jim smiled as he thought of all the jokes about why certain towns had their names.

A little over an hour later, he approached the outskirts of Houston and saw a noticeable increase in the traffic. Although his speed had dropped considerably, he knew that it would only take three hours or so to reach the base. His biggest concern was to make sure he was in the correct lane to take US 59 South. At least the signs were fairly prominent and gave adequate warning of the exits.

Jim saw the exit just about the center of Houston, took the ramp off I-10, and headed south. Now, he felt comfortable in finding a place to get gas and something to eat. Unfamiliar with Downtown Houston, he wasn't about to try finding anyplace and the way back onto the freeway.

Thirty minutes or so later, he saw a gas station that was on the same side of the road and a place called Venice Pizza and Pasta on the same block. Taking the next exit, he backtracked through the residential area until he knew he could join the access road and then have no trouble getting back on 59.

The gas tank was full, and his hunger was satisfied; Jim pulled back on the highway and figured it wouldn't take too long to get to the base, and there was no reason to stop again until he was there.

Watching for any signs pointing the way to the Naval Air Station Chase Field, Jim saw numerous jets flying overhead, obviously headed there. Slowing as he went through the town, it was almost one o'clock when he arrived at the gate to the base.

Presenting his ID and orders to the guard, Jim got the prepared information packet for Cadets and directions to the flight line. He headed directly there, hoping to meet someone who was also in the MARCAD program or one of the instructors who could help him.

Barely parked, Jim saw a Cadet with the insignia that all the Cadets wore. Stepping out of the car, Jim called out to get his attention. As the man approached, Jim identified himself and asked where he could find an instructor and where the quarters were for the Cadets.

Getting the information, Jim thanked him and entered one of the buildings adjacent to the flight line where the classes were held. Inside, Jim spotted one of the Cadets who had been at Pensacola when Jim had first arrived. Approaching him, Jim again asked for assistance in checking in and getting some study material.

The Marine Captain whom Jim met was cordial and helped him get the manuals for the F-9 and a couple of others covering operations at Chase. Carrying them back to the car, Jim then headed for the barracks and finished processing into the base.

Once established in his room, Jim emptied his bags, making sure to hang the uniform items in his closet and put his dirty clothes in a bag he found hanging from the clothes rack.

The next morning, Jim rose early as usual and hurried down to the flight line. As he arrived, he saw the Captain whom he had met and walked over to greet him. After a short conversation, Jim was shown where the lockers were located, how the scheduling was done, and what he could expect for the coming months.

As the room filled with other instructors and Cadets, Jim noticed several faces that he had seen during the earlier parts of the program. Knowing that they were ahead of him and some would be graduating soon, Jim watched as they settled into the routine. Excited to fly this new plane, Jim also looked forward to the end. Then, as a newly commissioned Second Lieutenant in the Marines and a pilot as well, he could regain some control of his personal life. Just what he'd do regarding Jennifer remained to be seen, but at least after graduation, he could make that decision.

Jim and Jennifer talked infrequently when Jim found time out of his demanding schedule of studying and flying. Occasional letters were sent with words of encouragement from Jennifer and a promise to try to get back to Florida from Jim.

Jim did manage one cross-country flight to Pensacola during his training and managed to spend the night with her. That reunion meant as much to him as it did to Jennifer.

Jim also continued to maintain some contact with Jewell, but as before, there was limited success because of her busy flight schedule and his twelve to fourteen hours spent trying to master the F-9 and the rigid courses as he pushed himself to stand above the other students.

The five months seemed to fly by, and when the day of his final flight arrived, only an hour or so remained before his goal was to be achieved.

After landing and the final debrief, Jim was ordered to report to the Base Commander's office in his dress uniform for the commissioning procedure. Knowing that it was somewhat abnormal, Jim put his flight gear away and hurried back to his room to shower and dress.

Arriving at the Commander's office, the secretary told him to wait while she notified the Colonel that he was there. A few seconds later, she told him to go on in. The minute he entered the office, the first thing he saw was General Barker standing beside the Colonel's desk, smiling at him.

"Cadet Lashley reporting as ordered, sir," Jim said, coming to attention just inside the door.

"Lieutenant Lashley," the Colonel said, correcting him, "please step forward to receive your Second Lieutenant bars and your gold wings as a Marine pilot. General Barker has asked to present them and will pin them on your uniform."

General Barker took a pair of gold bars from the top of the desk and stood in front of Jim, saying, "Lieutenant Lashley, it's my honor to pin these simple gold bars on you, designating you as our newest Marine officer. These are the same bars I received so many years ago, and I know you'll treasure them as I did when I got them."

Jim stood at attention as the bars were placed on his shoulders. "Now," General Barker continued, taking the wings from the desk, "again, it's my honor to present you with the gold wings of a Marine pilot."

Pinning the wings above the row of medals on Jim's chest, he finished, "Congratulations, Lieutenant Lashley, you have completed a very demanding course and have performed as I'd expected."

"Thank you, sir," Jim said.

"Now, there's one final thing," the Colonel told him. "Here are your orders for F-4 training at El Toro. General Barker personally directed your assignment and also ordered you to take thirty days of leave before you report."

Jim looked at General Barker and said, "Thank you, General. I don't know how to express my appreciation for all that you've done for me."

"You just keep doing what I've always expected of you," General Barker told him. "That'll be the only appreciation I need. Now you get your things packed, go wherever you want for the next month, and relax for a few days."

"Yes, sir," Jim said as he prepared to leave. "Again, thank you."

Jim pivoted and walked from the room, still in shock that General Barker had taken the time and interest in him. All he could think of now was to go home and try to sort out what he really wanted to do regarding either Jennifer or Jewell. Even though his contact with Jewell was almost nonexistent, she remained there in the back of his mind. He knew that things would never progress with Jennifer until he resolved that issue.

CHAPTER 15

As soon as Jim got back to his room, he packed everything he had except the clothes he intended to wear and his shave kit. Everything was locked in the trunk of his car; he called his dad and told him that he'd finished the program and would be back home late the next day. Another call was made to Jennifer, and he broached the subject of a trip to see her after visiting his parents. A futile attempt was made to contact Jewell.

Early the next morning, Jim showered, checked his room one last time, and headed for his car. He knew the almost 600-mile trip would take close to ten hours, but it'd been over a year since he'd been home, and he looked forward to the quietness of the drive.

Heading south out of the base, Jim joined I-37 North toward San Antonio. A little over an hour passed as Jim sped along with nothing demanding his time except the scant early traffic. It'd been such a long time, with almost every waking hour spent studying or reviewing flights, that he enjoyed the mental break.

On the outskirts of San Antonio, Jim found a truck stop

and pulled in, wanting to get a quick breakfast and refuel the car. Never really believing that truckers knew the best places to eat, Jim always thought that it was one of the few places they could park the 18-wheelers and get whatever food was available.

Again, looking around as he waited for the waitress to come to him, the obvious stares and disapproving looks reminded him of the contempt of most of the civilian population. Having spent the last year or so around primarily military people, he'd almost forgotten how the civilian world viewed him and his kind.

Eager to get back on the road, Jim ordered black coffee, two scrambled eggs, bacon, and toast. Figuring that his selection would be the quickest to make and least likely to be screwed up, he waited for it to be delivered. Trying to avoid eye contact with the other patrons, Jim sat staring out the window, wondering if any of these morons knew the hardships and effort that each member of the armed services went through so they could sit here safe and secure in their little buffered world.

As soon as the plate was noisily slammed down, Jim splashed a liberal dose of Tabasco over the eggs and wolfed the meal down more to get it over with than hunger. The thought of either the cook or waitress spitting in his food crossed his mind, but he refused to worry about things he couldn't control.

Finished, Jim left money for the bill and a meager tip before slowly walking out, intentionally sending the message that he wasn't going to run from the obvious disdain of these people.

Back on the road, Jim continued north into San Antonio and joined I-10 toward Kerrville. Again, the mindless monotony of the road soothed his anger at the civilians, and less than an hour later, he saw the exit for US 87 that'd take him to Brady. There, he'd join US 283 just north of Coleman, and remembering stories about his dad flying out of there during WWII, Jim thought about how much alike he and his dad really were.

After another hour of heading north, Jim approached Abilene, where he began looking for signs where he would join I-20 westbound. Less than an hour later, Jim took the exit for US 84 just before hitting Roscoe. Now, with less than two hours until he reached Lubbock, Jim watched familiar scenery pass as he drove past Snyder and Post. The melancholy feeling and nostalgia brought by memories of his past carefree and slightly rambunctious lifestyle reminded Jim of the dramatic change the Marines had made on him.

Approaching Lubbock, Jim decided to head to Luby's cafeteria for lunch. He wasn't a particular fan of the place, but his mother had always insisted on eating there whenever possible. Again, Jim was aware of the looks he was receiving as he walked down the buffet and selected meatloaf and mashed potatoes with gravy. As before, he tried to ignore the stares and ate quietly but quickly.

Finished and now slightly over an hour from home, Jim headed back to his car and wondered if he would ever understand why people held such hatred for service members. It was fine to oppose the war; hell, sometimes, he himself wondered about the wisdom of the continuing conflict, but those serving and dying were only doing what generations before them had done—follow the wishes of their elected officials. From the Revolution to today, men and women have taken up arms in support of their government. But Jim didn't think there had ever been such animosity against fellow citizens.

North of Lubbock, Jim passed Anton and Littlefield before reaching Sudan. There, he made the turn on State Road 303 that would take him home, smiling as he remembered his mother calling him The Terror of 303 when he was still a few years from high school. The little Cushman scooter had taken Jim all over the area within a couple of miles of their house as Jim pretended he was a desperate outlaw or on some secret mission to spy on neighbors' cattle or crops.

Over nine hours since leaving Beeville, Jim watched the familiar scrub brush and small sand hills pass as he thought about how welcome he'd be pulling into the driveway. He had no doubt that his father was telling his mother to quit watching for him but making excuses to be out of the house as often as possible to look down the road for the sight of Jim's 'Vette.

Stopping briefly at US 70 that ran west to Muleshoe and east to Earth, Jim remembered the number of times he had driven all these roads during his high school years, sometimes dating girls from either town, which was risky in Earth since it was a different school and the "local" boys resented strangers *befouling* their ladies. The strange thing was that Jim lived closer to Earth than Muleshoe, and some of the Earth "locals" lived closer than his classmates.

Two and a half miles later, Jim pulled onto the gravel drive that took him to the house. The first thing he saw was his father walking out of the single-car garage. Trying to look surprised and nonchalant, his dad waved as Jim drove up and parked in front of the house.

"Welcome home, boy," his dad said as soon as Jim had killed the engine.

"Hi, Dad," Jim said, climbing out of the car.

"Didn't expect for you to get here for another couple

of hours," John told him.

Noticing the lawn chair behind his dad's car, Jim smiled and said, "I don't suppose you were just sitting out here waiting for the sun to set, were you?"

John looked toward the garage and said, "Oh no, that chair's been there for a couple of days. I was just sitting out here the other day smoking my pipe and watching a hawk chasing a mouse in the pasture."

Jim looked up at the sky, smiling, and replied, "Guess he got the mouse and left."

"Let's get in the house," his dad gruffed. "I think your mother's been anxious for you to get home. And don't let on that you've seen her watching out the window. I think she's washed the same dish a dozen times over the last hour or so, looking out at the road."

As Jim opened the front door, John said, "You go on in, and I'll start bringing your bags in."

Jim walked into the kitchen, where his mother was pretending to be cleaning the sink, and said, "Hi, Mom."

She turned as she laid the wet towel on the counter and said, "I'm glad you're finally home. Your father's been walking down to the road every fifteen minutes looking for your car. But don't tell him I told you."

"Mum's the word, Mom," Jim said as she put her arms around his waist in a hug of relief.

Reluctantly letting him go, she said, "Your father took out steaks for dinner, and I'm pretty sure there's another batch of homemade ice cream. I swear, that man's been running around here like a chicken with his head cut off trying to think of things for you."

"He probably just wanted the ice cream himself," Jim joked, knowing his father.

"Then it's certainly strange that he drove all the way to

Texaco this morning after you told him you'd be in tonight," his mother said, "just for a bottle of Jack Daniel's. And then had to go back to town to get the stuff for the ice cream."

"Coincidence," Jim laughed, thinking about how his father had tried to anticipate the little things that they had shared over the years.

"What're you two jawing about?" John asked as he walked into the kitchen.

"Nothing," Jim's mother told him. "We're just talking about why you suddenly needed a bottle of Jack when there's half a bottle left from when Jim left last time."

"Oh, that," John answered. "I forgot that we had any, and I know how those Marine flyboys like to drink. I just didn't want Jim driving to Clovis, drinking with all his old buddies, and then driving home."

Jim shook his head and said, "I'll finish getting my stuff out of the car while you two finish this family feud."

John followed Jim back out to the car and helped carry in the last of Jim's bags. After putting them in Jim's room, he asked, "I don't suppose you'd like a little drink to wash the dust from your throat after that long drive, would you?"

"Maybe just a little." Jim smiled. "I'm pretty parched, and I haven't enjoyed a drink with my favorite *Dad* in a very long time."

Jim watched his father's eyes mist over as he turned away. "Well, we can't have a parched Marine in our house," his dad said, his voice almost breaking as he opened the cabinet where the liquor was kept. "Let's mix a couple and go outside. I've got to get some mesquite burning in the grill so it can ash over before we start the steaks."

The Jack and Coke mixed, Jim followed his dad out of the house and sat on one of the old lawn chairs, watching him pile a couple more sticks of mesquite wood in the grill.

After the fire was going, John came and sat beside Jim and watched the flames licking over the top of the old metal grill. Neither one of them said anything for several minutes, just relaxed, enjoying the occasional closeness that a man and his son sometimes have.

Jim's mother came out carrying three thick rib-eye steaks on a platter, saying, "If you two would get to work on these steaks instead of just sitting around, we might get to eat tonight."

John rose and took the platter, saying, "We've just been waiting for the fire to die down a little. If you've got everything else ready, we'll have these cooked in about seven or eight minutes."

"Everything's ready, and the table's almost set," she replied. "Now if you two think you can handle the steaks by yourselves, I'll go back inside and finish."

As soon as the steaks were cooked, Jim and his dad carried them in and put one on each of the plates at the kitchen table. Once everyone was sitting, John did the closest thing he ever did regarding prayer before eating as he said, "Thank goodness that you've made it home safely. Now, if it's okay with your mother, let's enjoy these steaks that I've cooked to perfection to celebrate your being here."

After chitchatting during dinner, John said, "I'm going outside for a smoke. Why don't you help your mother with the dishes?"

Jim and his mom talked about trivial things as they worked together, getting the leftovers put away and the dishes washed. Knowing that his mother would never say anything that revealed her true feelings about what the future held for him, Jim told her, "Mom, I know you've been worried about the flight training and the fact that I'll probably have to go back to 'Nam, but that's still almost a year away. If the war's still going on, I'll probably have to go back. But this time, I won't be on the ground, and we'll be based a long way from the actual fighting."

She turned to him and reminded him, "I lived with your father when he was flying during WWII, so don't try to tell me it's not dangerous for pilots. Just look at the number of planes that have been shot down over there and the number of POWs. Worse yet are those that are listed as Missing In Action, and the families may never know what happened to them. I don't care what you tell me about being careful. As long as you're over there, I'll worry every day. And so will your father. You may not know this, but I think that man worries more about you than I do. If anything ever happened to you, I think it'd just about kill him."

John came back in just as they were putting the last dishes away and said, "Well, I guess we better get to bed. I'm sure there are plenty of things Jim and I need to do tomorrow."

"You two go on," she said. "I've got a few more things to do before I come to bed."

Jim gave his mother a hug and whispered, "Thanks, Mom. You know I love you."

She hugged him and softly said, "I know, son, I know."

CHAPTER 16

For the next week, Jim and his dad piddled around the place, fixing small problems, going into town for various reasons, and just hanging out together. Jim spent as much time as possible with his mother, trying his best to reassure her. As they fell into the family routine of meals, TV, and visits to neighbors, but mainly just sitting around together, Jim began to feel the need to get back to his training. The week had been relaxing, but he wasn't one to sit too long before needing something to occupy his mind.

Having called Jennifer before leaving Beeville to tentatively plan a trip back to Pensacola, Jim checked airline flights and purchased a round-trip ticket from Amarillo through DFW. Selecting one that would give them almost four days together, he called and told her of his plans.

Once that decision was made, he told his parents of his intentions and promised that he'd be back before departing for El Toro. Both his mother and his dad knew that Jim was becoming bored at home and needed to find some outlet for the pent-up energy that had been typical of him since childhood.

Although they wanted to drive him to Amarillo, Jim refused the offer, reasoning that they would have to come back to get him. It was much simpler for him to drive himself and leave the car there while he was visiting Jennifer.

The morning he was to leave, his mother moved and sat beside him at the table as soon as John left the room. "Is this girl someone special?" she asked.

"I think so," Jim answered.

"How long have you known her?" she wanted to know. "How much do you know about her?"

"I guess I've known her for about a year," Jim said. "I met her right after I got to Pensacola."

"How involved are you?" she asked.

"We've gotten close," Jim told her, knowing exactly what his mother was asking.

"How does she feel about you being gone for months at a time?" she asked.

"She's not exactly excited about it," Jim replied. "But she understands that this is my life and that if she ever hopes to be a part of it, she has to accept it."

"Are you saying that you want her to be a part of your life?" his mother asked, wondering just how close Jennifer and Jim really were.

"I'm not sure yet," Jim told her. "I do know that I enjoy being around her, but there's still a big unknown ahead of me."

"There'll always be big unknowns in life," she reminded him. "I'm asking if you think this could be the woman that you want to live with for the rest of your life."

"I know what you're driving at," Jim answered. "The best answer I can give you is the same one I've given her. I've got to complete the training at El Toro and see if I'll have to go back to 'Nam before I make any lifelong decisions."

"I don't think you really do know what I'm driving at," she said. "What I'm driving at is—do you think, all other things aside, that this woman would be the right one for you?"

"All I know at this point," Jim told her, "is that she's made me happier than any other woman. And she's accepted my lifestyle with as much grace as I could expect of any woman."

"All right," she said, standing, "I'll quit meddling in your business. I just want you to make sure that she wasn't just some port in the storm while you were lonely down there. I've always hoped you'd meet someone that'd make you happy, and we could welcome her into the family."

John walked in as she was finishing talking and asked, "Who are we welcoming into the family?"

"Nobody," she said, walking to the sink. "We were having a private conversation when you so rudely interrupted."

"I suppose this is about that girl down in Florida," John said. "I say that any woman that'll put up with Jim, we should always welcome."

"Thanks, Dad," Jim replied, standing. "I'm glad to know that you have doubts about my suitability for a long-term relationship and should grab the first shiny thing that shows the minimal interest."

"Yep," John joked. "You ain't the prettiest thing around; you've certain tendencies to run off to foreign lands, and you still haven't figured out that you can't stay a kid forever."

"Thanks again, Dad," Jim said, smiling. "Maybe you'd like to call her and tell her about the huge mistake she's making just by seeing me. I've left her number by the phone in case you need to call, but I bet you can use it to warn her so she can change her plans before I even get to Amarillo.”

“No,” John grinned. “I think it’s too far along now for her to listen to the voice of wisdom. I suppose I can only hope that she’s got the good sense to understand that what she sees in you is exactly what she’ll get.”

“Seems she knows that,” Jim said, walking out of the kitchen. “If you’re finished belittling me, I’ll get the rest of my stuff and head north.”

Jim retrieved his single bag from his bedroom and headed for the front door. John was standing beside the ’Vette, watching as Jim put the bag in the trunk.

“How long will you be able to stay here when you get back?” he wanted to know.

“About a week or so,” Jim told him as he slammed the trunk.

Walking around to his father, he continued, “I need at least three days to drive to California, so add another day in case anything happens on the road. I guess I’ll have six or seven days.”

Putting his arm around Jim’s shoulders, his dad said, “I guess we’ll take what we can get, but each time you leave, it’s hard on your mother.”

Knowing that it hurt his father as much or more to say goodbye, Jim just smiled and said, “I know, Dad. She’s a tough old bird and will hold up as well as anybody.”

Giving his father a final hug, Jim climbed into the car as he looked at the house where his mother was watching from the window and said, “I’ve got to go so I can make the flight. You take care of Mom, and I’ll see you guys in four days.”

John watched as Jim shut the car door and told him, “You just drive carefully, and if you need anything, call me.”

"I'll do that," Jim told him as he started the engine. "You can reach me at Jennifer's if you need. Bye, Dad," Jim said as he waved to his mother at the window. "I think you may need to go back to Texaco for another bottle of Jack for my return. You seem to be sipping a little more lately, and I'm starting to worry about what the Baptists think."

"I'm blaming it on you," John said, raising his hand to wave as the car began to roll forward.

"No doubt," Jim said loudly over the exhaust noise as he waved goodbye.

The hour-long drive to Amarillo led Jim back through the small towns and countryside that had become so familiar over the years. As much change had taken place in his own life, he marveled at the lack of change around him.

Parked at the airport, Jim walked into the terminal, looking around to see if, by the most unlikely circumstance, he would run into Jewell. After checking in with the agent, he headed for the departure gate to wait. Although dressed in boots, jeans, and a starched shirt, Jim knew he stood out from the rest of the crowd because of his haircut. Again, the looks of disdain from the few young people around the gate bothered him, but he just smiled back and took a seat as far as possible from where they were sitting.

Finally, on the plane, Jim sat back and watched Palo Duro Canyon slide beneath the wings as they took off and headed southeast toward DFW. Now, with a broader experience in flying, he wondered what it'd be like to fly something this big. He was glad he hadn't been assigned to the transport part of Marine aviation, but he still wondered if the pilots enjoyed flying this type of plane the way he enjoyed the jets he'd been flying.

As the Flight Attendant approached with drink offers, Jim asked for a Dr Pepper and waited until she handed him the can and a small glass with ice.

"Army?" the Flight Attendant asked as she handed him a napkin.

"No, Ma'am," Jim said. "Marine."

"Well, regardless," she told him, "be careful. I lost a brother over there and just wish it was over."

"Me too," Jim said. "I'm sorry about your brother. We've all lost someone over there, and it never gets easier. But again, I'm sorry you've lost someone as close to you as a family member."

"Thank you," she said, continuing down the aisle.

The short stop at DFW passed quickly, and Jim was soon on the next flight headed for Pensacola. Again, he watched the terminal in hopes of seeing Jewell, but out of the sea of uniformed Flight Attendants, he recognized no one.

After takeoff, Jim found himself looking forward to seeing Jennifer. Thinking about his mother's questions, he knew that Jennifer was indeed something very special. But the fact remained that he still had almost six months of training ahead of him and very likely another year back overseas. He refused to even consider anything further until there was some stability in his life. That didn't keep him from dreaming about it, though.

CHAPTER 17

Jennifer was standing just outside the gate when Jim finally made his way behind all the other passengers. He could see her looking around the taller people who were heading for baggage claim or were greeting other people. When her eyes met his, he could see the smile and knew immediately why he'd made this trip.

As he exited the gate, she came running up to him and threw her arms around his neck. He kissed her gently on the lips and said, "You wouldn't believe how much I've missed you!"

Jennifer pulled her head back slightly and looked into Jim's eyes, saying, "I could hardly wait after you told me what flight you were on. It's only been a little over a month since you were here last, and you didn't get to stay long, but it seems like forever."

"Let's get out of here," Jim hurriedly replied. "I've grown to hate airline terminals, and I've been thinking about beer and pizza for quite a while now."

"Oh, so that's it?" Jennifer joked as they headed for the baggage claim. "I'd hoped you'd been missing me, not pizza!"

"Nope, just the pizza," teased Jim. "Okay, I'll admit that I've missed those cold Budweiser bottles in your refrigerator as well."

"You're such an ass," Jennifer said, hitting him on the arm.

"If you're trying to beat the truth out of me," Jim said, wincing, "I'll admit that maybe I've missed you serving me those beers and the pizza."

"Not near good enough," Jennifer joked, hitting him again.

"Okay, okay," Jim said. "It's true about the beer and pizza, but that thing about the way you serve is also true. I've replayed that first night in my mind over and over until I can just close my eyes and see the soap running down—"

"Stop it!" Jennifer laughed. "Let's not let all these strangers know what a pervert you really are!"

"Pervert? Me?" Jim asked incredulously. "Just who was it that lured me into the shower? Tempting me? If I remember correctly, I was completely satisfied drinking my beer and watching TV."

"Such a liar," Jennifer said as they waited for Jim's bag to arrive. "I remember it quite differently."

Jim smiled at her as he picked up the single bag and said, "Okay, little lady, suppose we just go back to your place and reenact the whole thing. I think you'll see that my version's indeed correct."

"Wishful thinking on your part," Jennifer told him. "Besides, that was something special for a poor little Cadet. I'm not so sure that'd be appropriate behavior for a Lieutenant in the Marine Corps."

"Oh, Lieutenants get treated much better than Cadets," Jim informed her. "But since we've known each other for so long, in private, you can still call me Jim. And I won't make you say 'Sir' each time you talk to me unless we're in public."

Jennifer just shook her head and said, "Not a chance, *Sir*! If you expect to be treated any differently than before, I'd suggest you use that return ticket right now." Stopping and turning to Jim, she said, "But I really am proud of you. I know it's been difficult, and I didn't make it any easier on you."

"No, Jennifer," Jim quietly said, looking into her eyes. "You're one of the reasons that I *did* make it. You've been the single bright spot through this whole thing, and knowing that you cared made it easier to put up with most of the crap that came my way."

Jennifer smiled as she looked at Jim and finally said, "You're right about that little beer and pizza thing. How 'bout we stop for the pizza on the way home? I've already got the beer, and I can have the shower running while you watch TV. Of course, I may have to ask for your assistance—again. How 'bout that?"

Jim laughed and said, "What're we standing here for? I can't wait to get that beer and watch TV!"

After a quick stop, they parked by Jennifer's apartment, and Jim followed her in, carrying his bag and the pizza box. "I'll put this in the kitchen," Jim said, sitting his bag on the floor.

"Fine," Jennifer replied as she headed toward the bedroom. "Grab yourself a beer and see if there's anything in particular you want to watch."

Vividly remembering those same exact words from before, Jim had barely opened the bottle when he heard Jennifer say, "Hey, Jim, can you come back here and give me a hand with something?"

Jim sat the opened beer back in the refrigerator, grinning, and thought, *Oh, I see you remember too!*

Almost an hour later, as they lay quietly in bed, Jennifer asked, "Are you ready to go eat, or do you want to stay here and let me feed you?"

"No," Jim answered. "I think those batteries need recharging again, so we better eat out there."

Jennifer rolled onto her side and put her head on Jim's chest, saying, "I'm so glad you're here. I know you can only stay a couple of days, but for now, I'm perfectly happy just having you with me."

Jim leaned down, kissing the top of her head, saying, "Me too. I wish I could stay longer, so let's not waste a single minute worrying about what'll happen later."

Jennifer sat up and told him, "You go get a quick shower, and I'll heat the pizza." As Jim got out of bed, she teased, "If you need a hand with anything, just call!"

"You'll be first to know," Jim retorted as he walked into the bathroom.

Standing under the warm water, Jim thought about how much he enjoyed his time with Jennifer. It was a combination of quiet satisfaction when they were just sitting together or immense pleasure when they were being romantic.

Smiling as he thought about their relationship, Jennifer poked her head around the curtain and said, "Just leave the water running. I'll jump in as soon as you get out."

Finished rinsing, Jim smiled and stepped from the shower, saying, "I'd stay in with you, but I've learned how devious you are when you've got something on your mind."

Jennifer smiled back as she got in and replied, "I don't seem to remember any complaints on your part!"

As Jim toweled dry, he said, "I'm not complaining, but

sometimes a guy just wants to go for long walks, hold hands, and talk about our feelings.”

From behind the curtain, Jennifer told him, “Liar, liar, liar! You are such a liar, Lieutenant Lashley! *Such* a liar!”

Jim walked back into the bedroom and pulled on his jeans before heading for the kitchen. Opening the refrigerator, he removed the beer he’d opened previously. Carrying it back into the living room, he sat on the couch and waited for Jennifer to get out of the shower.

A few minutes later, she walked into the room wearing nothing but a long T-shirt and remarked, “You seem to have made yourself right at home there, Mister. I don’t suppose you’d consider getting me a beer so I can join you?”

Jim sat his beer on the table and rose, saying, “It would be my honor, pretty lady. Why don’t you just sit here, and I’ll be right back.”

Returning with her beer, Jim saw her sitting on the couch with her legs partially curled beneath her. Sitting beside her, he remarked, “I may have to buy you a longer shirt if you insist on dressing so casually around me.”

Jennifer smiled as she took the bottle, her hand lingering on his for a moment, and said, “I didn’t know you had such sensitivities. But if my ‘attire’ bothers you, I’ll go get a long robe.”

Sitting beside her, Jim answered, “I’m a *very* sensitive man, but I can get used to seeing you like this over a long, long period of time. That’s if you continue to look like this over a long, long period of time.”

“Is that a proposal?” Jennifer joked.

“No, just a statement of fact,” Jim told her. “That fact is that I sort of like the way you look in that shirt. The other fact is that if we don’t get that pizza pretty quick, we may have to heat it again.”

Laughing, Jennifer got up and said, "I'll bring it in. You just sit there and behave yourself like a good little boy."

Later that evening when they had gone to bed, Jennifer asked, "Are you happy? I mean, do you enjoy being with me? Or is this just going to be a long series of one-night stands?"

Jim pulled her close to him and answered, "You know I'm happy being with you. I've never been with any other woman that makes me feel this way. And no, I don't think of this as one-night stands. But this is all I can offer right now. I can't make any promises about the future other than that I hope we can be together as much as we can." Jim whispered, "I do love you, and I do want more. It just can't be right now."

"I love you too," Jennifer said as she snuggled against him. "And that's enough for now."

The next morning, Jim was in the kitchen making coffee when Jennifer walked in, asking, "What do you want to do today?"

"How about we drive to Apalachicola?" Jim suggested. "They have some of the best oysters on the Gulf."

Jennifer put her arms around his waist and answered, "Sounds good to me. Maybe more oysters will keep your batteries charged more."

Jim laughed and said, "I don't think that old saying is true, but I'll try anything you want. However, if you're complaining, then that's an entirely different issue."

Jennifer smiled and slapped him on the behind, saying, "No complaints, except that you've been slow getting my coffee this morning. I thought you Marines were always up early."

She took her arms from around his waist and kissed him on the chest, saying, "You go sit down. I'll bring it in."

Later, after both had showered, Jennifer came into the living room where Jim was sitting and said, "Well, Lieutenant Lashley, if you're finally ready, let's storm the beach!"

Jim stood up laughing and replied, "I'm ready, but if you don't mind, let's drop the 'Lieutenant' stuff. Just call me Sir."

"Yes, *Sir*," Jennifer joked. "Now, *Sir*, let's go find those oysters you find so appealing."

Over the next couple of days, Jim and Jennifer spent most of their time just talking as they enjoyed the beach and restaurants or sitting around her apartment. The morning Jim had to leave came way too soon for either of their liking.

"Ready to go?" Jennifer asked as Jim came out of the bedroom with his bag.

"Ready," he told her as he put his arm around her.

"Then let's get this over," she told him as she headed for the door. "If you don't mind, I'll just drop you off at the airport. I'm not very good at long goodbyes."

Jim just nodded and followed her out the door. The short drive to the airport was silent as they both wished things could be different but realized that any future relationship would have to wait for now. At the airport, Jennifer stopped at the curb and looked at Jim. Without saying a word, Jim leaned over and kissed her.

Taking his bag from the rear seat, he opened the car door and said, "I do love you, I really do."

"I love you too," Jennifer said as tears slid down her cheeks.

Jim shut the car door and stepped onto the curb, watching as Jennifer took one last glance at him and drove away.

CHAPTER 18

The flight and drive back to Muleshoe were uneventful, as Jim's mind was preoccupied with the memories of the last few days. It wasn't until he pulled into the driveway and saw his dad sitting in a lawn chair, smoking his pipe, that Jim turned the memories off and started thinking about what the next months would bring.

The next few days passed quickly, and soon, the time to head for California arrived. As before, John reminded Jim of how much his mother would miss him and to make sure he called as often as possible. Never one to really show his own feelings, John used his wife as a safety conduit to keep everything in the second person and avoid the emotion.

The day before Jim was to leave, Jim and his dad took the 'Vette back into town to be serviced and for Jim to get a fresh haircut. After they returned home, John asked Jim if he wanted to go for a little drive before supper.

"Sure," Jim said, wondering what his dad was up to. "Where are we going?"

"Oh, nowhere in particular," John answered. "Just thought we'd wander around the country for a little while."

Jim followed his dad out to the truck and climbed into the passenger seat as he started the engine. Heading west on the dirt road that marked the edge of the farm, John drove silently as Jim watched the passing crops or vacant fields. Several of the old houses sat empty as the families of some of the kids Jim had known in school had left, and the farms were now leased.

About ten minutes later, they pulled into a narrow dirt road that led to a barn on a neighbor's property. Stopping in front of the wide-open doors, Jim recognized the owner as one of his dad's friends who had also been an aviator in WWII.

As they were getting out of the pickup, the man known to Jim as Mr. Murphy came walking out.

"Afternoon, Fred," John called out.

"Afternoon, John," Fred answered. "Who's that young fellow you've got tagging along?"

"Hi, Mr. Murphy," Jim said, sticking out his hand. "Been a while."

Fred shook Jim's hand and replied, "Yep, sure has. Your dad called and told me you were back for a few days, and I told him to bring you by."

Fred led them into the barn, where a couple of rear seats from an old car were sitting facing each other against one of the walls, and said, "Y'all have a seat. I'll get us a couple of beers."

Jim and John sat down as Fred opened the door to a dust-covered refrigerator and took out three bottles of Budweiser.

Using the bottle opener that hung from a string on the door handle, Fred opened them and handed one to each of them before sitting down, saying, "I hear you're heading for California tomorrow. Gonna be an F-4 pilot."

"Yes, sir," Jim answered, waiting for Fred to take a drink of his beer before he did.

"Well, I guess that's good," Fred said, taking a sip. "I suppose that means you'll be going back to 'Nam."

Jim took a small sip and answered, "Yes, sir, probably."

"I don't guess you know much about my past during WWII," Fred said, sitting his beer between his legs. "There aren't but a couple of people out here that do."

"No, sir," Jim acknowledged. "Dad only said that you were in the Army Air Corps."

"That's true," Fred said, leaning back. "I was a Flight Engineer on B-24s. I really enjoyed it. The crew always stuck together and generally got along quite well. But the part that most folks don't know is what happened after we were shot down over Italy."

Having never heard about this from his father, Jim just sat back and listened as Fred talked about the prison camps, forced marches where hundreds of men died, starvation, lack of sanitation, and overall misery of being a prisoner of war.

The story is finally over; Fred said, "The reason I wanted to tell you this little tale is that most people think that the aviators are immune from this sort of thing, that only the ground troops get captured."

Taking another drink from his almost-empty bottle, Fred continued. "I know you've seen the scenes on TV about pilots being shot down and pictures of them being led through the villages. What I'm trying to tell you is that any of us could be that person. Every time you fly your mission, there's a chance that you'll not make it back. Sometimes, I think those who died when they crashed were the lucky ones."

Finishing the beer, Fred rose and walked to the

refrigerator for another. As he opened the bottle, he turned back and continued. "The thing that has haunted me ever since we were rescued at the end of the war was how many men suffered for so long only to die before they ever saw freedom again. The whole truth about what happens in those camps in 'Nam may never be told, but the basic inhumanity is probably just as bad as it was during my war," Fred mused as he returned to his seat.

"Having said all that," he went on, "I know that your sense of duty is just like your dad's and mine back then. I hate to see all the demonstrations by those drugged-out, imbecilic, free love bunch of draft dodgers. We had our share of people who were opposed to our war, but these crap-for-brains kids have no shame.

"Now I want you to know that people like your dad and I support you every step of the way," Fred told him. "I personally don't understand what we hope to accomplish over there, but for the men and women who answered our country's call, I'm behind you all the way."

Jim was stunned to hear Fred's story and wondered just how many of his dad's other friends had similar stories. Jim sat quietly, looking at Fred for a few seconds, and then replied, "Thanks, Mr. Murphy. I know you and the rest of Dad's friends will always be there for me if I ever need you. And I'm sorry about what happened to you and your friends back then."

"Water under the bridge," Fred said, standing. "Just an old warrior reminiscing. You just take care of yourself if you have to go back. I've heard about your previous little encounter over there from your dad, and I feel sure you'll get back to us when this is over."

Jim sat his empty bottle on the ground beside the old car seat and offered his hand to Fred, saying, "I'll do my best, sir. I'm sure Dad will let you know everything that's going on with me. And thanks for the beer. It's been a pleasure talking with you."

Fred shook Jim's hand and said, "John, you take this young man home and make sure he enjoys every moment he has before he has to go. And if there's ever a time when you need to talk to someone who can barely remember the old days, you call."

John just nodded and answered, "Thanks for the beer, Fred. I'm sure I'll see you occasionally at the Dinner Bell. Take care."

Returning to the pickup, Jim sat quietly as they headed back to the house. Pulling into the driveway, John said, "Let's not tell your mother where we've been. She doesn't need to know Fred's story. If he wants to tell her, he will. We'll just say we drove around the country looking at the crops and talking about how many families have left the area, okay?"

"Sure, Dad," Jim answered as he climbed down from his seat.

That evening, John cooked the steaks that'd been taken out that morning and sat with Jim beside the grill, drinking Jack Daniel's while they waited. Jim's mom came out just before they were finished cooking and sat in the chair John had vacated to check on the steaks.

"I guess you know that I hate to see you leave again tomorrow," she said, putting her hand on Jim's arm.

"I know, Mom," Jim replied, placing his hand over hers.

She patted his arm and announced as she stood, "Well, the rest of the food is on the table, so if you boys are ready, let's eat."

After the meal, Jim helped his mother clear the table

until she finally said, "You go sit with your dad. I'll finish this and get ready for bed. John already set the alarm for six o'clock, so we can have breakfast together before you leave."

Jim walked up to her and put his arms around her, saying, "Thanks, Mom. I hope I can get back here after I finish the school. I should have a couple of weeks of leave by then."

She looked at him, smiling slightly, and said, "Don't forget that there's someone in Florida who'd probably like to see you during that time. If she's as special to you as I think, you better take a few of those days and get down there."

"I will, Mom," Jim said, turning toward the door.

The next morning, Jim woke to the sound of his father knocking on the door, saying, "Rise and shine, Marine. The cook has threatened to toss the food out if you're not there in five minutes."

Jim smiled and rolled out of bed. "Be right there," he said, pulling on his jeans and a T-shirt.

Everyone was quiet during breakfast as they each kept their thoughts to themselves. Finally finished, Jim excused himself and headed for his room. After one final check to ensure he had everything packed, he showered quickly, dressed, and grabbed his bag.

His mom was still doing dishes as he carried the bag to the car. His dad had already opened the trunk and took the bag, saying, "You go say your goodbyes to your mother. I'll take care of this."

Jim walked back into the kitchen and started to say something when his mother turned from the sink and said, "I know. You don't have to say it. Go give your daddy a hug and tell him goodbye."

Jim looked at the woman who had raised him and just nodded before turning back to the door. John was wiping imaginary dust from the windshield when Jim got back to the car.

"Thanks, Dad," Jim said, putting his hand on his dad's shoulder.

John turned and put his arm around Jim's shoulders and said, "You go on now, son. Just be careful and call if you need anything."

Jim returned the hug and again saw his mother looking out the window. Stepping away from his dad, Jim said, "You take care of Mom, and I'll call whenever I can."

As he got in the car, he saw his dad pull a handkerchief from his pocket and wipe his eyes. After starting the car, Jim smiled at his mother and headed down the driveway.

CHAPTER 19

Jim headed toward Muleshoe and watched the familiar farms passing by, knowing that most of the men who ran them would soon be in the fields, starting the day's work. Just north of town, he took US 70 toward Clovis, New Mexico, with the goal of making it to Las Cruces, New Mexico, where he'd spend the night. There, he'd join I-10 the next morning and continue to Phoenix, Arizona. The third day would make it a fairly easy drive to El Toro.

The monotony of the flat, barren countryside crossing New Mexico gave him plenty of time to reflect on the events that had led up to this point. Never imagining that he would end up as a pilot in the Marine Corps, a series of snap decisions had led him here. Sometimes, he felt as if he was just a passenger on a ride through life, and fate was the driver.

Granted, he'd been given choices, but the path he was following wasn't one of preplanning. He'd never considered the military as a career and certainly not the Marines. He'd never considered becoming an officer or a pilot once he'd enlisted. Now, here he was, heading toward another fork in the road of destiny that'd most likely send him back to 'Nam, the one place where he never considered returning.

And then there was Jennifer. He never planned on falling in love with her. He'd just wanted someone to befriend while he was in Florida, someone to go dancing and drinking with, just a female companion. Even the sex hadn't been a planned event, especially the emotions that'd developed. Now, here he was, leaving what he'd considered his plan for life before going to college, heading in a completely new direction.

Amazing, Jim thought as the past events rolled through his mind like a video. *So many opportunities to be going in a completely different direction, a different life, but fate has led me here. Where would I be if I hadn't gotten kicked out of college? Where would I be if I hadn't taken the assignment to MARCAD? Where would I be if I hadn't met Jennifer?*

Arriving in Roswell, New Mexico, Jim decided to take a short break and check out the paraphernalia regarding the infamous Roswell crash and the supposed "alien" that'd been found. Everywhere he looked, he saw references to the incident, stores that advertised shirts, hats, or anything else bearing the likeness of the alien's face.

After parking the 'Vette, Jim wandered around the town, stretching his legs as he looked at the obvious tourists and thought about what that little town might have been like if it hadn't been for the debatable crash twenty years ago. If Muleshoe had experienced a similar event, how much of the simple country town would survive the influx of strange, mostly weird, people he saw going in and out of the little shops?

Finally arriving at a café, again with the alien face depicted on its windows, Jim walked in and took a seat. Picking up the menu, he saw most of the entrées had been given an alien- or spaceship-related moniker.

Smiling as the waitress came to his table, pad in hand, Jim put the menu down and said, "Hi, would it be possible to get just a cheeseburger, fries, and a Dr Pepper? I'm having a little trouble figuring out what I'd be ordering if I tried using the names on the menu."

She smiled and answered, "Not a problem, sir. You're not the first to just ask for what they want, but a lot of our visitors seem to take great pleasure in using the ridiculous names on the menu."

Laughing, Jim replied, "You must not be from here, or you aren't a true believer."

"Both," she grinned as she turned to go. "Just a stop on my way to California. Had a little car trouble, needed some extra money for the repairs, and now here I am almost two years later."

"Well," Jim told her, "you could have broken down in a lot worse places. There's not too many places where you'd get help crossing so much barren country from Texas to California."

"You got that right," she agreed as she walked away.

As Jim sat waiting, he watched people with their alien T-shirts, ridiculous hats, stacks of books promising the "truth" about the crash, even some that purported to have uncovered an ongoing secret government program to insert alien DNA from one of the aliens recovered from a crashed UFO into a human embryo. The trilogy, *DNAlien*, was almost as far-fetched as most of the others.

"Here you go, sir," the waitress said as she placed Jim's order on the table. "Anything else?"

"No, thanks, though," Jim answered as he picked up the glass to take a drink.

"Just call if you do," she said, turning to head to

another table.

Jim finished his meal, put enough money on the table to cover the bill and tip, and headed for the door. Smiling to himself as he passed the other tables, he wondered just how many of these people actually thought there'd been an alien spaceship crash and that the government was covering it up.

Back in his car, he stopped at one of the last gas stations before leaving town and refilled the tank. Long stretches between towns out here, and he definitely didn't want to run out of gas.

More sparsely vegetated, dry brown land stretched in front of him as he headed west on US 380 to Las Cruces. The road was almost empty, and the miles rolled by with few radio stations powerful enough to send a signal into the barren countryside. Trying to keep his mind occupied, Jim tried to find animal shapes in the few wispy clouds that floated across the sky in front of him.

Finally arriving in Las Cruces, he pulled into the first motel that looked as if there might be clean sheets and a semi-clean bathroom. Checking in took very little time, and Jim hurried to his room. Sitting in the car for so long had been tedious and tiring. For now, all he wanted was something to eat, a shower, and a good night's sleep.

When the alarm went off at six o'clock the next morning, Jim showered and repacked his bag before heading to the office to check out. The half-asleep assistant manager gave him a receipt, thanked him, and told him to come back anytime. That done, Jim headed back along the road, looking for a decent place to eat.

Seeing a Mexican restaurant advertising breakfast, open from six to midnight, Jim wheeled in and parked. Being the only car in the parking lot, he figured that he was the first of the morning crowd or that the food was horrible and he would be the only customer.

Standing by the "Please Wait to Be Seated" sign, Jim looked around the theme-decorated room. The tables were spaced far enough apart that there was plenty of room for the waitresses and customers, but it still provided a sense that it served a fairly large crowd.

That and the smell from the kitchen told Jim that he just might have gotten lucky. A young lady with long black hair and a colorful dress came up carrying several menus. "How many?" she asked.

Jim looked behind himself and answered, smiling, "Looks like just me."

Following her to a table for four, Jim noticed that the walls were decorated with scenes from what appeared to be the Mexican-American war. As she placed the menu on the table, she asked, "Water and coffee?"

"Yes, please," Jim said as he sat in the heavy wood chair.

As he waited, Jim looked at the menu and saw one of his favorite breakfasts, Huevos Rancheros. As the girl returned with a mug of coffee and a glass of iced water, she asked, "Are you ready, or do you need a minute?"

"Huevos Rancheros," Jim told her as he picked up the coffee mug.

"Best thing on the menu," she said, scribbling on her pad.

As she walked away, a family of six came in and waited to be seated. Jim tried to figure out if they were locals or passing through based on their clothing. The man was wearing khaki pants and a knit shirt that suggested they were probably just travelers as he was.

It wasn't until they approached his table that he saw the "White Sands Test Facility" ID on his pocket. Knowing that this region was used by numerous government programs, Jim nodded at the man and his wife as they passed. At least he hadn't encountered any adamant anti-war attitudes since leaving Muleshoe.

A few minutes later, the waitress arrived with a steaming plate with a fragrant odor that made Jim's mouth immediately water. After she sat the plate in front of Jim, she placed a covered plate of hot tortillas beside it and asked if he needed anything else.

Telling her no, Jim picked up his fork and broke the yoke of the egg that sat on a flour tortilla. Taking another tortilla from the covered plate, Jim dipped it into the yellow liquid, forked on some Pico De Gallo, and took a bite. Smiling as he put some refried beans, pico, sour cream, and guacamole on the tortilla in his hand, Jim started eating in earnest. This was one of the best Huevos Rancheros he had ever had. *Might even be better than H3 in Fort Worth,* Jim thought as he plowed through the meal.

When the waitress came back to check on him, Jim told her, "That's about the best breakfast I've ever had. I'm surprised that this place isn't packed with people."

"It will be in about an hour," she replied. "Will there be anything else?"

"No, thanks," Jim said, standing and taking the check she had placed on the table.

Jim paid the cashier, leaving a generous tip, and headed for his car. Leaving the parking lot, he took the on-ramp for I-10 and sped westward, following the stream of eighteen-wheelers and the occasional early-morning travelers. Knowing that there were few places for gas, Jim decided that Lordsburg, New Mexico, would be about halfway and maybe three hours from Las Cruces.

There was practically nothing to look at out the

windows, and Jim decided that this was one of the most desolate roads anywhere in the United States. The quick stop at Lordsburg provided him with the opportunity to use the restroom, grab a quick Dr Pepper, and get back on the road.

As Jim approached Tucson, Arizona, he finally saw something besides brown or gray countryside. Looking out the window at the Huachuca Mountains, Jim remembered the stories about Geronimo hiding there and the effort to capture him. To the north was the Coronado National Forest, where Francisco Vasquez de Coronado searched for the mythical Seven Cities of Cibola.

Staying on I-10, Jim waited until he was almost out of Tucson before pulling over for gas again. Although it was just a little before noon, hunger was starting to announce its presence. The small taco shop just down the street looked inviting, and he decided to grab a couple to tide him over until he reached Phoenix.

Tucson to Phoenix would take a couple of hours, and the final destination for the day lay about fifteen miles to the west. He knew that Luke Air Force Base would be available for a room and a good place to have a beer. Now an officer, Jim wanted to see how well the Air Force took care of its officers. He had heard rumors about how much better their facilities were than any of the other services, so he was interested to see if that was true.

Close to three o'clock, Jim pulled up to the front gate and stopped for the enlisted guard to approach. When Jim showed his new ID identifying him as a Second Lieutenant, the guard came to attention and, saluting, said, "Welcome, sir."

Jim nodded his acknowledgment of the salute, got directions to the Visiting Officers' Quarters (VOQ), and drove off after thanking the guard. Pulling into the VOQ parking lot, Jim listened to the constant roar of the jets that were in the traffic pattern. The distinct sound of the afterburner's lighting boomed every few minutes as another one took off.

After checking into his room, Jim took a quick shower and pulled on his khaki uniform with the gold bars and wings proudly shining. This was to be his first time to be around any military people since General Barker had pinned the wings on his chest back in Beeville.

Walking to the Officers' Club, Jim watched the F-4s flying overhead and was suddenly anxious to get to El Toro and begin his own training. Entering the club, Jim noticed that the Air Force did make sure their officers had the most luxurious facilities. It was evident from the carpets, the paneled walls, and especially the well-accommodated dining room.

After eating, he entered the bar area, where several young officers were reliving their recent flights, and Jim sat apart, watching. *Regardless of the branch, flyers all behave the same,* Jim thought as he sat, sipping his beer.

Looking at the clock above the bar, Jim finished the beer and headed back to his room. Tomorrow would be a six- or seven-hour drive, and Jim wanted to arrive at El Toro early enough to get settled and find what he would be doing for the next five months.

CHAPTER 20

The sun was still a couple of hours from peeking over the Superstition Mountains to the east when Jim donned a clean pair of jeans and a T-shirt and put his bag in the car. It was just under four hundred miles to El Toro and an easy drive on I-10 into Los Angeles. The gas tank was full; Jim planned on making it to Blythe, California, before stopping.

Once clear of the base and on I-10, Jim pushed his speed to slightly above the posted limit and joined the westbound traffic that consisted mainly of the trucks that were carrying their loads toward Los Angeles. Again, the countryside became desolate, and the only signs of vegetation other than gray/brown scrub brush were a few saguaro cacti that poked into the sky like telephone poles with arms reaching heavenward.

Driving across such a desolate country made Jim appreciate the hardiness of the first people to brave the trip from the back east in search of the promises of the West. Endless miles of desert punctuated by strings of impassable mountains combined with a severe lack of local water would have been a most daunting task.

Three hours later, he took the exit for Blythe shortly after crossing over the Colorado River, barely a fraction of its size north of Parker Dam, which contained Lake Havasu. Knowing that most of the water that stretched for miles behind the dam was diverted to Los Angeles and some of the farms that lay around the lake, Jim wondered if there'd come a time when the expansion of Los Angeles and the surrounding towns would suffer from a lack of fresh water.

A quick bite to eat and a full tank later, Jim pulled back onto I-10, now only four hours or so from El Toro. As he neared Riverside, he saw the exit for California Highway 91 just before reaching Colton and turned southwest toward Corona. Just west of Corona, he exited onto California Highway 241, which would later merge with 133 and take him to the base.

Shortly after noon, California time, Jim pulled into the entrance of El Toro. Stopping and showing his ID, Jim nodded to acknowledge the guard's salute and asked for directions to the Visiting Officers' Quarters. Thanking the Corporal, Jim headed there to get a room for the night and change into his uniform before he reported to the 3rd Marine Air Wing to sign in. Now in his dress uniform, Jim returned to the desk and got directions to the Headquarters.

Pulling into the lot that served the wing, Jim took his orders and looked for the administrative offices. Finding them, he presented the orders and waited for the inevitable wait for the admin clerks to provide him with a room assignment, a base decal for entrance, and all the other mundane paperwork that accompanied reassignment.

Almost an hour later, Jim headed for the flight line to try to get any manuals for the F-4 and the course curriculum. The facility that housed the academic portion of the program was easy to find, and the first Captain that Jim encountered welcomed him and escorted him to where all the publications that Jim would need could be found.

Thanking the Captain, Jim took the books back to his room in the VOQ. Although he had been assigned permanent housing, he elected to stay in this room until tomorrow. Books stored on the small desk, Jim changed into his utility uniform and headed back to the lobby.

Having seen the Officers Club on his drive in, Jim walked over to see if he could still get a quick lunch before returning to his room to study. Seeing several officers wearing flight suits leaving the club, Jim knew that it would still be serving. His meal finished, Jim returned to his room and changed back into his jeans.

The next stop was the Exchange to replenish his dwindling supply of personal necessities—toothpaste, razor blades, shave cream, and all the other items that seemed to be used faster than he thought. Not knowing what laundry facilities would be available, Jim purchased a dozen pairs of socks and underwear.

Purchases in hand, he headed back to his room to hit the books. As before, Jim wanted to make sure he at least had some idea about the program, the airplane, and the procedures before he presented himself to his first instructor.

After a couple of hours of studying, Jim showered, donned his khakis, and headed back to the club for dinner and a beer. As he walked into the dining room, Jim spotted a face from the past sitting with two other officers at a table near the rear of the room.

Jim walked over and waited until Mark noticed him before asking, "Excuse me, but weren't you at Pensacola for the MARCAD program about a year ago?"

Mark looked up and answered, "Yes, I sure was." Mark stood and said, "I'm Mark Barber." Recognition showing in his eyes, Mark continued. "You're that Marine that came into the program from a tour in 'Nam, aren't you?"

"I guess that'd be me unless there are others. I'm Jim Lashley," Jim answered, shaking Mark's hand.

Mark turned to the others at the table and said, "Gentlemen, this is the guy I told you about. This guy shows up at Pensacola wearing a Silver Star and two Purple Hearts to be put with a bunch of college kids. Talk about having nothing in common."

Jim nodded at the other two and told them, "I'm still just a 2nd Lieutenant, just like you, guys. Don't let Mark tell you any different."

As the other two introduced themselves and invited Jim to join them, a waitress arrived to take their orders. That done, Jim and Mark talked about what had happened since their first meeting at Pensacola. Finally bringing themselves up to date, the conversation turned to the F-4 training the others were already halfway through.

"You're gonna love the plane," Mark told Jim. "It's unbelievable! If you thought the F-9 was a fighter, just wait until you strap this one on."

For the next hour, Jim, Mark, and the other two talked about the F-4, its weapons systems, radar, and everything else. It seemed a daunting task to learn such a sophisticated system in such a short time, but Jim knew that this school was just to get him qualified. Mastering the airplane and developing the skills to take full advantage of the plane would take years.

Dinner was finally over; Jim thanked them for letting him join them and for all the information and started to stand.

Mark rose from his seat and told him, "When you get settled tomorrow, let's meet at the O' Club bar and have a couple of beers."

"Sounds great," Jim said, standing. "I look forward to talking to all of you again tomorrow. Maybe y'all can help me get through this little program."

Mark shook his hand and replied, "Oh, I think you'll do okay. I still remember what the instructors said about you back in Pensacola. You seemed to have been the golden boy that they held up as what each of the Cadets should be aiming for."

Jim's face flushed slightly as he said, "I think they just got used to the college kids that didn't have my previous military training, not to mention that I had quite a bit of flying before I got there. Now we're more on an even playing field, and you guys are way ahead of me."

Mark laughed and replied, "Whatever one of us needs, we try to help. We're all Marines, and we're striving for the same goal. If we can help you in any way, we're here to do it."

"Thanks," Jim said, nodding. "It's been a pleasure, gentlemen."

The following morning, Jim put on his uniform, checked out of his room, and carried his bags to the 'Vette. Driving to where he would be living for the next five months or so, he carried everything up to his room and, taking just the manuals, headed for the academic facilities to begin training.

Jim developed a close relationship with Mark over the next couple of months, as well as several other pilots training there. Flying as often as he could, Jim spent every spare minute in the books or talking to the other students or instructors, trying to finish the program as quickly as possible.

At least once a week, he would call his parents and let them know that he was doing fine and not to worry. He'd also call Jennifer once or twice a week, and they'd discuss what was happening in her world and how he was doing. Both avoided any talk of what the future held for them at this point.

As graduation from the school approached, Jim was ordered to the Wing Commander's office one Friday afternoon after he had landed. Wondering what had brought him to the attention of the Commander, Jim listened to the debrief of the flight and tried his best to concentrate on what the instructor was telling him instead of worrying about why he'd been ordered to go see the General.

As soon as the debrief was over, Jim returned to his room to put on his dress uniform. Not sure what to expect, Jim wanted to look his best when he first met the Commander. Impeccably dressed, Jim drove to the Headquarters Building and announced his presence to the Sergeant Major sitting just outside the General's office.

Being told to go right in, Jim knocked on the heavy wooden door and entered when he heard the invitation from within. Stepping through the door and closing it, Jim stepped to the front of where the General was sitting and, at attention, announced, "Lieutenant Lashley reporting as ordered, sir!"

The General looked up at Jim and said, "Lieutenant Lashley, it has come to my attention that you're about to graduate from our school, and barring any difficulties, you've been personally requested to be assigned to VMFA 115 when they have an opening. If I'm not mistaken, and I seldom am, a certain General Barker has signed the orders."

"Yes, sir," Jim acknowledged, still at attention.

The General rose from his desk and said, "At ease, Lieutenant. I've known General Barker for years, and he asked me to keep an eye on you while you were here."

Jim relaxed slightly as he waited for the General to

continue.

Walking around the desk, the General continued. "I have kept an eye on you, Lieutenant, and I must admit that everything General Barker told me has been correct. I was happy to relay that information to General Barker when he made the request."

"Thank you, sir," Jim said. "May I ask where General Barker is assigned?"

"I'm afraid that old warhorse is flying a desk at the Pentagon," the General told him. "He flew his last flight as a Marine pilot back in 'Nam and has been given the dubious reward of sitting at a desk for the rest of his career."

"Yes, sir," Jim replied, having nothing else to add.

"Well, Lieutenant," the General said as he returned to his chair, "that'll be all. As soon as you complete the program, you'll be assigned to VMFA 531 until they need you overseas. Unless you have anything to add, you're dismissed."

Jim snapped back to attention and replied, "No, sir!" Doing a sharp about-face, Jim marched back to the door and left.

The next few weeks flew by as Jim gained more and more experience and confidence in flying the F-4 in formation, range missions, and carrier landings. The day of his last flight arrived, and he anxiously awaited the final landing.

The formal portion of the training was now complete; Jim merely transferred to the 531st while waiting for his assignment to the 115th, which was already deployed overseas.

CHAPTER 21

Having been granted two weeks' leave, Jim called home and told his parents that he'd finished training and was trying to get tickets home for the next day.

Next, he called Jennifer and asked her if she wanted to see him in a week or so. Hearing that she was anxious for him to come back, he told her he'd call as soon as he had tickets. He then called the airlines to arrange a ticket from Los Angeles to Amarillo, another with an open date from Amarillo to Pensacola, and a final one from Pensacola back to Los Angeles with another open date.

Returning to his room, Jim neatly put all his clothes away and packed a few things he'd need at home and in Florida. When everything was satisfactorily put away or packed, he headed for the Officers Club for a quick meal. The first flight out of Los Angeles was early, and he wanted to get a good night's sleep.

The next morning, Jim rose early, showered, put the final items in his bag, and took a cab to the airport. Once he arrived and had his ticket in hand, he made another call home and told his father which airline, what flight, and what time he was due to land in Amarillo. Hearing that his father and mother would be there to pick him up, he sat in one of the chairs close to the boarding gate and waited for the boarding announcement.

Immediately after takeoff, the plane made a slow turn eastward, and Jim watched the barren countryside slide beneath the wings. Having driven across most of this land scant months ago, he was glad to be flying at over six hundred miles an hour instead of driving at sixty.

As Jim deplaned in Amarillo, his mom and dad were standing there, waiting. Smiling, Jim walked up and hugged his mother, gave his dad a quick one-arm hug across the shoulders, and said, "This is my only bag, so if you're ready, let's go."

John was driving, and Jim was sitting in the front passenger seat, and his mom was in the back; they started the drive back to Muleshoe. The scenery did not catch anyone's attention; Jim and his dad talked mostly about the training, what was next, and how he liked the airplanes.

Not quite to the house, his mother asked, "I suppose you're going back to Florida before you return to California?"

Turning in his seat, Jim answered, "Yes, Mom. I'll go out there in a week or so."

"I guess I don't need to ask again if this is serious," she responded.

"No, you really don't," Jim told her. "Nothing's really changed since I saw her last. I'm still worried about having to go back overseas."

"You do know that you can leave a wife at home when you go, don't you?" she retorted.

"Why don't you let him make his own decisions?" John said, looking at her in the mirror.

"I'm just saying that if this is the right girl, he doesn't need to wait for another year or more," she told him. "There were plenty of young wives at home during WWII and Korea," she continued.

"Yes, and there's plenty of them now," Jim told her. "And now, as back then, there're plenty of wives with children whose husbands and fathers aren't coming back."

"That's no excuse," she told him, sitting back and crossing her arms.

"Let the boy do what he feels best for himself," John sternly said. "He'll know when it's right. Until then, just let it rest."

The rest of the trip was made in silence while each of them made silent arguments to themselves.

Finally pulling into the driveway, John said, "Look, let's forget anything about the way we feel on this issue. Jim's here for a week, and we need to just relax and enjoy what time we have."

"You're right," Jim's mother said. "I just want my baby boy to be happy."

"I am, Mom," Jim said, reaching over the seat and squeezing her hand. "I'm probably the happiest I've been in a very long time. I've done things in the last year that I never imagined, and yes, I've met someone that just may be the right one."

As the car stopped in front of the house, Jim opened his door and continued, "But for right now, Dad's right. I just want to enjoy the next couple of weeks."

And they did. For the rest of the first week of leave, Jim spent many hours with his father just sitting around or driving around the country. Jim spent as much time as he could with his mother, sitting at the table while she did the dishes or helping her.

One morning after breakfast, John asked, "Like to go fly?"

"Sure," Jim said. "Where do you want to go?"

"I just want to fly," he answered. "Doesn't matter where."

"I can go nowhere as easy as I can go somewhere," Jim joked. "I'd say that if you're going nowhere, you're already there. But if you're going somewhere, you've got a ways to go."

"Fine," his dad said, smiling. "Since we're already here, and that's nowhere, we better go somewhere."

"Why don't you two just get out of here and go?" Jim's mom said, smiling at the easy manner between the two that had been there since before Jim had become a teenager.

"Let's go before she starts throwing things," John said as he winked at his wife. "You don't want to be around that woman when she gets riled."

Jim grinned as he followed his dad out the door, saying, "I think she'll calm down by the time we get back. Maybe if we promised to take her to Luby's, it would soothe her feathers."

Ducking the pot holder that was thrown at their backs, they hurried out of the house.

"Is there anywhere in particular that you'd like to go?" John asked as they opened the hangar doors.

"How about taking the same trip we did about a year ago?" Jim suggested as they pulled the little Ercoupe out of the hangar.

"Sounds good," John said. "Want the left seat?"

"No," Jim answered. "I've flown enough for a while. You just enjoy flying while I marvel at the pristine countryside."

"If by pristine you mean flat," John joked as he started

the engine, "there's certainly a lot of 'pristine' land around here."

"I know," Jim acknowledged, smiling and nodding. "Sometimes I think the Governor of Texas should apologize for so much of his state looking like a tabletop."

John took off, and they followed basically the same path as they had before Jim first left for Pensacola. Both sat silent as John weaved back and forth across the flat ground until reaching the Caprock.

A few miles later, John reversed directions and headed back. Indicating for Jim to take the controls, John watched as his son's hand caressed the wheel as he took control and began a rhythmic waltz across the sky on the way home. *He really does have a knack for this,* John thought, realizing that Jim had truly found his calling.

Fifteen minutes later, Jim flew across the house and made a low 180-degree turn to line up with the runway. Touching down, he taxied the airplane to the hangar and returned control to his father. As soon as the engine sputtered to a stop, John turned to Jim and said, "Not bad for a jet jock."

Jim just smiled back and said, "You didn't do too bad for a man who learned to fly from Wilbur and Orville Wright."

As soon as the plane was put away, they walked back to the house, where Jim's mom had the old hand-crank ice cream maker sitting on the back steps, ready for the ice.

"What's this?" John asked as he approached.

"You know exactly what this is," she told him. "You're the one that told me last night to have it ready when you came back. Don't you play like this is all my idea."

Jim just laughed and said, "I don't care whose idea it was. Come on, Pop, let's make some ice cream."

Knowing that Jim would be leaving the next morning, they spent the rest of the day sitting around, making small talk. Again, steaks cooked over mesquite, corn on the cob, and baked potatoes were the evening's fare. After supper, Jim and his dad sat outside sipping Jack Daniel's as John smoked his pipe.

The dishes were put away, and Jim's mom came out and sat quietly with them, enjoying the company of two of her favorite men.

CHAPTER 22

The next morning, Jim showered, repacked the clothes his mother had washed, and joined his parents in the kitchen, where his mother was cooking sausage and eggs for breakfast.

"Where's Dad?" Jim asked as he gave her a hug.

"He's outside," she replied. "I think he's checking the oil or something on the car."

"Okay," Jim said as he took a mug from the counter and filled it with coffee.

"How long are you going to stay in Florida?" his mother asked as she turned to look at him.

"Four or five days," Jim answered.

"I promised your dad that I'd leave this alone," she said, wiping her hands on her apron. "But have you considered Jennifer's feelings about this relationship?"

"Yes, Mother," Jim responded, sitting his mug on the table. "We've talked about it, and she understands why we can't go any further right now."

"I'm sure she says she understands," she told him. "But women think differently than men. When she says she understands, that generally means that she will put up with it for now. But if something doesn't change, she'll lose that understanding."

"I can't help that," Jim replied, picking up the mug and twisting it in his hands.

"What if she decides that enough is enough while you're sitting around in California? Or if you do go back overseas for another year? How long do you think this woman's going to wait?" she questioned.

"I don't know, Mother," Jim said, looking her directly in the eye. "I do know that I've been as honest with her as I can be. I've made no promises that I don't intend to keep. If she decides that what I can give isn't enough, then I'll accept that and go on with my life."

"Without her?" she asked.

"Yes, if that's what happens," Jim said with a tone of finality in his voice. "I hope Jennifer and I can continue to see where this leads, but it's got to wait until I see if I'm going back to 'Nam."

"What if you wait around for a year?" his mother asked. "What if you wait around for two or three years? Do you think she'll wait around that long?"

"I don't know," Jim repeated. "I'm not going to make any decisions that'll affect the rest of my life until I'm certain."

"As much as I'm opposed to it in general," she said as she turned back to the sink, "have you considered letting her come to California while you wait?"

"Yes," Jim answered. "I've thought about that, but what if she comes out to stay, and I'm sent away a month or so later? Where does that leave her?"

"Don't you think that should be her decision?"

Exasperated, Jim sat the mug down and answered,

"Yes, that's her decision if I give her the option. I'm not going to do that. If she wants to come out for a visit, regardless of the length, that's one thing. But moving there with some implied promise, no."

Turning back from the sink, she said, "All right. But I think you should talk the options over with her. That's if you truly feel this may be the right woman for you. Just give her some options that'll give her hope. That's all I'm saying."

"I'll talk about it with her," Jim said, putting his hand on her shoulder. "I know you're only concerned with my happiness. But please let Jennifer and me determine what's best for both of us."

"I will," she said as she stepped close and put her arms around his waist. "Just don't let the uncertainty of things that may never happen cause you to lose something that I think you really want."

"What does he really want?" John said, stepping into the kitchen.

"I want sausage and eggs," Jim answered, winking at his mother. "And I want you two to stop worrying about me. I'm a big boy now and can take care of myself."

John looked between the two of them and finally said, "Fine! Now, if there's nothing else, let's eat and get headed to Amarillo."

Breakfast over, Jim took his bag out to the car, where John was waiting beside the open trunk. "Mom giving you a hard time?" John asked, slamming the trunk closed.

"Not really," Jim told him.

"You've got to understand her," John said, leaning back against the fender. "What she really wants is for you to have a family and a home. She thinks that means you're safe and happy. But as you know, that also means you have more to lose. Sometimes, it's best to have nothing to lose."

"I don't believe that, Dad," Jim said, leaning against the car. "I think that having something you don't want to lose gives you a reason to try harder."

"If that gives you strength," John said, looking at his son, "then hold on to those things that give you that strength. And hopefully, you'll never have to need it."

As they were finishing their talk, Jim's mom came out of the front door and told them, "If you two are through plotting whatever you two do when you're together, we need to get going so Jim doesn't miss his flight."

The drive to Amarillo was mostly silent. Sporadically mundane subjects were brought up, but they each danced around the things they had discussed earlier.

Arriving at the terminal, Jim opened his door and left it open for his mother. Opening her door, he helped her onto the curb, while John opened the trunk and retrieved Jim's bag.

Hugging her, Jim said, "Mom, I promised I'd let Jennifer know that she's always welcome to come for extended visits, and I'll do that. It's not that I think you're meddling in my life, but I've got to do what I think is best for me."

"I know," she said, returning the hug as long as she could. "I'll support any decision you make. I just want you to be happy."

"Let the boy go," John said as he sat Jim's bag on the curb. "We've got an hour's drive home, and he's got a plane to catch."

Jim waited until his mother had slid into the front passenger seat and leaned in, kissing her on the forehead before shutting the door.

He turned to John, stepped close, and put his hand on his shoulder, saying, "Thanks, Dad. I'll keep in touch as often as possible, and I'll let Mom know if or when Jennifer comes out."

John put his arm over Jim's shoulder and said, "That'd make her happy. Now get out of here."

John quickly turned and walked around the car, pausing briefly as he looked at Jim before climbing in. As the car moved away from the curb, Jim waved at the back of their heads before bending to pick up his bag and enter the terminal.

After checking in at the ticket counter, Jim got his seating assignment for the next flight to Pensacola and walked to the gate to wait.

CHAPTER 23

The flight arrived on time, and Jennifer was there, waiting, wearing a pair of well-fitting cutoffs and a snug T-shirt. As she waved discreetly, Jim smiled and returned the wave as he trudged along behind the other passengers. When he finally cleared the gate, he stepped around the others and strode up to where Jennifer was standing.

"Hello, pretty lady," Jim said as he kissed her softly on the cheek.

"Hello yourself," Jennifer told him as she responded by throwing her arms around his neck and kissing him on the lips.

"How was your visit with your mom and dad?" she asked as they made their way toward the exit.

Jim shifted the bag to his left hand and took Jennifer's in his other. "Really good," he answered. "I guess it was one of the best."

"Why's that?" she asked.

"Oh, I think it was because I wasn't worried about going to another school, concerned about what it'd be like and how I'd do there," Jim replied.

"Well, I hope this is your best visit here, too," she smiled.

"Me too," Jim said as they left the building and headed for Jennifer's car.

"What do you want to do first?" she asked as she opened the rear passenger door.

"Go to your place, put on some shorts, get some beer, go to the beach, and think about nothing for an hour or so," Jim told her as he tossed his bag into the rear seat.

"You got it," she said as she walked around the car. "You jump in, and I'll take care of the rest."

As soon as she had parked, she ordered, "Grab your bag and follow me, Marine."

"Yes, Ma'am," Jim grinned, pulling his bag from the car.

"You know where everything is," Jennifer said. "You go change, and I'll fix us a picnic basket for the beach."

A few minutes later, Jim came out in a pair of cutoff jeans and a loose T-shirt draped across his shoulder. "Need any help?" he asked as he walked up and kissed the back of her neck.

"Nope," she answered, pushing her neck against his lips. "You're here to do nothing but relax. If I need your help, I'll ask. These next few days are for me to cater to your every whim and desire."

"Sounds like you've been thinking about this," Jim queried.

"Yes, as a matter of fact, I have," Jennifer told him. "I know that you've been absorbed with getting done with all the schools and training for about a year and a half. Now it's time for you to forget all that and enjoy a few days."

"That doesn't sound half bad," Jim agreed. "But I didn't come out here for you to be my slave or handmaiden."

"This is what I *want* to do for you," she said, turning into him. "I know that I wasn't the most supportive person over the last year. And I know that I could've been. So now I'm going to try to make up for any pressure I put on you, and for all those times I hated what you were doing."

"You don't have anything to make up for," Jim said, taking her hands in his. "If anything, I should apologize for not paying enough attention to you. And I do know that it's been hard on you, but you were always there."

"Okay," she smiled as she turned away, her eyes beginning to tear. "Let's just head for the beach and enjoy an hour or so of sun."

As she took the basket from the countertop, she asked, "Could you please get the beer out of the refrigerator and put it in the cooler on the table?"

Jim opened the refrigerator door and joked, "I thought I just heard you say that I was just here to relax?"

Jennifer frowned at him and retorted, "And if your brain isn't fried from a lack of oxygen or too many 'G's,' you'd also have heard me say that if I need your help, I'd ask. Well, I just asked. So, move your ass, or I'll be having a picnic by myself!"

Jim ducked as she threw a roll of paper towels at him and said, "Hey, look out for the eyes! I'll need both of them if I stay a pilot."

"Then you better use them to watch your mouth," Jennifer joked as she grabbed the roll from the floor.

Jim took two six-packs of Budweiser from the refrigerator and put them in the cooler. Opening the freezer compartment, he filled the cooler from the bag of ice that he found inside.

Leading the way, he opened the front door and held it as Jennifer walked out. Making sure it was locked, he followed her toward the car, thinking the same thing he always did: watching her from behind.

At the beach, Jim carried the basket and cooler while Jennifer retrieved a couple of large beach towels from the rear seat. Once they'd been spread over a secluded sandy spot, Jim sat the basket and cooler on the sand beside them.

He pulled two bottles from the cooler and asked, "Did you remember to bring an opener?"

"Yes, I did," Jennifer smiled deviously. "Your job is to find it."

Looking in the basket, Jim asked, "I don't suppose it's in here?"

"Nope, you'll have to keep looking," she replied.

"Do I need to go back to the car?" Jim asked, knowing where this game was going.

"If you want," she answered, leaning back on her elbows, her ankles crossed.

"Hint?" Jim pleaded, facing her on his hands and knees.

"You're looking in the right direction," she teased.

Jim crawled over to her and asked, "Am I getting warmer?"

"Yes," she answered, grinning and lying back.

Jim stretched forward and lay beside her, asking, "Where should I start?"

"Tell you what," she answered, "you keep your hands on the blanket, and I'll tell you when you're either getting warmer or getting colder."

"Just what am I supposed to use?" Jim asked, knowing the answer.

"Your teeth," Jennifer said.

Jim rose to his knees and bent over her, taking the front of her shirt in his teeth, mumbling, "Shall I rip it off? Or do you want to give me another hint?"

Laughing, Jennifer told him, "It's not in the shirt."

Jim lifted his head and said, "I know that, but it seemed like a fun place to start. And I still think I'll rip it off unless you tell me where it is."

"Okay, okay," she said, rolling over. "Look where you'd expect to find it, you dumb-assed jarhead."

Seeing the outline of the opener in her back pocket, Jim bit her there, saying, "I guess I'll just have to tear the pocket off since I can't get my teeth in there."

Jennifer reached behind her back and quickly extracted the opener. "Here, spoilsport," she said as she rolled back over and sat up.

Jim smiled and told her, "I saw it there when you were walking to the car. I just wanted to play with you for a little while."

She tossed the opener at him and pouted, "You really are such an ass. I don't know why I put up with you."

Jim caught the opener in the air and said, "Me neither. Me neither."

The rest of the afternoon they spent dozing or talking about things that had been happening in their lives or what they wanted to do for the rest of Jim's visit.

Back home, they showered together and stumbled into the bedroom. Now, knowing what gave each other pleasure, they took their time making love. Finally, exhausted from the sun and the sex, they fell asleep, lying together, holding hands.

The days that followed drifted by quickly yet slowly as they spent their time just being together. The last night together, Jim sat beside her on the couch, quietly staring into space.

"Something on your mind?" she softly asked.

"Yes," Jim told her, turning to look into her eyes.

A moment passed until he finally said, "You know I'm going back to California tomorrow, and I don't know just how long I'll be there."

Watching his eyes, Jennifer answered, "I know."

Pausing for a few seconds, Jim continued, "I also expect that within the next few months, I'll be assigned to one of the squadrons overseas."

Jennifer sat quietly, while Jim struggled to tell her what he was thinking.

"If I do go," he resumed, "I'll probably be gone for a year."

Still silent, Jennifer continued waiting, now apprehensive about what was to come next.

"What I'm saying, what I mean to ask," Jim hesitantly told her, "is that while I'm waiting out there if you want to come out and spend some time . . ."

Tears began trickling down Jennifer's cheeks, both from relief and from joy. "I'll come to you anytime you want. I'll stay as long as you want. And I won't ask for any more than you can give for now. If you want me."

As she put her arms around Jim's neck, he softly said, "I want you forever."

CHAPTER 24

The next morning, Jim rose and headed for the shower as Jennifer started a pot of coffee brewing. By the time Jim had finished and dressed, she came in, saying, "The coffee's ready, and I'll be out in a few minutes."

Out in the kitchen, Jim poured a cup and headed for the living room. Turning the TV on, he sat back to watch the early news while he waited. As always, the leading stories were of the Vietnam War and the number of Americans killed, wounded, captured, or missing in action.

Jim paid close attention to the number of aircraft that had been lost as the slick-haired newscaster showed graphs of the totals for each successive year and the total for the war. Seeing what he already knew, the numbers were still staggering in their implication.

Jim was still watching when Jennifer came in and sat beside him, asking, "Are you concerned about what'll happen if you have to go back?"

"Of course," Jim answered. "But if I don't, somebody else will have to."

"Why not let them go?" she wanted to know. "You've

already been there. Twice. Let someone else go."

Jim turned to her and said, "I've taken an oath to follow any orders that are given by my superiors. If that means going back, that's what I'll do. I knew that when I accepted this job instead of finishing my enlistment."

"You wouldn't have had to go back if you had," she argued.

"And I'd never have met you," he reminded her. "So, which would you rather have? Me or having me safe somewhere in South Carolina?"

"I want you safe with me," she responded.

"Can't have it both ways," he said. "Besides, I fully intend on coming back to be with you if I do have to go."

"I know," she said, rising from the couch. "I can still want you safe with me regardless of what might have happened if you hadn't come here. I can wish all I want."

Jim rose and followed her into the kitchen, rinsing his cup and placing it in the sink. "I wish lots of things," Jim said, turning to her. "But I have to live in reality for now. And that reality is that I have to get back to California and see what happens."

"I know," Jennifer resignedly said.

The ride to the airport was unusually quiet. Once there, Jim opened his door and stepped to the curb. As he was opening the rear door, Jennifer came around and put her arms around Jim's waist. As he pulled her closer to him, he said, "I do love you. And I'll call when I get back and see what arrangements I can make for you to come out and stay for as long as possible."

Finally letting him go, she reached up and kissed him, saying, "I know. You just call, and I'll work out how long I can stay."

Jim returned the prolonged kiss and finally said, "We'll

work it out. In the meantime, don't worry about things over which we have no control."

Releasing him, Jennifer stepped back and crossed her arms, saying, "Okay, you just get back there and get things settled so I can spend as much time with you as I can."

Pulling his bag from the rear seat, he told her, "I will. It may be a week, or it may be a month. But I'll work it out."

Jim kissed her quickly, said his final goodbye, and headed into the terminal. Jennifer watched him disappear into the building and walked back to the driver's side. Unable to hold the tears back, she sat quietly for a few minutes until her eyes cleared, and she drove away.

The flight from Pensacola passed back through DFW with a short wait before leaving for Los Angeles. Sitting beside the departure gate, Jim watched the crowd of travelers passing by. For once, he wasn't looking for Jewell.

The flight to Los Angeles was what every traveler wanted—on time, smooth, and uneventful. After taxiing to the terminal, Jim waited for the rest of the people to deplane and then pulled his bag from the overhead and followed.

Hailing the first cab he saw, he hurried out of the airport and back to the base. Showing his ID and passing through the gate, he went to his room and put his clothes away before going to the club for something to eat.

The next morning, Jim rose early, showered, and put on his uniform before leaving for the flight line. Once there, he reported in and asked what he needed to do. When told where to go and how the flights were scheduled, he spent the rest of the day getting acquainted with the squadron's operations.

The following day, Jim found he had been scheduled for a flight that afternoon with a Radar Intercept Officer (RIO) instructor. When they met shortly after lunch, the instructor briefed Jim on the flight and who they would be "fighting." The flight went smoothly, and Jim tried to absorb each bit of information. After the debrief, Jim took several manuals back to his room to prepare for the next day's flight.

For the next few days, Jim studied and flew. Some days, he went in formation with three other aircraft to practice air-to-air combat. Most days, he was on the range dropping practice bombs or strafing the various targets that simulated convoys of troops or equipment.

Having settled in with his new squadron, Jim felt confident in calling Jennifer to let her know that he was looking for an apartment for them. Hearing that she was ready anytime he found something or that she'd share his Spartan quarters on base, Jim began to look forward to spending his free time with her instead of hanging out at the club.

Finding a small one-bedroom furnished apartment was relatively easy, and Jim quickly put a deposit down and told Jennifer to come out whenever she was ready.

Three days later, Jennifer called to tell Jim that her flight would be arriving the next afternoon. Jim checked with the flight scheduler and rearranged his flight for the early morning so he could meet Jennifer when she landed.

Additionally, he asked the scheduler to keep him off the flight schedule for the following day as well so he could move his few belongings to the apartment.

That accomplished, Jim went to his room and began packing. After getting everything as close to ready as possible, he headed to the club to meet some of the other pilots for dinner and a few beers.

Early the next morning, Jim arrived at the flight line, ready to go. This morning's flight was to be a formation of four against two aircraft simulating enemy MIGs. Three hours later, the flight was successful; Jim sat listening intently as the adversarial pilots discussed the good points and the flaws in the mission. Reviewing the gun camera films, Jim saw his mistakes vividly displayed on the screen.

One of the advantages of flying with the RIOs was that most of them had already served a tour back in 'Nam and could provide the experience that can't be gleaned from a textbook.

Jim was waiting at the airport, watching the planes land and take off several minutes before Jennifer was due to arrive. Watching the airline pilots changing airplanes or just coming in to get out of the cockpit, Jim smiled to himself that he didn't think he'd ever enjoy their job.

Hearing the announcement for Jennifer's flight, Jim stood against the wall opposite the arrival gate. Being slightly over six feet, he could see over most of the others who were there to greet the other passengers.

Jennifer was one of the first ones coming into the terminal, and Jim waited until she was clear of the majority of the crowd before walking to her. Seeing a suitcase in her hand, he asked, "Is that it? I'm surprised you can fit enough in that little thing to last more than a couple of days."

"Maybe that's all I'm staying, jarhead," she said as she slid her arm around his waist.

"I must be really something," Jim joked as they headed toward the baggage claim. "To think you'd spend that much money just to see me for two days."

"Oh, I'm used to spending much more than this for my weekends with the boys," she smiled as she squeezed him.

"Okay, I'm a cheap substitute for the lifestyle you're accustomed to," he replied. "I guess I'll have to work twice as hard to make you as happy as those other 'high dollar' guys do."

"Oh, I expect you to work three times as hard," she told him.

As the bags began to arrive, Jennifer pointed out the ones that were hers. Three large bags later, Jim looked at her and asked, "What'd you plan? Moving in? It's a good thing that I borrowed a friend's car because the 'Vette wouldn't hold all this."

Taking the smaller of the three, she replied, "That's exactly what I planned. If you have any doubts about it, say so now. I can get a return ticket and be back on the same plane headed back."

Jim took the overstuffed suitcases that remained and answered, "Not a chance, little lady. I happen to know the Chief of the Airline, and he's informed me that there are no open seats for the foreseeable future. You're stuck here with me!"

Jennifer smiled and walked beside Jim as he headed for the exit, saying, "We'll just see who's stuck with who."

CHAPTER 25

For the next several months, Jim went to the base every day for eight or nine hours, while Jennifer stayed in their apartment or went shopping. Evenings were spent at the Officers Club with some of Jim's squadron mates, out on the town, or quietly sitting at home.

Jennifer met several of the wives from the squadron, a few of the girlfriends, and a scattering of people from the apartment complex. Listening to the stories of the wives whose husbands were overseas and those whose had returned, she knew that having some support from people who had firsthand knowledge of the hardships the families endured was important.

The ladies she felt the worst for were those whose husbands or boyfriends were missing. At least those in the POW camps were known to be alive and had a good chance of coming home. Those who were known to have died were certainly heartbreaking, but the ones who remained as MIAs left such a gaping hole in the lives of the family, and the uncertainty was always evident when the ladies met.

Jim was flying almost every day, and he was aware of

the frequency with which other pilots who had been there before he arrived were leaving for their tour overseas. He knew that it was just a matter of time before he'd have to go.

It was almost as if you could take a roster of the arrival dates of each pilot and see how many were in the queue ahead of you. Given the average number of pilots transferred each month, you had a very good idea of when your time would come. The major difference with Jim was that he knew he would be joining VMFA 115 and was waiting for an opening there, not any of the other squadrons.

Jim didn't know if the wives had a similar system for estimating when their loved ones would be sent. But he never mentioned his assignment. They'd discussed what she'd do if he had to leave, but Jennifer preferred not to dwell on the countdown that ticked by each day.

Finally, the day arrived. Jim was called into the Squadron Commander's office and officially presented with his orders to VMFA 115 based in Da Nang. Well-prepared mentally, Jim accepted his orders and began the now-familiar process of departing one duty station for another.

The one thing that had a bit of a bright spot was that he could take two weeks' leave before he had to leave for 'Nam. It was later than normal when he returned to the apartment, and Jennifer had begun thinking that something abnormal had happened.

When Jim walked in, she asked, "Long day?"

"Yeah," Jim said, walking to the small refrigerator and taking out two beers. "Let's go sit outside for a few minutes."

Now Jennifer knew for certain that her fears were about to be realized. She followed Jim out to the small patio and waited for him to let her know what was happening.

Jim handed her one of the beers and composed his

thoughts before beginning, "We need to decide what you plan to do when I leave."

Jennifer sat back and closed her eyes. Having dreaded this moment, she knew that it had been rapidly approaching as she and the other women had watched so many from the squadron leaving.

"How much time do you have?" she asked.

"A couple of weeks," Jim answered.

"I don't suppose that you're not going back over there?"

"I'm going back," Jim said, looking into her eyes.

"Any way of changing that?" Jennifer asked a lump that felt like it weighed a ton settled in her stomach.

Jim took a small sip from his bottle and simply answered, "No."

"What do you want me to do?" Jennifer finally said, accepting the fact that she was about to lose Jim for at least a year.

"I've told you what I think," he replied. "But it's ultimately your decision. I can keep the apartment here if that's your choice."

Jennifer sat quietly for a few moments before she gave the answer that she'd known since coming here. "I'm going home."

Jim just nodded and then told her, "I have to be in St. Louis for the flight to 'Nam. Until that date, I'm free to go wherever I want."

"Where do you want to go?" she asked.

"I need to go home for at least a couple of days," he answered. Pausing for just a few seconds, he continued, "I'd like for you to go with me."

Jennifer was somewhat taken aback but had also been waiting for the day that he would introduce her to his parents.

"When do we need to leave?" Jennifer asked, letting him know that wherever he wanted her to go with him was what she wanted.

"It will take at least a day to finish what I need to do at the base," Jim told her. "And I need to let the apartment manager know that we're leaving."

"What do I need to do?" she asked.

"Just pack your bags, I guess," he said. "Pack one for the trip to Muleshoe and the others we'll have shipped to Florida."

For several minutes, they sat quietly, absorbed in their own thoughts, until Jennifer finally rose and said, "All right, we knew this day was coming. I've always figured that I'd go home, but now I'm positive. So, I'll go figure out what clothes I want to take with me and pack the others."

Jim looked up at her as she demonstrated that, in addition to the other traits that had drawn him to her, she could be decisive and in charge of her own life regardless of what happened to him.

Smiling as he rose, he said, "Why don't we delay that until tomorrow? I'd like to spend the rest of the evening with no thoughts of tomorrow coming between us."

"I think you have a great idea there," Jennifer said as she slid to his side and wrapped her arms around him. "Tomorrow will arrive soon enough."

The next morning, Jim rose early and started the coffee. When he finished showering and walked into the bedroom, he heard Jennifer on the phone talking to one of the wives she'd met, listening to her tell the other that she was going to donate all the items she'd gathered so the next new arrival would have some of the basics.

Jim ran his hand down her neck, kissed her softly, and started pulling his clothes from the closet. With still no more than his uniforms and a few civvies, Jim packed everything except one uniform and his traveling clothes.

Uniform on, he went into the tiny kitchen and poured two cups of coffee. Handing one to Jennifer as she continued talking on the phone, he motioned that he was leaving.

Jennifer placed her hand over the phone and asked, "When'll you be home?"

Holding up two fingers, Jim answered, "Two hours, maybe three."

Nodding, Jennifer returned to her conversation as Jim finished his coffee and headed for the door.

Orders in hand, Jim cleared all the required places on base, took a pay advance, changed his permanent address to his parents' house, and collected all the documents he'd require for the trip from St. Louis, Missouri, to Da Nang.

That done, he swung by the flight line to say goodbye to all his fellow aviators and hear their well wishes. Knowing that he'd be issued new flight gear upon arrival in 'Nam, he made sure he had left no personal items in his G suit or anywhere else.

Driving back to the apartment, he stopped by the manager's office and told him that he'd be leaving the next day. The manager was well accustomed to the erratic lifestyle of the majority of his tenants. Also, knowing that word spread quickly among the military, he wanted to keep his reputation for fairness and honesty.

Telling Jim that he hated to lose him as a tenant and neighbor, the manager gave him a check for the deposit and for the remaining days of the month-to-month contract. Somewhat surprised, Jim thanked him and told him that if he ever came back or knew of anyone coming, he'd recommend these apartments.

Back at their apartment, Jim walked in to see the

closets bare, suitcases sitting closed, and several boxes filled with food, cooking utensils, dishes, and various other items from the house.

One of the squadron wives was helping Jennifer use newspaper to wrap the remaining items as he said, "Did you at least leave me a beer or two?"

Jennifer smiled and said, "Nope, it's all gone. Mary's husband is coming over in a few minutes with a pickup to take all this over to their house. There's a new Lieutenant and his wife that just checked into the base, and Mary will contact her to see if they can use this."

"Do you know where they are staying?" Jim asked.

"In the VOQ for now," Mary answered.

"Don't haul this stuff away just yet," Jim said, turning and heading for the door.

Fifteen minutes later, Jim came back with an almost-new Chevrolet following him. Leading the Lieutenant and his wife to his apartment, Jim introduced everyone and told them that it was now available, and if they desired, all the boxed items could stay.

It took less than ten minutes for them to decide that they wanted the apartment. Jim took the Lieutenant to the manager's office and introduced them. Five minutes later, they were back at the apartment. Hearing the news, Jennifer smiled at the couple whose lives had just improved.

Thanking Mary for her help, Jennifer told the couple that they'd need a couple of hours to get their personal things out. Just as Mary was about to leave, her husband arrived an
d knocked on the door.

Quick arrangements were made for him to take Jim to the airport with Jennifer's excess bags. There, Jim would have them flown back to Pensacola and be waiting for her parents to get them.

It was barely after one o'clock when all the arrangements had been completed, and Jim stood with Jennifer, looking at what had been their first home together.

"Gonna miss it?" Jim asked, standing with his arm around Jennifer's waist.

"Actually, I will," she replied, looking at the disarray left by the abrupt change in plans. "I really will."

Jim turned to face her, put his hands on her shoulders, and asked, "How would you like to leave right now?"

Somewhat surprised, Jennifer asked, "Is that what you want to do?"

Nodding, Jim answered, "Yes, there's no reason to go to the base for a room, and we could make it to Flagstaff, Arizona, today. That would be about a seven-hour drive." Watching her face for any sign of doubt or concern, he continued. "Then tomorrow morning, we'll leave as early as possible and drive the rest of the way."

"How long would that be?" she wondered aloud.

"A little over nine hours," he told her.

"Are you in that big of a rush to get home?" she asked.

"I don't see any reason to wait," he responded. "I'd like for us to spend a week or so with Mom and Dad, then fly to Florida for the rest of my leave."

"What'll they think about you leaving them with that much time off before you go overseas?" Jennifer asked, thinking that Jim's parents may resent her taking him away from them.

Jim smiled knowingly and answered, "They'll be okay with it. As a matter of fact, my mother would probably insist on it even if it meant having me leave a few days early."

"Why would she do that?" Jennifer asked.

"I'll just let you figure that out after we get there," he said. "Now, if we're to go, let's fill up the tank and get out of here."

One last look around the apartment was accomplished, their bags tossed in the trunk of the 'Vette, and they pulled out of the apartment complex.

CHAPTER 26

Heading east on California 91, he concentrated on the traffic as Jennifer watched for the exit to join I-15 just past Corona. Merging with the traffic onto I-15, they sped north toward Barstow, where they'd join I-40 eastbound.

The traffic was relatively light, and Jim pushed the speed limit every chance he got. Slightly less than two hours after leaving the apartment, they arrived at Barstow and pulled off for gas and something to eat.

As soon as the car was refueled and they'd eaten a quick meal, Jennifer told Jim that she wanted to find a grocery store to get some snacks and drinks for the road. Spotting a small store just blocks from where they were, they parked in the almost empty lot and went in.

Her basket full, she headed toward the checkout area to see if she'd find Jim there. As she started to turn from the aisle, Jim almost ran over her as he came around the corner.

Looking at her basket, he asked, "No butterfingers?"

"If you want one, they're by the cash registers," she answered. "I'll just stick with fruit and nuts."

"You've been in California too long." he grinned as he

joined her heading to the front of the store. "I've had about all the *fruits and nuts* I need for the rest of my life!"

Jennifer returned his smile and replied, "Don't worry, these will never make it out of California alive."

"I hope not," he agreed. "I don't think Texas would put up with them. We just have to make sure to dump anything that might be remaining before we leave New Mexico."

After paying for their purchases, they iced the drinks and put the cheese and fruit on top of the cooler. After Jennifer had gotten in, Jim handed her the cooler, and she sat it on the floor between her feet.

"Not much room left," she said as she put the bags of chips on the cooler. "You could've packed a lot more food if you'd left me behind."

Jim walked around the car and said as he got in, "Yeah, but I don't care to talk to fruit and nuts. Plus, since you know how to drive a standard transmission, I'll let you drive some of the time. Bananas don't have driver's licenses either."

About two hours later, they were approaching the Colorado River just south of Needles. Crossing the river into Arizona at Topock, Jim told her how much smaller the river was where he had crossed it on I-10 and where the water went.

As they neared Kingman, Arizona, Jim pulled into the first clean-looking gas station to refill and to allow Jennifer to use the restroom. That was one thing that Jim hadn't paid a lot of attention to previously, but Jennifer was extremely picky about the restrooms. As far as his needs, just about anything would do.

Jim had gathered all the trash they'd accumulated and put it in the wastebasket when Jennifer came back. "Want to drive?" he asked, holding the passenger door open.

"Sure," she said, walking around the front of the car.

"I've had to just sit there and listen to you ramble on about schools, rodeos, kids I don't know, and every other boring detail of your life for too many hours. Now you just sit back and listen to mine."

Jim shook his head as he climbed into the passenger seat and tried to arrange the cooler and remaining bags between his feet. "I guess your stories are going to keep me on the edge of my seat with anticipation."

Jennifer got in, started the engine, and smiled, saying, "There isn't room in this car for sitting on the edge. You'll just have to sit back, don't step on the chips, smile, and nod every time I say something, and I might let you ride with me to Flagstaff. Or you can hitchhike and meet me there."

Jim nodded and smiled quietly as she put the car in gear and drove out of the station. Watching him smiling and nodding, she said, "You learn fast for a jarhead. Just keep doing that, and we'll get along fine."

Arriving at the outskirts of Flagstaff, Jennifer pulled into the first nice-looking motel along the road and parked. Almost crawling out of his seat, Jim stretched and tried to get the kinks out of his legs. Sitting almost motionless for the last couple of hours had stiffened his legs as he tried to avoid the things on the floor of the car.

Jennifer climbed out, stretched her arms over her head, and remarked, "This has been a *long* day."

"Yep," Jim replied. "And tomorrow will be just as long."

"How far from here to Muleshoe?" she asked as she walked around the car.

"Probably nine or ten hours," Jim told her as she put her arms around his waist.

"That's even longer than today," she protested.

"Driving, yes," Jim replied. "But we didn't get started

until after noon today. Tomorrow, we'll have a five- or six-hour earlier start."

"Do your folks know I'm coming?" Jennifer asked as they headed for the lobby.

"I'll call them after we check in," Jim told her, holding the lobby door open for her.

"You should've told them yesterday," Jennifer criticized as they walked to the front desk.

"I wasn't sure when we'd get there," Jim told her as they waited for the desk clerk.

"You could've at least told them I was coming with you," she protested.

"That would've just given my mom more time to fret," Jim said as the clerk arrived. "This way, she only has one day to worry about what she'll do, what she'll say, or what you'll think."

Paying for the room and giving the key to Jennifer, Jim said, "If you go unlock the room, I'll drive over and bring in the bags."

Kissing him on the cheek, Jennifer grinned and said, "You know, this is our first motel room."

"I know," Jim smiled back. "And don't think you can have your way with me just because we're sharing a room."

"I think I can have my way with you anytime I want," she teased. "And this just feels so naughty!"

Jim lightly slapped her on the behind and said, "Leave it to you to smut up my honorable intentions."

Jennifer laughed as she walked down the line of rooms to theirs, and Jim headed to the car.

Holding the door open as Jim parked and retrieved their bags, Jennifer asked, "Do you want to go eat or take a shower first?"

Jim sat their bags on the bed and answered, "Let's eat.

I'm going to call home right quick, so if you want to shower or anything, go ahead."

"Nope," she answered. "I'll wait until we get back. I'll just wash my face a little and freshen up while you call."

Jim's mother answered the phone while Jennifer was in the bathroom with the door closed. "Hi, Mom," he said.

"This is sort of a surprise," she responded. "Is anything wrong?"

"Nope," Jim told her. "I finished the training in California, and I'm on the road heading your way."

"When will you get here?" she asked.

"Tomorrow afternoon," he answered. "And I'm bringing a guest."

A few seconds of silence followed until his mother said, "I'm assuming that it's Jennifer."

"Yep, who'd you think it would be?" Jim laughed.

"I'm just surprised," she replied. "And I wish you'd given me more time. There's so much I need to do around here before she sees this place."

"I doubt if anything needs to be done, Mom," Jim answered. "Jennifer won't care."

"What about your father?" she asked.

"I don't think Dad will care either," he said. "Just relax and don't worry. I'm guessing it will be four or five o'clock before we get there. The only things we'll need are already there, so just tell Dad we're coming, and we'll see you tomorrow."

Resigned to the short notice, she answered, "Fine, but if the house isn't perfect, it's your fault for not letting me know ahead of time."

Jim laughed and said, "I'll let Jennifer know. Now we've got to get something to eat and try to get a few hours of sleep. I'll see you tomorrow."

Jim hung up the phone as Jennifer came out, asking, "What'd she say?"

Jim took the motel keys from the desk and said, "I'll tell you over dinner. She's just being my mother."

Back in their room later, Jennifer walked into the bathroom and started the shower. A few seconds later, Jim heard her say, "Jim, could you come in here and give me a hand with something?"

CHAPTER 27

The next morning, Jim woke before the alarm chimed five o'clock. He rose as quietly as he could and headed for the bathroom. Shutting the door, he started the shower and tentatively tested the water before getting the temperature he wanted. As he was rinsing off the remaining soap, he heard the door open.

"Morning," Jennifer said as she peeked around the shower curtain.

"Morning," Jim replied. "Want me to leave the shower on?"

"Please," she asked.

Jim stepped to the back of the tub and pulled a towel from the rack, saying, "There you are, pretty lady. I'll go get some coffee while you're taking your shower."

Jennifer gave him a quick kiss and stepped into the tub, pulling the curtain closed. "Will we have time to clean up just before we get to your parents' house?"

"Do you think that's necessary?" Jim asked as he finished drying.

"I just don't want to meet your mother looking like I've

been on the road for two days," she said from behind the curtain. "I'd prefer to stop somewhere and get my hair done, put on some nice clothes . . . you know. I just want to look my best."

Pulling his razor from his shave kit, Jim told her, "She knows we've been on the road, and she doesn't expect you to look like you're dressed to go out. Mom's a pretty simple lady and is used to a very relaxed style. If you try to impress her, she'll wonder why. A simple T-shirt, jeans, and a smile will do more for her impression of you than all the fancy in the world."

"I'd still feel better if we'd at least stop for an hour or two so I can take another shower. If it's going to be nine hours of driving, I don't think that's asking too much," she pouted.

"Okay," Jim relented as he rinsed the remaining shave cream from his face. "We can stop in Muleshoe, get a room so you can *refresh*, then go home."

Jennifer looked around the curtain and smiled, "Thank you."

Shaking his head, Jim walked over to his open bag and pulled out clean underwear, socks, and a T-shirt. Those on, he took his jeans from the chair where he had tossed them last night and pulled them on. Finishing with his boots, he announced, "I'm heading to the lobby for some coffee. Will you be ready when I get back?"

"Doubt it," he heard her say. "But if you relax a little, it won't take me long."

"Okay," he said as he grabbed the keys to the room and the 'Vette. "I'll go fill the car before I get the coffee. That'll give you fifteen or twenty minutes."

Jim shut the door and headed for the car. As he was leaving the gas station on his way back, he saw a small pancake house that appeared to be open. He pulled in to check and found that it was. Asking for two coffees to go, he checked the menu while waiting and liked what he saw.

Back at the motel, Jim parked and took the coffee in, hoping to find Jennifer ready to go. As he opened the door, he knew it was still going to be a little while. She was standing in front of the sink and mirror, fussing with her hair and makeup.

Sitting her cup on the counter beside her, Jim said, "There's a nice little breakfast place just down the road that's open." Flipping on the TV, Jim sat on one of the barely comfortable chairs to watch the news while waiting for Jennifer. "If you'd like," he said between sips of coffee, "I'll pack your bag."

"No, thanks," she said, rechecking the eyeliner she'd been applying. "I'll get it when I'm done."

"Okay," Jim said, looking at his packed bag. "I'm not sure that café is open for lunch, so . . ."

"Just hush," Jennifer tried to say as she applied her lipstick. "You're starting to get on my nerves. I've got enough to worry about without you rushing me."

Jim knew better than to continue this conversation, so he switched topics. "We'll be going right by Meteor Crater less than an hour from when we leave. We can stop by and look if you want to."

"How long would it take?" she asked, fingering her hair, unsatisfied with the way it looked.

"Maybe thirty minutes, surely less than an hour," Jim answered.

"Tell you what," she proposed, picking up her coffee and turning, "I'll take that thirty minutes or hour to clean up in Muleshoe. So, I'm really not adding any time to the trip. And I really don't care about seeing a hole in the ground."

"Fair enough," Jim agreed, smiling. "I'll sacrifice my tour of a famous landmark so you can do your nails."

Jennifer walked over to him and kissed the top of his head and whispered, "You're such an ass, Jim Lashley."

"I hope you get all the name-calling out of your system before we get home," Jim told her. "I don't think you'll impress my mother by calling me names."

"I bet she'd agree with me," she argued as she started packing her bag.

"Probably so," Jim said, nodding and standing. "And I'm sure Dad will side with you on that. While you finish packing, I'll get some ice for the cooler. We can get some drinks later when we stop for gas."

A few minutes later, Jim carried the bags to the car, stowed them in the trunk, and put the cooler on the floor of the passenger side. Leaving the door open to the room, he returned the keys to the desk clerk and made sure there were no additional charges. Jennifer was walking out as he returned, and he asked, "Did you recheck everything?"

"Yep," she said, walking to the car. "I think I'd like breakfast now, if you're finally ready."

Jim shook his head, amazed that she would even joke that it'd be his fault for being too late. "I guess I'm *finally* ready. Sorry, it took *ME* so long."

"You're forgiven," Jennifer said, smiling from the passenger seat. "Now that we've established who'll *always* be at fault, I'm starving."

After breakfast, Jim drove as they continued east on I-40 toward Albuquerque, New Mexico. There was no mention of Meteor Crater as they sped by the sign pointing to the road that led to the site just before reaching Rimmy Jims.

Crossing into New Mexico, Jim decided to stop in

Gallup to refill the gas tank and stretch his legs. They were still ahead of his mental timetable, and he knew that he could push the speed limit a little more than usual out here in the almost-desolate country. Most of the land they were driving through was Indian Reservations, and very little local traffic would be on the road, especially this early.

Jim went in and got four Dr Peppers for the cooler and two packs of beef jerky. Seeing a bag of barbecue-flavored chips, he grabbed that as well and paid for the food and gas.

He was just finishing putting the drinks in the cooler when Jennifer returned from the restroom. "Need anything?" he asked, shutting the lid.

"Nope," she answered. "I'm just ready to get this drive over. I don't think I've seen so much barren land in my life."

"This isn't that bad," Jim said as she got in the car. "You should see what you've got to look at on I-10. This is scenic compared to the drive from El Paso to Los Angeles."

"I'll take your word for that," she told him. "Next time, let's fly."

Jim just got in, started the engine, and pulled back onto I-40. In a little over two hours, they should be in Albuquerque, and that would be a good time to stop for lunch.

As before, there were few towns as they skirted the Reservations, but at least there were plenty of trees as the elevation rose. Not quite the pines Jennifer was used to seeing in Florida, but it was a welcome change from the raw land they'd left behind.

Arriving in Albuquerque, Jim spotted a Mexican restaurant that looked to be popular by the number of cars in the parking lot. Pulling in, he smiled at Jennifer and asked, "How 'bout a Chile Relleno for lunch?"

"What's that?" she asked as she got out of the car.

"It's a poblano pepper stuffed with cheese, dipped in a special batter, and deep-fat fried to a golden brown," he replied, "normally served with refried beans, rice, chips, some guacamole, and red or green chili sauce."

Jim held the door open for Jennifer, and the fragrant odor of cooking hit them. "If it tastes as good as it smells, this should be very good," Jim said, shutting the door behind him.

Seated at their table, Jim waited for Jennifer to look at the menu before saying, "I'd still recommend the Chile Relleno, but tacos are hard to screw up. Now, tamales are something different. They're really hard to make well. But your choice."

When the waitress returned, Jennifer laid the menu down and asked, "Are the Chile Rellenos good?"

"The best thing we have," the waitress told her. "But the Carne Asada is excellent as well."

"I'll take the Chile Relleno, please," Jennifer said. "And unsweet tea with lemon."

Writing the order, the waitress turned to Jim, asking, "And for you, sir?"

"The same," he told her. "And some Pico De Gallo, please."

Turning as she wrote, the waitress said, "I'll be right back with your drinks and some chips."

"How much longer?" Jennifer asked, taking a chip from the bowl that had just been delivered.

"About four hours to Muleshoe," Jim said, dipping a chip in the green sauce. "Then it's about fifteen miles to the house."

"So, four hours to Muleshoe, one hour at the motel, and fifteen minutes to the house is that what you're telling me?" she smiled, trying a taste of the red sauce.

"Yep, exactly," Jim said, nodding. "We'll be at the house in five hours and fifteen minutes."

"Unless my hair needs some more work," Jennifer joked as the waitress arrived with their food.

After they'd eaten, Jim told Jennifer that he was going to use the pay phone and call his folks to let them know where they were and when they'd arrive.

"Do you really think you should do that?" Jennifer asked. "If you tell them you are in Albuquerque, they'll know how long the drive is. How're you going to explain the extra hour?"

"I'll just tell them we stopped so you could clean up," he replied.

"You'll do no such thing," she said. "I certainly don't want your mother to see me and know that I just spent an hour trying to look good. I'd rather let her think that we just finished a nine-hour drive, and I still look fresh and clean."

Jim thought about it for a second and shook his head, saying, "As always, you're right again. How could I have been so dense to think that you'd be devious about how you look? I should've known better."

"Yes, you should've," Jennifer said, climbing in the car.

Jim walked around the rear and got into the driver's seat. Glancing at Jennifer as he started the engine, he just shook his head again and pulled back onto the road that led back to I-40.

Crossing the mountains east of Albuquerque, they sped across the flat plateau that would ultimately take them to the state line. Eager to get back to Texas and to get home, Jim pushed the speed as much as he dared.

Finally, in Muleshoe, Jim pulled into the only motel and parked. "I'll be right back," he said, climbing out.

Minutes later, he returned with a key and drove to the room. "What do you want me to bring in?" he asked as he parked.

"Just my bag," Jennifer told him, taking the key from his hand.

Jim got out and opened the trunk, taking Jennifer's bag from inside. Shutting the trunk, he carried it in and sat it on the bed. "Anything else I can do?" he asked as he turned on the TV.

"No, thanks," she answered. "I'm just going to take a quick shower, redo my makeup, and run a brush through my hair."

And that'll take an hour? Jim thought, settling into the chair.

A few minutes later, Jennifer appeared in the doorway to the bathroom, one towel around her as she dried her hair with another. "Could you open my suitcase, please?" she asked, smiling.

"Sure," Jim said, rising from his chair. "Anything in particular you need?"

"I just want clean underwear, a clean shirt and jeans, and socks," she answered, walking to the bed where Jim was opening her suitcase.

Resigned to waiting, Jim returned to the TV and patiently waited. Thirty minutes later, Jennifer announced that she was ready. Jim turned the TV off, took the closed suitcase from the bed, and picked up the room key from the desk.

"I'll put this in the car and go check out of the room," he said, opening the door to the room.

"Okay," she said. "I'll just take a quick look around and be ready to go when you get back."

Knowing that she'd be constantly rechecking her

makeup for the last time, Jim gave the desk clerk the keys, paid, and offered no response to the curious look he received. *Guess they don't do a lot of hourly rate business here,* Jim thought as he walked out.

Jennifer was closing the door when Jim got back to the room. "Ready?" she asked as she walked to the car.

"I reckon," Jim responded. "Are you?"

Jim started the car and drove the very familiar route from town to where he'd grown up. It was a little after five o'clock when they pulled into the driveway. Jim was slightly surprised not to see his father sitting in a lawn chair, *not* waiting for them.

It was shortly after Jim killed the engine that the front door opened, and his dad came out. "Thought I heard someone," John said, walking up to the car. "Didn't expect you for another hour or so."

Jim got out of the car and said, "We made good time, Dad."

Jim gave him a quick squeeze on the arm as he walked around the car to open Jennifer's door. "Dad, this is Jennifer," he said as he helped her out of the car.

John walked around and put out his hand, saying, "Good to meet you, Jennifer. Welcome to our house."

Jim's mother was just coming out of the house as John was shaking Jennifer's hand. "It's about time," she said. "Your father's been antsy for the last hour or two." Walking around the car to Jennifer, she said, "You must be Jennifer. I've heard so much about you from Jim. You just come on into the house and let the boys bring in the bags. You certainly don't look like you've spent the last ten hours sitting in that little cramped car of Jim's. Can I get you a glass of tea?"

Jennifer turned and winked at Jim as she walked into

the house with his mother.

CHAPTER 28

Jim and his dad watched the women enter the house before they turned to the car. "I guess we better get the bags," John said, waiting for Jim to open the trunk.

"I reckon so," Jim said, lifting out Jennifer's bag. "There's only two, and I'll get them both, Dad. Why don't you go on in and see if there just might be a little of that Jack Daniel's left from my last visit?"

"You mean you didn't stop in Texaco when you drove through?" John asked, taking Jennifer's bag from Jim. "You expect me to keep you in booze every time you drop in unannounced?"

Laughing, Jim replied, "The answer to the first part, no, I didn't stop. Next, yes, I expect there to be the appropriate beverage here when I arrive. Finally, it wasn't unannounced. Now, think there's a sip or two remaining in that bottle?"

"I can tell you for a fact there's not a drop left in that bottle," John told him.

Jim stopped abruptly and said, "No Jack Daniel's?"

"Didn't say that," John answered.

"What'd you say?" Jim asked, going along with the running narrative that'd taught him to listen to the question, not assume, and only give the answer to the asked, nothing more.

"I said there wasn't a drop left in *that* bottle," John said, sitting Jennifer's bag in Jim's room. Turning to Jim, he said, "I suppose you know your mother doesn't approve of men and women sleeping together unless they're married."

Jim threw his bag on the bed and said, "I think she'll make an exception this one time, don't you?"

"I suppose so," John answered. "I do know that she's mighty keen on you finding and keeping the right one. And she seems to think that you believe this is the right one."

Jim put his hand on his dad's shoulder and whispered, "Let's not worry about what either of them think for now. I seem to have gotten the impression that there just may be another bottle hiding in the cupboard. Let's go look."

Jim followed his dad to the dining room, where he knew the wine and whiskey was kept. As John opened the bottom door, Jim told him he was going into the kitchen to visit with his mother.

As he entered, he saw Jennifer and his mother sitting at the table, drinking coffee. Both were leaning toward each other and paying attention to what each was saying. When they saw Jim, both straightened up and became suddenly silent.

"What're you two ladies plotting?" Jim asked as he got two glasses from over the counter.

"Nothing," his mother answered. "Just talking about y'all's drive from California."

Jim looked at Jennifer as she nodded, agreeing, "I just told her about what barren country it was and how many hours we were on the road."

"If it wasn't an interesting drive, what makes it an interesting conversation?" Jim wanted to know.

"Not to change the subject," his mother said, "I suppose you and your father are going to sit out there and make boy talk?"

"I guess you could say that," John said, walking in with the bottle in his hand. "Don't forget to put some ice in those glasses. I'll get a couple of cans of Coke and see you outside."

Both women sat quietly, watching until Jim and his dad were out of the room. "Think we should join them?" Jennifer asked.

"In a minute," Jim's mom answered. "Let them get their hellos out of the way, and we'll take the steaks out and join them. Would you like something else to drink?"

"Water's fine," Jennifer answered.

Jim's mother looked her in the eyes and said, "Around here, we tend to speak our minds. I'm pretty sure that if it was just you and Jim, you'd be having more than just water."

After pausing for her words to sink in, she continued, "If you intend on hanging around with my son, you better learn that I'd prefer for you to be the same with me as you are with him. Now, if you'd like water, there's the sink. Me, I don't often drink John's whiskey, but tonight, I think I'll join my boys in a drink."

Jennifer reevaluated Jim's mom and concluded that there wasn't going to be much that slipped past her. "Now that you mention it," Jennifer said, getting up, "I'd like having a drink with you and your boys. I'll get the glasses and some ice."

"Pleased to have you join us," Jim's mother said, smiling at Jennifer. "You take the glasses out, and I'll be right behind with the steaks."

John was puffing on his old pipe when Jennifer came out. He stood and said, "Here, you sit by Jim. I'll get the other two chairs and bring them over."

"Thanks," she said, still standing. "Why don't you put the other chairs facing yours, and we ladies will take them?"

"That'll be just fine," John said, pulling two well-worn lawn chairs over.

"Take a seat, and I'll fill those glasses for you," John said as he picked up the bottle of Jack from between his and Jim's chairs.

Jennifer took the chair opposite Jim's and held the two glasses out as John poured about half of what he and Jim had in their glasses and said, "That's about what she usually has if she's nipping. If you want more, just ask."

"This'll be just fine," Jennifer replied. "I think we're going to sit with you guys for a few minutes while you get the steaks going, and then we'll head back inside to finish cooking the rest."

Jim's mother came out with four large steaks on a platter and sat them on the small ledge attached to the grill. "Potatoes need about fifteen more minutes; corn will be done by then, and the salad's made," she said, taking the glass Jennifer offered before sitting down.

Regardless of the seating arrangement, Jennifer mainly talked to Jim's mom while he talked to his dad. An occasional question or comment was directed the other way, but the conversation may just as well have been with the ladies still in the kitchen.

The mesquite now a dull ashen gray, John rose and arranged the steaks on the grill, asking, "How'd you like yours, Jennifer?"

"Medium rare," she answered.

"Reckon that'll be four medium rare," he said, putting

all the steaks the same distance from the hottest part of the grill.

A few minutes later, Jim's mother rose and said, "Ten minutes. Don't overcook those steaks."

As the women went inside, John whispered, "Almost forty years I've been cooking steaks, think she'd know by now that I know what I'm doing?"

Jim smiled and took another swallow of his drink. "How often does she remind you?"

"Damn near every time," John said, toasting Jim with his glass. "Damn near every time."

"Think she'll ever change?" Jim asked, standing and walking to the grill.

"Not a chance," John said, checking the bottoms of the steaks.

Once the meat was cooked, they loaded the steaks back on the platter and headed for the house. Jim held the door as John walked in, announcing, "Steaks are done."

The kitchen table was set, and the only thing left was to put the platter in the center. Jennifer brought a large pitcher of iced tea and sat it by John's seat at the head of the table.

Jim took his usual seat on John's left, and Jennifer took the seat across from him as the last of the food was placed in the center of the table. Once his mother had taken her seat, John looked at Jennifer and said, "You're the guest. You take your steak first."

Jennifer politely replied, "Thank you. I'd be pleased if you'd pick one for me."

John took her proffered plate and stabbed a steak, placing it in the center, saying, "They're pretty much all the same, but I think this one had just a little more marbling than the others."

As the others passed their plates, John divided the steaks and removed the platter. "I guess all I need now is a tater and an ear of corn," he said, returning to his seat.

After supper, Jim helped Jennifer and his mother clear the table while John took out the trash. After being told to leave the dishes to Jennifer and his mother, Jim went outside to join his father.

Few words passed between them as they sat there, but the unspoken said more about their closeness than any conversation could. A few minutes later, Jennifer came out and joined them. Watching the two men, she realized that they were almost identical in their mannerisms and gestures, and Jim looked like a younger version of his father.

When his mother came out with a tray carrying four bowls of ice cream, Jim asked, "Where'd you get this?"

She passed the bowls around and answered, "Yesterday, your father decided that he wanted some homemade ice cream. He called it a sudden yearning. Of course, it had *nothing* to do with you coming home today."

Jennifer watched the look that passed between Jim and his dad, knowing that neither of these two would ever acknowledge the bond between them or their feelings about each other. But it was unmistakable to everyone who watched them.

The ice cream finished. Jennifer gathered the bowls and headed inside. Jim's mother announced that she was going to bed so she could get up early the next morning to cook breakfast.

Mere minutes later, John rose, saying, "I'm hitting the sack as well. You kids stay up as long as you like, and I'll see you in the morning."

"It's still early," Jennifer told Jim as they watched John go into the house.

Jim just smiled and told her, "That's just their way of not acknowledging that we are sleeping in the same room. If they're asleep or pretending to be, they don't know what we're doing."

After a few minutes of talking about Jim's family and what they'd be doing for the next few days, Jim rose and said, "Let's go to bed. You know that we have to get up before them and be in the kitchen when they get up."

Jennifer smiled as she got up and took Jim's hand, saying, "I suppose that's so they didn't see us leave the same room."

"Pretty much," Jim acknowledged. "And we have to make some noise in the kitchen that woke them. Then they can complain about it and not acknowledge what they don't normally approve of."

"Guess we'll have to be quiet," Jennifer whispered as they entered the house.

"Yes, unless you want to sleep in another room," Jim said, softly shutting the door.

CHAPTER 29

The next few days slipped by as Jim spent most of the days with his dad, sometimes with Jennifer in tow. They went to the normal haunts, where Jennifer got to know the type of people who lived in the small rural farmland and how their lives differed from what she'd known growing up in the Florida Panhandle.

Trips to town were rare as they wanted to spend as much time as possible with just the family. The one evening they decided to eat out was spent at El Monterrey in Clovis, New Mexico. Jennifer spent a lot of her time helping Jim's mother around the house, and they took the occasional trip to neighbors or to town.

As the time approached for Jim and Jennifer to leave, the issue of his return to Vietnam was never mentioned but was apparent in the subjects they skirted during their conversations. The night before they were due to fly from Amarillo to Pensacola was almost painfully subdued.

"How long will you be in Florida?" John asked as they were sitting outside, watching the evening stars.

"Three days," Jim said, reaching down to get his glass

of Jack and Coke.

"Not a lot of time," John remarked.

"No," Jim agreed.

"Your mother worries about you," John said, putting his hand on Jim's arm.

"I know," Jim said, turning to look at his father.

John pulled his hand back and continued, "She's glad you brought Jennifer. I think she'd like to stay in touch with her after you leave."

"I'm sure Jennifer would like that," Jim agreed. "I know they've spent most of their time huddled together plotting something."

John laughed and said, revealing, "Your mother would never say it, but she was impressed that Jennifer took time just before she got here to shower and put on clean clothes."

Jim smiled and said, "I figured she'd notice. Somehow, that woman seemed to know every time I tried to sneak something by her."

"Yeah," John admitted, taking a pull on his pipe. "She has that gift, but the evidence about your stop in Muleshoe before you came home was provided by a neighbor that shall remain nameless."

"What do you mean?" Jim asked.

"Seems that someone saw your 'Vette at the motel and called your mother to see if you were home," John told him.

"You were ratted out by nosy neighbors." John explained, "Now, don't you say a word to Jennifer. Your mother said that she'd have done the same if she were meeting the parents for the first time, and she'd never embarrass Jennifer by letting her know that the secret was out."

"I'll keep it a secret," Jim said, smiling to himself.

Jennifer and Jim's mom walked out of the house as

they were laughing about the motel incident. "What're you boys laughing about?" Jennifer wanted to know.

"Nothing," Jim said, smiling at her. "We were just remembering some of the stupid things I did as a kid and how Mother always knew about it."

"Mothers have a way of finding out things," his mom said. "You boys always think you're getting away with something, but we know."

She sat beside John and continued, "Even your father thinks I don't know about some of the things he's pulled over the years, but I know."

"What things?" John asked incredulously. "I've never tried to keep secrets from you."

"What about that time you ran out of gas in the plane and had to borrow some from the rancher whose pasture you landed in?" she asked.

"I don't remember anything like that," John huffed.

"I guess I never got that phone call asking if you finally made it home," she informed him. "The poor man was more worried about you than I was."

"I never should have given him my phone number," John said, pouting. "He should have known to keep his mouth shut anyway."

"Well, just remember that we women have our ways of finding out what you boys are up to when you think you're so sneaky," she told him. "Now I think we better get to bed. We need to get up early tomorrow and get Jim and Jennifer to Amarillo for their flight."

John rose and followed her toward the house, saying, "We'll see you in the morning."

Jim and Jennifer remained outside for a few more minutes to allow his mother time to get in bed. Then quietly, as every night before, they went into their own bedroom.

Jim was up early the next morning making coffee while Jennifer showered. John came out and sat at the table while the pot brewed. Content to just sit there, he watched as Jim took the cups from the shelf and placed them on the table.

"Morning," Jim said, putting his father's favorite mug in front of him.

"Morning," John said, slowly turning the mug between his hands.

As the pot finished, Jim brought it to the table and was pouring for his father when his mother came in.

"Morning," she said as she took her seat at the table.

"Morning, Mom," Jim replied as he poured her cup. "Jennifer's in the shower," he continued as he filled his own cup. "She'll be out shortly."

"That's fine," his mother told him. "I'll start breakfast as soon as she's out. Do you have your bags packed?"

Jim returned the pot to the counter and took his seat, saying, "Yeah, I put most of my stuff in it last night except for what I'm wearing to Florida." He took a tentative sip and continued, "I think Jennifer packed her suitcase also, but she had to leave out a lot of stuff. Couldn't decide what to wear, so about half of it's still spread out."

A few minutes later, Jennifer came out wearing a pair of jeans and a T-shirt, saying, "Good morning!"

She walked to the pot and came back, asking if anyone needed a refill, and then poured her own cup.

Sitting down, she asked, "Can I help with breakfast?"

"No," Jim's mother told her. "I've got that taken care of. You just relax and drink your coffee. Then, while I'm cooking, you and Jim finish packing. Breakfast will be ready when you get done."

Jim rose and put his empty cup in the sink, announcing, "I'm heading for the shower and getting dressed. I'll be done in ten minutes or so."

Showered and shaved, Jim put the remaining things in his bag and started to carry it to the front door. Jennifer came into the bedroom and put her things into her suitcase for him to carry also.

"Breakfast is about ready," she said as she snapped the suitcase closed.

"Okay," Jim said, heading for the bedroom door. "I'll come back and get yours and meet you in the kitchen.

The bags were delivered to the small foyer by the front door; Jim headed for the kitchen, where he could hear his mother and Jennifer talking. John was still sitting quietly at the table as he entered.

"Take a seat," his mother said as she sat a large bowl of scrambled eggs on the table beside a platter of biscuits. "Sausage and gravy are about ready."

Jim retrieved his cup from the sink, refilled it, and sat while Jennifer stirred the skillet with the gravy.

As the remaining items were placed on the table, they each took what they wanted and passed the plates and bowls around.

Conversation stopped as they each ate and thought about what would happen in the next few days. When the meal finished, Jennifer rose and started carrying the dishes to the sink. As Jim's mother started the water running, Jennifer put her arm around her shoulders and hugged her.

Jim watched and wondered just how tight the bond between them had grown over the few days they'd spent together. John looked at them also, rose, and headed for the back door.

Leaving the women to themselves, Jim followed his dad out and walked with him to the garage. John started the car and backed it to the front door as Jim went in and got the bags.

Looking in the kitchen window, Jim watched as his mother and Jennifer finished the dishes. Knowing that he might be seeing his mom for the last time made him realize how much he loved her. That and the fact that she and Jennifer shared their feelings about him brought on a strange feeling of serenity. It was as if whatever happened over the next year or so, he had what every man could possibly hope for.

The trip to Amarillo was devoid of conversation except for occasional remarks by Jim's mother to Jennifer about how she'd enjoyed the visit and that she was welcome to come anytime. Jennifer also told her that she'd be glad for them to come visit Florida while Jim was gone if they wanted.

Pulling up in front of the terminal, John killed the engine and got out to open the trunk. Jim exited the front seat and opened the door for Jennifer. All of them standing on the curb, Jim hugged his mother, gave his dad a quick squeeze, and picked up the bags.

Jennifer hugged John and, thanked him for the hospitality, and then put her arms around Jim's mother. After several seconds of holding each other, Jennifer reluctantly let go and followed Jim into the terminal.

CHAPTER 30

The flight to DFW was unremarkable, and they arrived with plenty of time to catch the connecting flight to Pensacola. After grabbing a bite to eat from one of the numerous food kiosks, Jim and Jennifer sat beside their departure gate, watching the travelers passing back and forth in front of them.

The boarding call for their flight was delayed a few minutes while some minor maintenance problem was resolved. As soon as the announcement that the plane was ready, Jim and Jennifer joined the line of passengers waiting to be processed and allowed to board.

Their seats near the rear of the airplane, they stood in the aisle while those ahead of them stowed their suitcases in the overhead compartments. Having checked their bags at Amarillo, the only thing they carried was Jennifer's purse.

Less than two hours later, they arrived in Pensacola and sat waiting for the others to retrieve their bags and deplane. Finally able to get off the airplane, they headed into the terminal, where Jennifer's mother and dad were waiting.

"Hi, Mom," Jennifer said, smiling as they met.

"Hi, baby," she replied. "How was your flight?"

"Fine," Jennifer answered.

"Welcome back," her father said to Jim, shaking his hand.

"Thanks," Jim said. "I'm glad to be back, even if it's only for a few days."

Turning toward the exit that led to the baggage claim, Jim said, "We checked two bags, and if you haven't gotten the ones we sent from Los Angeles, we need to get them as well."

"We've got those already," Jennifer's dad told him. "They're at Jennifer's apartment. As soon as these get here, we'll take you there."

Jennifer and her mom stood back and talked as the men waited for the bags to arrive. When Jim's bag and Jennifer's suitcase made their way to where they were standing, Jim grabbed his while her dad got Jennifer's.

"I guess we're ready," Jim said, walking back to where Jennifer was waiting. "I appreciate you getting all the others we sent."

"No problem," Jennifer's dad answered. "I don't think we could've gotten all of them and both of you in the car anyway."

"Yeah, there was a lot of luggage," Jim responded as they headed out of the terminal. "I had to borrow a pickup to take them to the airport before we left. Seems strange that I can live for over a year with one bag, and she needed four big suitcases for a couple of weeks."

"You should see what her mother has to pack for a weekend trip," Jennifer's dad said, shaking his head. "Women can't seem to get by with a couple of changes of clothes. They've got to have at least four changes for each day, just so they can have different choices."

"I figure a pair of jeans will last four days, a clean shirt for each day, and fresh underwear," Jim agreed. "If it's more than four days, I look for a laundry and wash everything I'm not wearing."

"I agree," her dad said as he opened the trunk. "I don't know if I could live on what you've got in your bag for a year, but I can get by on a hell of a lot less than the typical woman needs."

Once the bags were loaded, Jim got in the back with Jennifer while they drove to her apartment. Questions about what they'd do for the next couple of days passed for conversation as they followed the thinning traffic out of the airport and across town.

With promises to have dinner together the next day, Jim and Jennifer thanked her parents for the ride and took their bags into the apartment. The first thing Jennifer did was to start unpacking the three large suitcases and separating her things into piles to wash, send to the cleaners, or put away.

Jim took everything out of his bag and hung his uniforms in the closet after making sure they didn't need to be cleaned. Then, all the clothes he'd worn for the trip were set aside to be washed.

The next couple of hours were spent on laundry and just busy work around the house. Jennifer's mother had obviously cleaned the apartment, and there was little to do except wait for the washer to finish each load before putting it in the dryer.

When the last load was finally done, folded, and put away, Jennifer looked in the refrigerator and checked to see if there was sufficient food for dinner that evening. Not surprised to see it freshly stocked with milk, juice, hamburger meat, vegetables, and beer, Jennifer asked Jim what he wanted to eat that evening.

Looking over her shoulder, Jim said, "How about we call for a pizza and do nothing but sit around this evening?"

Taking out two Budweisers, Jennifer handed one to Jim and answered, "That sounds fine for me. As much as I enjoyed spending time with your folks, I'm ready for some us time."

"Me too," Jim said, opening his bottle and switching it with hers. As he opened the second bottle, he continued, "I'm glad you and mom got along so well, but having to pretend we weren't sleeping together was getting to be a pain."

Jennifer tapped her bottle against Jim's and laughed, saying, "Your mother knows what's going on. Even if she doesn't really approve, she has to keep up the pretense of 'if I don't see it, it didn't happen.' But deep down, I think she's glad we're together."

"I know," Jim said, walking into the living room. "She'll never change her ideas about how unmarried people should behave, but she also understands that she has to let me live my life according to my own values."

The rest of the evening was spent sitting together and watching TV. Jim was content to just sit with Jennifer, holding her hand or stroking her arm. Lying on the couch with her head on Jim's lap, Jennifer could think of no better way to spend the rest of her life. The impending separation seemed a distant point in her mind, and for the next few days, she wanted to focus on enjoying the little time remaining.

The next afternoon, they went to her parents' house well before dinnertime. Jim wanted to spend some time with her father, and Jennifer wanted to let her mother know about the new developments in their relationship.

Jim had talked to her dad on various occasions, but there'd never been a serious conversation about his relationship with Jennifer. Even this evening, it was more of a getting to know personally each other than a discussion about him and Jennifer. But Jim wanted Jennifer's father to understand the type of man he was and that he cared for Jennifer.

When Jennifer and her mom came out carrying a pitcher of margaritas, Jim smiled and said, "I don't know what more a man could want—beautiful women, pleasant conversation, dinner cooking, and booze. We've got to do this more often!"

Sitting around with their drinks, Jennifer's parents wanted to know about his training in California, where he'd be going when he left, when he'd get back, what type of missions he'd be flying over there, and if he'd be in any danger.

Jim tried to answer each question as best he could, and although he told them about the dangers of flying in Vietnam, he tried to stress the fact that he was much safer flying than he'd been on the ground.

Dinner finally over, Jim and Jennifer said their goodbyes and headed for her car. Almost there, Jim whispered to her, turned, and walked back to where her parents were standing.

He walked up and put his arms around Jennifer's mother and again tried to reassure her that he'd be back for Jennifer. Shaking her father's hand, he repeated that nothing was going to keep him from coming back.

As he climbed into the car, Jennifer said, "Thanks. I know that meant more to them than any other thing you've done."

The next day, Jim spent most of his time making sure his uniforms were packed for the trip and what personal items he needed were in the bag. Rechecking his flight information and putting his orders and records in an envelope, Jim realized that he was excited to get going.

The rest of the day was again spent sitting quietly or napping together on the couch. That evening, Jim and Jennifer lay in bed quietly, talking about their plans for the year that he would be gone. Finally falling asleep in each other's arms, their last night together slipped away.

The next morning, Jim eased out of bed and headed for the shower. When he finished, he put on his uniform trousers and padded in his bare feet to the kitchen, where Jennifer was making breakfast.

"Good morning," he said as he kissed the back of her neck.

"Good morning," she responded, turning into his arms. "I promise not to be sad about this being our last morning together."

Jim kissed her softly on the lips and told her, "This *isn't* our last morning together. Our last morning together is still years away."

After they'd eaten, Jim finished putting on his uniform and closed his bag for the last time until he arrived in Vietnam. The trip was silent until they pulled up to the terminal, and Jennifer finally said, "I love you, Jim Lashley. You hurry home. I'll be waiting."

Jim leaned over and kissed her, repeating, "I love you too. And I'll be back before you know it."

He took his bag from the rear seat and sat it on the curb. Leaning in the passenger door window, he told her, "I'll write every chance I get. I know Mom and Dad would love to hear from you almost as much as I'd love it."

He stood up and watched as tears ran down Jennifer's cheeks, wishing there was more he could do to comfort her. Knowing that there wasn't, he picked up his bag, waved, and headed into the terminal.

CHAPTER 31

Jim's flight to St. Louis, Missouri, was over in a little under two hours. He'd sat close to the rear of the airplane and purposefully ignored the people sitting around him.

Although he'd hated leaving Jennifer, he was missing flying the F-4. And as much as he knew he shouldn't feel this way, he looked forward to combat in 'Nam.

The conflicting thoughts rumbled through his mind. He barely noticed that they were landing. Off the airplane, he took the envelope with his orders and the tickets to Da Nang to the counter of the airline that had been chartered by the military to support the massive number of troops that needed to be taken to or back from the war.

Given his seat assignment, Jim went to the United Service Organization (USO) to wait for his flight. As he entered, he saw members of each service sitting around, waiting for their flights either to their next duty station or going home. Finding an empty seat beside an Air Force Lieutenant, Jim nodded and sat down.

As he was looking at his orders, for the millionth time, the Lieutenant beside him asked, "Heading to 'Nam?"

"Yes," Jim answered. "How about you?"

"Same" came the reply. "Where'll you be stationed?"

"Da Nang," Jim said, turning to the Lieutenant. "What about you?"

"Biên Hòa," he answered. "I've been assigned to fly the OV-10 for the next year or so."

"Forward Air Control (FAC)," Jim said, nodding. "I'll be flying the F-4, so we just may meet on the radio someday."

"Possible," came the response. "You never know who you'll meet or who'll be there to save your ass."

"That's the truth," Jim acknowledged. "If I'm in trouble, I don't care if it's the Boy Scouts that come pull me out."

They continued discussing the war, airplanes, home, girlfriends, and every other thing that military men discussed while killing time. When the time came to head for the flight, both men headed for the same gate.

The flight was long and boring, but being filled with military members from all branches, there was always someone to talk to. Jim listened to several pilots who were on their way for a second tour. Most of them would talk about things that'd happened during their first tour and what they'd learned.

Jim listened closely to each of their stories and remembered some of the things the RIOs had taught him during training. Knowing that he'd never fully appreciate the things he was hearing until he experienced firsthand what it was like to be in the middle of a fight, he tried to envision each incident.

Finally landing in Da Nang, Jim waited for the bus that was taking them to sign in with their units. As he was dropped off at VMFA 115 headquarters, Jim noticed one of the F-4s being repaired by the mechanics. The numerous holes along the side of the airplane attested to the strength of the plane and that flying there was a deadly serious game.

Checked in, Jim was assigned his quarters and told to report to the flight line for his equipment the next morning. He carried his bag to where he'd be spending the next year and thought about how different this was from his last tour as an enlisted man.

The following day, he was shuffled from place to place, getting everything he needed to start flying with the squadron. The last stop was to talk to the squadron scheduler and be paired with a seasoned RIO. The next day would be their first flight as part of their in-country checkout.

The following morning, Jim was early for the brief and was looking at all the maps covering the walls when his RIO walked in with three other men in flight suits. After introductions, they sat around talking about the upcoming flight while they waited for the rest of the formation to arrive.

The Captain who was leading the flight walked in a few minutes later and began the brief. Knowing that this was Jim's first mission, the Captain covered specific things that were unique to the checkout. Finally over, Jim and his RIO went with the rest to get their flight gear and be taken to their airplanes.

Three hours later, Jim took his turn, landing as the formation broke over the airfield. Although there'd been no confrontation with enemy aircraft, nor were they fired at from the ground, the stress of knowing that death could be seconds away wore out all of them.

After putting their gear away, they met for a quick debrief and then headed for the club to have a beer and something to eat. During their time at the club, Jim learned more about what he'd seen and how things really worked than during the formal debrief.

In the more relaxed atmosphere of the club, and over several beers, more instruction and advice were given than in all the formal briefs put together. Not only was wisdom gained from experience offered, but getting to know who you were flying with and knowing that they were watching out for you also made each man more confident that they were a team.

Over the next few months, Jim moved from flying the wing position to flying as number 3 with a man on his wing. Now more experienced, he helped the new men as they arrived and tried to give them the same assistance he'd gotten from those who came before him.

Almost eight months into his tour, Jim finally became the flight commander for a mission that was to provide cover for a search and rescue mission. Although he had flown numerous missions like this as the wingman, this was to be his mission, and success or failure rested on his shoulders.

He briefed the flight and headed for his plane. *This is the reason I wanted to come back,* Jim thought. *Now, I get a chance to help out some poor, trapped men struggling to stay alive while waiting for rescue.*

The four-ship formation took off and headed for the assigned coordinates. Recognizing the area from his previous tour, the first thing that crossed Jim's mind was the hill where he'd been trapped almost two years ago.

Circling just south of the area where the rescue was to take place, Jim's formation floated lazily about twenty thousand feet above the ground. From this vantage point, he watched the FAC weaving back and forth along a small ridge line, trying to pinpoint the exact location of the men on the ground.

Listening to the radio chatter, Jim knew that there was an enemy formation approaching, and time was becoming critical. When the FAC finally spotted the Marines on the ground and determined what would be the fastest way to get the awaiting helicopters in, he then requested for Jim and his flight to provide cover and try to disperse the enemy that would soon be there.

As Jim pulled the throttles to idle and started a roll to bring the nose of his F-4 toward the advancing enemy, he adjusted his flight path to run parallel with the small set of hills that were between the Marines and the enemy troops. Knowing that the rest of the formation would be following him several seconds later, he scanned the area for his target.

As he was making his final adjustment for his pass, the FAC fired a Willie Pete (white phosphorus) rocket to mark the forward edge of the enemy's line. Mere seconds later, he fired another to bracket the troop concentration.

With the plumes of white smoke rising, Jim began his strafing run from the first rocket toward the last. Pulling up as he finished his run, he looked over his shoulder and saw his number 2 plane making the same run.

Pushing the power back up, Jim climbed back toward ten thousand feet and searched for any ground-launched missiles or antiaircraft gunfire. Seeing none, he began an orbit to wait for the rest of the formation to join.

Watching the FAC make pass after pass, Jim waited for the call to make another run. Finally, he heard the FAC direct the helicopters toward the Marines and turned his attention to the other members of his flight.

Knowing about how much fuel they'd used, he quickly calculated that they'd have to head back to Da Nang in the next fifteen minutes or be dangerously low on gas.

As he watched, the last of the helicopters took off and

headed off to deliver their load of relieved Marines. Hearing the FAC announce his departure also, Jim turned his plane and headed back to base.

Back at Da Nang, Jim debriefed the Operations Officer and the other members of his formation as quickly as he could. That completed, he checked to see if he was due to fly again tomorrow and then headed to his quarters.

He'd been writing Jennifer at least once a week and his parents every couple of weeks. There'd been almost daily letters from Jennifer and the occasional one from his mother. From Jennifer's letters, he knew that she was maintaining contact with his mom and that she was planning a trip to Muleshoe to visit them in the near future.

The end of his tour was now less than four months away, and Jim was almost counting the days until he could return to the States. The flying was always exciting but fraught with danger.

Now with almost one hundred missions under his belt, he felt confident in his skills and comfortable with the other pilots in the squadron. Now a First Lieutenant, he had gained the respect of every pilot because of both his abilities and his readiness to accept any mission.

Some of the pilots who were getting within a month or so of rotating back stateside were less than eager to fly unless absolutely necessary. It was understandable since every time you took off, the

flight was potentially the one that caught the golden BB that brought your plane down. Death or capture was hovering nearby on each mission.

Finally, the week before he was to go home, Jim was called into the Squadron Commander's office. Not unusual but always some concern about being summoned, Jim reported as ordered.

The Commander, a Lieutenant Colonel, motioned for Jim to have a seat as he finished a phone call. Hanging up the phone, he told Jim that he had two things for him. The first was orders to Yuma, Arizona. There, he'd be assigned to VMFAT 101. Since Jim had now served three one-year tours in Vietnam, assignment to a training squadron would mean not coming back for at least three more years.

The second thing was a set of double silver bars denoting his promotion to Captain. Then Jim was told that effective immediately, he was being taken from the flying schedule, and he should begin out-processing.

After being dismissed, Jim headed for the administrative offices to collect the necessary paperwork to get him back to the United States. Flight arrangements had already been made, orders transferring him to Yuma had been cut, two weeks of leave had been granted, and what seemed like reams of paperwork were handed to him in several envelopes.

Using one of the few phones available to call the United States, Jim tried to call Jennifer but got no answer. Then he called his mother and told her that he was leaving the next day, going through St. Louis, and would call her from there to tell her what flight would bring him to Amarillo.

Jim returned to his quarters and reviewed everything. Seeing that he'd be departing in two days, he returned to the flight line to turn in all his flight gear and say goodbye to those he probably wouldn't see over the next couple of days or maybe never again.

That evening at the Officers' Club, he was congratulated by his fellow aviators and was forced to drink a toast with each until he knew that tomorrow would be spent with a bad headache. When the final farewell drink was gone, Jim stumbled back to his bed and passed out.

Minor details completed the last full day in country and Jim packed everything for his early flight tomorrow morning. As much as he had looked forward to coming here and flying, he was ready to go home, hopefully never to return.

CHAPTER 32

The following morning, Jim boarded another chartered flight that would take him back to St. Louis. As before, this one was filled with servicemen from all branches, but this time, the relief of leaving was written clearly on each face.

Jim slept most of the way, as did many of the others. When the airplane crossed the western coast of the United States into California, the Captain announced it over the intercom. The cheer probably could've been heard on the ground.

As Jim exited the airplane, he watched tearful reunions as families struggled to find each other in the madhouse atmosphere. Heading toward the baggage claim, he hoped to get his bag as quickly as possible and then find the first available flight to Amarillo.

Luckily, there was one leaving in an hour that would pass through DFW with only a forty-five-minute layover. Paying for the ticket, Jim checked his bag through and headed for the departure gate. Stopping at one of the pay phones, he called home and gave his mother his arrival time in Amarillo. Hearing her say that they'd be there waiting for him, Jim hung up and tried to call Jennifer again. Still no answer.

Still in his uniform, Jim drew more stares and looks of disapproval as he waited for the flight to depart. It seemed to him that the country's attitude toward the military had gotten worse since his departure a year ago.

His seat on the airplane to DFW was thankfully next to an empty seat, and he could lean against the window and ignore the passengers around him. Opening the envelope that contained all his records, Jim reread everything just to keep busy.

The change of planes in DFW went smoothly, and Jim barely had time to grab a sandwich before the call to board was announced. Jim handed the agent his ticket and prepared to join the line. Looking at the seat assignment, the agent checked a note she had been given and reassigned Jim to one in the very rear of the plane.

Trying to avoid meeting anyone's eyes, Jim concentrated on looking at the seat numbers as he waited for those in front of him to find their seats, place their bags in the overhead compartment, and climb over the already-seated passenger beside their seat.

Finally, at the rear of the plane, Jim slid into his seat by the window and pulled the emergency card from the seat pocket in front of him. The continual movement of people at the front of the plane told Jim that it would be several minutes before they left the gate.

At last, he heard one of the engines start and heard one of the flight attendants begin to explain how the seat belts worked. After hearing the other engine start, Jim felt the sudden jerk as the airplane backed from the gate. Still not looking up, he dug around the seat pocket for something else to keep him occupied.

As the plane taxied out, Jim watched the terminal slide away and several taxiways pass as they neared the runway. Hearing the Captain tell the Flight Attendants to prepare for takeoff, Jim leaned back and closed his eyes.

Ten or fifteen minutes later, he saw the Flight Attendants moving behind him as he glanced toward the aisle. The service cart passed his seat on its way to begin providing drinks to the coach section of the plane, and Jim reclined his seat as much as he could and waited for the cart's return.

He had barely leaned back when he felt someone sit down in the open seat beside him. Jim opened his eyes and turned to see who had decided to change seats. He just hoped it wouldn't be someone with an anti-military attitude.

As he turned his head, he heard someone say, "Hey, Marine, where've you been?"

Jim's eyes opened wide as he looked at the smiling face of Jewell.

The next two hours flew by, and they had barely caught up on each other's lives as Jewell had to keep getting up and down to take care of the rest of the passengers. Once the descent into Amarillo began, she returned to sit beside him.

"Where are you headed now?" she asked.

"Home," Jim answered. "My folks are picking me up. I've got a couple of weeks before I have to go to Arizona."

"How long will you be in Arizona?" Jewell asked.

"Not sure," Jim replied. "Could be three or four years."

"What then?" she wanted to know.

"Not sure," Jim said. "I'll have about two or three years commitment left with the Marines."

"Think you'll stay for twenty?" she asked.

"Don't know," Jim told her. "That'd be another twelve years or so. I'll just wait and see what happens over the next couple of years."

"Now," she questioned, "are you seeing anyone? Anyone special, I mean."

Jim hesitated for just a second and replied, "Yes."

Disappointment obvious on her face, Jewell said, "Well, I guess that means that you don't want me to find you in Arizona."

"That wouldn't be good," Jim told her. "But if anything happens, I still have your phone number. And I'd like to stay in touch."

"I'll think about it," Jewell said. "I'd like to stay in touch too, but that might not be the best thing for either of us."

"Up to you," Jim said. "I'd still like to be friends. You can never have too many good friends."

"I'll let you know," Jewell said as the plane taxied to the terminal. Getting up, she continued, "If you call, leave your number, and I'll decide then."

Jim stayed in his seat until the plane was almost empty before standing and heading toward the exit. Passing Jewell at the front of the plane, he said, "It was good to see you again. Take care, and I'll call from Arizona when I get settled."

Seeing her slight smile, Jim left the airplane, wondering if he'd ever see her again.

His mom and dad were standing in front of the gate when Jim stepped into the terminal. Hurrying up to them, he gave them both a hug and headed toward the baggage claim with his arms still around them.

Standing at the carousel with his dad, waiting for his bag to appear, Jim wasn't paying attention until someone stepped around him and looked up at him. Glancing down, he saw Jennifer smiling as she said, "Welcome home, gyrene!”

Jim swept her into his arms and kissed her, saying, “I guess I know now why you didn’t answer your phone for the last couple of days.”

Laughing, she said, “Your mother called me right after she talked to you and asked me if I wanted to come. I wanted to surprise you.”

Setting her back down on her feet, Jim turned to his mother and complained, “You should’ve told me she was going to be here.”

His mother smiled and said, “Then it wouldn’t have been a surprise, would it?”

Jim looked at his dad and stated, “You were in on this too, weren’t you?”

John just smiled and answered, “It wasn’t my idea. I just do as I’m told around these two.”

Jennifer frowned and asked, “Aren’t you glad to see me?”

“Of course!” Jim answered, paying no attention to the carousel. “I can’t think of a better welcome home than having all of you here.”

“Good answer,” Jennifer said, smiling. “However, this wasn’t my idea.”

“Just whose idea was it?” Jim asked, looking at his mother.

“Does it matter?” she asked.

“I guess not,” Jim replied. “I was just going to thank them.”

“In that case,” John said, “it was mine.”

“Oh, you hush,” his mother said. “If you must know, we’ve all been planning this for weeks now. So you can say it’s all of us.”

“Then thanks, all of you,” Jim told them. “You’ve all

made this one of the best days of my life."

Jennifer leaned her head against Jim's chest and answered, "Mine too. Mine too."

The last bag on the carousel, Jim waited until it was in front of him before picking it up and saying, "Let's go home."

CHAPTER 33

The next week flew by as Jim and Jennifer stayed in Muleshoe with his parents. Jim's mother and Jennifer spent more and more time together, letting Jim and John do whatever they did away from the house.

There was never a word said about the sleeping arrangements, and now Jim's mother and father were usually up early and making breakfast when Jim and Jennifer came into the kitchen. Even when they went to visit neighbors, Jim's mom just introduced Jennifer as a friend who was visiting from Florida.

Wanting four days to drive to Yuma, Jim flew with Jennifer back to Florida for a few days. Driving his 'Vette to the airport, they finalized the decision for her to come out to Arizona after he got settled.

Jennifer's parents picked them up at PNS and welcomed Jim home just as his own folks had done. Over dinner the first night, Jennifer told her parents about their plans and got their approval.

Hating to see Jim leave, Jennifer nevertheless was anxious for him to get to Yuma and find a place. She also knew that she needed quite a bit of time to move her stuff into storage since she no longer needed the apartment.

Three days later, she drove Jim to the airport and kissed him goodbye, saying, "You let me know when you've found something, and I'll be there as soon as I can. I'll miss you even more now that I know we're going to have lots of time together, and I really do love you!"

Jim returned her kiss, saying, "I love you too. I'll find something temporary for now, but when you get there, I want you to help pick where we'll want to live."

Flying back to Amarillo, Jim considered just what he was getting into. He knew he wanted to be with Jennifer and knew he loved her, but this was a major step in his life.

Landing in Amarillo, Jim got his car out of the long-term lot and headed back to Muleshoe. Now in a hurry to get to Arizona, he sped south to Canyon and then southwest to Hereford on US 60. Just outside Hereford, Jim turned south on State Road 1055, which would take him to the little town of Earth.

Six miles west of Earth, Jim made a right-hand turn on 303 that would take him to the house two and a half miles later. Pulling into the gravel drive, Jim saw his dad washing his car, obviously waiting for Jim's return.

Not quite noon, Jim pulled onto the grass beside the driveway and parked. John tossed a towel to him as he got out of the 'Vette and said, "Here. You can give me a hand drying this one, and then we'll wash yours."

Smiling as he walked to the side of his father's car, he replied, "Be glad to help, but I don't think washing mine will do much good. I'll be on the road for the next two or three days, driving across New Mexico and Arizona. The way the winds blow across that country will screw up a wash job faster than a dust storm in Lubbock."

"At least we'll clean the windshield and vacuum out the inside," John said, wiping the last water from the hood.

"That'll be fine," Jim said, wringing out his soaked towel. "I do need to change the oil and check everything else before I leave tomorrow."

"Then let's take it into town and get that done while we let Mother do a little shopping," John said, taking the wet towel from Jim.

"Does she need to do any shopping?" Jim asked as John dumped the soapy water from the bucket beside the car.

"Constantly," he answered as he put the sponges and towels into the bucket. "There's not a day that goes by that that woman can't think of something to go shopping for."

"I'll just take my bags inside," Jim told him as he walked back to the 'Vette. "I'll ask Mom if she wants to go."

As Jim was closing the trunk, his mother came out and asked, "How was your visit? Did you get a chance to talk to Jennifer's parents? What do they think about her coming to live with you in Yuma?"

Jim smiled and said, "Good, yes, they approved—in that order."

"Don't be such a smarty-pants," she said as she hugged him. "I want to know all the details."

Heading for the house, Jim told her, "Why don't we talk about it on the way to town?"

"Oh, are we going to town?" she asked, following him into the house.

"Dad wants to take the 'Vette to get serviced before I leave," Jim answered. "I thought I'd let him drive it, and I'd ride with you. That'd give us plenty of time to discuss the *details* you want to hear."

"Well," she murmured, "there are a few things I could use from town. Your dad never wants to go shopping, so yeah, I can get a few things while we're there."

Jim went to his room and pulled all his dirty clothes from the bag and checked his uniforms that were hanging in the closet. The uniforms looked fine, so he gathered up the dirty things and headed for the washing machine in the small mudroom inside the back door.

"Let me do that," his mother said as she started pouring detergent into the washer. "You go help your dad while I get this started. We can put them in the dryer when we get back."

"Help me with what?" John asked, coming in the back door.

"Nothing," she replied. "You guys just get ready to go. I'll be done here in a minute."

John just shook his head at her and said, "I'm ready."

Watching their natural banter, Jim said, "Dad, you take the 'Vette. I'll ride with Mom, and we'll pick you up."

"Fine," John said, turning back to the door. "Just don't leave me sitting around the mechanic's shop too long."

"We're leaving in five minutes," Jim's mother said. "You just do as you're told. I bet we have to wait for you to finish your long-winded stories when we get there anyway."

As soon as the top of the washer was closed, Jim's mother said, "You go start the car. I'll be right out. And I'd rather you drive."

"Okay, Mom," Jim said, watching her head toward her bedroom.

Jim was sitting in the car when she walked out, shutting the front door. Knowing this was going to be fifteen minutes of questions and answers, he told himself to just be patient and tell her everything she wanted to know.

His mother still had hundreds of questions left to ask when they pulled into the mechanic's station but knew they'd have to wait.

John came over to the car as Jim pulled in, got in the back, and asked, "Where to now?"

"Piggly Wiggly," Jim told him. "Mom wanted to get some fresh vegetables for tonight. How long did the mechanic say it'd take?"

"About thirty minutes unless he finds something wrong," John said. "Why don't we go to the Dinner Bell and have lunch before we go to the grocery store?"

"Sounds good to me," Jim agreed. "How about you, Mom?"

"That's fine," she answered, "but don't eat too much. I've got steaks, baked potatoes, corn on the cob, a big salad, and peach cobbler planned for dinner tonight."

"We better pick up some chips and drinks for Jim's trip," John said as they pulled into the Dinner Bell parking lot. "That cooler you brought from California is still sitting in the garage."

After lunch, they drove back to check on Jim's car and were told that it was ready. Jim and John decided to head back home while his mother did her shopping.

"Did your mother bend your ear a little on the way to town?" John asked, knowing she did.

"A little," Jim answered.

"A little, my ass," John laughed. "She's been walking around just thinking of things to ask. I bet she'd spend the next week asking all sorts of things, like what was Jennifer's mother wearing, what kind of shoes she had, whether she dyed her hair. There'd be no end."

Jim smiled and replied, "Well, you know how women are. Those things are important to them. I couldn't tell you what dress or shoes she was wearing, about her hair, or anything else. I just don't notice."

"Me neither," John agreed. "We'll come home from

someplace, and she'll ask what I thought about some other lady's clothes, or shoes, or hair. She really doesn't care what I think. She just wants to talk about it. So I listen and agree with everything she says."

"That seems to be the way it is around women," Jim said. "Just agree with whatever they say."

"And they say a lot!" John laughed.

"That they do," Jim agreed, smiling and nodding. "That they surely do."

CHAPTER 34

The next morning, Jim rose early, only to find his mother already cooking breakfast and his dad taking the cold drinks from the refrigerator and icing them in the small cooler.

"Morning," Jim said, kissing his mother on the cheek before pouring a cup of coffee. "Y'all are up early."

His mother turned and simply said, "You said you wanted to get an early start."

As she turned back to scrambling the eggs, John closed the lid to the cooler and asked him, "Where do you plan to spend the night?"

"Probably Las Cruces," Jim told him. "That's a pretty easy drive and about halfway."

"That's where you stayed when you drove to California, isn't it?" John asked, picking up the cooler.

"Yeah," Jim answered. "There was a little restaurant there that made some of the best Huevos Rancheros I've ever had. I'd stop just for that, even if I wasn't spending the night."

Jim carried his cup as he followed John out to the car,

watching the sun peek above the horizon. John had always said that sunrise was the best part of living there, but Jim thought sunset was just as pretty and meant the end of the long days on the farm.

"You'll have plenty of room since you don't have a passenger this trip," John remarked as he sat the cooler on the floor of the passenger side. "I don't know how you kids drove halfway across the US cramped in this little car."

Jim smiled, remembering the long drive, and said, "It was a little cramped, but certain aspects of having Jennifer along made the trip more fun."

Shutting the car door, John looked across the roof at Jim and asked, "Are you sure you want her to come live with you in Arizona?"

"I'm sure," Jim told him. "I'm not sure if I'm ready to get married, but I do want her with me for now."

Rounding the front of the 'Vette, John told him again, "You know your mother would rather have you two married. I sort of feel the same way, but I can understand your reluctance. Either way, your mother and I think the world of Jennifer."

"Me too, Dad," Jim said, putting his arm across his dad's shoulders. "Me too."

When they walked back into the house, Jim's mother was calling for them to come eat. "On our way," John said, stopping in the living room and turning to face Jim.

"Son, I just want you to know that your mother and I are very proud of you," John said quietly as he put his hands on Jim's shoulders. "Sometimes we don't always say what we feel, but we're glad you're back from 'Nam safe. We were both very worried, but now that you're home, your mother can relax a little."

"I know, Dad," Jim replied, smiling. "I'm glad that I

made it back too. I suppose now that Mom isn't worried about that, she'll find something else to worry about."

"Oh, she'll always worry about you," John said as they resumed their walk toward the kitchen. "Now she'll just worry about you and Jennifer, if you'll get married, when she'll have grand kids. Sometimes, I think she just likes to worry."

"Gives her and her lady friends something to gossip about," Jim whispered before they entered the kitchen.

"What're you two whispering about?" his mother wanted to know as she put the plate of bacon on the table.

"Man stuff," John told her as he took his seat.

"Man, stuff my foot," she retorted, taking her seat. "Jim, sit down and eat before the eggs get cold."

"Yes, Ma'am," Jim said, taking his seat and smiling at his dad.

Breakfast over, Jim headed for the bathroom to shower and get ready for the trip. Twenty minutes later, he came out dressed in jeans and a T-shirt, carrying his bag. As he walked out of the front door, he saw John looking under the hood of the car.

"What're you looking for?" Jim asked as he opened the trunk.

"Just making sure everything's all right," John answered, shutting the hood. "I put a couple of quarts of oil and two gallons of water in the trunk just in case you need them on the road."

"So I see," Jim said, slamming the trunk lid. "Thanks."

Jim's mother came out carrying a brown paper sack, saying, "I've put some sandwiches and snacks in here for you."

Jim took the sack from her, saying, "Thanks, Mom. You didn't need to do this. I could've stopped along the road.”

“You eat way too much junk food anyway,” she told him. “At least I’ll know you’re eating something healthy for a day or two. After that, you’ll probably go back to burgers and fries. At least when Jennifer comes out, she’ll make sure you eat right. When do you think she’ll move out there?”

“Not sure,” Jim answered, sitting the sack on the passenger seat. “Depends on how long it takes me to find an apartment or house.”

“If you need any help with the finances, you let me know,” John told him, standing with his arm around Jim’s mom.

“I will,” Jim said, walking up to them. “I’ve got quite a bit saved from the year overseas, but I’ll let you know if I need anything.”

Jim put his arms around his mom and dad, saying, “Thanks for everything. I’ll give you a call when I get settled in Yuma. I’m sure Jennifer would love to have y’all out after she gets there and builds her nest.”

“You better not let her hear you saying that,” his mother replied, hugging him.

“I won’t, Mom,” Jim said, returning her hug. “I may be a dumb-ass, but I’ve learned when to keep my mouth shut.” Turning to hug his dad, he concluded, “Sometimes anyway.”

“You’ll never know when you’re about to say something dumb,” his dad said, smiling as he hugged Jim. “After all these years, I still occasionally manage to stick my foot in my mouth around your mother.” Patting Jim on the back, John finished. “Now, you get on the road. And drive safe!”

Jim nodded and climbed into the car. As soon as the engine started, he gave a slight wave at his parents, who were standing with their arms around each other. Seeing them wave, he headed down the gravel drive toward the road.

Making a right turn onto 303, he saw them still standing in the front yard, watching him drive away.

Following the same route he had taken to El Toro, Jim stopped in Roswell, New Mexico, as before, to refill the gas tank. Seeing the same restaurant where he had eaten on his last trip, Jim drove over and parked in front.

As he entered and took a seat, he saw the same waitress who had served him before. "Hi," he said as she walked over to him. "Still haven't made it to California, I see."

She smiled and replied, "Nope, still here. What can I get you?"

"Cheeseburger, fries, Dr Pepper," Jim said without opening the menu.

"Be right back with your drink," she said, scribbling on her pad and walking away.

Guess she doesn't remember me, Jim thought, watching her head for the cook's window. *But then why should she? Just another face among the thousands that pass through here.*

Waiting for his food to be delivered, Jim sipped the Dr Pepper she had brought and watched the crowd of tourists that came and went. *Nope, just another face.*

The meal over and paid for, Jim left a tip and headed back to the 'Vette to drive the last half of the trip to Las Cruces.

Almost three hours later, he found the same motel as before and checked in. After unloading his bag, Jim brought in the cooler and the sack his mother had packed.

Taking out fresh clothes for tomorrow, Jim found a bottle of Jack Daniel's hidden beneath a pair of jeans. Pulling the bottle out, he smiled and shook his head, knowing that his dad had been the culprit.

Getting a glass from the counter by the sink, he took some of the remaining ice from the cooler and poured the glass half full of Jack. Topping it off with Coke, Jim sat back to see if there was anything on TV to interest him.

Channel surfing for a few minutes, he finally settled on *Get Smart*. Sitting there sipping his drink, Jim's thoughts kept returning to his relationship with Jennifer. For the next couple of hours, he alternated between watching TV and not paying attention to what was on. Finally deciding that the next year of living with her would determine the outcome, he finished his drink, undressed, and slipped into bed.

CHAPTER 35

The next morning, Jim rose early, showered, slipped into his jeans with a clean T-shirt, repacked, and tossed his bag into the trunk. Carrying the cooler, he left his room and refilled it with ice before placing it on the floor of the passenger side.

Putting the two uneaten sandwiches on top of the ice in the cooler, he put the bag with the chips in the passenger seat and headed to the front desk to check out.

A few minutes later, he pulled into the parking lot of the same Mexican restaurant and parked. Walking in, he waited to be seated as he looked around the room again.

As he was being led to a table, he told the waitress, "Huevos Rancheros, black coffee, and a glass of water, please."

Acknowledging his order, she told him she would be right back with the coffee and water.

Sipping the hot black coffee, Jim watched a few other patrons enter and be seated before the waitress returned with his breakfast. He thanked her and immediately dug into the fried egg that rested atop the flour tortilla.

Several minutes later, the plate wiped clean with a tortilla, Jim pushed the plate to one side and concentrated on finishing his coffee. He knew it was about eight hours of driving and figured he would get to Yuma while the sun was still up.

Leaving a tip, Jim took his check to the cashier and paid, telling the waitress that it was one of the best meals he'd ever eaten. Again thanking her, he exited the restaurant and got back in the 'Vette.

After filling the tank with gas, Jim pulled back on I-10 and joined the meager stream of traffic heading west as the sun was just rising above the horizon behind him. Again, the early sun painted the desert with shades of brown, red, purple, and yellow.

Two hours later, he passed Lordsburg, knowing that he would be entering Arizona in just a few more miles. And in another two or so hours, he would be in Benson, Arizona. There, he'd stop for gas and eat the sandwiches his mother had made yesterday.

That accomplished, Jim sped on westward toward Tucson, along with the truckers and the occasional dusty pickup that entered the highway from the barren countryside on both sides of the road.

Just south of Phoenix approaching Casa Grande, Jim exited onto I-8 toward San Diego, California. Another two and a half hours would put him at Yuma with plenty of time to check into the base and get quarters for the night.

Seeing a clean gas station just after entering Yuma, Jim pulled in and killed the engine. Taking the clean uniform from where he had placed it at the top of his bag, Jim went into the restroom and changed clothes. Tossing the jeans, boots, and T-shirt into the trunk, Jim climbed back into the car and headed for the base.

Arriving at the front gate of Marine Corps Air Station Yuma, Jim showed his ID and got directions to the administrative offices. After returning the guard's salute, Jim followed the directions and signs that led him to the unimposing building that housed the administrative personnel for the base.

After presenting his orders, Jim told the admin clerk that he would require base housing and was then assigned a room at the Bachelor Officers' Quarters (BOQ). Taking all the paperwork that had been generated, Jim left the building and headed for the BOQ.

Carrying the cooler from the car, Jim found his room and looked around at the fairly modern apartment-like facility. A small kitchen with a table, living room, bedroom with a single bed, and bathroom comprised the entire thing. Still, this was a giant step up from the barracks he had been assigned as an enlisted man.

Returning to his car, Jim finished bringing in the remaining items and separated his uniforms from his civvies. Hanging the uniforms and checking to ensure that they didn't need cleaning, he put his underwear into the small chest of drawers and his toiletries in the bathroom.

After taking a quick shower and shaving, Jim put his uniform back on and headed to where his squadron was located. Knowing that they'd still be flying for at least the next hour or two, he wanted to check in with his new Commander and be prepared for whatever needed to be done the next day.

Jim parked his car, where he saw the VMFAT 101 Sharpshooters patch displayed on the side of the building, and took the packet with all his records and orders inside.

Finding the Squadron administrative office was easy, and Jim handed a set of his orders to the enlisted clerk behind the desk. The clerk checked the paperwork and asked Jim to wait for a minute and headed toward the Squadron Commander's office located just a few doors down the hall.

Minutes later, the clerk came back and told Jim that Lt. Col. Bill West, affectionately known as Wild Bill, wanted to see him. Thanking the clerk, Jim headed toward the Commander's door.

Entering the office, Jim told the secretary sitting behind a gray metal desk that he'd been summoned by the Commander. She smiled pleasantly and told him to go right in.

Jim stepped to the Commander's door and announced, "Captain Lashley reporting, sir!"

Lieutenant Colonel West rose from behind his desk and said, "Welcome, Captain. I'm glad to have you aboard." Coming around the desk, Bill continued. "At ease. I was a little surprised that you got here as early as you did."

Jim relaxed his posture slightly and replied, "Sir, my orders were to be here no later than tomorrow."

"I know," Bill told him. "I'm just surprised that you weren't given a full month's leave. Most men coming back from a year in 'Nam take the entire leave they've accumulated, and that's almost always over thirty days." Motioning for Jim to take a seat, Bill took one of the two chairs in front of the desk and sat, saying, "Either way, I'm glad you're here. But if you need some more time off, let me know."

Jim took his seat once Bill had sat, saying, "Sir, I don't need any more time off for now. I'd like to just get processed into the Squadron and get to work."

"Not a problem," Bill said. "Since today's Thursday, why don't you take the rest of the day and tomorrow to get settled in your quarters, and we'll take care of the Squadron business Monday?"

"Yes, sir," Jim answered, standing. "Anything else, sir?"

Bill stood and offered his hand, saying, "No, but if you need anything, call me. You can get my number from my secretary."

Jim shook his hand and snapped back to attention before turning to the door. As he approached Bill's secretary, she held out a packet and told him, "Here's everything you need to know about the Squadron—the personnel roster, emergency numbers, numbers of all the supervisors, and a brief Squadron history."

Jim took the packet, thanked her, and headed back to his car. The first thing he needed to do was to get a base sticker for his car and then find the Exchange and replenish most of the things he had used over the last two weeks. He also needed new underwear, socks, towels, and washcloths and then a trip to the Commissary to stock the cupboards and refrigerator.

That done, Jim spent the rest of the afternoon putting things away and finding that there were several things he still needed. Returning to the Exchange, he purchased a set of dishes, cooking pots and pans, flatware, glasses, and cups. He also needed a mop, broom, dustpan, cleaning supplies, and dish rack. So many things he'd never thought about over the last couple of years.

Next came a trip to the liquor store for beer, and then Jim headed back to the BOQ to start putting everything away. It was dark when he finally had the bed made, beer and soft drinks in the refrigerator, dishes washed, and most of the place livable.

Looking around, Jim decided that he didn't want to cook this evening, so he headed for the Officers Club.

Entering the bar, he saw several men in flight suits with the Squadron patch on their sleeves. Not knowing them, he took a seat close by and ordered a Jack and Coke. After an initial glance his way, the pilots and RIOs went back to their conversations.

Having been in this Squadron for his initial training at El Toro slightly over a year ago, he hoped he'd see some of the people he'd known there. So far, there were none, but come Monday, he'd see.

Taking his drink, Jim headed for the dining room to get something to eat. It had been several hours since he had eaten those sandwiches, and his stomach was beginning to complain. Selecting a steak, mashed potatoes, and green beans from the menu, he sat back and waited.

After the meal was finished, Jim paid and headed back to his room. One final thing to do before turning in for the night. He found a pay phone and called his parents to let them know that he was there safely.

Then he dialed Jennifer's number.

CHAPTER 36

Jim spent the next day shopping for a few items he'd neglected to purchase, found a copy of the local newspaper, and went back to his room. After putting everything away, he scanned the "Apartment for Rent" and the "House for Rent" sections of the paper.

Armed with a local map, he selected houses and apartments he might be interested in and began calling to see if they were still available. Starting with the houses, he plotted a tour of them before contacting the owners or managers.

Back on base, Jim began calling the numbers listed for those rentals he'd selected and made arrangements to see them the next day. The apartments were available to see that afternoon, so he scheduled times to see both.

After lunch at the O' Club, Jim headed to the apartments. Although one of them appeared to be satisfactory, Jim told the manager that he'd call him later in the week. If he wanted it, he'd be back. If it was no longer available, that'd be fine also.

That evening, Jim called Jennifer and told her about the

apartment and his plan to see four or five houses the next day. Hearing that she didn't care what he decided, he told her that if she wanted, he would postpone any decision until she arrived.

Jennifer told him to make the decision. If it turned out that things needed to change, they could finish their lease and look for something else. Her main concern now was getting out of her apartment, packing what she needed, and getting to Arizona.

On Saturday morning, Jim began his inspection of the houses he'd selected. After the fourth one, he decided that the second one he'd looked at was as good as he could get with the money he was making. Returning to meet the owner, Jim signed a six-month contract and accepted the keys, promising to bring his security deposit and first month's rent the next morning.

On Sunday, Jim took the required amount in cash and met the owner again. Explaining that he hadn't had time to open a local checking account, Jim handed him the money. Now that the house was officially his for the next six months, Jim wandered through the rooms, trying to decide what furniture he'd need.

Finally deciding that a simple bed, two chairs, TV, and kitchen table would suffice until Jennifer arrived, he left and headed back to the base.

After calling the squadron the next morning, Jim went to the local bank and opened a checking account. Taking the available checks they provided, he headed downtown to get the furniture he needed.

After arrangements were made to have the furniture delivered that evening, Jim went to the Squadron and asked to have the rest of the day and the next to move from the BOQ. Permission granted, Jim went back to his room and repacked everything.

Once it was put away in his new house, Jim took the cleaning supplies and did a quick job of making sure everything was ready when the furniture arrived. An hour or so before the sun went down, all the furniture was in place, and Jim decided to cook for himself that evening.

The next morning, Jim called all the utility companies and made arrangements for everything to be billed to him at that address. The phone company said it would be out later in the day and for him to please be available for the installation. Nothing to do now but wait. Jim walked around the house, looking at the lawn, and realized that he would need a mower and a few more items. Those could wait until Jennifer arrived.

Back at the Squadron, Jim began flying sorties as scheduled, got to know most of the other members, and fell into the normal routine. The last call from Jennifer had told him that she'd be arriving the following week.

Jim was at the airport as she walked off the plane. Seeing him, her eyes lit up, and she hurried through the crowd to hug him.

"I guess you're glad to be in Arizona," Jim said, hugging her.

"I'd be glad to be in Oklahoma if it was with you," she said, smiling up at him.

"Don't say that," Jim teased. "I'd never drag you to Oklahoma. I wouldn't do that to a stray dog. Hell, I'd rather have a sister in a whorehouse than a cousin in Oklahoma!" Turning toward the baggage claim signs, Jim asked, "How many bags this time? I've still just got the 'Vette."

"Just three," she answered. "I had some stuff shipped that should be here in a couple of weeks, so all I brought was just enough to get me through until then." Waiting for her bags to arrive, she asked, "What's the house like? Have you got all the furniture? Does it need to be cleaned?"

"You'll see in a few minutes," Jim told her. "As I told you earlier, I just got enough for me to survive until you got here. I'll let you pick out what else we need."

"What about the cleaning?" she frowned. "Did you leave that for me, too?"

"No," Jim answered. "But I'd bet that you won't think I've done all that needed to be done. And I don't mind you criticizing my work. I'm not the best house cleaner, but I tried a week or so ago."

"Oh, I can't wait to see what's accumulated over the week or so," Jennifer joked. "You'll just blame anything I find on that week or so, not on your cleaning."

"You're right about that," Jim said, grabbing the bags from the carousel. "Even if I didn't do it right, I'll blame it on it just getting dirty again."

Pulling up to the house, Jim said, smiling, "This is it. I know it doesn't look like much from out here, but it's worse inside."

Jennifer looked at the house as she got out of the car and said, "It looks just fine. It does need a little paint, maybe some flowers, but it'll certainly do."

Jim opened the front door for her and watched her walk around, looking at the bare rooms. As she wandered into the kitchen, she opened the refrigerator and smiled. "At least you have Budweiser," she said, pulling two bottles from inside. "What say we celebrate our first house together?"

Jim took the bottles and opened them, joking, "I thought we'd celebrate in a different room, but if this is your choice, so be it."

Taking one bottle from Jim, Jennifer smiled and said, "I plan on celebrating in *every* room."

Once Jim had her bags in the house, he went out to watch TV while she put everything away. When she finally came into the room, she asked, "Why'd you just get two chairs? How about a couch?"

"Thought I'd let you pick that out," Jim replied. "Same for everything else. I just got the bare essentials, nothing that I can't toss and not worry about what it cost."

"Looks like I'm going to have lots of fun decorating this place," she told him, sitting on his lap. "You may have wasted money on that other chair since I don't plan on leaving your side."

Jim leaned back and smiled. "If I'd known that, I'd have bought the couch and let you pick the chairs."

That evening, after they'd showered and gotten dressed, Jim drove her out to the base, where they had dinner at the O' Club. As they ate, Jim talked about the Squadron, flying out here in the desert, and other facets of his day-to-day life.

The next morning, while Jim was showering, Jennifer got up and started breakfast. When he came walking in wearing his flight suit, she smiled at him and asked, "How do you like your scrambled eggs?"

Kissing her on the neck, he replied, "Scrambled."

"Good answer, good answer," she said, turning to the stove. "You just have a seat, and I'll finish the bacon."

Jim took the cup sitting beside the coffee maker and poured it full. Leaning against the counter, looking at Jennifer, he said, "I think I'm glad you're here."

"Think?" Jennifer teased.

"Think so," Jim teased back. "Yep, pretty sure. I think I'm glad you're here. I'll let you know after I eat the eggs if I'm positive that I think that I'm glad."

"As always, Capt. Jim Lashley," Jennifer said, taking

the pan with the eggs from the stove, "you are such an asshole! You know good and well that you're glad I'm here."

"Yes, I am," Jim said seriously. "I've been ready for you to be here since our first night together back in Pensacola."

CHAPTER 37

For the next two years, Jim and Jennifer looked like any other military couple. Jim spent his days flying with the Squadron, and Jennifer got a part-time job in a women's dress store downtown. They went to Squadron parties, hung out with couples from the Squadron, and blended in with the husbands and wives.

In late 1972, a secret peace agreement was reached between the United States and North Vietnam. The South Vietnam President wanted major changes to the agreement, and North Vietnam made the agreement public. Releasing the information made President Nixon mad, and he ordered Operation Linebacker II to put pressure on them. A combination of the bombing and pressure on the South Vietnam President resulted in Paris Peace Accords in January of 1973.

With the war officially over, many of the pilots of all services were no longer needed. Many were offered early outs, while others were simply told that they'd be discharged because of the reduction in force (RIF) that had been ordered.

Jim still had another three years of his commitment left and wasn't considering getting out. Many of his peers were ready to return to civilian life, but Jim didn't know of anything else he'd rather do than be a Marine pilot.

He'd just finished flying for the day when the Commander, Lieutenant Colonel West, stopped him in the hall. "Got a minute, Jim?" Bill asked.

"Certainly, sir," Jim responded.

"Let's talk in my office," Bill told him as he headed down the hall.

Jim followed him, wondering what his boss wanted from him. He wasn't due for any performance reports, and he knew of nothing that'd bring him to the Commander's attention.

Entering the office, Bill said, "I believe you know General Barker."

"Good afternoon, Captain Lashley," General Barker said, extending his hand.

"General Barker, it's good to see you again, sir," Jim said, shaking the General's hand.

"Jim, the General asked me to bring you in for a little talk," Bill said. "Now, if you'll excuse me, I've got a couple of errands to run." As Bill turned to leave, he continued. "General, please feel free to use this office as long as you like. If there's anything you need, just let me know."

As soon as Bill was gone, General Barker smiled and said, "Have a seat, Jim. It's been quite a while since I last saw you."

Jim waited until the General was seated before sitting, saying, "Yes, sir, it has been."

"I suppose you're wondering why I'm here," Gene said, leaning back in his chair.

"Yes, sir," Jim told him. "Is there anything I can do for

you?"

"Maybe so," Gene answered. "You probably don't know it, but I retired a little over a year ago."

"No, sir, I didn't know that," Jim said.

"You do know that there's a RIF going on," Gene said. "I also suspect that you want to stay in the Marines."

"Yes, sir, I do," Jim told him, wondering what the General was getting at.

"Have you ever heard of an organization known as Black Water?" Gene asked.

"Vaguely," Jim acknowledged.

"They're a civilian company that provides security for overseas organizations or personnel," Gene informed him. "They're mainly ex-military men that have specialized training that can't be found in the civilian world."

"Pardon me, sir," Jim said. "But anything I knew about that sort of operation from my enlisted days is badly out of date."

General Barker smiled and said, "I'm not talking about them offering you a job. For now, I'm just giving you some background information."

"Yes, sir," Jim replied, accepting the mild chastisement.

"Now, after I retired," Gene said, "I was approached by a member of one of our government agencies to become an 'advisor' to the Black Water group."

He explained, "That advisory position was to be funded by the companies or individuals that contracted with Black Water for their services. That way, the agency that 'hired' me never had to disclose my position since I drew no salary. And since I wasn't an employee of Black Water, I never appear on their personnel sheets other than as miscellaneous contract expenses."

Jim sat quietly, listening as Gene continued, still wondering what this had to do with him.

"That's the basics of Black Water. But like some other operations that you may have heard about, such as Air America, the interesting point is their connection to US government agencies," Gene said.

"Now, before I go on, there are some papers I need you to sign," Gene said, picking up a briefcase that was beside his chair. "I'll give you the basics of the documents, and you can take them home with you to study before you sign them if you desire."

Opening the briefcase, Gene took out a folder that contained four sheets of paper. "This first one is your agreement to never divulge this conversation or any other that may take place regarding any offers I, or others, may or may not make."

Handing that sheet to Jim, Gene looked at the next sheet, saying, "And this one is your agreement to never discuss any of the organizations we're about to talk about with anyone other than with Black Water personnel unless cleared to do so."

Jim scanned the first two sheets as Gene explained the third. "This one gives Black Water, or any of its subsidiaries, the right to conduct background checks on you, your family, or friends as they feel necessary."

Gene said after handing the fourth sheet to Jim, "This final one is your oath to the US government to never divulge any ties with Black Water or its subsidiaries, its operations, or personnel with any organization or individual unless specifically authorized."

Jim took the last sheet and asked, "What are you leading up to, General?"

"I can't go any further until you've signed all the

agreements I just gave you," Gene told him. "If you need some time, we can meet again later."

Jim sat for a moment, thinking about the oaths he was being asked to sign. *Nothing different than those I signed with the military,* Jim thought.

"All right, sir," Jim agreed. "I have no problem signing these since I don't know anything about these organizations anyway."

Gene handed Jim a pen and said, "That's right, but what I'm about to tell you falls within the scope of these oaths. So, once you sign, everything we talk about can never be discussed."

Jim signed each page and handed them and Gene's pen back, saying, "I understand, sir."

Gene looked at each page and then signed the bottom of each, signifying that he'd witnessed Jim's signatures.

Putting the papers back in the briefcase, Gene smiled at Jim, saying, "Black Water has a certain affiliation with our Central Intelligence Agency (CIA), but that can never be traced. There are numerous companies, as I said earlier, that have ties to government agencies. Some can be traced, some can't."

Gene explained, "As a private company, Black Water is not bound by the same constraints that hamper some of our governmental abilities to perform certain missions."

Gene continued. "As an advisor, I can make certain *suggestions* or recommendations. It's up to the company to either follow my recommendations or not. And since I'm not officially a government employee, nothing I suggest to them has any ties to any government agency."

Gene said, "As we discussed earlier, the RIF will have a major impact on our forces. A lot of pilots will be looking for civilian employment, whether or not that's what they really want. You've said, and I already knew, that you want to remain a Marine pilot."

"That's correct, sir," Jim acknowledged, nodding.

"Even if you stay in the Marines, there is going to be a slowdown in promotions since many of our higher-ranking officer positions won't be filled. That'll certainly trickle down to Lieutenant Colonels and Majors," Gene explained.

"What I'm about to suggest is for you to join a Marine Reserve unit back in Texas," Gene said, leaning back to gauge Jim's response.

"I thought the Reserve units were filled separately from the regular Marines," Jim told him.

"That's true," Gene acknowledged. "But during my last years at the Pentagon, I did make a few friends. One of them just happens to be in charge of the Marine Reserves."

Gene added, "And upon his recommendation and the fact that you're a native Texan, I can just about guarantee you'll be welcomed to VMF 112 at the Dallas Naval Air Station."

"So, what you're telling me, if I may, is that I should request a release from active duty, apply for a position with VMF 112, and wait for Black Water to contact me with a job offer," Jim summarized the conversation.

"That's the basics," Gene agreed. "But you'll never be contacted by Black Water. As we discussed, you no longer have the skills they require. And it'd take too long and be too expensive to retrain you. There're plenty of volunteers for those positions anyway."

"Then why did I need to sign those papers concerning Black Water?" Jim asked.

"As I mentioned," Gene said, "there are subsidiaries, and I can suggest that they might want to give you preferential consideration in employment."

"Anyone in particular?" Jim asked.

Gene sat forward and said, "Dark Water."

CHAPTER 38

That evening when Jim got home, he headed straight for the refrigerator and grabbed a beer. Taking it into the living room, he sat on the couch and thought about what General Barker had told him.

He knew that he might possibly be let go with other pilots in the RIF, and he didn't know what he'd do should that happen. The opportunity to keep flying the F-4 had been dangled, and the bait was tempting.

The part about transferring to the Reserves and being stationed at NAS Dallas was appealing in several respects. One, it would give him the opportunity to go back to college and finish his degree. Two, it would put him and Jennifer closer to both their parents. Three, he'd still be flying the F-4.

The biggest question he had right now was what he'd be doing for the company Gene had called Dark Water. Obviously, a subsidiary of Black Water, but its function was yet to be discussed. He'd told Gene that he would discuss it with Jennifer, and he was to meet Gene the next morning. Then he'd learn what he'd do should Dark Water offer him a job, and he'd just about been promised that would happen.

Jennifer came in from her job less than thirty minutes after Jim got home. When she came through the door, Jim got up and said, "Have a seat, baby. I'll get you a beer while we discuss something."

Jennifer walked to him, kissed him, and asked, "Is anything wrong?"

"Nope," Jim said, returning the kiss. "Just have a seat, and I'll tell you when I get back with your beer and another one for me."

Jennifer sat on the couch, waiting for Jim to return, wondering what had happened.

Jim returned a moment later, handed her a beer, sat down, and asked, "How'd you like to move to Texas?"

Stunned, Jennifer asked, "What do you mean? Are you being transferred?"

"No," Jim answered. "You know about the RIF that's happening. This has something to do with that."

"Are you being released?" she asked, worried about what would happen.

"Not that I've heard," Jim told her. "What I'm talking about is leaving the Regular Marines and joining the Reserves."

"You mean just flying on weekends or something?" she asked.

"It's more than just weekends," Jim explained. "They have full-time people, they have long exercises, they aren't just 'weekend warriors' as they're usually called."

"What would you do when you're not flying?" she asked.

"I'd try to go back to school and finish my degree," Jim answered. "And if necessary, I'd find a job that would allow me to do my Reserve duties."

"How long until you'd have to leave?" Jennifer asked, holding her beer without taking a drink.

"I'm not sure," Jim answered. "You remember the General that helped get me into MARCAD?"

"Yes, he's the one that came to your graduation in Beeville, isn't he?" she said.

"Same guy," Jim told her. "Well, he came by to see me today."

"What'd he want?" she asked.

"He's the one that wants me to go to the Reserves," Jim told her.

"Why does he want you to do that?"

"General Barker is convinced that the RIF will affect me at some point," Jim explained. "He wants to help me get a position with the Reserve unit in Dallas so I can keep flying."

"Can he do that?" she wanted to know.

"I think so," Jim told her, taking another drink of his beer. "He's retired now but still has a lot of pull in Washington and lots of friends that are still active Marines."

"What does he do now that he's retired?" Jennifer asked, finally taking a drink of her beer.

"I'm not sure," Jim admitted. "We just talked about what was going to happen to all the services now that the war is over."

"What do you want to do?" she asked.

Jim thought about it for a few seconds and then said, "I really don't know. I trust General Barker's judgment, but this is a major step."

Jennifer looked at Jim and reminded him, "He's the reason you're here. If it hadn't been for him, we'd have never met, and you'd never have gotten to fly your beloved F-4."

Jim smiled and said, "I know. I owe him a lot. I really

don't know why he singled me out to take care of, but he did."

"You said that you're supposed to meet him tomorrow. Do you have to give him an answer then?" she asked.

"Yes," Jim replied.

"Then you'd better make up your mind," Jennifer stated.

"What about you?" Jim asked.

"I'll go with you anywhere you go," she said, reaching out to hold his hand. "You know that."

"I know," Jim said, looking into her eyes.

"So, the decision is all yours," Jennifer told him. "Whatever you decide, I'll be there." She sat quietly, watching him, and then said, "You know your mother and dad would love for you to be back in Texas."

"I know," Jim agreed.

"And I know that my mom and dad would love to have us that close," she continued.

"That's not 'that' close," Jim told her. "That's still over six hundred miles away."

"That 600 miles is better than over 1,800," she argued.

"True," Jim said, "but it's still a long drive."

"Or a short flight," Jennifer countered as she finished her beer. Standing, she asked, "Do you need another beer, or will that affect your thinking?"

Jim smiled and handed her his empty bottle, saying, "I don't think three beers is going to make any difference. But I think we need to go out to dinner and celebrate."

"Celebrate what?" she asked, taking both empties to the kitchen.

"Celebrate my decision," Jim said, following her.

Jennifer turned and asked, "What decision?"

"I'm going to accept General Barker's offer," Jim told

her.

Shocked, Jennifer finally asked, "What made you decide?"

"You," Jim said, taking the bottles from her hand and setting them on the counter.

"Me?" she asked. "What'd I do that made you decide to do this?"

Jim took her in his arms and said, "You said you'd go anywhere I went. That was really the only thing that I didn't know."

Jennifer kissed him and said softly, "I'll always go wherever you go."

CHAPTER 39

The following morning, Jim arrived at the Squadron earlier than needed for his noon flight. When he checked with the scheduler to see if any changes had been made, he was informed that his flight had been canceled. He was also told to go see Lieutenant Colonel West.

Knocking on his door, Jim said, "You wanted to see me, sir?"

"Come in, Jim," Bill said, laying down his pen. "General Barker asked me to remove you from the schedule today. Apparently, he's under the impression that he has a meeting with you this morning and doesn't know how long it will take."

"Yes, sir," Jim replied, nodding. "He told me he was leaving sometime today and needed me to make a decision about joining VMF 112 at NAS Dallas."

Bill leaned back in his chair and asked, "Can he guarantee you a position?"

"I believe so, sir," Jim answered.

Bill straightened up and said, "I have no doubt that he has quite a bit of influence, but if I were you and wanted to leave the Regular Marines, I'd wait to turn in my papers until I was sure."

"I agree. This morning's meeting is just to let General Barker know if I'm interested," Jim told him.

"And are you interested?" Bill asked.

"Yes, sir, I am," Jim answered.

Bill stood and walked around his desk to the door behind Jim. Closing it, Bill sat in one of the chairs opposite from where Jim was standing and said, "Have a seat, Jim."

Jim sat down and waited to hear what Lieutenant Colonel West wanted to say.

"I hate to give you this advice," Bill said, looking at Jim. "You've been a great pilot and an asset to this Squadron, but I think you would be wise to take the offer. If it's offered, that is."

He continued. "There're going to be substantially fewer pilot slots in the very near future. I'll fight for each of my men as much as I can, but the fact remains that the Marines have too many pilots now."

Bill added, "Not only are we going to be losing pilot slots, but I think the Reserves may lose a few also. They won't get hit as hard as we will, but those slots will be hard to get."

"I understand, sir," Jim said. "And as I said this morning, all I intend to do is to let the General know that I'm interested. I have no intention of applying for a discharge until I have a firm commitment from the unit in Dallas."

"What time is your meeting with General Barker?" Bill asked.

"Not sure, sir," Jim answered. "I came in early just in case he called."

Just as Jim was finishing talking, Bill's secretary knocked on the door, announcing that he had a visitor.

Jim stood, anticipating that Lieutenant Colonel West would rise also, and said, "Sir, if there's nothing else, I'll go back to Operations and wait."

"That'll be fine, Jim," Bill said, standing. "I'd like for you to come see me after you talk to the General if you could."

Bill opened the door as Jim answered, "Yes, sir."

When the door opened, General Barker was standing by the secretary's desk, talking to her.

"General," Bill said as he saw him, "what can I do for you today?"

"Good morning," Gene answered. "I was just wondering if I could borrow Captain Lashley for an hour or so."

"Not a problem," Bill said. "He's been taken off the flying schedule for the day, and he's all yours."

"I appreciate that," Gene replied. "Captain Lashley, if you don't mind, I'd like to go over to the O' Club and have breakfast."

"Yes, sir," Jim replied. "I'll be glad to drive us over."

Gene chuckled and said, "Not in that cramped little car of yours! I've got a staff car outside. We'll take it."

Turning to leave, Gene told Bill, "I'll have him back before noon. Maybe you can get a little work out of him today after all."

Jim followed the General out to the car as Gene tossed the keys over his shoulder, saying, "You drive, please."

Jim caught the keys and replied, "Yes, sir."

Nothing was said on the drive over to the club. Once there, Jim parked in one of the slots reserved for Colonels or above. The three stars affixed to the front license plate would let the Military Police know that it was the General's car.

Entering the dining room, Gene walked to a corner table that had been previously reserved and said, "Have a seat, Jim. We can discuss what we need to talk about here."

Waiting for the General to sit, Jim took the chair opposite and sat down. Almost as soon as they were seated, a waiter arrived with a carafe of coffee and two menus.

As he walked away, Gene asked, "Have you made your decision?"

"Yes, sir. If the Squadron will accept me, I'll turn in my papers and join them," Jim answered.

Gene signaled for the waiter and said, "Good. Now let's eat, and I'll try to answer any questions you may have."

As soon as the waiter left, Gene leaned forward and put his elbows on the table, saying, "I can't tell you much about the Dark Water company right now. They have to do their checks and actually make an offer to you before I, or anyone, can talk about their operations."

"I understand, sir," Jim said, leaning forward. "What can you tell me about my chances of getting orders to VMF 112?"

"That I can assure you," Gene said as the waiter brought the orange juice. "As a matter of fact, I'd expect the orders to be on your boss's desk when we get back."

"When would I have to be there?" Jim asked, surprised at how fast things were moving.

"That's negotiable," Gene told him. "The orders will be to report 'on or before the end of the year.'" He continued. "That way, you'll have time to wrap up anything here, but more importantly, it'll give Dark Water time to investigate your background and make their decision about recruiting you."

After their breakfast was delivered, Jim asked, "Do you think they will?"

Picking up a muffin and spreading butter across it, Gene smiled and said, "I can almost guarantee it."

Jim broke the yoke of his egg and asked, "Is there anything that you can tell me about what Dark Water does?"

Glancing around the room, Gene said, "All I can tell you is that they solve problems for the parent organization."

Intrigued, Jim asked, "What problems?"

"Let's say that if a certain group whose interests are opposed to those interests of a Black Water operation become known and may cause the failure of the operation, then Dark Water is called in to remove the threat," Gene said quietly.

"Isn't that sort of like mercenary operations?" Jim wanted to know. "And isn't that one of those types of things that we agreed I didn't have the skills to do?"

"Not necessarily," Gene told him. "It may be as simple as offering a certain sum of money to change the views of the opposition. But it can be that a certain individual must be removed from his position within the opposition's leadership."

"That still sounds like mercenary operations," Jim argued. "I know we have snipers that are sent out to assassinate people. We did that in 'Nam frequently." Jim concluded, "And I'm certainly no sniper. I couldn't sneak up on a deaf, blind, crippled cow."

"Not necessary," Gene said. "The whole point of what Dark Water does is to eliminate the problem without anyone knowing it was done or who did it. Let's say, for example, the target is suddenly called away to another location the day of our operation or that he's given information that an attempt may be made on his life by another competing group from a neighboring area."

Gene continued. "Now, with him removed, the operation is no longer in jeopardy. Not all operations require the target to be eliminated, just incapacitated for the period we need."

"How will I know which method to take?" Jim asked.

"That's left up to the people who make the big bucks to make decisions," Gene told him. "You'll be brought in to execute that decision."

He continued. "Now I can tell you there is a contingency of indigenous people who are under contract with both Black Water and Dark Water who do most of the work. They do the surveillance, recommend a solution, and provide the materials needed to implement the final decision."

"Why don't they do the operation themselves?" Jim asked.

"Too close to the operation," Gene told him. "The whole issue is to provide deniability and ironclad alibis for the local people. If anyone involved in the surveillance is known to be associated with either of our organizations or has any connection that can be known or suspected, they must be able to prove they were elsewhere when the 'action' happened. There can be no provable tie to either them, Black Water or Dark Water."

"How do I get there, do the job, and not be suspected?" Jim asked.

"That's where the Reserves come in," Gene answered. "Occasionally, you'll be sent as an advisor to some unit in whatever country where we have concerns, be briefed, equipped, and provided with the necessary tools. If it's a money issue, you'll merely take it and make the offer. If it's refused, you return to the men that set up the meeting and report."

"What happens then?" Jim asked.

"That's up to the local unit," Gene answered. "Generally, they have a backup plan, but that's seldom necessary. They do a lot of research on their target and usually know which approach will work."

Jim sat back for a moment and then asked, "When will I hear from either of these organizations about the job?"

"They're already running their investigations," Gene said. "With most of the work done by the military when you first got your clearances, it shouldn't take long. I'd guess within two or three months."

Nodding, Jim asked, "What about pay?"

Gene wiped his lips with the napkin and said, "I'm not surprised that you didn't ask that at the beginning. It's never been about the money with you. I can't say exactly what the pay is. It varies with the operation. But I know that most of our other 'operatives' earn around $150,000 a year."

"How many operations do they perform each year?" Jim asked, amazed at the sum.

"Ten to twelve," Gene told him. "Depends on the needs of Black Water. Some years, the average man will go out three or four times. Other years, that may be fifteen. Sometimes, you'll get two assignments for the same operation."

"How do I explain that much money on a Marine's salary?" Jim wanted to know.

Smiling, Gene told him, "Easy. That's one of the good things about this program. The money never comes to you directly. It's deposited with a money management fund that trades stock. You just happened to have been investing in that fund since you joined the Marines. And it has done, and will continue to do, very well!"

"I haven't invested in anything like that," Jim countered.

"Not according to the fund's records," Gene told him. "That's if you're working for the Black Water organization as I suspect you will be." Gene said, standing, "Now let's get out of here. And I'm sure you'll remember that everything I've told you falls under the agreements you've signed."

Jim nodded as he stood, shocked at what he had just heard.

Leaving the money for the meals on the table, Gene headed for the exit, saying, "I'll drop you off at the Squadron. As I said, your orders are probably already there, and I'll be in touch with you as soon as Black Water finishes their part."

CHAPTER 40

When Jim walked back into the Squadron building, he was told that Lieutenant Colonel West wanted to see him. Jim assumed it was both his conversation with General Barker and the orders that had arrived while he was gone that interested his boss.

Knocking on Bill's door, Jim waited until he heard the "Come in" and then stepped inside, saying, "You wanted to see me, sir?"

"Have a seat, Jim," Bill said, rising from his chair and rounding the desk with a single sheet of paper in his hand. "How'd your visit with the General go?"

"Fine, sir," Jim answered, waiting for Bill to sit first.

"Good," Bill said, sitting across from the chair he had indicated for Jim to take. "I'd bet that you're not surprised that orders to VMF 112 arrived while you were gone."

Jim sat down and replied, "Yes and no. The General told me that they might be here when I returned."

Looking at the sheet of paper, Bill said, "These orders give you almost seven months before you have to report. Have you decided when you want to put in your papers?"

"No, sir," Jim answered. "First, I want to make sure the Squadron won't suffer any loss of capability when I leave."

"I thought you might think about that, but you don't have to worry," Bill said, sitting back and looking at Jim. "Actually, your volunteering to leave means that at least one other man won't be forced to go." He continued. "What are the other things that concern you about when you leave?"

"Just finding a place to live near Dallas, setting up the move . . . just normal stuff, I guess," Jim answered.

"Have you thought about what you'll do outside of the Reserves?" Bill asked.

Remembering the restrictions about discussing potential employment, Jim answered, "Not really. I'd like to finish my Bachelor's degree, and there are several good colleges in that area."

"Have you considered trying to get a job with the airlines?" Bill asked.

"Not really, sir," Jim said. "I'm not sure that I'd want to do that. That seems to me that it'd be like being a bus driver, although faster, and I'm sure they earn more."

Bill laughed at the image of a bus with wings and agreed, "Yeah, but nothing will ever compare to flying fighters. If I were you, I'd consider it. It does pay very well, and nobody's shooting at you."

Jim smiled and agreed, "That's true, but boredom can also kill a man, at least his spirit. And those guys live out of a suitcase almost half of every year. That's gotta be tough on the families."

"Well,"—Bill finally got to the point of wanting to see Jim—"you know these orders to VMF 112 are only valid if you're out of the Regular Marines."

Wondering what Bill was getting at, Jim asked, "What are you trying to say, sir?"

"It's just that if you change your mind in the next few weeks or months, these orders are invalid," Bill explained. "But it also means that you can hold off putting in your papers until the last minute if you need the time to get everything done."

Bill concluded, "I guess what I'm trying to tell you is that you can keep working here up until the day before these orders will expire and still draw your pay, keep flying, and be eligible for promotions and transfer within the regular forces."

"I appreciate you telling me that," Jim said, nodding. "You've always been a fair Commander and looked out for your troops. I honestly think I'll accept the orders, and I also appreciate you letting me stay on the payroll until I finish everything."

"Not a problem, Jim," Bill said, handing Jim the sheet of paper that gave him the chance to join VMF 112 almost at his leisure. "If there's anything I can do to help you, let me know."

"Thanks," Jim said, rising as he saw Bill about to stand. "The only thing I can think of right now is that I'll take terminal leave however many days I have available right before my resignation takes effect."

"We'll make that happen," Bill said, shaking Jim's hand. "If you want to talk about this any further, my door's always open."

Jim nodded as he turned away, saying thanks before heading for the door. Pausing there and turning, Jim asked, "What about you, sir? How's this RIF going to affect you?"

Bill reached into his desk drawer and removed a pair of silver eagles, saying, "I've just been informed that the next O-6 Colonel's list will include my name. That guarantees me at least three more years and that I can retire after that if I choose to do so.”

“Congratulations,” Jim said, smiling. “It’s always good to see good men rewarded. In my estimation, there have been way too many who got promoted more because of a brown nose than leadership. Again, congratulations!”

Jim left the office and took a quick look at the scheduling board. Seeing his name for an afternoon flight the next day and nothing for the rest of today, he told the scheduler that he was taking the rest of the day off, but if needed, he’d come back.

Jennifer wasn’t due home until much later that afternoon, so Jim made himself a quick bacon, lettuce, and tomato (BLT) sandwich, poured a glass of milk, and parked in front of the TV.

Rerunning what General Barker had told him about the operation of Dark Water, he tried to envision how he’d be used. He didn’t worry about the security checks. He already possessed a Top Secret clearance from the US government, and nothing had changed since they’d done their background checks.

If it was only going to take two or three months for Black Water to do their checks, he could be ready to leave as soon as the job offer was made. Now, he needed to call home and tell his mother and dad that he’d be moving to the Dallas area within the next three or four months.

Knowing that it was just after noon back home, Jim dialed the number at the house. His mother answered it on the third ring, saying, “Hello?”

“Hi, Mom,” Jim said. “How’re things back there in Texas?”

“Oh, they’re fine,” she said. “Is anything wrong? I mean, aren’t you supposed to be at work?”

“Nothing’s wrong, Mom,” Jim assured her. “I just got

some news today that might make you and Dad happy."

"What's that?" she asked.

"I'm moving back to Texas," Jim informed her.

"What about Jennifer? Is she coming too?" his mother asked.

"Of course, she's coming with me," Jim told her.

"When are you coming?" she asked.

"Probably in three or four months," Jim said.

"Are you moving back here?"

"No, Mom, I'm being stationed in Dallas, so we'll find a place down there," Jim told her.

"So, you'll still be in the Marines?"

"Sort of," Jim said. "I'll be in the Reserves."

"Does that mean you'll never have to go overseas again?"

"No, the Reserves are there to augment the Regular Marines if they need us," Jim explained. "I'm still a Marine but not full-time."

"What'll you do when you're not flying?"

"Oh, there's lots of things that need to be done," Jim told her. "But my primary job is to fly, and that's what I'll mainly do when I go to the Squadron."

She paused for a few seconds and then said, "Good. I'm glad. And I know your father will be glad to have you back here, even if it is in Dallas. Don't they have something in Fort Worth, maybe Lubbock?"

Jim laughed and told her, "If you're in the Air Force, maybe. But I'm a Marine, and Dallas is the closest place."

"Okay, I guess I'll have to settle for that," his mother relented. "I'd still rather have you in Fort Worth! Oh, here's your father. Tell him."

"Hey, Jim," his father said, taking the phone. "What're you supposed to tell me?"

"I'm moving back to Texas," Jim replied.

"Oh, why's that?" John asked.

"I'm turning in my papers and being assigned to the Marine Reserve Squadron at NAS Dallas," Jim answered.

John paused and then said, "Good. Your mother will like that."

Jim laughed as he said, "I know. Now she's pissed that I can't move to Lubbock or Fort Worth."

"Dallas is only five hours away. She'll want to visit every week, you know," John informed him.

"I know, but I'll still be flying, going to school, working . . . you know. I won't be sitting around the house all day every day," Jim replied.

"I know, but you better be ready for her to come to Dallas as soon as you move in," John told him. "I reckon Jennifer's happy too?"

"Yep, she's glad that I'm getting into the Reserves and life will settle down," Jim answered.

"I suppose she's mentioned that 'settle down' thing a few times," John said.

"Actually, no. She's been pretty quiet about it, but I'm sure that once we get to Dallas, she'll start thinking about something more permanent," Jim admitted.

"No doubt," John said. "Anyway, I'm glad you're moving back here. For your mother's sake."

"I know, Dad," Jim said, smiling to himself. "I know."

CHAPTER 41

Jim continued flying with the Squadron in Yuma as if nothing had happened. Although he'd told the other pilots and RIOs that he was getting out, nothing changed as far as the way the Squadron operated.

One evening, less than a month after Jim had talked with General Barker, he received a call at home from an individual whose identification was never divulged. The man only told Jim that there would be a package delivered within the next few days that contained an offer of employment with Black Water.

Jim was instructed to review the offer and, if acceptable, follow the instructions that were included, complete any forms required, and return the documents within one week of receipt. Additionally, no one was to be told of either this call or the package.

When Jennifer asked who'd called, Jim merely told her that it was a realtor from Dallas. Since Jim and Jennifer had met, and especially now that they were living together, he'd never intentionally lied to her about anything.

Before this, he always told her that he couldn't discuss

certain things. Jennifer knew better than to press him on issues that concerned the military or operations that he didn't want to talk about. Like most military wives, Jennifer had learned to live with classified subjects.

Three days later, at the Squadron, he was told that he had a phone call at the operations desk. Picking up the phone, Jim said, "Captain Lashley."

"Captain, are you able to meet me within the next few minutes here on base?" the caller said.

"Who is this?" Jim asked.

"A couple of days ago, you were told to expect a package to be delivered," the man said. "I'm the delivery-man."

Jim paused for a couple of seconds and then replied, "Okay, I can meet you at the Exchange in five minutes. Do you know where that is?"

"Yes, I'll be there," came the answer.

"How will I recognize you?" Jim asked.

"I'll recognize you," the caller answered.

"Okay," Jim replied, "I'll be there in five minutes, maybe a little quicker."

The line went dead as Jim was waiting for some response that never came. Hanging up, Jim glanced at the clock and headed for the door. When he got to his car, he noticed a car sitting next to the 'Vette with the motor running.

As he approached it, the passenger window rolled down, and he heard the driver say, "Captain Lashley."

Jim walked to the open window and said, "Yes."

The driver took a package from the passenger seat and passed it through the open window, saying, "No need to go to the Exchange. Here's your package."

Jim took the package and started to say thanks when

the window began to roll up. Standing there, he watched the car back up and drive away. Somewhat taken aback, Jim realized that he hadn't really seen the driver and wouldn't be able to recognize him if he ever saw him again or if he had ever seen him before.

Not wanting to take the package into the building where someone might question what he was reading, Jim opened the trunk of the 'Vette and placed the unopened package inside.

Back in the Squadron, Jim rechecked the scheduling board for his afternoon flight and decided to head to the O' Club for lunch. Seeing his RIO for the flight, Jim asked him if he wanted to have lunch.

When he agreed, Jim said, "Great. Let's take my car."

"Sounds good," came the reply. "Mind if I drive it?"

"Not a problem," Jim said, tossing him the keys.

The short drive to the club took several minutes longer than necessary as the RIO drove around the base. "Having fun?" Jim asked as they passed the turn to the club for the fourth or fifth time.

"Yep," he answered as he accelerated down the street. "I've wanted to do this since I first saw your car."

Jim shook his head and just waited until the fun was over. Several minutes later, they pulled into the club's parking lot and sat there for a couple of minutes, listening to the low rumble of the engine.

Finally turning off the motor, the RIO smiled and said, "Sweet," tossing Jim the keys.

Throughout lunch, Jim's thoughts continually drifted to the package in the trunk of his car. He knew that it contained an offer of employment, but exactly how specific the terms would be and how much information about the actual job it would contain were unknown.

After they'd eaten, Jim drove back to the squadron for the flight brief. Now that he had something tangible to think about, he forgot about the package and concentrated on the afternoon's mission.

Three hours later, following the debrief, Jim told everyone he'd see them tomorrow and headed home. He'd have a couple of hours alone at home to review the contents of the package before Jennifer was due back from work. He definitely didn't want her to see it and start asking questions.

Parked at the house, Jim opened the trunk and removed the manila envelope that he'd been handed almost five hours ago. Carrying it into the house, he tossed it on the counter while he got a beer from the refrigerator. Taking his first sip, Jim stared at the envelope for a few seconds before picking it up and bringing it into the living room.

Turning on the TV, Jim set the volume low enough that he'd hear if Jennifer drove home earlier than expected. Setting the beer on the end table, he removed the red hatched tape from the flap and opened the package.

Taking out the first sheet, Jim read it completely and started to read it again. There was nothing in the terms of employment that stated what he'd be doing, where he'd be required to go, or what he'd be paid. It basically said that Jim would perform on an "as needed" basis, receive compensation commiserate with the requirements of the tasks, and be provided with transportation to and from the locations yet to be determined.

The second sheet was another declaration of confidentiality and a "hold harmless" agreement absolving the company of any responsibility should any harm come while on an assignment.

The third one contained specific instructions as to how to return the signed documents.

From his original conversation with the man who had called telling him to expect the offer, Jim knew he had a week to respond. He didn't know if that included whatever time would be required to get the package back to Black Water or if he could take the extra couple of days to make his final decision.

Returning to the first sheet, Jim tried in vain to find something concrete in the verbiage that would give him a clue as to what he could expect. Thinking back to what General Barker had told him, Jim decided that until he was actually an employee of the company, he'd never know what his job would be.

Almost an hour had passed as he sat there, rereading everything over and over. Finishing his beer, he picked up the three sheets and returned to the kitchen. Laying the first two sheets on the table, Jim pulled his pen from his flight suit pocket and quickly signed them.

That done, he got another beer and sat, looking at the instructions. Although the decision had been made, Jim was reluctant to follow through. Until he'd gone into the Marines, Jim had never really considered the long-term ramifications of his decisions. Since the first day at boot camp, he'd let the Marines make most of his decisions.

The first time he'd made a conscious decision that would affect the rest of his life was when General Barker had offered him the slot with MARCAD. Now, he was faced with making another life-altering decision. Struck with the sudden realization that General Barker had been at the cause of both decisions, Jim wondered why he'd been picked.

Also, knowing that General Barker had been right the first time, Jim decided to trust the man's judgment again. Taking a long pull from his bottle, Jim then set it down and carried the instruction sheet to the phone.

Dialing the number, Jim noticed that it had an Arizona area code. Waiting for it to be answered, he wondered if there were operatives living here, as Gene had mentioned earlier, discussing operations in foreign countries.

On the third ring, Jim heard a voice announce, "Light Industrial Waste."

"This is Jim Lashley," Jim said.

"I know," the voice replied. "Have you completed the paperwork?"

"Yes," Jim answered.

Before he could say anything else, the voice said, "Put everything back in the envelope and wait for me to call you back."

"Okay," Jim said.

Again, before he could ask any questions, the voice asked, "On second thought, can you meet me in five minutes at the gas station on the west access road on I-8 and West Eighth Street?"

Jim looked at his watch and said, "Yes."

Again, before he could ask anything, the line went dead.

Damn, Jim thought as he finished his beer, *these folks aren't long on conversation!*

Setting the empty bottle on the counter, he picked up the three sheets and returned to the living room for the envelope. Looking at what amounted to volunteering for an unknown mission, not knowing the risks or the rewards, Jim finally shoved the sheets back into the envelope and headed for the door.

Three minutes later, Jim pulled into the gas station and parked. Sitting there, not knowing what to expect, the tap on the roof of his car mildly surprised him. Looking out the window, all he could see was the top of a pair of jeans and the lower portion of a white T-shirt.

"The envelope, please," said the man whose hand was now resting on the door.

Jim handed him the envelope and watched as the man opened it, glanced at the first two sheets, and then closed the flap.

As he turned, Jim heard him say, "We'll be in touch," and then he walked away.

Jim sat watching until the man turned the corner of the building and disappeared. Again, he never saw the face and could only describe the man as average height, average build, and with brownish hair.

Jim started the 'Vette and returned home, wondering if this was the way it would always be, strangers meeting and leaving him without ever knowing who they were or what they looked like.

Tossing the empty bottle he had left into the trash, Jim took another bottle from the refrigerator and returned to the couch. His mind was occupied with the weirdness of how this company operated; Jim was hardly aware when the front door opened and Jennifer walked in.

"Hi, honey," she said as she sat beside him. "Anything interesting today?"

Without looking at her, Jim simply said, "Nope, just another day."

CHAPTER 42

Two days later, Jennifer had just left for work and Jim was getting ready to leave when the phone rang.

"Hello," Jim said, looking at his watch.

"Good morning, Captain," Gene said. "I have some good news for you."

"Good morning, General," Jim replied. "I guess I can stand some good news."

"Oh, anything wrong?" Gene asked.

"Oh no. I'm just always ready for good news," Jim answered, smiling. "I really don't like it when somebody calls telling me that they have bad news."

"I understand," Gene told him. "Well, everything is in place with the company, and you can turn in your papers whenever you're ready. The Squadron in Dallas is ready for you to report any time now."

"That's pretty fast, considering that we only started this a little over a month ago," Jim said.

"No need to hold off, is there?" Gene asked.

"I guess not, but I still need to take care of some business here. And there's the little issue of a place to stay

270

in Dallas," Jim told him.

"I understand," Gene answered. "How long do you reasonably think it'll take to clear the base there?"

"Maybe less than a month, depending on when I can schedule the movers, get the house ready to give back to the owner, yeah, less than a month," Jim said, mentally running down the checklist he'd performed with each previous move.

"All right, let's say a month, just to give you plenty of time," Gene said. "What about any leave you have?"

"I think I have about thirty days or so," Jim answered.

"How's this sound for a timetable?" Gene suggested. "You put in your papers to get out in two months. Take the first month to process out of the base, have your household goods packed, and get the house cleaned and returned. You did have a thirty-day notice on the rental, didn't you?"

"Yes, sir," Jim answered.

"Fine. That way, you get your deposit back, and we keep the owner happy with the Marines," Gene said. "Then you'll find round-trip tickets waiting for both of you at the airport to Love Field in Dallas (DAL). I'll have a realtor who works primarily with servicemen meet you there and take you on a tour of the local area." Gene concluded, "And if I may be so bold as to suggest an area, I think you'll like Frisco."

"My knowledge of that area is somewhat limited," Jim told him. "Where is Frisco?"

"It's a small community about forty miles north of NAS Dallas," Gene informed him. "You may not know it, but I'm rather a fan of small towns that have a unique history. Frisco just happens to be one. Also, I think it has a lot of potential for growth over the next few years."

"I sure don't want to live in Dallas," Jim told him. "And I'm basically a small-town-type guy. What're the prices like out there?"

"Reasonable," Gene assured him. "Don't forget, you'll be making just a little more than the average Marine Captain."

"That sounds all right with me," Jim said. "When'll I sign in at NAS Dallas?"

"At the end of your leave," Gene said. "That way, you'll be drawing your pay from the Regular Marines up until your leave expires. Then you'll be full-time with the Reserves for the next six months or so."

"Who's buying the tickets to Dallas?" Jim asked.

"A certain company that I advise on occasion." Gene chuckled. "You're going to have to get used to a different lifestyle when you get here."

"I suppose so," Jim acknowledged. "Is there anything else that's going to surprise me?"

"Assuredly so," Gene answered. "But just keep in mind that as far as the rest of the world knows, you're just a Marine Reserve pilot who made some shrewd investments."

"All right, sir," Jim said. "I'll tell Lieutenant Colonel West that I'm putting in my papers when I get to work this morning. Is there anything else I need to do over the next thirty days?"

"Nope," Gene answered. "Just go do your job and behave like any other Marine that's getting out. If anything comes up in the meantime, I'll call you."

"Yes, sir," Jim said as he heard the phone disconnect.

As soon as he arrived at the Squadron, Jim requested to see Lieutenant Colonel West. Bill came out of his office as Jim approached and said, "Come on in, Jim."

Leaning against his desk, Bill asked, "What can I do for you today?"

"Sir, I'm requesting my discharge effective in sixty

days," Jim reluctantly told him.

Bill looked at Jim for a few seconds and then said, "We knew this was coming, so try not to look so down in the face."

Jim looked down for a moment and then up at Bill, saying, "I know, sir. I just never really thought it would come this fast."

Bill stood and offered Jim his hand, saying, "You're making the right decision, and the sooner you get going, the better you'll be."

"Thanks, sir," Jim said, shaking Bill's hand. "I have to admit that I'm a little concerned about leaving. Although I never thought about being a Marine pilot up until a few years ago, it seems to be the thing I've liked best in my life."

"You're still a Marine pilot," Bill said, putting his hand on Jim's shoulder. "And at least this way, you're guaranteed that you won't get kicked under the bus when the RIF finally hits. Again, you're making the right decision. Both for you and the Marines."

"Now," Bill said as he turned back to his desk, "you still have a sortie or two to fly before your time is up. But start getting everything in order for your departure. If you need to be removed from the schedule, let me know."

"Yes, sir," Jim said as he turned for the door.

Checking the scheduling board, he saw that he had a formation flight that afternoon going to the range. Seeing who the other pilots were, Jim was positive that the flight would go perfectly as planned.

Taking his orders, Jim headed for the administrative offices to start the process of being discharged. Like everything else, there was a mountain of paperwork that needed to be filled out and notices sent to various base offices to process his medical records, flight records, personnel records, and anything else that had to do with his years in the Marines. Finally, he stopped by to make arrangements for his household goods to be packed and held until an address was determined.

That afternoon, after the debrief, Jim headed home to tell Jennifer that they would be leaving in thirty days. He stopped by the owner's house to give him the notice and promised to make sure the house was clean before they left.

At the house, Jim called all the utility companies and notified them to stop service two days after Jim figured they would leave. Giving them his parents' address to forward the bills, Jim called home to give them the news.

When his mother answered the phone, Jim said, "Hi, Mom. Looks like we'll be heading to Texas in about thirty days."

Hearing her ask if he was coming home, Jim told her, "Not right now, Mom. Jennifer and I are flying into Dallas to look at some houses. If we find something we want, we'll make an offer."

"Do you want your father and I to come help?" she asked.

"No, that's not necessary," Jim told her. "When we find something, we'll let you know. Besides, we've got to fly back to Yuma and get the car."

"You'll stop by on your way from Yuma, won't you?" she asked.

"I don't know, Mom," Jim answered. "It mainly depends on how much time it takes us to find a house. I've got thirty days of leave after I leave here, so if I'm lucky, I'll have time to drive through on the way to Dallas."

Finally telling her that his closeout bills would be sent to their address, Jim said goodbye and hung up.

Jennifer was just walking in as Jim was saying goodbye, and she asked, "Who was that?"

"Mom," Jim said, walking into the living room to take her in his arms. "I just told her that we're moving to Dallas in thirty days."

"What?" Jennifer said, pushing him away. "Why didn't you tell me first?"

"It sort of slipped out," Jim said, wondering why she was getting upset. "I just called to tell her that I'm forwarding our final bills to her house."

"You didn't think it important to talk to me about it first?" Jennifer pouted.

"We 'talked' about this over a month ago," Jim reminded her. "I just found out this morning that they want me at NAS Dallas sooner than I'd expected," Jim explained. "And since I needed to give thirty days' notice on the house, I just started taking care of all the little things that need to be done."

"I still think you should've talked to me first," Jennifer told him.

"Would it have changed anything?" Jim wanted to know.

"Probably not, but I just think that you should always tell me first about anything that involves us," Jennifer stated.

"Fine," Jim said, smiling. "I'm planning on having a beer in five minutes, and I'd love for you to have one too. Now you're the first to know."

"You just don't understand," Jennifer said.

Taking two bottles from the refrigerator, Jim told her, "Oh, by the way, we're flying to Dallas to look for a house before we go see my folks."

Jennifer took one of the bottles from his hand and said, "I suppose you told your mother that as well."

"As a matter of fact, I did," Jim told her. "Let's get

something straight right now. I follow orders. That's my job. Sometimes, I may have to make a decision that I can't tell you about first. But I'll never do anything that involves both of us without your consent." "Now, do you want to go look at houses with me? Or would you rather worry about who heard what first?" Jim asked, looking in her eyes.

Jennifer waited a few seconds and then said, smiling, "I get to pick the house."

CHAPTER 43

The next month rolled swiftly by as Jim tried to maintain a normal schedule at work and juggle the demands of preparing to move to Dallas. Thinking back to what General Barker had told him about Frisco, Jim did a little research on the town and found that the town of Lebanon was established on the old Shawnee Trail, later named the Preston Trail, along which wagon trains and cattle herds were driven north from Austin.

When the railroad finally arrived, Lebanon was situated too high on the Preston Ridge for the watering station the steam engines required, so several of the residents moved their houses down to the lower level. The town that grew from that was named after the St. Louis-San Francisco Railway. Then, Frisco City became just Frisco.

Finally, moving day arrived. Jim and Jennifer stayed around the house while the moving company came and began packing their meager belongings. Although they had completely furnished the house, and Jennifer had amassed a rather large assortment of clothes, the entire process took less than half a day.

They stored the few items they'd need for the next thirty days or so in one bedroom, being careful not to have too many things to fit in the 'Vette. That accomplished, they took their packed clothes and moved into the single-bedroom VOQ for their final night in Yuma.

The farewell party at the O' Club was a bittersweet experience for Jim. He was leaving a lot of people whom he knew he'd probably never see again, but he was becoming more anxious to get to Dallas and start his new life.

After the last toast was made, Jim and Jennifer walked back to their room and prepared to go to bed. Jim had barely undressed when the phone rang.

"Hello," he answered.

"I guess you've said your final farewells to the folks there in Yuma" came the response.

Recognizing General Barker's voice, Jim said, "Yes, sir. We're flying out in the morning, and I'm looking forward to joining VMF 112."

"Good," Gene replied, "but let's not get ahead of ourselves here. You're still a Regular Marine until your leave has been used. As I recall, that's about thirty days."

"That's correct, sir," Jim acknowledged. "But I thought I'd stop by while we're down there and let them know we're coming."

"That's a good idea," Gene continued. "They're a good unit, and I know you'll be happy there. However, I've got a man who'll pick you up at Love Field and take you up to Frisco. I told him to find you something with an acre or so, three or four bedrooms, somewhere in the neighborhood of $60,000."

"That's a little rich for my blood," Jim complained. "Given my financial situation, I don't see how I can afford to spend that much on a house. I may even have trouble getting the down payment."

"That's been taken care of," Gene reminded him. "All that money you invested over the years will more than cover that."

"I didn't think that was available yet," Jim said.

"Let's just call it an advance on your first assignment," Gene replied. "I told you, things are going to change, and you've got to get used to a little better lifestyle than you've lived up to this point."

"I'll trust your judgment on that," Jim told him. "But I'm still a little uncomfortable about exceeding my salary at this point."

"Well, you just take a look at what's available, and I'm sure you and Jennifer will make the right choice," Gene concluded. "I'll contact you after you've settled in, and we'll work on your 'education' for your new employer."

"Yes, sir," Jim said.

"Now, you kids get some sleep, and Mr. Rob Brown will meet you at the airport when you arrive. He has your flight information, and I'm sure he'll take good care of you," Gene said before hanging up.

"Who was that?" Jennifer asked, coming out of the bathroom.

"General Barker," Jim said, hanging up the phone.

"What'd he want?" she asked.

"Just to tell me that Mr. Brown will meet us at the airport tomorrow and show us some houses," Jim told her.

Jennifer jumped onto the bed and exclaimed, "I'm getting excited about looking for our first house! It's going to be so much fun decorating and getting stuff! I can hardly wait!"

"Easy, lady," Jim said, smiling at her exuberance. "This is a major step, and I want to take our time picking out what may be the only place we live for the next hundred years or so."

"Is that a proposal?" Jennifer asked.

"No," Jim emphatically said. "You'll know when I propose. For now, if you want, we'll keep the same arrangement."

"For now," Jennifer told him. "But you know that both your mother and mine aren't going to be happy unless we're married."

"I know," Jim said. "But I'm not going to let their desires override ours. Let's just wait until things settle down, and I see if this new job will meet our needs. I want to be sure I can support us, and we like living down there."

"All right," Jennifer said. "But I don't care about where we live as long as we're together. That's the main thing for me."

"Me too," Jim said, kissing her and turning out the light. "Now, let's get some sleep. Tomorrow's going to be a long day."

The next morning, Jim woke Jennifer and told her that he was going to the VOQ office to pay their bill and asked her to get ready to go to the airport. As soon as he returned, he saw that she was in the shower, and a few items were left to be packed.

Jim's uniforms were already in storage, and the only clothes he had kept were two pairs of starched Wranglers, three crisp long-sleeve shirts, enough socks and underwear for a week, a few T-shirts, and his boots.

Hearing the shower stop, he undressed and poked his head around the corner, asking if he could get a quick shower while Jennifer did her hair and makeup. As he stepped into the shower, Jennifer started a small pot of coffee and resumed getting ready.

Five minutes later, Jim came out of the shower and wrapped a towel around his waist as he watched Jennifer blow-drying her hair. "Coffee?" he asked, walking to the small pot that had finished brewing.

"Please," Jennifer said, putting the finishing touches on her hair. "What do you think I should wear?"

Jim carried a cup to her, saying, "We're going to Texas. Jeans and a shirt will do fine."

"What about when we're looking at houses?" Jennifer asked as she finished her makeup.

"We're not applying for a job," Jim told her. "We're just going to be sitting in a car, driving from house to house, and the realtor doesn't care what we look like, just how much commission he'll make if he sells us a house."

Finally finished and their bags repacked, Jim waited for the knock on the door announcing that Lieutenant Colonel West had arrived. Knowing that it could be several days before they returned to get his car, Jim had made arrangements for Bill to drive them to the airport and leave his car on base.

Jim was rinsing out his cup when Bill knocked on the partially open door, asking if they were ready.

"Yep," Jim said as he watched Jennifer close her suitcases. "Just three bags."

Bill reached for one of them, saying, "My wife needs at least three bags to spend the weekend away. I don't know how you expect to get by with so little for the next couple of weeks."

Jim took the other two and followed Bill out to the car, saying, "I reckon they sell clothes in Dallas, and I'm pretty sure that shopping will be high on Jennifer's list when we get there."

Smiling, Bill put the suitcase he was carrying in the

trunk and said, "They seem to do that, don't they?"

"Sure do," Jim said, holding the rear door open for Jennifer. "But as much as Arizona has in common with Texas, I'm sure Jennifer will need to upscale her wardrobe."

As Bill got behind the wheel, he said, "Especially around Dallas. If you were on the Fort Worth side, you don't need to be quite as dressy."

The ride to the airport was short, and little was said as Jim watched the gates of his old home pass behind them. Turning to Jennifer, he said, "Well, I guess we're finally really leaving."

Jennifer looked at what had been their first assignment together and smiled, saying, "I prefer to think of it as we're going, not leaving."

Bill looked at Jim and said, "It's always better to be heading somewhere than looking behind. If you're always checking your six, you've already lost the fight."

CHAPTER 44

The flight to Love Field in Dallas, Texas, was just a little over two hours, and the small talk between Jim and Jennifer was mainly about what they thought they each wanted in a house.

As they left the airplane, a medium-height man wearing a charcoal gray suit, light-pink silk shirt, and a gray tie was standing just off the exit door. When he saw Jim, he waved and walked toward him, saying, "Hello! I'm Rob Brown, and I'd bet that you're Capt. Jim Lashley."

Jim shook the outstretched hand and replied, "Yes, sir, I'm Jim, and this is Jennifer."

Rob gently shook Jennifer's hand and told her, "I'd heard that you'd be accompanying Captain Lashley. So glad to meet you both."

"To start with," Jim said as they headed for the baggage claim, "I'd prefer to be called Jim. No need for the formality of rank since I'm leaving the service in a few weeks."

"Oh, I heard that you'd be joining VMF 112 over at NAS Dallas," Rob said.

"That's true," Jim told him. "But still, I prefer just plain Jim."

"As you wish, Jim," Rob said. "How many bags are we waiting for?"

"Three," Jim told him. "And I see the first two now."

As the bags arrived, Rob said, "I've got these two, and I'll take them out to the car. You'll find me parked right outside."

The last bag arrived just as Rob was leaving the building, and Jim hurried with Jennifer to catch up.

They arrived just as their bags were being loaded in the trunk of a new glossy black Lincoln Continental. "Just toss that one in here," Rob said, holding the trunk open.

Once the last bag was in, he asked, "What'd you like to see first? I've previewed five houses that seem to fit what I believe are your requirements."

"I don't know about Jennifer," Jim said. "But I'd like to see a restaurant first. It's been a while since I had a real meal."

"That sounds good to me," Jennifer agreed.

"Fine," Rob said as he held the door for Jennifer. "There're several nice restaurants on the way to Frisco. Just yell if you see something you like."

As they left the terminal, he told them, "We'll take Mockingbird east and then turn north on Preston Road."

Maneuvering through the traffic and exiting the airport, he continued. "You may not know this, but Preston Road is one of the oldest north-south roads in Texas. It's not necessarily the fastest way from Frisco to the base, but it's convenient to Frisco from here." Rob asked, "Any particular type of food you'd like?"

"Actually, I'd like a good chicken fried steak," Jim said as he watched the buildings flow past the dark-tinted windows.

"I know just the place," Rob said. "Just a little way up the road. Called Babe's. Small place but some of the best chicken fried steak in the state. How 'bout you, Jennifer? That sounds all right with you?"

"That's fine," Jennifer answered, amazed at how congested Dallas seemed compared to Yuma or Pensacola.

"By the way," Rob told her, "there's a folder with the houses we're scheduled to look at today lying there on the seat beside you. Feel free to take a look, and maybe we can discuss them over lunch."

Jennifer picked up the folder and looked at each listing. As she finished, she passed them to Jim. "Oh, I like this one," she said, handing Jim the sheet that described a ranch-style house on two acres. "I'd like to start with this one."

Jim looked at the price and whistled, saying, "A little expensive, don't you think?"

"I know the place you're looking at," Rob told him. "It's been on the market for over a year and needs some work on the interior. I think they'd take quite a bit less than the asking price about now."

Pulling into the restaurant lot, he continued. "Just bring those in, and I'll tell you what I know about each after we order."

As soon as the waitress took their orders, Rob took the folder from Jennifer and started talking about each of the houses. The ranch house was the only one that was currently unoccupied, and they decided to visit it last since there were already appointments with the others.

When the check arrived, Rob took it, saying that today was his treat. Leaving the tip, he checked his watch and said, "Now we're just in time to see the first one."

Handing the listing to Jennifer, he opened her door and

then went around to the driver's side. Getting in, he told them, "This is a very nice house, almost three thousand square feet, about three-fourths of an acre, four bedrooms, and a two car garage. I think it's a little over priced at $65,000, but it might not go for less right now. It's only been listed for less than a month."

Pulling into the drive, Rob killed the car and asked, "Are you interested in going inside?"

"Of course," Jennifer said, climbing out of the car. "I'd like to look at every one of them, even if they're not the one we'll buy."

"That's perfectly all right," Rob said as they walked to the front door.

Ringing the bell, he told Jim, "Most ladies like to just look at everything, sometimes to get ideas or to see what the rest of the community looks like."

As soon as the door opened, Rob said, "Good afternoon. I'm Rob Brown, and we've got an appointment to look at the house if that's all right with you."

Welcomed in, he said, "Why don't you two just walk around and I'll wait here if you have any questions?"

A few minutes later, Jim and Jennifer returned and thanked the lady who had opened the door. Rob thanked her as well and left her one of his cards before escorting Jim and Jennifer back to the car.

"What'd you think?" he asked as he backed into the street.

"Nice," Jennifer told him. "But I thought the kitchen was a little small for such a large house."

"You're right about that," Rob said as he accelerated down the road. "But I think you'll love the next one."

Pulling into the drive, he glanced at the listing and said, "This one's priced about right at $60,000. The house on the left sold last year for 58, and this one's slightly larger."

"How big is the lot?" Jim asked as they walked to the front door.

"Almost an acre," he answered. "But it looks larger because of the open land behind."

After being invited in, Rob again told Jim and Jennifer to look around while he waited. Fifteen minutes later, they came back to where he was talking to the owner. Again thanking the man Rob was talking to, Jim and Jennifer headed back to the car.

"Next," Rob said as he got in the car, "is a nice three-bedroom on about an acre and a half. The house is not quite as large as the first two, but it's in a great location. All the lots in that area are at least one acre, and several are two or more."

Pulling into the drive again, they walked together to the front door and rang the bell. After waiting for a few minutes, Rob opened the lockbox attached to the knob and opened the door.

"They said they may not be back when we arrived," he explained as he replaced the key. "Have a look."

Almost twenty minutes passed before Jennifer came into the living room, where Jim was talking with Rob. "What'd you think?" Rob asked, opening the door.

"Nice," Jennifer told him. "I don't care for the master bath, though."

Jim just shook his head as they walked back to the car, saying, "It has a sink, a toilet, and a tub. What more do you want?"

Climbing into the rear seat, Jennifer told him, "I'd like a place for all my stuff, you know, a countertop for when I'm putting on makeup, my own sink. Things like that make it much better."

"That's been my experience," Rob said as they headed for the last house he had an appointment to see today. "Most ladies put more emphasis on kitchens and bathrooms, while men look at garages and family rooms."

Pulling into the ranch house, he restated, "As I said, this house has been vacant for a while and has been on the market for over a year. And it definitely needs some work."

"What's it listed for again?" Jim asked as Rob opened the door.

"For 75,000," he answered.

As they stepped into the entryway, Jim noticed that the floors were oak and that each room they passed through had oak crown molding and baseboards. The kitchen was large, with an island in the center, a small dining table off to the side, and space for a large refrigerator. Additionally, there was a six-burner gas stovetop and oven.

The slate floor in the kitchen needed refurbishing as did most of the oak floors they'd seen. The master bath was larger than the living room in their house in Yuma. Jim could see Jennifer's eyes light up as they walked from room to room.

"You go ahead and look some more," Jim told her. "I'm going outside with Rob and look at the garage and the lot." "What's your best guess at what they'd take?" Jim asked when they walked out of the back door.

"I'd say probably sixty-five," Rob told him. "But an offer of fifty-seven or fifty-eight would be a good starting point."

"I'm going to say draw up the contract," Jim told him. "But I'll let Jennifer tell you as if it's her idea."

Rob simply smiled and said, "You're a smart man, Captain. Ever raise cattle?"

Surprised, Jim said, "Yes, back when I was a kid."

"Well, you know it's a lot easier to herd them when you're taking them where they want to go," Rob said, grinning. "And I think you know where this one's wanting to go."

"Pretty sure," Jim said, smiling. "Let's go back in and watch her decide she wants this one."

CHAPTER 45

After Jennifer spent another hour wandering around the house, telling Jim what she thought needed to be done in each room, she finally said, "I think this is the one. What do you think?"

"You sure you want it?" Jim asked, knowing the answer.

Jennifer looked around the massive kitchen, nodded, and emphatically said, "Yes, I'm sure!"

Jim turned to Rob and said, "That's the decision. Draw up a contract this afternoon, and let's get this started."

"Excellent," Rob said. "I just happen to have a blank contract in my car. I'll go get it, and we'll fill in the blanks."

"How long before we know if they accept our offer?" Jennifer asked, running her hands along the countertop.

"Could be today, could be tomorrow, could be the next day," he answered, coming back in with the contract.

"You go look around some more if you want while we fill this out," Jim said as he and Rob sat at the small table in the kitchen.

A few strokes of the pen later, Jim signed the contract

offering $58,000 for the property with a seventy-two-hour expiration date. Rob reviewed the contract, signed it, and told Jim he'd be back in thirty minutes or so to contact the owners.

Jim followed Jennifer around the house, listening to her decorating ideas while he waited. As soon as Rob came back smiling, Jim knew that he had probably bought the house.

"Good news," Rob said. "The owners countered with an offer of $62,000, but since I'm the listing *and* selling agent, if you accept their counter, I can cut my commission in half. That would make the actual cost to you just a hair over $60,000, $60,140 to be exact, and I'll waive the $140."

"Jennifer?" Jim asked.

Jennifer looked at Jim and said, "Your decision. You're the one that has to pay for it."

Jim looked at her for a minute, turned to Rob, and said, "We'll take it. When can we finish this?"

"Probably in a couple of days," he answered. "I've got a title company that I work with, and I was authorized to get preapproval for your loan up to $70,000. Also, the house was inspected, and an appraisal was done previously by the same bank. So, I'd say two days, three at the most."

"Great," Jim said. "Now, I guess we need to find a hotel and wait for your call as to where and when we need to meet again."

"Not a problem," Rob said, replacing the contract inside his jacket. "I've taken the liberty of booking you a room just a few miles south of here. Reasonable rates, walking distance to a couple of restaurants, and a nice bar. Shall we go?"

Reluctant to leave the house she now considered hers, Jennifer asked, "Can we come back tomorrow and look some more?"

"Of course," Rob said as he led them out of the house. "I'll even let you borrow one of the company's cars for the next couple of days."

After dropping them off at the hotel, Rob waited until their bags were inside, and then he pulled Jim to the side, saying, "I'm sure you'll enjoy the new house, Jim. A certain Mr. Barker was the one that previewed the listings a week or so ago and told me to make this work."

Surprised, Jim just nodded, wondering how far General Barker's reach really extended. More than that, how powerful this company was. Or if it had ties with the government that went beyond what Gene had told him.

For the next two days, Jim and Jennifer returned to the house several times as she made a mental list of what furnishings needed to be bought. Trips to different furniture stores, department stores, and appliance stores combined with meetings with contractors to take care of the minor problems inside the house consumed the two days quickly.

Finally, everything was completed; Jim called home and told his parents about the house. Telling them that he was flying back to Yuma in a couple of days and would stop by on the drive back to Frisco, he handed the phone to Jennifer. Reminding her that he didn't want any visitors until the house was completely ready, he listened to her tell his mother about what she planned to do to the house.

Jennifer made another call to her mother, telling her in great detail what was going on, and promised to have them visit as soon as the house was ready.

As soon as the final documents were prepared and signed, Rob took Jim and Jennifer back to Love Field for their flight back to Yuma. Dropping them off at the airport, he thanked them and told Jim to call if he needed anything.

Three hours later, they landed in Yuma, and Lieutenant Colonel West was there waiting as he had promised. Taking them to the VOQ, he shook Jim's hand and reminded him to stay in touch.

Early the next morning, Jim woke to find Jennifer showered, dressed, bags packed, and a pot of coffee ready. "Anxious?" he asked as he crawled out of bed.

"Yes," she answered as she took a clean pair of Jim's jeans out of his suitcase and laid them on the bed. "You get a shower, and I'll finish packing your stuff."

Shaking his head, Jim headed for the bathroom, saying, "I suppose you want to make this a two-day drive to Muleshoe."

"Nope, one day," she said as she set out his socks, underwear, and T-shirt. "Let's get moving, Marine. I can't wait to talk to your mother."

Ten minutes later as Jim finished showering and shaving, Jennifer had everything except his shave kit packed and sitting by the door.

"You get dressed and go take care of the bill while I load the bags," she said, taking the car keys from the table. "I want to make it to Roswell by noon."

Ten minutes later, Jim returned to the room to find Jennifer standing beside the car. "You drive first," she said, tossing him the keys.

I-8, I-10, and US 70 were a blur as they sped eastward. Stopping just long enough for gas, snacks, and to change drivers, they passed through Muleshoe just after seven that evening. Fifteen minutes later, they pulled into the drive of the house of Jim's parents. Sure enough, John was sitting on the front lawn smoking his pipe, watching them pull in.

"Didn't expect you for another couple of hours," John said, standing. "Your mother's been a nervous wreck waiting for you though.”

“Hi, Dad,” Jim said, stretching as he got out of the car. “I don’t suppose you have a little Jack sitting around to wash the trail dust from my throat, do you?”

“Just might, son, just might. Let’s go look,” John said, putting his arm across Jim’s shoulders. “We’ll get the bags later.”

CHAPTER 46

Disappointed that they could only stay a couple of days, Jim's folks understood that he and Jennifer were anxious to get to Frisco and get settled. Just having Jim back in Texas mitigated any other feelings at this point. Plus, tentative plans had been made between Jim's mom and Jennifer for an initial visit in two weeks.

Jennifer had also called her mother and invited them for the same visit. She figured it'd be a great housewarming if both of their parents finally met there. Jim agreed with the plans, knowing that to do otherwise would be inviting disaster.

The morning before they left, Jim's dad took him aside and asked, "Do you need any help with the finances? I know that your salary over the last few years hasn't been much, and I'd be glad to help out."

"That's not a problem, Dad," Jim answered. "I've saved just about everything I've made since joining the Marines, especially the three years in 'Nam. Thanks, but I've got it covered."

"What about while you're finding a job besides the

Reserves?" John asked. "My offer still stands. You don't want to get in over your head financially."

"For the next six months, I'll be drawing the same salary as before," Jim explained. "That gives me time to find something, or maybe I can get one of the advisor jobs out there."

"What's the 'advisor' job?" John asked.

"I'd be traveling some to help other units overseas that come up shorthanded or need someone from the Marine Aviation branch to coordinate with their units," Jim explained, making sure he didn't breach his agreement with either Black Water or Dark Water.

"All right, if you say so," John said. "But don't hesitate to call if you find yourself a little short. The initial cost of furnishing a big house can be unbelievable."

Jim smiled and replied, "I've been finding that out. Jennifer's just about exhausted my reserve funds with her selection of furniture."

"Tell you what," John said, "your mother and I will buy the furniture for the living room as our gift to you. How's that sound?"

"That's too much, Dad," Jim complained. "How 'bout just a bottle of Jack Daniel's when you come for the 'family' visit?"

"Nope, it's done," John firmly stated. "I won't take no for an answer, and I'll make Jennifer give me the receipts when we get there. And don't you go trying to hide anything from me. Your mother and I want to do this for you kids, so consider it your obligation to provide me with every single receipt."

"Fine, Dad," Jim said, smiling and putting his hands on his dad's shoulders. "I know better than to argue with you. You're way too stubborn."

"Never stopped you before," John said, smiling back. "But this time, I mean it."

Jennifer and Jim's mom came out as they were finishing their conversation, and Jennifer asked, "Are we about ready?"

"Yep," Jim answered, looking at his dad. "Dad was just giving me some last-minute instructions about the perils of homeownership."

"You going through Plainview and Wichita Falls?" John asked as Jim opened the driver's door of the 'Vette.

"Nope," Jim said as he got in. "I'm taking 114 from Lubbock to Bridgeport, 380 through Denton, and then down. I want to show Jennifer the old ranches along the way. It's about the same distance, but the drive's much prettier."

"Okay," John said. "Just drive carefully, and call if you need anything."

Jim started the car and waved out of the window as they pulled away. Once away from the house, he told Jennifer about his dad's offer, more like a demand, to pay for the furniture.

"He's so nice," Jennifer told him. "And you'll never guess what my dad wants to do."

"What?" Jim asked as he sped toward Sudan.

"He and Mom are buying our bedroom furniture," she told him. "Isn't that great?"

"Yes, makes you wonder, though," Jim said. "You don't think your folks and mine planned this, do you?"

"I don't really know," Jennifer answered. "I do know that your mother said she'd talked to my mom about their visit, but other than that, I haven't a clue."

"You may not," Jim said, smiling at her, "but I'd bet the ranch on it."

After a short stop in Seymour for gas, Jim abused the

speed limit until they were approaching Highway 289 that would take them to Frisco. Finally pulling into the drive, Jim told Jennifer that Rob had kept a set of keys and had been watching the house for them. The last thing Jim had heard from him was that most of the floors had been done, and some of the furniture had been delivered.

Stopping in front of the house, Jim said, "With luck, we'll have a bed to sleep in tonight, but I'm sure we'll need to eat out."

Jennifer climbed out of the car, looked at the house, and said, "I don't care if we sleep on the floor tonight. And I don't care about where we eat. I'm just glad to be back here and make this our home."

For the next week, Jim and Jennifer spent almost every waking hour getting everything put away and getting utilities connected, shopping, or rearranging what they'd done just days before. When their household goods arrived from Yuma, Jennifer decided that most of it needed to be donated to one of the local charities.

With almost two weeks of leave left before being officially discharged from the Marines, Jim was starting to look for ways to get out of the house. Just before dinner one evening, Jim was sitting in his new recliner when the phone rang.

"Hello," he answered, thinking it was either his folks or Jennifer's.

"Captain Lashley," the caller said, "I hope that I'm the first to congratulate you on your new house."

"Of course, you are," Jim answered, knowing the voice well by now. "How're you this evening, sir?"

"Fine," Gene said. "I just happened to be in the area doing a little work and thought I'd give you a call."

"Any chance you can come for dinner?" Jim asked.

"Jennifer's finally learned how to make a decent chicken fried steak, and there's plenty."

"I'd like that," Gene told him. "How 'bout in an hour?"

"Great. I'll let her know you're coming," Jim answered. "Do you need directions or a ride?"

"Nope," Gene said. "I've got a company car, and I know the way. I'll see you in an hour or so."

Replacing the phone, Jim called Jennifer and told her that they were having company for dinner and to make sure there was plenty. Hearing that she'd made enough for tomorrow's dinner as well, Jim walked into the dining room and started setting the table.

Not quite an hour later, the knock on the door announced Gene's arrival. Opening the door, Jim said, "Welcome, General Barker! Please come in."

"Thanks, Jim," Gene said. "I hope I'm not interrupting your evening."

"Not a chance," Jim said, leading him into the kitchen.

"Jennifer," Jim said, "this is General Barker. General, I'd like you to meet Jennifer."

"Just call me Gene," Gene said as he shook Jennifer's hand. "I've heard lots of good things about you and am pleased to finally meet you."

"Thank you, General," Jennifer replied, somewhat embarrassed to be meeting the man who'd mentored Jim's career up to this point. "It's so nice to finally meet you as well."

"Can I get you anything to drink, sir?" Jim asked.

"Think you can round up a Jack and Coke?" Gene asked, looking around the kitchen.

"Just happen to have one or twelve," Jim told him, taking the bottle of Jack from the cabinet.

"Let's take them into the living room," Jim said as he

added the Coke and handed Gene a glass.

"Would it be all right to walk around the place?" Gene asked, accepting the drink.

"Of course," Jim answered, realizing that Gene didn't want Jennifer to overhear their conversation.

Walking out the back door, Jim asked, "This isn't just a social visit, is it, sir?"

Making sure they were several yards from the closed door, Gene said, "Some social, some business."

"What sort of business?" Jim asked, wondering what the real purpose of Gene's visit was.

Standing by the back fence, Gene answered, "The company has requested for you to come to Langley for a few days' orientation. If it's convenient, you'll fly back with me in two days."

"How long will I be gone?" Jim asked.

"Four or five days," Gene told him. "It can be rescheduled if it's a problem right now. But I'm guessing that you're getting tired of sitting around, burning the last couple of weeks of leave."

"Yes, I am," Jim agreed, nodding. "I haven't had so much time to just sit on my hands or agree with every change Jennifer makes to her decorating since I was a kid. To be honest, I'm about to go nuts."

Gene laughed and said, "I thought so. This'll be painless and give you a better perspective of what you're going to be doing over the next few years."

"I suppose you have a plan to tell Jennifer as to why I'm leaving?" Jim asked.

"Of course," Gene replied. "I always have a plan, a backup plan, or a way out."

"What is it this time?" Jim asked.

"My way out," Gene said, smiling. "You think of something and tell her tomorrow! Now let's go get some of that chicken fried steak I smelled back in the kitchen."

CHAPTER 47

The following morning, Jim told Jennifer that General Barker had requested him to come to Quantico to review some records that pertained to the battle that had won him his silver star. Still in heavy shopping mode, all she asked was when he'd be back.

Later that afternoon, Jim received a call from General Barker asking if he'd made a suitable excuse for going to Langley. When Jim finished telling him about the cover story, Gene just laughed and said that impromptu reasons or excuses were a very necessary part of the job and that an agile mind was the most desirable characteristic he knew of.

After a few moments, he told Jim to be at Love Field at ten o'clock the next morning for the flight to Langley. Casual attire, boots, and jeans were perfectly acceptable, and the company plane they'd be using would ensure confidentiality for the passengers.

Expecting Jennifer to become inquisitive later that evening, Jim was surprised when the subject never arose. Finally, he told her that he needed to be at the airport for the flight no later than nine o'clock. Her only response was to ask him if she could select the furniture for the spare bedrooms without his concurrence.

Waking at six the next morning, Jim walked into the kitchen and started a pot of coffee without waking Jennifer. Walking through the bedroom as quietly as possible, he quickly showered and shaved with the door closed.

As he opened the closet door to get a freshly starched pair of Wranglers, he heard her ask, "Where'd you say you're going?"

"Quantico," Jim answered, realizing that she hadn't been paying attention to anything he'd said about the trip.

Sitting up in bed, Jennifer asked, "And when'd you say you're coming back?"

Pulling on his jeans, Jim told her, "Probably in three, maybe four days. I'm not sure how long this is going to take."

Sliding out of the bed, she said, "Well, I guess I better get dressed so I can drive you to the airport."

"No big rush," Jim said, pulling on his boots. "We've got a couple of hours."

Jennifer walked into the bathroom wearing nothing but one of Jim's T-shirts, asking if the coffee was ready.

"Yep," Jim answered. "Are you coming out?"

"No," she said. "I'm going to take a quick shower and get dressed first. I plan on being at this little store I saw in Addison as soon as they open. Is it okay if I drop you off a little early?"

"What're you looking for?" Jim asked as the bathroom door closed.

"Just stuff," Jennifer said as she turned on the water in the shower.

"Early's fine," Jim said, pulling on his shirt. "I'll see you when you're done in there."

Almost an hour later, Jennifer came out to the kitchen and took the last cup from the pot, asking, "Do you want me to make more coffee?"

"Not unless you want it," Jim answered from the living room.

Coming into the living room and sitting beside Jim, she asked, "What exactly are they going to ask you about something that happened almost six years ago?"

"I don't really know," Jim said. "I suspect that it involves something about why we were sent on that mission, but I just don't know." Jim asked again, "What stuff are you shopping for?"

"Just decorating stuff," Jennifer told him. "Pictures for the spare bedrooms, things to set on tables, lamps, nothing big."

"Okay," he said, looking at his watch. "You know our mothers will be here next week. Don't you think they'd enjoy helping you?"

"Probably," Jennifer answered, "but I want to do this myself. This is about the last thing I want to do before everybody gets here, and I know pretty much what I'm looking for."

Finishing her coffee, she rose and headed for the kitchen, saying, "If you don't mind, I'll brush my teeth, and we can go."

"I'm almost ready," Jim said, following her. "All I've got left is to put my shaving stuff in the bag."

"No uniforms?" Jennifer asked.

"Nope," Jim answered, putting his cup in the sink. "This is sort of an informal thing, and if they decide to make an official inquest, I'll have to go back in uniform."

A few minutes later, Jim came out with his suitcase and told Jennifer that he was headed to the car. Putting the bag in the trunk, he closed it and waited for her to get there. As soon as she shut the front door, Jim asked, "You want to drive?"

Heading for the passenger side, she told him, "No, I really don't like driving down around that airport. If I had my way, you'd drop me off at the store and pick me up when you get back."

Laughing, Jim said, "I don't think I can afford to leave you in a store for three or four days. The only good thing right now is that you can't get much in the trunk of this little car."

"They do have delivery service," Jennifer said, smiling at Jim.

"There goes my weekend bar money," Jim joked, backing out of the drive.

Forty minutes later, Jim pulled off Mockingbird Lane into the airport and stopped in front of the terminal. Taking the keys, he went to the rear of the 'Vette and opened the trunk as Jennifer came around to meet him. Shutting the trunk, Jim handed her the keys and kissed her.

"Have fun shopping," he said as he lifted his suitcase from the ground.

"I will," Jennifer said, hugging him. "You just hurry back."

Jim watched as she drove away and then entered the terminal. Walking to one of the ticket agent's positions, he asked, "Which gate do corporate jets use?"

"Not sure, sir," the lady answered. "I'll have to ask."

A minute later, she returned, saying, "You'll have to go to the General Aviation (GA) area."

"Where's that?" Jim asked.

"At the northwest end of the field," she told him.

"How do I get there?" Jim asked.

"I guess you have to take a taxi, sir," she replied.

"Okay, thanks," Jim said, heading back out of the terminal.

At the curb, Jim waved for the closest taxi and waited for him to pull up beside him.

"Where to, sir?" the driver asked.

"General Aviation terminal," Jim said, climbing into the back seat.

"Yes, sir," the driver told him. "But there's a minimum charge of $5."

"That's fine," Jim said.

Ten minutes later, the cab pulled up to one of the fixed base operators, and the driver said, "Here you are, sir."

Jim handed him a $10 bill, saying, "Thanks. Keep the change."

Still over an hour to wait, Jim carried his bag into the waiting room and looked around to see if maybe General Barker had arrived. Not seeing him, Jim set his bag beside one of the chairs and headed for the complimentary coffee/snack area.

About forty-five minutes later, Jim saw General Barker come in. Standing to get his attention, Jim waved and waited for Gene to come join him.

"Good morning, General," Jim said, shaking Gene's hand.

"You too," Gene replied. "You ready for your first day on the job?"

"As much as possible," Jim answered. "If knowing nothing and not knowing what to expect makes you ready, I'm about as ready as anyone could be."

Gene laughed and said, "As I told you, this is just an orientation. No specifics will be divulged, only general operating procedures. Each mission is unique, and flexibility is the key ingredient."

"Is this one of those 'flexibility is the key to airpower' type things?" Jim asked.

"Same thing, except no air, just power," Gene answered.

"You know what the key to flexibility is, don't you?" Jim asked, smiling.

"What's that?" Gene questioned.

"Indecision," Jim joked. "And you know what the key to indecision is? Lack of information. Therefore, the less you know, the more you can accomplish."

Gene smiled and said, "Interesting take on it but, in some ways, very true."

As they were sitting talking, a Lear jet with BW 3 on the side was seen through the window, stopping in front of the GA. "That looks like our plane," Gene said, standing.

Jim stood and waited while the Lear's door opened, and a man wearing blue trousers and a white shirt with four silver strips on his shoulder epaulets came down the steps. After talking briefly with one of the ground personnel, the man headed for the door that led to the waiting area.

Seeing Jim and Gene standing together, the man walked over and asked, "Langley?"

"Yes," Gene answered. "Two of us."

"Fine," the man said. "I'll be your pilot, and we'll be ready to go in about fifteen minutes as soon as they top off the tanks. If you don't mind, I'll take your bags, and you can wait on board."

"No need," Gene said, picking up his bag. "We'll carry our bags. Any other stops before Langley?"

"No, sir," the pilot said, leading the way to the door. "We should have you on the ground in about two hours."

"Great," Gene replied. "How was the ride down?"

"Smooth," the pilot told him as they got to the plane. "Little bit of headwind, but that'll help us going back. Go on in, gentlemen. I'll be back as soon as I sign for the fuel, and we'll be on our way."

CHAPTER 48

Jim and Gene sat in the rear of the luxurious aircraft as they sped northeast toward Virginia. The company had provided several selections of snacks, sandwiches, and a fully stocked bar. Except for the two pilots, Jim and Gene had the aircraft to themselves.

During the flight, Gene told Jim as much about the entire operation as he could. The basics were that Black Water was partially funded with discretionary funds provided through the CIA; other funds came from the people or companies that hired them for their services.

In addition to US companies and personnel, various other countries used their services as well, both at home and abroad. Black Water was considered the premier of security in any country in the world.

Their only discoverable tie with the United States in any form was the single advisory position that General Barker held. Even that would be considered minor if discovered since he was an advisor on several different boards.

Gene's salary from Black Water was minimal as far as

the records were concerned. However, General Barker had obviously made some very shrewd investments with his former military salary, his current retirement, and the *meager* pay recorded with Black Water.

Jim learned that all funds, whether CIA or Black Water, that went toward the operations that Jim would be involved in were held in offshore accounts under various money management funds. These funds actively traded with one another as well as worldwide financial institutions.

Not on any country's publicly traded stock or bond market, the privately held funds were immune to the scrutiny of any financial monitoring agency. The fact that some of the accounts were growing at astronomical rates could be explained by the intuitive ability of the fund managers to buy in great quantities when certain targeted stocks or bonds were at below-average costs and sold well above normal averages.

Not having to have their books examined, the fact that in some cases, backdating of either purchases or sales could never be determined as the reason that some individuals seemed to do extremely well while others within the same fund groups did the opposite. Never would anyone outside the company see that for each dollar one individual earned as profit, another lost an equal amount.

Also, since most of the moneys paid were not considered as revenue earned within the United States, there would never be any tax issue. Even the requirement to be overseas when a salary was earned, except for the few days an individual could be within the United States, didn't apply since the salary wasn't earned overseas, nor was it truly earned within the States.

Gene explained how the company's lawyers and accountants had researched every country's statutes and laws to determine the exact means of sheltering the payments and to prevent anyone from ever determining whether it was a salary, an investment, or capital gains and exactly where the money came from.

"All in all," Gene told Jim, "this is probably the most sophisticated money laundering system ever devised. This makes some of our drug dealers or organized crime schemes seem juvenile."

"I was skeptical at first," he continued, "but I contacted several different Certified Public Accountants (CPAs), and each told me the same. The money could never be touched by our Internal Revenue Service (IRS)."

"Even if you take funds from your account at some later date, the company's accountants are the ones that prepare your W-whatever forms that the government requires for capital gains, investment income, wages, salaries, or tips. Trust me, the money in your overseas account can never be traced or taxed by any government agency in the world." Gene finished. "The tax system of the country where each individual resides is taken into consideration when structuring their earnings. As I said, this system is amazing in its complexity and its thoroughness. Simply amazing."

Gene then went on to discuss the Dark Water operations. "As I told you at the start," he said, "you don't work for Black Water. However, as they 'own' and control Dark Water, they perform all accounting, procedural, and oversight programs for each of their subsidiaries."

"Are there other companies below, either Black Water or Dark Water?" Jim asked.

"That subject is closed to discussion," Gene answered. "One of the basic tenets of the organization is that all, I mean all, information is extremely compartmentalized. If you aren't involved in the activities of any other group, you aren't told about it, and it'll be vehemently denied should anyone ask."

He continued. "You're familiar with the military's procedures. Just because you possess a Top Secret clearance doesn't mean you're authorized to read all information at that classification. We called it need to know. If you didn't need to know the information, you weren't authorized to see it."

Gene warned, "Here, the rules are even stricter. Even if you might need to know something, only the portion that *they* think you have an actual need to know will be shown to you. And operations of either the parent company or any other subsidiary, should any exist, are strictly off-limits. The bottom line is if they think you need to know something to perform your mission, they'll give it to you."

Gene concluded, "If you think you don't have enough information, think you need other assets or just want to explore other options, you might voice your concerns. But never, never ask questions that could even hint at trying to find out things that you don't need to know."

"I do have one question," Jim said.

"What's that?" Gene asked.

"Let's assume that everything you told me about the financial arrangements is working as you described," Jim said. "What would happen if one of the CPAs, or bookkeepers, or anyone that has any information that the IRS or other US government agency might desire gave it to them?"

"First," Gene lectured, "that'll never happen. No individual has enough pieces of the puzzle to even start to piece together the process. For example, the people who provide you with your W-whatever forms get their information from another group. The group that sends the information gets the numbers from an entirely different group. That group only sends the totals from sums sent by other groups. It's a circle where information is flowing back and forth, round and round, and nobody can put the whole thing together.

"For example, you are sent to X country by an office within Dark Water. They got the directive from an office within Black Water. When you get to X country, you'll be met by someone who has possibly never heard of either Black Water or Dark Water. All they know is that someone working within country X told them to do certain things, provide you with certain things, and that's the end of their knowledge.

The things that take place before you arrive have been arranged by someone, unknown to the group doing these things, and they don't know what or who'll follow up on their initial work. Once they complete their assignments and are paid, they never hear about what happened or why it happened. If any news that might seem to tie their work to an actual event leaks out, they still don't know who ordered it or who did it."

Gene concluded, "As I've tried to explain, this is one very *HUGE* operation. "They have more assets than the entire Marines, Army, and Air Force combined in the little country of Vietnam. And as far as I can tell, they use their assets wisely. Hell, if we'd let them have the 'Nam problem, they'd probably have had it resolved in the first year. But like I said, they operate without the constraints of a President, a Senate, a House of Representatives, a Judicial Branch, and certainly no public opinion. They, in effect, are the perfect war machine."

Still unconvinced, Jim pressed the issue. "Okay, just

for the sake of argument, let's say that two or more individuals from different areas just happen to find that they are both involved in parts of the organization that neither knew existed. Maybe they happened to meet in a bar; it doesn't matter, they met."

Jim went on, "Then once the conversation started, maybe some boundaries were crossed, both determined that they held the key to interlocking information. Then unauthorized, of course, one or both decided to do a little backtracking of information. That led them to another group, and then another, and then another. Sooner or later, they might have enough to present it to someone outside the organization, especially if they knew that it would lead to some perceived financial or publicity reward. What then?"

"What you're surmising is only remotely, *very remotely* possible," Gene explained. "These various groups are not only separated by office. They are separated by city, state, and continent. Chance meetings between different offices are a virtual impossibility."

"Again, just asking what if?" Jim queried.

"There'd be vacancies within the organization," Gene sternly stated. "Within hours of the *chance* meeting, there'd be vacancies."

CHAPTER 49

After landing in Langley, the Lear jet taxied to a spot reserved for civilian aircraft and stopped at the command of the ground personnel. As the door opened near the cockpit that provided the steps for exit, a limousine arrived and stopped just clear of the left wing.

Gene came out first and waited for Jim to deplane and stand beside him. "This car will take us to the facility where you'll be given your orientation. Once we arrive, I'll be leaving you with the instructors. You'll be staying within the building for your brief visit, and arrangements have already been made for your return to Dallas."

"Will you be coming back with me in the Lear?" Jim asked.

"No," Gene answered. "And the Lear won't be taking you back. A commercial flight's been arranged, and you'll fly back alone when you're done here."

Gene stopped and looked at Jim quizzically, asking, "Do you think you get your own personal jet every time you travel?"

"I just thought—" Jim started to say.

"The company may have plenty of assets," Gene told him, smiling, "but they're not for field personnel. No, son, you fly commercial. And in coach."

As they approached the car, the driver held the rear door open for them and put their bags into the trunk once they were inside. Once back in the car, the driver closed the window that separated him from the passengers and headed out of the base.

Thirty minutes later, they left the main roads and headed down an unmarked narrow road leading into a dense growth of trees. The only thing Jim noticed out of the ordinary was the almost invisible glint of sunlight off the lenses of well-camouflaged cameras at frequent intervals along the road.

Almost three miles into the trees, the road curved sharply left, and a nondescript concrete building came into view. Surrounded by two parallel fifteen-foot chain-link fences topped with razor-sharp concertina wire, the single entry was guarded by double gates on each fence line.

After stopping at the first gate, a guard appeared from a small building and approached the car. The driver rolled down his window and presented a sheet of paper for the guard to see. Taking the sheet to the guardhouse, Jim and Gene waited patiently for clearance into the facility.

Moments later, the guard returned with the paper and nodded at the driver. Back in the guard shack, the gates began to swing outward, allowing the vehicle to enter the first portion of the facility. Once the gates were fully closed behind them, the interior gates began to open into the grounds.

Past the last fence, they drove to the only apparent entrance into the building. After the car had stopped, the driver opened the rear doors and headed back to the trunk as

Gene and Jim exited the car.

"I'll escort you inside," Gene said, picking up his suitcase. "You'll be in their capable hands after that."

As Jim followed Gene toward the door, he noticed that there were no windows on this side of the building and that there was an abnormal number of antennae covering the roof. Numerous dishes that pointed skyward were on the outer perimeter, while tall masts dotted the space further away from the walls.

As they approached the door, Jim noticed cameras on either side tracking their movements. Looking along the walls on either side of the door, he saw several more just below the roofline that constantly swept across the area between the building and the interior fence.

Gene tapped a code into the display beside the door and then reached for the handle. Swinging the door open, they both stepped into a small room that had a glass panel on the left side. Jim turned to face the glass as Gene did and waited for whoever was on the other side to allow them into the interior of the building.

Gene held up an ID card and spoke. "General Barker and Jim Lashley."

An audible click was heard, and Gene opened the door that led into a hall that stretched through the building. As Jim followed Gene down the hall, he noticed doors on either side numbered much as houses on streets. Passing several perpendicular hallways, they finally turned left and stopped at a door on the right.

Again, Gene tapped a code into the pad beside the door and swung it open. Entering, they were met by a man wearing khaki pants and a knit shirt with a logo and the words "Dark Water" embroidered beneath.

"Good afternoon," the man said as he shook Gene's

hand. "How was the flight?"

"Excellent," Gene answered. "I'd like to introduce Jim Lashley, our newest member."

The man turned to Jim and said, "Good to meet you, Jim. I'm Rob."

Jim shook Rob's hand and said, "Good to meet you too."

Gene shook Jim's hand and said, "Good luck. I've got to get back to work. Rob will show you to your quarters and spend the rest of the day giving you a tour of the facility. He'll be your guide for your time here and get you to the airport when you're finished. Any questions?"

"None that I can think of, sir," Jim said.

"Fine," Gene said, turning toward the door. "Rob, let me know how things go, please."

"Yes, sir," Rob replied as Gene opened the door. "I'll have a formal report for you the day Jim leaves."

"Now," Rob said as the door closed, "let's get you settled first. You'll be sleeping in a private room with a bath, much like a cheap motel, but don't let the Spartan accommodations worry you."

Leading Jim to a hallway that branched out of the room, he continued. "We have one of the finest cafeterias around, and it's open twenty-four hours a day. All your instruction or orientation will take place within this portion of the facility. Unfortunately, you won't be permitted to leave this area or make any contact with people outside until we're complete. The only exception is to go to the cafeteria, and I'll escort you to and from all your meals."

Opening an unlocked door, Rob continued. "Here's your room. If you'll just toss your bag on the desk, we'll head down to get something to eat."

Jim set his suitcase on the small desk and looked

around the room. A single bed positioned along one wall, a chair that faced the desk where he had set his suitcase, a mini refrigerator, a small closet that covered about half of the wall, and a door leading into the tiny bathroom were the extent of his quarters. *Comfort's not high on their list of priorities,* Jim thought, shutting the door.

Following Rob down the hall, they passed several other numbered rooms until reaching a door that led out of the area. Rob pressed a code into the pad and swung the door in, holding it for Jim to exit.

Down several more halls, they finally arrived at a large room that reminded Jim of the O' Clubs at most of the military bases he had seen. Taking a seat near one of the walls, they waited until a young lady wearing what was rapidly becoming apparent as their uniform, khakis and knit shirt, approached.

As she handed them the menus, she said, "Good afternoon, Rob. What would you guys like to drink?"

"Tea for me," Rob told her and then looked at Jim.

"Tea's good," Jim said.

"I'll be right back," she said, turning away.

Jim looked at the menu and noticed that the selection was fairly extensive, but there were no prices for any of the entrées. Looking questioningly at Rob, he asked, "Any recommendations?"

"Just avoid the Mexican plate," Rob said, not looking at his menu. "Everything else is good, especially the seafood."

After they'd eaten, Rob led Jim back into their area and told him, "After we get back to your room, I'll bring you some organizational charts, a few other pamphlets, just a quick overview of things, and we'll start in earnest tomorrow."

Not knowing if he was allowed out of his room, Jim began putting his few clothes away while he waited for Rob's return.

Hearing the knock on the door, Jim opened it and saw Rob standing there with a folder, saying, "If you need anything, the phone on the desk is connected directly to mine."

Jim took the folder and asked, "Do I need to call you if I want to leave the room?"

"Yes, unfortunately," Rob said. "I know it's quite an imposition, but that's just the way it is here. But within reason, I'm always available. If you need anything, give me a call, and I'll get here as soon as I can."

Jim thanked him and shut the door. Taking the material he'd been provided, Jim sat and reverted to his normal means of coping with new information. He studied each piece until he had a good grasp of each part of what was obviously a very complex organization.

That, along with what General Barker had told him, had him well prepared the next morning when Rob knocked on his door. Following breakfast, they returned to their area and used one of the vacant rooms to discuss what Jim had read and to see if there were any questions.

Every time Jim asked a question, it was considered, and as accurate an answer as possible was given. Several times, Rob just said, "Not to my knowledge."

Jim came to understand that the phrase "not to my knowledge" covered a host of things but generally meant you don't need to know, so don't ask again.

The first full day was spent looking at how various missions had been planned, the resources used, and the success of each—everything from simple invitations to a dinner on a certain day, outright bribery, kidnapping, sudden illnesses, and, of course, the demise of certain individuals.

By the end of the day, Jim had seen hundreds of examples of how Dark Water removed any obstacle to Black Water's success in performing whatever contract was being executed. Although never explicitly told, Jim knew that failure on the part of Dark Water would probably mean failure in some aspect of Black Water's operation.

The next day covered a more in-depth look at some of the resources at Dark Water's disposal. This included various bacteria, viruses, or poisons that could be dispensed in various ways; having a bartender or café waiter provide the opportunity to "doctor" a cup of tea or drink by turning their back at the right time; someone distracting the target long enough for the operative to slip something into the drink; canes and umbrellas with needles at the tip and a syringe in the handle; and, of course, knives and rings with a coil of thin steel wire hidden within. The list seemed endless.

In addition to the actual mechanics of completing an assignment, the more important aspect was protecting the in-country resources and the operative. Stores of blood samples, skin tissues, DNA from undeterminable sources, hair samples, and other types of physical evidence that could be left at the scene were available that would match any location in the world. Much emphasis was placed on completing the assignments and even more on protecting the individuals and, therefore, the company.

By the end of the day, Jim understood why Gene had said that, given the company's assets and methods of operation, they were the perfect war machine. When Rob arranged for Jim to be dropped off at the airport for his return flight, Jim knew two things: whoever ran this organization probably had more power than the President of the United

States, and they didn't tolerate either failure or breach of their own security.

Jim certainly knew what Gene had meant when he said that there'd be vacancies should any protocol be violated. There was no doubt that once in the organization, it was a lifetime commitment.

CHAPTER 50

After Jennifer picked Jim up at Dallas Love Field, they went straight back to the house while she talked about all the things she'd done to get the house ready for their parents, who were due to arrive in two more days.

It was only after they'd gone into the house and Jim was getting the bottle of Jack Daniel's from the cabinet when she asked, "How was your trip?"

"Fine," Jim said, taking two glasses from the cupboard. "Rather boring, I'd say. I'm not exactly sure what they were looking for, but I don't think any of my answers solved their problem."

Mixing two Jack and Cokes, Jim handed one to Jennifer and said, "Show me what you've done."

Jennifer took her drink, leading Jim through the house, pointing out what she'd bought, how she'd arranged the furniture, which room each of their parents would have, and what else needed to be done prior to their arrival.

Jim nodded as she explained everything, made appropriate comments when he felt it needed, and when the "tour" was finally over, said, "Looks good, baby. Looks really good.”

Jennifer smiled and said, “I’m glad you like it.”

Jim held his drink up, and she tapped it with hers as he said, “I do like it. I think our parents will, too.”

The next two days were spent taking care of the minute details. Jennifer spent her time in the house, and Jim used his new mower and weed eater around the outside. The night before everyone was to arrive, Jennifer made a final pass before coming to bed.

“I guess we’re ready,” she said as she lay with her head on Jim’s chest. “What time do you think your mom and dad will get here?”

“Well,” Jim said, stroking Jennifer’s hair, “it’s almost a seven-hour drive. I’d guess a little after noon.”

Jennifer raised her head and asked, “Do you really think they’ll get here that early?”

“Oh yes,” Jim said, smiling at her. “If Dad had his way, they’d be here for lunch. And he’d say that Mom just couldn’t sleep and she kept nagging at him until he finally gave in.”

“You know what you ought to do?” Jennifer asked, laughing.

“What?” Jim asked.

“Be sitting in a chair on the front lawn when he pulls in,” she said, remembering the way John was always waiting for them to arrive.

“No,” Jim told her seriously, “that would be mocking Dad. I’d never do that.”

The next morning, while Jennifer was finishing cleaning the table, Jim went to a local meat market and picked out six two-inch-thick rib-eye steaks. Taking them home, he sprinkled on a generous helping of Montreal Steak Seasoning and set them aside.

Although he hadn't located any mesquite while shopping, he had found briquettes with small slivers of mesquite embedded inside. *Not quite the same, but it'll have to do,* Jim thought.

They were just sitting down to have a light lunch when Jim heard a car pulling in the driveway. He looked at Jennifer and said, "I'll be damned. He had to have left just after four this morning to get here this early."

Jim left his unfinished sandwich and headed for the front of the house. Pulling the door open, he saw John holding the door open for his mother. Walking out to greet them, he said, "Look what the wind blew in. It must've been one helluva wind to blow you here this fast."

"Oh, your mother," John said, walking up to hug Jim. "I told her last night when we went to bed that we should wait until seven or eight this morning before we left. But she just couldn't wait. She kicked me out of bed just a little after three and said we're leaving."

Jim hugged him and replied, "Well, you always said to get an early start if you want an early finish."

Jennifer came out of the house as Jim was walking toward his mother and said, "I'm so glad you got here early. Let's get your things inside, and I'll show you around."

Jim got the suitcases from the trunk while Jennifer took his mother and father into the house. As he entered, he saw his dad walking around the living room and could hear Jennifer and his mother back in the room where they'd stay.

"Looks nice," John said as he took one of the suitcases. "If you gotta live in a town, this is about as nice as you'd find anywhere."

"It's not a ranch, that's for sure," Jim said, heading through the house. "But it doesn't take the work to keep it up either."

John followed Jim into the bedroom, where he would spend the next couple of nights, and looked around, saying, "You kids have a nice place here. If I could get Mother off the farm, I wouldn't mind living in a town if it was as nice as this."

"Thank you, John," Jennifer said as she opened a closet door. "Y'all put your things down, and I'll go make you something for lunch."

Jim followed Jennifer to the kitchen and took down two plates and glasses. Setting them on the table, he asked, "What time does your mom and dad get in?"

"Three this afternoon," Jennifer said as she made two more sandwiches. "I told her to call when they got a cab." Turning to Jim, she said, "We really need to get another car, you know. If I want a job, I'll need one, especially since you'll be at the base. Besides, that car of yours only has two seats and is useless if there's more than just us."

"I know," Jim said. "It's just that I figured the house came first. When I start work with the Squadron, we'll start looking for you a car."

"Y'all need another car?" John asked, walking into the kitchen.

"Yeah, Dad, we'll need another one pretty soon," Jim answered.

"Tell you what," John said, "why don't we take my car and go pick up Jennifer's folks when they get here? That'll leave some time for your mother to visit with Jennifer alone."

"Sounds good to me. How about you?" Jim said, looking at Jennifer.

"That'll be fine," she replied, "but it doesn't solve the problem of having one car with only two seats."

After everyone finished their lunch, Jim took his dad

around the outside, and John finally said, "Oh, I almost forgot."

"Almost forgot what?" Jim asked as he followed John back to the front of the house.

Opening the trunk of the car, John pulled out an old burlap sack and handed it to Jim, saying, "I didn't figure you could find seasoned mesquite around here, so I brought you a bag."

Jim opened the bag and looked inside, saying, "Thanks, Dad! I looked around town this morning for some and had to settle for some charcoal briquettes that had chips."

"Nothing beats the real thing," John said, smiling. "I bet you went out and found a couple of steaks too."

"Sure did," Jim said, carrying the sack of mesquite around the house.

"Isn't there a town named Mesquite around here someplace?" John asked knowingly as he followed Jim to the back of the house.

"Yep," Jim answered. "It's just a little way south and east of here."

John stood looking at him and asked, "Do you think they named the town for an oak tree?"

"You're probably right, Dad," Jim admitted. "I just haven't had time to find the best place to get things around here yet. But maybe while you're here, we menfolk can do a little scouting while the ladies do whatever they do."

Jim and his dad left just a little after two to go to the airport and get Jennifer's parents. The flight from Pensacola was only a couple of minutes late, and once everything was loaded, they headed back toward the house.

Being the first time John had met Jennifer's parents, he remained quiet during the drive and listened to the conversation between Jennifer's mom and Jim.

Back at the house, introductions were made, and Jim went with his parents to the living room while Jennifer got her parents settled.

"I believe we have something to settle before we get this visit officially underway," Jennifer's dad announced as he came into the living room, winking at John.

"I believe you're right," John said, coming to his side.

"What's that?" Jim asked, wondering if these two had entered into a conspiracy.

"I believe that you promised to give me the receipts for all the things in this room," John said, looking around the living room.

"And I believe that you promised me the same thing about that bedroom of yours," Jennifer's dad told her.

"I'm sorry," Jim said, looking at each of the men. "Those seem to have been misplaced."

John looked at Jennifer's dad and said, "I told you he'd try to get out of it." Looking at Jim and Jennifer, he said, "But I'm still one step ahead of you."

Looking at Jennifer's dad, John continued, "With your consent, why don't we go together and get these kids another car for a housewarming present?"

Jennifer's dad smiled and said, "That's about the best idea I've heard today. They can't misplace what they don't have yet, can they? I bet that there's probably a good car dealership around here somewhere that might take care of this little problem."

"Good," John said, shaking Jennifer's dad's hand. "Tomorrow, you and I will go get a car and bring it back."

"Don't I have a voice in this?" Jennifer asked.

Almost in unison, the three men said, "NO!"

CHAPTER 51

The visit was finally over; Jim spent the next couple of days preparing to report to VMF 112 for duty with the Squadron. All his uniforms cleaned and pressed, he waited for the day that'd been agreed upon to drive to NAS Dallas and be sworn in as a Captain in the Marine Reserves.

For the next six months, Jim spent ten to twelve hours a day during the week at the Squadron, learning all their procedures and flying as often as possible. Although it was similar to life at a regular Squadron, the few men who worked full-time comprised a small portion of the Squadron's strength.

During exercises, there was virtually no difference other than the players changed more frequently. Jim learned that the majority of the pilots had normal nine-to-five jobs and only came out to meet the service requirements that would ensure their retirement at age sixty.

Several of the pilots flew for various airlines, American being the major employer. Some flew for a small carrier named Southwest Airlines, which had recently begun operations out of Dallas.

The Squadron Commander, Lt. Col. Andrew "Andy" Jackson, had tried to get Jim on as a full-time pilot but was unable because of budget constraints and other issues. Jim started looking around for some other job to provide the income that he'd been expecting from Black Water since he hadn't heard from them or General Barker since his orientation.

Early on Saturday afternoon, just days after his six months of full-time flying were up, Jim was alone in the house, reading the newspaper, when the phone rang.

"Hello," Jim said, not really expecting any calls.

"Captain Lashley," the familiar voice responded, "how are you today?"

"Fine, sir," Jim answered. "It's been a while."

Gene laughed and told him, "You're not the only fish in the ocean. I do have other things to do besides hold your hand."

"Of course, sir," Jim protested. "I only meant that I thought—"

"I know," Gene interrupted. "You've gone from working for a living to sitting around, waiting for something to happen. That gets boring real fast, doesn't it?"

"Yes, sir, it does," Jim agreed. "What can I do for you today?"

"We've got a mission for you," Gene told him. "You're going to be sent to Turkey as the Marine Aviation Liaison to a small US Army unit over there."

"When do I need to go?" Jim asked, becoming excited about finally getting a mission.

"In one week," Gene told him. "You'll get a call about five minutes after I hang up, and a meeting will be set up for this afternoon. There, you'll be given a package describing the situation in broad strokes and your part in more detail."

"How'll I get to Turkey?" Jim asked.

"In a minute," Gene reprimanded. "First, you need to learn to trust that everything that is needed will be thought out well before we contact you. The entire mission may have been taking place for months, if not years and every detail has been reviewed again and again under differing scenarios. Nothing is left to chance."

"Sorry, sir," Jim apologized.

"Don't worry about it," Gene told him. "This being your first mission, I understand the issues of lack of control and not quite trusting someone you've never seen. Just think of this as a deployment with the Marines. You get your orders, follow them to the letter, and let the command structure worry about the logistics. You still remember that, don't you?"

"Yes, sir, I do," Jim answered.

"All right, back to the package," Gene said. "In the package, you'll find basic instructions, contact points, photos of the target, and the desired result. Commit these to memory and burn the entire package once you're satisfied that you no longer need them. Make sure no one sees this package once it's in your possession. And make sure any ashes are unrecognizable. Everything is printed on paper, much like your newspaper, so I'd recommend burning it in the grill out on the back porch. Then char a piece of newspaper, leaving enough to identify it as a newspaper, and lay it among the ashes in case anyone sees it."

"Yes, sir," Jim acknowledged.

"Now, in three days, orders will arrive at the Squadron, tasking them for an F-4 pilot with previous ground experience to go to a small Army detachment in Turkey. The on-station date will be four days later. The temporary additional duty (TDY) will be for one week, including travel time," Gene explained.

"Since you're currently the only pilot that meets these requirements," Gene continued, "you'll be the one sent. Had there been other possibilities, we'd have requested you by name. But as long as assignments seem to be in your Commander's hands, fewer questions will ever arise."

"I understand," Jim said.

"We're leaving the logistics of getting you in and out of Turkey to the Marines. You will, in fact, be the liaison to the Army unit that requested assistance and will spend the majority of your time with them," Gene explained.

"At some point during your first day, someone will greet you with the name Rob and provide you with further instructions," Gene went on. "Once Rob has given you your instructions, follow them to the letter. But do not attempt to contact him again."

Gene told him, "Should anything go wrong with the mission, he'll already know and will either provide you with further instructions or cancel the mission."

"Regardless of the outcome, you're to merely follow your instructions, complete your TDY with the Army, and return home." Gene finished. "Do you think you can handle that?"

"Yes, sir," Jim answered. "Will I know if the mission is a success?"

"Does it matter to you?" Gene asked.

"I'd just like to know if I've done my job," Jim told him.

"You just follow orders. That's your job," Gene reminded him. "You don't need to know what the ultimate goal of the mission is. Hell, you just may be a minor player in the initial phase of a longer-term mission. You might even be sent back at some point as another piece of the overall puzzle."

Gene tried to explain, "The thing you need to understand is that sometimes there are many players, many acts, and sometimes the ultimate goal is years away. Think of it as a chess game. We move. They look at our move and make one. Over and over, the pieces are moved about the board, trying to force the King into an untenable position. Then the game is won."

"Yes, sir," Jim said, somewhat chastised. "I've just never had a mission where I didn't know the desired result or know if I'd done what I'd been sent to do."

"Again, I understand," Gene said. "But the rules are different here. You can consider your mission successful if you do exactly as you're told and get home unscathed."

As Jim was about to say something, the phone went dead in his hand.

Sitting back, going over the conversation in his head, Jim had hardly begun to realize that he was being activated when the phone rang again.

"Hello," he answered.

"Good afternoon," the caller said. "My name is Rob, and I believe you've been instructed to meet with me this afternoon."

"Yes," Jim replied. "I just finished—"

"I know," the caller interrupted. "Be outside by the street in two minutes. A brown Ford pickup will be sitting two houses down to your right. Walk toward it. When you get close, an envelope will be dropped on the curb, and the truck will drive away. That's your package."

"I understand," Jim said into the now-dead phone.

Getting out of the chair, Jim headed for the door. *How many fucking "Robs" does this fucking company have?* Jim wondered as he left the house. *It seems like everybody I've met, other than Gene, is some fucking Rob.*

As he walked down the driveway, Jim looked down the street. Not seeing a brown pickup, he turned and looked the other way in case he'd misunderstood his instructions. The only thing he saw in that direction was a white Chevrolet passenger car driving toward him.

Turning to his right, as directed, Jim was somewhat surprised when the car stopped beside him, and a voice said, "There's no brown pickup. Here's your package."

Jim stepped off the sidewalk over to the car as a hand extended from the passenger window, holding a large brown envelope. He barely had the envelope in his hands when the car sped away.

Never seeing more than the back of the driver's head, Jim took the envelope and returned to the house. *Two houses down,* Jim thought. *I never left the front of my own house. Brown pickup, white car. Are these people paranoid? And if they are, why?*

CHAPTER 52

Jim said nothing about the TDY assignment to Jennifer when she came in that afternoon. There was no way of explaining that he knew he was being sent out before the Squadron even knew, assuming, of course, that they hadn't received the tasking orders.

No, either he'd get the orders in three days, as General Barker had said, or he'd just wait for the General to call back. He certainly couldn't know about Squadron tasking before the Squadron Commander. That would be a little hard to explain.

Three days later, when the phone rang, Jennifer answered it and called out, "Jim, it's your boss, Lieutenant Colonel Jackson."

Taking the phone from her hand, Jim said, "Colonel Jackson, what can I do for you?"

Listening to his Commander tell him that he was being sent TDY for a week to Turkey, Jim looked at Jennifer and frowned. When the call was over, Jim shook his head as he replaced the receiver.

"Bad news?" Jennifer asked.

"Yes and no," Jim answered. "I'm being sent to Turkey as an advisor to a bunch of Army grunts."

"Army?" Jennifer asked. "I didn't know we had any people over there."

"It's a small detachment of 'Advisors,'" Jim explained. "We have units like that in several countries around the world."

"Isn't that what we had in Vietnam before we got into the war?" Jennifer asked.

"Yes, but don't compare the two," Jim told her. "Most of these units are there to liaison with some diplomatic corps. They don't actually advise the Turks of anything unless requested by the State Department."

"How long will you be gone?" she asked.

"Probably six or seven days, maybe more, counting the travel time," Jim told her. "I'll be leaving in three or four days, depending on how the Marines want to get me there, about a week there, and then a day or two to get home."

"Will you be flying over there?" Jennifer asked.

"No, I wish I were, but this is strictly a ground assignment," he answered.

"Then why don't they send some ground guy?" she asked.

"Because the person they want needs to be a pilot and have ground combat experience," Jim explained.

"I just wish they'd send someone else." Jennifer pouted.

Jim put his hands on her shoulders and said, "You knew I'd be sent somewhere sooner or later. I'm still in the Marines, even if it's the Reserves. We get orders just like the Regular Marines."

"I guess I thought you'd go as a unit, like before," Jennifer explained.

"Well," Jim told her, "sometimes they only need one special person or team. I feel pretty lucky that they never made me a FAC. That'd have me stuck on the ground most of the time, although the OV-10 would be an interesting plane to fly."

The next morning, Jim went down to NAS Dallas and picked up his orders. There was already a ticket for a flight leaving DFW, passing through La Guardia (LGA), Heathrow (LHR), and on into Turkey. He saw from there he'd be driven across the border to meet the Army unit.

The only special instructions from the Marines were that he traveled in civilian clothes and wore only his utility uniform with no unit patches or rank insignia. The only document he was to carry across the border was his civilian passport.

Two days later, Jim kissed Jennifer goodbye and headed west to catch his flight. Now anticipating the assignment, he was ready to get there and see what he was being asked to do.

Combining the flying time, the waiting for the connecting flights at LGA and LHR, and the nine-hour time zone change, it was almost dark the next day when Jim arrived in Turkey.

The man meeting Jim quickly gathered him and his single bag, hurried them to his car, and left the airport. A few miles south, he pulled over and told Jim to change into his uniform. After changing, Jim was instructed to leave his suitcase in the car and promised that it would be waiting for his return.

A few hours later, the driver crossed the border into Syria along some remote trail, and Jim was deposited at a small clearing on the side of a mountain. The only thing Jim could see was the faint outline of a tent.

Walking to it, he heard a voice asking, "Jim?"

"Yes," Jim answered.

"Come in," was the reply.

Pulling the flap aside, Jim stepped into the tent and could barely make out a man with long, unwashed hair, wearing a robe and sandals, sitting at a small table.

"Please sit," the man said.

Jim took the only vacant chair and looked at the man. It was impossible for Jim to determine exactly what nationality the man was. The attire resembled that from pictures Jim had seen of tribesmen from several of the Middle Eastern countries.

"My name is Rob. Welcome to Syria," the man said, looking at Jim. "I understand you were told to expect me."

"Syria? I thought I was working in Turkey," Jim protested, still unsure of what was happening.

"Things change. You know what your target looks like, don't you?" Rob asked.

"Yes, I can recognize him," Jim finally answered, realizing that the parameters of the mission had changed dramatically.

"Good," Rob said, nodding. "Tomorrow, I will take you to a location where I can show you where this man lives. It'll take a couple of hours to get there by foot."

"What will we do then?" Jim asked.

"Observe," Rob replied.

"What're we looking for?" Jim asked.

"To see what he does, who he sees, where he goes," Rob explained.

"Anything else?" Jim asked.

"No, that's all," Rob told him.

Rob stood and pointed to the cot along one wall of the tent, saying, "This is where you'll sleep. This'll be your home until you're ready to leave."

Bowing at the entrance to the tent, Rob finished. "I'll be back with appropriate clothing for you in the morning. Don't leave the tent. Should you need to relieve yourself, there's a container in the corner. Please replace the lid when you've finished."

Before he could say a word, Rob dropped the flap and disappeared into the darkness. There was nothing to do now except sleep; Jim pulled his clothes off and climbed onto the cot. The thin pillow and coarsely woven sheet were a long way from comfortable, but life in the field for a Marine can be worse, much worse.

Jim was sound asleep when the tent flap was thrown open. The brightness of the light almost blinded Jim as he looked toward the noise. Silhouetted against the glare was a figure dressed in a robe.

"Rob?" Jim asked, sitting up on the cot.

"No, I'm Major Biggs," the figure answered. "May I come in?"

"Of course, Major," Jim said, reaching for his pants.

"Take these," the Major said, setting a robe, a pair of sandals, and a sash on the table. "You'll also need a head wrap, but Rob is getting one that's common to one of the local tribes."

Jim picked up the robe and draped it across his shoulders. Taking the sash, he tied it around his waist and then put on the sandals. As he was dressing, the Major had stepped back outside.

Once finished, Jim called out, "Major Biggs."

The tent flap opened, and the Major reappeared, saying, "I just saw Rob coming up the mountain. He should be here in an hour or so. In the meantime, I've brought you some breakfast."

"That's great," Jim told him. "I haven't eaten since yesterday, or tomorrow, or whatever day it was when I left the States."

"Yeah, sometimes you never know what day it is," the Major said. "Sometimes I go to sleep in one country and wake up half the world away. Then it depends on whether I flew east or west as to what day it is."

Jim looked at the small cup of a mushy-looking substance and asked, "No eggs over easy?"

The Major just smiled and said, "No, but there's some cold goat meat in the bottom. Beats fish heads and rice."

"This'll do," Jim said, taking two fingers of his right hand and scooping the mush into his mouth.

"I'm leaving now," the Major said. "If you need me for anything, tell Rob. He'll find me."

"Is his real name Rob?" Jim asked.

"Hell, if I know," the Major answered. "I was just given a location, a description of the man, and a code to verify the person. I was told to wait for him to introduce himself as Rob and then proceed with my orders."

Turning to the door, the Major said, "My orders were to provide you with these luxurious accommodations and remove them when you leave. Enjoy your stay."

Almost thirty minutes later, Rob arrived in front of the open flap, asking, "Are you ready to go?"

Jim sat up on the couch where he'd been resting and asked, "Did you bring a head wrap?"

Stepping into the tent, Rob answered, "Of course, but the question remains: are you ready to go?"

Jim stood and faced Rob, saying, "Yes, I'm ready."

Rob pulled the head wrap from his sash and set it on Jim's head, saying, "Then, by all means, let us go."

For the next two hours, they picked their way down the

steep decline of the mountain. The biggest problem Jim had was that the sandals kept letting his feet slide forward, and soon, a blister was forming between his big toes and the adjacent ones.

Not about to admit that he was struggling to keep up, Jim fought back the pain and remained only a foot or so behind Rob as they worked their way down the mountain.

Stopping about a mile up from the small village, Rob motioned for Jim to squat beside him behind a large boulder. Pulling a pair of binoculars from within his robe, Rob covered the top of both lenses, making sure the sun wouldn't glint off the glass.

Speaking softly, Rob told Jim where to look and what robe and head wrap to look for before passing the binoculars. Jim took them and mimicked Rob's hand, covering the end of the glasses. Spotting the target and recognizing him from the pictures he'd seen, Jim nodded and continued to watch.

"When he turns in this direction, looks up here for a few seconds, and then walks to a building," Rob whispered to Jim, "that's where you'll meet him tomorrow night."

"Why am I meeting him tomorrow night?" Jim asked, still watching the man in the village.

"To give him a package," Rob said. "I'll give you the package when we get back to the tent. You'll come back here tomorrow afternoon and give it to that man tomorrow night."

As Jim was watching, the figure in the village turned to his right and stared at where they were. Behind the boulder and with the sun in the man's face, Jim knew that they couldn't be seen, but the feeling wasn't good.

The figure then turned back in the direction he had apparently come from and walked to a small hut on the edge of the village. Stopping momentarily, he disappeared into the hut.

"Let us return," Rob told Jim, sliding backward away from the boulder. Following Rob, Jim climbed the mountain for the next two hours, wishing he had his boots.

Back at the tent, Jim went inside to pull the sandals from his aching feet. A few minutes later, Rob come in and put a large package on the table.

"You'll take this tomorrow afternoon as we discussed," Rob stated. "After the sun goes down, you'll set it against the side of the house we observed. Put it below the window that faces the mountain. Then you'll return here."

"I thought I was supposed to give it to the man we watched?" Jim asked, still wondering if his feet would take another trip down and back up the mountain in the sandals.

"Plans change. You'll be taken back to Turkey the next day," Rob told him.

Jim just nodded as Rob turned and left the tent. A few minutes later, Major Biggs reappeared and asked, "Want some company for supper?"

CHAPTER 53

Jim slept until past noon the following day. The trip down and back up the mountain had worn him out. The time difference was just an additional factor contributing to his fatigue.

Sitting up on the cot, Jim noticed a bowl sitting on the table. Getting up and walking to it, he saw a note beneath the bowl. Knowing what the bowl held, he opted to read the note first. The note read,

It's cold, it tastes like shit, be glad you've got it.
Biggs

Smiling at the attempt at humor, Jim wiped his fingers on the inside of the robe he'd fallen asleep in and dug into the coagulated mess within the bowl.

Knowing that it was at least six hours until sunset, Jim calculated that it'd take three hours to descend to the hut. That left three hours to kill. Previous instructions were to not leave the tent. But there was no one around to enforce those instructions.

Jim opened the flap to the tent and peeked outside. Nothing except scrub brush, some gray-green brownish grass, widely scattered among the boulders. Looking down the hill, there was one new item. Jim glanced around and made his decision.

Keeping low, he eased down the mountain a few feet and dropped behind a boulder. At the base of the large rock was the pair of binoculars he'd used yesterday. Picking them up, he leaned around the side of the boulder and looked down the mountain.

He could see the path they'd taken down and noticed there was a slightly worn trail that led from where they'd hidden down to the village. Looking from here, after the trek yesterday, Jim decided that he'd take the same route. Not only did it look like the most expeditious, but it'd also be much easier to retrace on his way back in the dark.

Slipping back into the tent, Jim finished the cold gruel that constituted his meal, maybe the only thing he'd get until tomorrow, and stared at the package. There was no way of knowing what was wrapped inside the brown cloth.

Picking it up and holding it, Jim could determine its weight within a few ounces, but that meant nothing. A package this size of $100 bills would probably amount to several thousand dollars. A package of Syrian pounds, who the fuck knew what that would be worth?

Jim decided to spend the rest of his time trying to rest and not worry about what was in the package. The one thing he could do was to try to devise a way to keep the sandals from causing any further damage to his already sore and swollen feet.

Taking some of the remains of his meal, Jim pressed a glob between his toes and pulled on the pair of dark socks he'd been wearing when he was picked up in Turkey. Tearing two small strips of canvas from the tent flap, he pressed them between his toes where the strap would rub.

Taking a few tentative steps with the sandals on proved to be some improvement. At least the leather strap wasn't pressing directly on the already-blistered skin.

Smiling at his ingenuity, Jim took the binoculars and returned to the boulder to watch the village. If he'd learned nothing else in Vietnam, it was to reconnoiter your target as often and as long as possible before going in.

Time passed slowly, and the sun was a constant irritant. Jim decided to leave slightly early and ease down the mountain at a slower pace than before. Not only would this give him time to watch what was happening below, but it'd also allow him to place his feet more sideways and avoid direct pressure from the strap that held the torturous device on his foot.

The sun was still just above the horizon when Jim reached the spot where they had stopped yesterday. Using the binoculars, he noticed nothing different. The few people who occupied this collection of huts seemed to be going about their normal routine. The man he'd been watching never appeared.

As the sun passed below the horizon, Jim leaned back against the boulder, holding the package in his hands on his lap. Still wondering what he was delivering and why the directions were to leave it in a specific location, he waited a few more minutes for the twilight to dissipate.

He was most likely being watched. Somewhere up on the mountain, Major Biggs or Rob was probably looking at him right now. Earlier, the faint trail from where he sat to the village had been somewhat noticeable. As the last rays of sun faded and darkness gathered rapidly around him, Jim slipped around the boulder and began a quiet descent. Although not visible, the texture of the ground provided enough clues for Jim to feel his way along the narrow path.

Almost an hour later, Jim was merely yards from the wall he was seeking. A flicker of light from within the hut clearly defined where the window was. Now Jim slipped the sandals off and crept the last few feet. Crouched beneath the window, he could hear the voices of a man and a woman inside. Not understanding a single word, Jim couldn't tell if this was a meeting or a normal family evening.

The brown cloth that held the package made it invisible in the dark as Jim sat it against the wall directly beneath the window as directed. Looking at it lying there, it closely resembled one of the adobe-looking bricks with which the hut had been constructed. There were even a few other pieces of broken bricks along the base of the wall. Taking even more care to avoid any noise, Jim crept back to the spot where he'd left his sandals and put them back on.

Still making almost no noise, Jim cautiously climbed back to the boulder where he'd waited for the sun to set. There, knowing that it'd be almost impossible for anyone from the village to see him, Jim increased his stride and speed on his return to the tent.

Now almost seven hours since he'd started down the mountain, Jim was exhausted when he felt the canvas of the tent. Knowing better than to have any light that could be seen for miles around, he took the devil sandals off and tossed them to the side.

Pulling his socks off, Jim wiped the mush from between his toes and pulled the socks back on inside out. This hadn't been the longest, the most difficult, or the most dangerous mission he'd ever been on, but it had worn him out. Maybe he just wasn't in as good shape as he'd been. *Nah,* Jim thought as he collapsed on the cot. *It's the altitude.*

It was still dark outside when Jim heard the tent flap open. "You awake?"

Relieved to hear at least it was English, Jim answered, "Barely. Who's there?"

"Rob," the voice said as the flap closed behind him. "You need to gather your things and come with me."

"Now?" Jim asked, trying to rub the sleep from his eyes.

"Yes, now," Rob said. "The car is waiting about a mile up the mountain, and the driver's very anxious to get going. Just put on your robe and come with me."

Sensing the urgency in Rob's voice, Jim was immediately wide awake and jumped off the cot. Pulling the robe around him, Jim slipped his feet into the hated sandals and rolled everything else into a wad. Making sure he had everything he'd brought, he slipped out of the tent behind Rob's disappearing figure.

"Quietly," Rob said as he led the way up the mountain. "It'll take us about an hour to reach the car. That should give you at least an hour to get over the ridgeline and close to the border."

Jim had no options other than to follow and wonder why they were having to leave so early. The sandals were now rubbing raw skin from where the blisters had broken, and the pain was becoming more pronounced with each step.

Almost at the end of his endurance, Jim heard a slight sound from somewhere ahead of them. "There's the car," Rob whispered. "We're almost there."

After five more minutes of agony, Jim saw movement in the darkness in front of him. Recognizing the faint outline of the car that'd brought him here, Jim knew that the worst must now be over.

"Throw your stuff in the car," Rob ordered Jim as he grabbed him by the arm. "Hurry up and get in."

As Jim tossed the wad of his uniform and boots into

the rear of the car, he thought he saw Rob heading back down the mountain. Climbing into the passenger seat, Jim was barely seated when the driver started the engine and accelerated over the ridgeline.

The cross back into Turkey went unnoticed by Jim. Not only didn't he know exactly where they were, but the slowly evaporating darkness also hid every feature of the surrounding land.

A few minutes later, the driver pulled the car to the side of the road and said, "Take the robes off and put your uniform back on."

Jim did as he was directed, and as the sun broke over the horizon, they were once again on their way. For the next few hours, Jim leaned against the door of the car and slept.

He woke to the gentle shaking of his shoulder and the driver's voice telling him, "We're almost at the airport. There's water for you to wash in the building on the right. You need to do it quickly: put your uniform back in your bag and put your civilian clothes back on."

Jim blinked his eyes and glanced into the back seat. The suitcase he'd brought from the States was sitting where he'd left it. Stepping out of the car, Jim carried the bag into the building and stripped down. The small pitcher of water was cold, the tiny rag was coarse, and soap was nonexistent, but washing the grime and dust away was a welcome luxury.

Packing the stinking uniform back in the bag, Jim donned the remaining clean underwear and socks. Pulling his boots over his swollen feet was unpleasant, but having clean clothes made up for the discomfort.

Back in the car, the driver quickly took them the few remaining miles to the airport. Stopping at the curb, he simply nodded at Jim and waited for him to get his bag and leave.

Jim slid out of the car, grabbed his suitcase from the rear seat, and had barely gotten his hand away from the door handle when the car sped away. Shaking his head, Jim reached inside his jacket and found his return ticket.

Walking into the terminal, he thought, *So much for private jets, limos, and the good life. This ain't much better than the grunt Marines.*

CHAPTER 54

The flight back to the States was just as long as the trip over, but the time zone changes worked in his favor. Jim even had a little time in LHR to wash a little more in the men's room during his wait for the connecting flight to New York. Carrying his suitcase into the restroom, he slipped off his shirt and took the razor from his ditty bag. Using the soap from the dispenser at the sink, he scraped the stubble from his face and washed his underarms.

Arriving in New York, Jim cleared customs again and headed for the departure gate. Seeing the flight number and on-time status, Jim went to one of the kiosks that provided a quick meal. Sitting at one of the small tables, eating his sandwich, Jim was surprised when a passing lady laid an envelope on his table.

Having barely gotten a glimpse of her as she passed, Jim picked up the envelope and opened it. Inside was a single black-and-white photo of what remained of a small building against a bleak background. Recognizing the terrain, Jim knew that the photo was of the hut where he'd left the package.

Taking the picture into the restroom, Jim tore it into tiny pieces and flushed them down the toilet. Now, he was certain that he hadn't been delivering either US dollars or Syrian pounds. So much for self-delusion, he was officially now an assassin. The thought was unsettling, but surprisingly, he felt disconnected from what he'd done. Even after seeing the destruction, Jim had no proof that there'd been any people within the building when the bomb went off.

A flashback of booby traps in 'Nam and comrades who'd been killed or maimed passed through Jim's mind as he watched the bits of paper swirl down the drain. Knowing enough about the situation in the Middle East, Jim realized that the wars between tribal chiefs in that area were an ongoing situation. He was just another pawn in forcing the opposition to make a move.

Settling into his coach seat, Jim looked out the window as the plane rapidly filled. Wondering which side of which skirmish he was working for prevented him from noticing any of the people taking their seats or the usual instructions as to how to fasten his seat belt, where the exits were located, or any of the other standard spiel the Flight Attendants were making.

It was almost an hour into the three-hour flight when Jim heard a familiar voice asking, "Would you care for a drink or a snack?"

Looking toward the aisle, Jim saw Jewell smiling at him across the two passengers seated between them. Returning her smile, he said, "Dr Pepper, please."

Mouthing "I'll be back," Jewell passed the can and a glass of ice before shoving the service cart down the aisle. Several minutes passed until she returned and nodded in the direction of the restroom located in the tail of the aircraft by the galley area.

Jim excused himself as he stepped over the center seat occupant's feet and around the man who had risen from the aisle seat. Walking to the rear, Jim stopped where Jewell was latching the service cart within its bin.

Turning to Jim, she said, "Been a while, Gyrene."

"Yes, it has," Jim replied, smiling at her.

Jewell looked him up and down and stated, "You look like you've been traveling some."

Careful not to reveal how much traveling he'd done, Jim lied, "Not really. Spent some time in Upstate New York camping, hiking, just enjoying the countryside."

"Are you still in Arizona?" Jewell asked, leaning against the side of the airplane with her arms crossed.

"No," Jim told her. "I'm living in Texas now."

"Still a Marine?" she asked.

"Reserves," Jim answered.

"Still have a girlfriend?" Jewell asked.

"Yes," Jim told her. "She lives with me just north of Dallas."

"Pretty serious, I guess," Jewell said. "I'm assuming it's the same one you told me about."

"Same lady," Jim acknowledged.

"Oh well." Jewell sighed. "This airline business isn't the greatest to make or keep relationships."

"Neither is the Marines," Jim agreed.

"What else are you doing besides the Reserves?" she asked.

"Not much," Jim told her. "I'm looking for a job and thinking about going back to school to finish my degree."

"Are you going to marry this girl?" Jewell suddenly asked.

Jim looked at her for a few seconds, thinking about

how to answer her, and then finally said, "Probably."

"What's stopping you?" she asked.

"Lots of things," Jim admitted.

"Such as?"

"Uncertainty, I guess," Jim said. "That'd be a major change in my life."

"How do you figure that?" Jewell asked. "Haven't you been living with her for several years now?"

"Yes, we've been together for over three years," Jim told her. "What's that got to do with being married?"

"Seems to me you just want to keep an escape route," Jewell told him. "If you've gotten along for the past few years, what do you expect to change if you get married?"

"Nothing, I guess," Jim admitted.

"Well, if you really want to keep this woman, you need to take the next step," Jewell advised. "The little piece of paper that means marriage is more important to a woman than you realize."

Jewell finished. "Now, if you don't want to take my advice, that's your choice. But you need to return to your seat so I can do my job."

Jim saw the look in her eyes and realized that not only was the conversation over, but any thoughts about a relationship with Jewell were over as well. Nodding at her, he went back up the aisle and took his seat.

Jim sat quietly for the remainder of the flight and didn't pay any attention to the Flight Attendants as they walked up and down the aisles. About thirty minutes out of DFW, Jewell passed Jim's row, checking to make sure all the seats were up, tray tables stowed, and seat belts fastened. Smiling faintly at him, she disappeared as she headed for the rear of the airplane and her jump seat.

When the plane was finally at the terminal, Jim sat and

waited for the passengers seated in front of him to head down the aisle before he rose and took his suitcase from the overhead bin. Nearing the front of the plane, Jim didn't see Jewell standing, telling the passengers 'Bu-bye'. Nodding at the Captain, who was also telling everyone goodbye, Jim headed up the ramp to the terminal.

Outside, Jim walked to the long-term parking and found the 'Vette. Tossing his suitcase in the trunk, he headed to the exit gate, paid for his parking, and pulled onto the road that led south to Mockingbird Lane. There, he turned left and drove east to Preston Road.

Pulling into the drive, Jim parked in front of the garage and stopped. Leaving the motor running, he used the remote to open the garage door and drove in. As he opened the car door to get out, Jennifer opened the connecting door to the house.

"I thought you were supposed to be gone for another day or so," she said, watching Jim get his suitcase from the trunk.

"Well, you know how these things go," Jim said, walking up to her and giving her a quick kiss. "Sometimes you stay longer than planned. Sometimes, you get lucky and go home early."

"What was it like?" Jennifer asked.

"Normal Army stuff," Jim told her. "Crappy accommodations, lousy food, bad information, lack of leadership—normal Army stuff."

"How'd you like Turkey?" she asked, following Jim into the bedroom.

"Sort of like living in the foothills in New Mexico," Jim answered as he sat his suitcase on the bed. "Not much to see where we were unless you like looking at rocks and dirt."

"What's that smell?" Jennifer asked, holding her nose

as Jim pulled his dirty clothes from the bag.

"That's the smell of staying in the field." Jim smiled. "If you think this is bad, you should have smelled our clothes when we came back from a week in the field in 'Nam. This is nothing."

"I don't care what it was like in 'Nam," Jennifer protested. "You take those smelly things straight to the washing machine."

Laughing, Jim gathered everything into his arms and headed out the door as Jennifer told him, "And throw those clothes you're wearing in with them. They smell almost as bad."

CHAPTER 55

The following morning, Jim drove to NAS Dallas and reported to Lieutenant Colonel Jackson. "How'd it go?" Andy asked, seeing Jim at the scheduling desk.

"Fine, sir," Jim answered. "Shorter than expected, as you know. But all told, I think everything went well."

"I did get a call this morning, thanking me for sending you," Andy told him. "I guess if the Army's happy, you did all right."

"Thanks, sir," Jim said as he looked for his name on the schedule.

Andy had turned away and then said, "By the way, my secretary has a number for you to call. Judging from the prefix, it's a Virginia number, and I guess they didn't have your home phone."

"Thank you," Jim said. "I'll go see her right away."

Walking away, Andy said, "If it's something I need to know or can help you with, let me know."

Not seeing his name scheduled to fly for the next two days, Jim walked into the secretary's office and got the slip of paper with the number. Not recognizing it and knowing that General Barker would probably have called him at home, Jim left the base to look for a pay phone.

"Light Industrial Waste," the voice answered when Jim called.

"Uh, this is Jim Lashley. I was told to call this number," Jim said.

"Hold, please, sir," the voice instructed him.

A few seconds later, another man came on the line, asking, "Jim?"

"Yes," Jim replied.

"Hold for General Barker," the man said.

Jim stood watching traffic pass in front of the gas station while he waited, wondering why Gene hadn't called him directly.

"Jim, how'd it go?" General Barker said, coming on the line.

"Fine, I guess, sir," Jim answered.

"Anything out of the ordinary happen?" Gene asked.

"Only that I wasn't in the place where I thought I'd be working," Jim told him.

"Matter of expedience," Gene said. "Anything after the mission?"

"Well," Jim said, knowing that Gene probably already knew about the photograph, "there was a photo that showed up in New York that I hadn't expected."

"I know," Gene said. "We'll discuss that in a couple of days. I'm flying out to Dallas tomorrow, and if you're free the next day, we'll talk about a few things that might be concerning you about

now."

"That sounds good," Jim said. "I just looked at the schedule, and I'm not scheduled to fly either of those days."

"I know," Gene said. "How 'bout if I take you and

Jennifer out for a steak dinner the next night? I'll come by a couple of hours early, and we can have a Jack and Coke while she finishes getting ready. That'll be plenty of time to cover what we need to discuss."

"Look forward to it, sir," Jim said.

"Fine. Now, don't worry about anything. This is just an after-action brief that we do for most of our missions," Gene explained, "especially after the first one."

"I understand," Jim said.

"All right, I'll see you in two days. Shall we say four o'clock that afternoon?" Gene asked.

"Four's fine," Jim agreed. "I'll see you then."

Driving back home, Jim stopped and bought a new bottle of Jack Daniel's just in case the one at home was getting empty. Seeing nothing else in the liquor store that interested him, he paid for the bottle and headed for the house.

Pulling into the open slot in the garage, he carried the bottle into the kitchen and said, "Honey, I'm home!"

Jennifer came out of the bedroom and asked, "No flying?"

"No," Jim said as he put the bottle in the cabinet. "I wasn't due back for another day or so, and they filled the schedule with the other pilots." Taking the nearly empty bottle of Jack down, Jim asked, "Join me for an afternoon sip?"

"Kind of earlier than usual," Jennifer said, looking at Jim. "But we can call this a welcome-home drink."

Jim poured the two drinks and carried them into the living room, with Jennifer following him. "Have a seat," Jim said, indicating the couch.

Jennifer sat down, and Jim handed her a glass. Tapping the rim of hers with his glass, Jim said, "Here's to coming back to the girl I love."

Jennifer raised her glass and said, "Welcome back."

Jim sat beside her and said, "I just talked to General Barker, and he wants to take us to dinner the day after tomorrow. Is that all right with you?"

"Of course," Jennifer said. "What's he doing back here so soon?"

"I don't know," Jim lied. "Must be something to do with his job."

"What does he do?" Jennifer asked.

"Not sure," Jim told her. "Some sort of advisory job. Lots of Generals get hired after they retire by companies that deal with the military." Jim sat his glass on the coffee table and said, "That's not the real reason I wanted to have this drink."

Surprised, Jennifer looked at him and asked, "Just what reason do you have?"

Jim studied her face for a few seconds and finally said, "I think maybe now's the time to talk about getting married."

"What?" Jennifer gasped, setting her drink on the table. "Did you just say you want to talk about getting married?"

"Yes," Jim said, nodding, "that's exactly what I said."

"I'm asking you to marry me," Jim continued. "I want you by my side for the rest of my life. Now the question is, will you marry me?"

Jennifer sat in shock for scant seconds and then threw her arms around Jim and said, "Yes, of course, I'll marry you!"

Smiling, Jim eased her away and looked at her, saying, "Make sure you're positive about this. I'd hate for you to jump into something you haven't given adequate thought."

"You're such an asshole, Jim Lashley. I've known the answer for a long time," Jennifer said, tears running down her cheeks. "You've known it too. You were just too stubborn to admit it."

"You're probably right," Jim said, laughing. "I just always wondered if you'd marry a stupid, dumb-assed asshole!"

Jennifer leaned over and kissed Jim lightly and softly said, "I've dreamed of marrying a stupid, dumb-assed asshole ever since I met you."

Jim put his arms around her and said, "You're right. I've known this was going to happen for a long time now."

Laying her head against his chest, Jennifer asked, "If you've known for so long, why'd you wait?"

"I don't know," Jim admitted. "It's just that after the last year or so, I knew that I didn't ever want to be with anyone else. Now that I'm no longer concerned with having to leave you and go back overseas, possibly to never return, I just knew that now was the time."

Jennifer sat up, smiling, and picked up her drink, saying, "Next time, don't take so long. If you'd waited much longer, I don't know if I'd have said yes."

"Liar," Jim said, laughing. "You think there are lots of dumb-ass people like me out there just waiting for someone to come along? Nope, you found the only one. And I'm lucky to find someone that admires those qualities in a man."

"No," Jennifer quietly said, "I'm the lucky one."

CHAPTER 56

Later that evening, Jennifer called her mother and told her about the engagement. For the next hour, Jim occasionally overheard one-half of the conversation and wondered just how long it took a woman to tell her mother that she'd accepted a proposal they both knew was coming.

After hanging up, Jennifer asked, "Are you going to call your mom?"

"I was just waiting for you to finish," Jim said, smiling.

"Well, after you tell her, I want to talk to her," Jennifer stated.

"Fine," Jim said, reaching for the phone.

Dialing the number from memory, Jim waited until he heard his mother's voice.

"Hi, Mom," Jim said. "Is Dad around?"

Jennifer quietly demanded, "You tell your mother first!"

Holding his hand over the phone, Jim said, "I will. Just hold your horses."

A second later, Jim's mother told him, "He's not in the house right now. Is there something you want me to tell him?

Or should I have him call when he gets in?"

"That's okay, Mom," Jim said. "You can tell him, and if he wants to call, I'll be home for the rest of the evening."

Pausing for a second, Jim told her, "I've asked Jennifer to marry me."

Listening to her response, Jim then said, "No, we haven't set a date. I just asked her this afternoon."

"Of course, she said yes," Jim said after hearing the question.

"All right, Mother," Jim said, exasperated. "Here's Jennifer."

Jennifer snatched the phone from Jim's hand and said, "Isn't that wonderful? I'm so happy."

Jim listened to a few minutes of the conversation and headed into the kitchen to refill his drink. Smiling as he listened to Jennifer repeat all the same things he had heard her tell her own mother, Jim just shook his head and walked outside.

Almost an hour later, Jennifer came out to join him, saying, "Your mother's so excited. I don't know who's the happiest, me, my mom, or yours."

"Probably me, your dad, and mine," Jim said, deadpan. "Our little hearts are all aflutter."

"Men," she said, lightly punching him on the shoulder. "You're just as excited as we are, but you're afraid to show it."

"Of course, you're right," Jim said, smiling and knowing that any other answer would spell trouble. "I'm sure right now Dad is pouring a Jack and Coke to celebrate."

"Oh pppppst," Jennifer said, sticking her tongue out at him. "You just wait. Your dad will be the proudest man there, except for maybe mine."

"Of course," Jim agreed again. "Now, don't you think

we should go to Dallas tomorrow and find the ring?"

"I've already found it!" Jennifer exclaimed. "I just *happened* to be looking at some jewelry the other day, and just *happened* to see these rings, and just *happened* to see one that I really, really liked."

"What a surprise," Jim said, smiling at the excitement in her face. "I don't suppose you'd like to go down tomorrow and get it, would you?"

"I can make time," Jennifer teased, "since it's that important to you." "OH," she said, squeezing his arm, "I'll have it when General Barker comes."

Releasing Jim's arm, she continued. "And I'll wear it to the restaurant so everyone'll see. This is going to be sooo much fun!"

"Let's order a pizza for tonight," Jennifer said, smiling. There's plenty of Budweiser in the refrigerator, and I'm too excited to go out right now."

"That's fine," Jim agreed.

"All right," she said. "I'll just take a quick shower, and we'll go get the pizza."

"Okay," Jim replied as she headed inside.

About five minutes later, as he was rinsing his glass, he heard Jennifer call from the back, "Jim, can you come back here and give me a hand with something?"

Jim was barely out of the kitchen when he remembered those exact words the first time he had spent the night with Jennifer.

"Need a towel or something?" Jim said, stepping into the bathroom, already undressed.

CHAPTER 57

The next morning, Jennifer slipped quietly out of the bed to let Jim sleep as long as he wanted. She went to the kitchen, started a pot of coffee, and prepared all the ingredients for Huevos Rancheros. She'd found a Mexican restaurant while Jim was gone that was willing to give her their recipe. Asking them if they had ever heard of H3 Restaurant in Fort Worth, one of the men said he'd worked there several years ago.

Asking him if their Huevos Rancheros were as good as H3's, he grinned and told her it was the same recipe. Jennifer copied it down and tipped the man. "I promise to be back some morning for breakfast, but I'm going to try to make these myself once."

Almost an hour after she'd gotten up, Jennifer heard Jim coming through the house. "Good morning, baby," she said, greeting him with a kiss.

"Good morning," Jim said, grabbing a cup from the counter. Pouring his cup, Jim glanced at the bowls sitting on the counter by the stove and asked, "What're you making?"

"A surprise," Jennifer told him. "You go sit down

somewhere, and I'll call you when breakfast is ready."

Jim took one more look at the bowls, egg carton, and other things he didn't recognize right away and headed for the living room.

Twenty minutes later, Jennifer called him into the kitchen and told him to have a seat.

As soon as Jim sat down, Jennifer set the plate covered with the Huevos Rancheros in front of him, saying, "Try it."

Jim looked at the plate and said, "I've seen this before."

Scooping some Pico De Gallo onto the fried egg, Jim took his first bite. Looking at Jennifer and smiling, he asked, "Where did you learn to make this?"

Smiling back, Jennifer answered, "I'm sorry, sir, that's classified information."

Jim just grinned and kept eating while she brought her plate and sat with him.

After breakfast, Jim helped her clean the table and waited for her to go freshen up for the trip to the jewelry store. When she came out, Jim merely stood and followed her out to her car.

"By the way," Jim asked as she backed out of the drive, "how do you like this little Honda?"

"Just fine," she answered. "But I still think you guys should've let me pick what I wanted."

"Look at it this way," Jim replied. "If they'd just driven up in it and said, 'It's yours,' would that have made it any different?"

"They didn't," Jennifer argued. "They just went out and got me what they wanted to get."

"Sometimes you don't get a choice in the present you get," Jim reminded her. "What if I'd gotten your ring in the old-fashioned way and presented it to you?"

"That would've been fine," she told him. "That's sort of the tradition, isn't it?"

Realizing the impossibility of winning the argument, Jim just said, "Well, let's say it makes it even. You didn't necessarily get the car you wanted, but you got exactly the ring you wanted. That's even, isn't it?"

"Of course, dear," Jennifer said, smiling at Jim. "That's even."

Now Jim knew for sure he'd lost the argument and certainly knew better than to try to reopen it.

At the store, Jennifer led Jim to the counter and waited for the salesman to assist them.

"Yes, ma'am," he said as he approached. "What can I do for you today?"

Jennifer pointed to the display case and said, "I want to see the ring set in the top row on the left side."

Unlocking the case, the salesman put his hand in and started to select the ring. "No," Jennifer said, "I mean, the one on my left."

"Fine, madam," the salesman said, picking up the blue velvet box and placing it on the top of the display. "I assume this is the one you want."

"Yes," Jennifer said as she took the engagement ring from the box.

Sliding it on her finger, she held her hand out to Jim and asked, "What do you think?"

"I think it is perfect," Jim said, wondering just how much this was going to cost him.

"We'll take it," Jennifer said, holding her hand in front of her eyes and admiring the ring.

"Excellent," the salesman said. "Shall I wrap it?"

"Can you size it here?" Jim asked.

"No, sir," came the answer, "but I can recommend an

excellent shop, and they will give you a 10 percent discount since the ring came from here."

"How far is it?" Jim asked.

"Just a couple of blocks," the salesman said as he picked up the box. "If you'd just follow me."

Jim followed him to the sales department and waited for the final bill. Looking at it, he just shook his head and pulled out his checkbook.

"Will the lady be wearing the ring, or should I put it in the box?" the salesman asked as he handed Jim the receipt.

"If you want your hand still attached to your arm, I wouldn't try to get that ring off her finger right now," Jim said, smiling as he turned to walk away.

Driving straight to the small jewelry and watch repair shop, Jim followed Jennifer in. The shop owner immediately came to them, asking what he could do to assist them.

Explaining that she'd just bought the ring and needed it sized, the owner nodded and pulled a tapered rod from beneath the counter. Also, taking out a large ring that held dozens of brass rings, he proceeded to eliminate several sizes until he found the one that fit Jennifer's finger.

Sliding Jennifer's new ring down the tapered shaft, he noted its size and said, "I need to take out a very small section of the band."

"It won't show, will it?" Jennifer asked, afraid that her perfect ring might have a flaw.

"No, ma'am," he assured her. "I've been doing this for many years now. If you can even see where I've made the adjustment, there'll be no charge."

Jennifer stood staring at the ring for a moment and then said, "Okay, when can we pick it up?"

"Would tomorrow morning be too late?" he asked, smiling at Jennifer.

"I suppose that'd be fine," Jennifer answered, unable to take her eyes off the ring.

Turning to Jim, the owner asked, "Is there a wedding band also that you need sized?"

Jim handed him the box and said, "Yes, sir, but there's no rush on this one."

The owner gave him a knowing look and said, smiling, "I'm sorry, sir, but I'm afraid that they'll *both* be ready by ten tomorrow."

CHAPTER 58

When Jim woke the next morning, Jennifer was in the kitchen making breakfast. Smelling the coffee, he climbed out of bed and slipped on a T-shirt. After using the bathroom, he walked in to find her talking on the phone to her mother.

Pouring a cup, Jim sat at the small table and listened to her describe the ring in every possible way you could describe a two-carat, princess-cut ring. Shaking his head, he got up and went into the living room to watch the news. Knowing that Jennifer would make life miserable if they weren't there to pick up her rings at ten o'clock, Jim flicked through the channels until something caught his eye.

There on the screen was the exact picture of the hut in Syria that he'd seen in New York. Listening closely, he heard the newscaster describe how warring factions of one tribe were blaming another tribe for the assassination of their Chief because he had been sympathetic to the interests of an outside group.

Looking at the robes and head wraps, Jim noticed that the tribe being blamed wore the exact same as he'd worn. Trying to remember what the man who had walked toward the hut was wearing, Jim could almost swear that he'd worn the same design as he and Rob.

Not knowing for sure if each tribe had distinguishing headwear, Jim could only rely on his past, where each side usually wore some sort of distinguishing clothing so that during a conflict, you could tell who was the bad guy and who was the good guy.

As the scene changed from Syria to US news, Jim lost interest and started thinking about questions he'd ask Gene later that evening.

Hearing Jennifer call from the kitchen, Jim carried the remaining tepid coffee in and dumped it into the sink.

Taking his seat at the table, Jennifer told him how excited her mother was to be coming back when they planned their engagement party and how she wanted to let Jim's mom help plan it.

Keeping his mouth shut, except to eat the eggs and bacon, Jim waited until Jennifer had finished all her planning and finally said, "Isn't this just a little overboard for a simple engagement? I mean, who, besides our families, will be attending this event?"

Seeing the look on her face, Jim continued, "Look, it's fine to have our folks out again. I really look forward to seeing them, and they get along so well. But besides them, we don't really know anyone besides a few people at the Squadron."

"That's who I really want," Jennifer explained. "For the last three years or so, I've just been 'Jim's girlfriend.' That's sort of been the way it is here, too. I want the other wives to know that I'm not just your 'girlfriend.' I want them to know that I'm as much a part of this Squadron as they are."

Jim thought about it for a minute and then said,

"You're right, honey. You *are* a part of this Squadron as much as any of them. If this shows them that you're as serious about my involvement as they are about their husbands, I'll stand behind you all the way."

Taking her hand, Jim said, "I never knew that you thought of yourself as less a part of my life just because we weren't married. I do know that sometimes military wives seem to assume things that aren't necessarily true, but I never dreamed that they'd look down on you."

As soon as breakfast was over, Jennifer asked Jim to clear the table while she got ready. "Ready for what?" Jim asked as he started putting the dishes in the sink to soak.

Jennifer smiled at him and answered, "To pick up my rings at ten o'clock, dummy."

"How could I have forgotten?" Jim teased, wiping the table. "Is this going to be a formal affair, or can I wear jeans to the 'fitting of the ring' ceremony?"

"Wear what you want," she teased, walking out of the room. "Everyone'll be looking at me and my ring anyway."

Jim had everything put away and the dishes in the dishwasher when Jennifer came back in. "Ready to go?" she asked.

Jim looked at the clock and said, "We still have two hours. It's only about a thirty-minute drive."

"I know," she told him, "but I need to do a little shopping before we get there."

"Don't you want to wait and wear your new ring while you're shopping?" Jim teased. "That'd give *soooo* many more people the opportunity to see it."

"Are you going with me or not?" Jennifer stated. "I'm leaving in ten minutes with or without you."

"I'm going," Jim said. "Just let me go brush my teeth."

At precisely ten o'clock, Jennifer pulled into the store's

parking lot and walked inside with Jim following.

"Good morning, ma'am," the owner said. "I guess you're here for your ring?"

"Yes, sir. I was hoping it would be done," Jennifer answered.

"Finished it about a half hour ago," he told her. "Wait just a second, and I'll get it."

Returning with the blue velvet box, he handed it to her, saying, "I hope you like the way it looks and fits."

Jennifer took the engagement ring out and examined it before slipping it on her finger.

Turning to Jim and holding her left hand out, she said, "It fits perfectly! What do you think, baby?"

Jim took her hand and told her, "It looks great."

"Please try on the wedding band also," the owner said.

Jennifer took the other ring out of the box and put in on. Smiling, she showed Jim and said, "It's perfect."

"Well," Jim said, "I guess that's been taken care of. Now, let's take care of the bill."

After they got back to the house, Jennifer put both rings back in the box and said, "I'm going to clean the house before General Barker gets here. Do you have anything you need to do?"

"Just a little mowing and cleanup in the yard," Jim answered.

An hour before Gene was due to arrive, Jim went in and told Jennifer he was going to take a shower and put on some clean clothes. After he finished, he checked his watch and still had half an hour. Walking into the kitchen, he set the new bottle of Jack Daniel's and two glasses on the counter.

Just as he made sure there were cold Cokes in the refrigerator, the phone rang. "Hello," Jim answered.

"Good afternoon, Jim," Gene said. "I'm running a little ahead of schedule. Would it be all right to come over a few minutes early?"

"Of course," Jim told him. "Any time's fine."

"Good," Gene said. "I'll be there in about ten minutes."

Hanging up the phone, Jim walked through the house one more time to make sure everything was put away and stopped by the bedroom to tell Jennifer that General Barker would be a little early.

Just as Jim was walking back into the living room, the doorbell rang.

"General Barker," Jim said as he opened the door, "please come in."

"Thanks," Gene said. "I hope my being early hasn't inconvenienced anyone."

"Not at all," Jim told him. "Would you care for a drink?"

"Naturally." Gene smiled. "But only if you'll have one with me."

"My pleasure," Jim said, leading Gene into the kitchen.

After Jim made the drinks and they toasted each other, Gene asked, "Could we step outside for a few minutes?"

"Sure," Jim said, opening the back door.

Once the door was closed, Gene said, "I assume you saw the picture on the news this morning and recognized it as the same as the one you got in New York."

"I did," Jim acknowledged. "I was just surprised to see the one in New York. I didn't expect to find out what the results of the mission were after our last discussion."

"Normally, you don't," Gene informed him. "But since this was your first mission, I thought it might be helpful if you got some information about what happened.

"This started off as a pure bribery mission. Up until the

day you got there, the company was almost certain that a deal had been made. Then word came back that the amount was inadequate, and the man demanded twice what had been agreed upon.

"That couldn't be accepted. When a sum is agreed upon, the company stands by its word and expects the other party to do as well. Now, if anybody else wants to 'renegotiate,' the example of how well that works has been provided."

Gene took a drink and went on, "The original plan was for you to take the package with the money, meet the recipient in the hut that night, and give it to him. After the 'renegotiation' attempt, the backup plan went into effect.

"The man you actually saw in the yard wasn't the man we'd negotiated with. He was part of the backup. His mission was only to identify the specific hut where the original man would be that evening."

Gene concluded, "His clothing was unique to another tribe in the area, as was yours. This was merely in case either of you were seen. We actually planned on one of you being seen, hopefully not you, but the intent was for the blame to be placed on the other tribe. And as you heard on the news, it went as planned."

"What about Rob? Was he supposed to have been seen?" Jim asked.

"Didn't matter," Gene answered. "All three of you were wearing almost identical clothing. As long as one of you was seen by anyone in that village, the blame would be shifted."

"Speaking of Rob," Jim said. "Is everybody with the company named Rob?"

"Are you named Rob?" Gene asked, smiling. "Am I?"

"I get your point," Jim said. "But I'd be willing to bet

that at any given time or place, I may be Rob."

"Misdirection, misidentification, misinformation. At the heart of any project, any tool that improves success or denies the opponent awareness of the program or the operation will be used," Gene said as he heard the back door open.

Turning, Gene smiled and said, "Jennifer, you look lovely. Is that an engagement ring? How beautiful!"

CHAPTER 59

For the next twelve years, Jim continued to work with Dark Water and fly with VMF 112. He and Jennifer were married one year after he proposed, and they stayed in the house they bought in Frisco.

During those twelve years, Jim was promoted to Major and then Lieutenant Colonel. His contact with General Barker remained sporadic, but every few months, Gene would contact him for both personal and operational reasons necessitated by Jim's involvement with Dark Water.

Jim traveled throughout the world, working with Dark Water during those years. After his initial mission, Jim's instincts that'd been originally honed in the jungles of Vietnam became one of his most valuable assets.

As he gained more and more experience in the field, he was occasionally brought in to evaluate the plans or techniques that would be employed on future missions.

Throughout the period, he returned to Langley numerous times to be trained on the newest technologies that could be employed in the field to incapacitate or eliminate designated targets. The explosion of new viruses, bacteria, or other chemical weapons that were virtually undetectable during any normal autopsy and could only be found if tested for that specific compound provided a wide-ranging arsenal for the type of operations used by Dark Water.

Training in mechanical methods was also extensively covered. Anything from a knife, garrote, silenced weapons, to blunt instruments was taught, and techniques were perfected. Over the years, Jim had earned the reputation of following orders without question, and the result was always as desired.

The number of aliases and the supporting documents that Jim employed were continually changed or eradicated. Each new assignment would incorporate his duties either as a military liaison, a contract advisor, or any of a multitude of identifications that fit the particular circumstance.

General Barker was invited as the guest of honor at Jim's promotion party to Lieutenant Colonel and to pin the silver oak leaves on Jim's shoulders. His unofficial reason for coming wasn't disclosed until the day after the party.

Gene arranged to come by Jim's house while Jennifer was at work. This gave them plenty of time to discuss what Gene considered the next phase in Jim's mentoring.

Jim answered the door as the bell rang precisely as Gene had said he would arrive. "General," Jim said as he opened the door, "please come in."

"Thanks, Jim," Gene said, following Jim into the now-familiar living room. "How's your head after last night's party?"

"Fine, sir," Jim said, motioning for Gene to take a seat.

After Gene sat down on the couch, Jim sat on the other end and asked, "What's on your mind these days?"

Gene took a second to compose his thoughts and then said, "You know that your flying days are numbered now that you're a Lieutenant Colonel."

"Yes, sir," Jim agreed. "They've been giving me more desk assignments, more trips to Quantico, and more paper shuffling than I ever thought possible."

"Welcome to the real world of field-grade officers," Gene said, laughing. "You wouldn't believe how much more of that you have to put up with as a General. Hell, I was lucky to get to fly twice a year. Even that stopped when I left 'Nam."

"I think I'd rather have stayed a Major and kept flying," Jim told him. "I'm just not cut out for office work."

"I know that," Gene agreed. "That was one of the reasons you were recruited for Dark Water. Granted, you could probably do well in the planning department or anywhere else they decided to use you. But it's your instinct for fieldwork that makes you exceptional."

Gene told him, "I knew that after your last mission as a Recon Marine back in 'Nam. If there was ever a situation that demanded natural instinct for survival, that was it."

Gene explained, "That specific trait is something that can't be taught. It's got to come from somewhere deep within a man. It can't be determined under normal circumstances, either. It really only becomes evident during periods of high stress, unknown situations, extreme danger, and a limited range of options."

Jim smiled and said, "Sir, with all due respect, I hope you never see me in another situation where you can judge my instincts. And that leads me to a question that has bothered me since that day you offered me a slot at MARCAD."

"What question is that, and why has it taken you so long to ask it if it's important?" Gene asked. "And it must be important to you for you to carry it so long."

Jim hesitated a few seconds and then looked Gene in the eyes and asked, "Why me?"

Gene leaned back and took a deep breath before answering, "Do you know anything about the original mission to 'Howard's Hill'?"

"Of course, I'd heard about it," Jim answered.

"What you probably never heard was that I lost a son on that mission," Gene said sadly.

"No, sir, I never knew," Jim said. "I'm sorry to hear that."

"Thanks, Jim." Gene continued. "The worst thing about the loss is that his body was never recovered. To this day, I don't know if he died on that hill or was captured. That's the agony of it. I could accept his death if I knew it to be certain."

Gene told him, "Even after all the POWs were supposedly released, there's still doubt. Every so often, there's information about a hidden camp somewhere, or something else happens that indicates there are still US troops being held over there. There's just no final closing of that chapter, it seems."

Gene paused for a minute and then said, "Another thing you never knew was that I had a nephew on that hill with you. My only sister's youngest son."

"No, sir, I didn't know that either," Jim said.

"As you well know, he died on that mission," Gene reminded him.

"Yes, sir, I remember it all too well," Jim told him.

"There was nothing anyone there could have done to save him," Gene said. "The only thing that I'm so very thankful for is that you brought all those boys out. If you hadn't done that or been killed yourself, I might've had another family forever, MIA, as would possibly several other families.

"Hell, if it'd been left up to me, I'd have given you the Medal of Honor for your actions. But having such a personal interest, I left that up to others who could view it without the prejudice that I had. The possible years of pain and anguish your actions spared my entire family made it impossible for me to even hint at any recommendations."

Gene said, smiling, "However, that didn't keep me from doing everything in my power to ensure you were rewarded. It's not just that you brought my nephew home. I knew that you were the right person for each step along your career."

"I appreciate everything you've done for me, sir," Jim said. "And I—"

"I don't need to be thanked for doing what was right for the Marine Corps, son," Gene admonished him. "If it hadn't been right for the Corps, I'd never have given you the chance. You've earned everything you've gotten."

Smiling slightly, he admitted, "Now, maybe I had a *little* influence on some of your assignments. But the Corps was the primary reason I helped you." Gene sat up straight and asked, "Do you think we should have a Jack and Coke now that we've bared our souls about the past?"

Jim stood and said, "Yes, sir. If you'd please follow me, I believe I happen to know where we can find just that exact thing." After Jim handed Gene a glass, he took his and said, "To the Corps."

"To the Corps," Gene said, tapping Jim's glass with his. "Now, let's go discuss the future."

Jim followed Gene back into the living room and waited for him to sit before he took his seat. "Whose future?" Jim asked.

Gene took a sip and answered, "Yours. As we've

agreed, your flying days are numbered, not to mention the fact that you've enough time with the Marine Reserves and your previous service to fulfill your obligations and earn your retirement."

"Yes, sir," Jim said, "I'm aware of that."

"So, with flying at a virtual standstill, no real need to go to the Squadron, and do things you don't want to do, what're your plans for the future?" Gene asked.

"I hadn't thought too much about that," Jim admitted.

"Airlines," Gene stated. "Have you given that any thought?"

"I think I'm a little past their hiring cutoff for old farts." Jim laughed.

"Not so," Gene informed him. "It just so happens that most of the major carriers are experiencing a shortage of qualified pilots. I know for a fact that American Airlines is hiring well-experienced pilots up to the age of fifty."

"I'm not sure, sir," Jim said. "I imagine that there are lots of pilots applying for those jobs. I'd think that they'd look more favorably on guys with heavy experience. You know, bomber pilots, cargo pilots, even tanker pilots."

"Again, not so," Gene reiterated. "I just happen to know that fighter pilots are given more priority than heavy drivers. Granted, they don't have the number of flying hours the cargo pilots have. But the hours a fighter pilot has is equal to at least ten times each hour a heavy puke has."

Gene admitted, "And I also just happen to have a friend or two over at American Airlines that might, *just might*, find a slot for an old F-4 driver."

"Let's say you're right," Jim said. "If I go to the airlines, that pretty much shuts down my ability to travel for Dark Water. Have you planned for that?"

"I believe a few years ago I told you that I planned for

everything," Gene said, smiling. "A plan, a backup plan, or a way out."

"I remember," Jim said, smiling.

"The plan is for you to work for another little organization that has close ties with both Black Water and Dark Water," Gene told him.

"What organization's that?" Jim asked.

"Muddy Water," Gene said. "You'll never have to leave the States again, and it ties in perfectly with an airline pilot's job."

CHAPTER 60

Jim discussed quitting the Marines when Jennifer came in that evening. He told her that his chances of getting a real flying job were negligible and promotion to full Colonel was possible with the right jobs for the next few years, but basically, he didn't want to do the things required to fill the squares, not for just a promotion.

He explained what he'd learned from General Barker, although he didn't credit Gene with the information. He attributed it to talk around the Squadron, and there *had* been that.

Neither did he reveal the true reasons Gene had picked him to follow the career path with the Marines. He absolutely never said a word about his "extracurricular" activities with Dark Water or the discussions about the as-yet-unknown Muddy Water.

Telling her that he was going to apply to interview with the airlines and that upon acceptance, he'd turn in his papers for retirement, Jim discussed the problems with the constant travel and days away from home.

Jennifer listened to all the good points and all the bad

points about being an airline pilot and how it could possibly affect their family. When Jim finished talking about his plans, she merely told him to do what he thought was right for him. She'd stand beside him regardless of the path he chose.

Although Jim's dad had died several years ago, he'd still occasionally sit out in the yard drinking a Jack and Coke, pretending his father was sitting there as they'd done so many times in the past, and Jim would tell him about his plans. Even though there were never any voices from the past, Jim felt as if he knew exactly what his father would have said had he been there.

Every time he had these "conversations" with his father, he'd ask himself the exact questions his father had always asked: Have you thought this through? Is this what you really want? How will this affect your family? Why haven't you already done what you know you're going to do?

In the end, Jim would smile, raise his glass to the memory of his father, and say, "You're right, Dad. It's time I got off my ass and did it."

For the next week, Jim sent résumés to every major carrier in the United States. During the next ten days, he had interviews set up with Delta, Northwest, American, TWA, United, and Continental. He never applied with Southwest because they required a 737-type rating, and Jim didn't possess one. Strangely, none of the airlines asked about his F-4-type rating. Guess they didn't care.

Buying a new suit and a pair of "accountant" shoes, dress shirts, and dark socks was necessary because he'd never needed them during his career with the Marines. He hadn't had a pair of civilian shoes since he was a kid, and those were long gone.

The interview process was fairly straightforward. The first stage was to take physical and drug tests, take the Minneapolis Multiple Personality Index (MMPI) test, fly a simulator occasionally, and talk to two or three various people from the company.

Northwest was one of the few that required you to talk to a psychiatrist and makeup stories about pictures he showed you. Delta seemed more interested in your family status, marital problems, or other issues that had nothing to do with flying the airplane.

United was more interested in your minority status than anything else. If you were female, black, Hispanic, American Indian, or any other minority, they wanted you.

American was much like the others for Phase 1. By the time Jim had his interview with them, he'd learned what to say and, more importantly, what not to say, and his chest had been scraped for the EKG so many times that rubbing a paper towel across the electrode points would bring blood. Having never taken drugs, Jim had no problems with the repeated urine tests, but the veins in his arms would retract at the sight of the needle they used to draw blood.

After each interview, Jim would fly home and wait for the letter that told him either when Phase 2 would start or, more frequently, thanks, but no thanks.

The call for Phase 2 with American came almost a week after he'd returned from the initial interview. Jim assured the human resources lady that he'd be there at the appointed time and told Jennifer the good news.

Phase 2 with American went well, and Jim drove home that evening feeling confident. The nagging thought that Gene had somehow ensured that he would be hired constantly bothered him. He appreciated Gene's help, but he wanted to be hired because of his abilities, not his connections.

Almost two weeks later, he received a letter notifying him of the final phase of the interview with American. Putting his new suit and shiny shoes back on, Jim drove over to the American Airlines Center just south of DFW. Walking in, he saw several people there for one of the interview phases. It was obvious once you knew what to look for.

Just about everyone there was busy filling out some form and dressed almost identical—gray pin-striped suit, red tie, light-blue or white shirt, brown wingtip shoes, a haircut that'd do an Air Force officer proud, and a smile that never left their faces.

Phase 3 was the easiest and most reasonable of all the others. Jim met with several pilots, and they questioned him about his flying career, his outside interests, his family, his background, and a host of random subjects. Finished, Jim thanked them and headed home. *Hell, that was nothing but a fucking personality/beauty contest,* Jim thought. *They just wanted to see if they could stand being trapped in the cockpit with me for hours on end for three or four days.*

That evening, Jim took Jennifer out to dinner to celebrate. "Just what are we celebrating?" she asked as they got ready to go.

"My last interview," Jim said as he snapped his starched Wrangler shirt closed.

"How do you know that was the last one?" Jennifer asked.

"Because if American doesn't hire me, I'll stay in the Marines until I'm sixty!" Jim replied. "I've had enough poking and prodding, enough questions that mean absolutely nothing, enough competing with incompetent idiots that only got there because of some ancestor. If I'm not good enough based on my merits, not my personality, I'll get a job as a Walmart greeter and live happily for the rest of my life!"

Almost a week later, a letter arrived from American, assigning a training class for Jim. He immediately called the phone number provided and accepted the job. Additionally, he wrote a quick acceptance letter, signed the enclosed forms, and sent them back as requested.

His scheduled class date was still six months away, but Jim decided to go ahead and put in his papers with the Squadron. That decision was made and enacted. If there were assignments with Dark Water, they could figure out the logistics of using him as a civilian.

The retirement party was less than a week away when Jim received a phone call from Gene.

"Congratulations," Gene said. "I hear you've been accepted with American Airlines!"

Smiling, Jim said, "Yes, sir. I managed to pull the wool over their eyes. They think I'm a nice, polite, easygoing, professional pilot who knows some good jokes."

"I doubt if that's the reason," Gene told him. "But whatever the reason, again, congratulations."

"Thanks," Jim said earnestly. "If it hadn't been for your help over the last almost twenty years, I'd be out sweeping sidewalks in Yuma after a sandstorm."

Gene laughed and said, "I doubt that also. But we need to set aside a day after you retire to further discuss that little issue we briefly talked about a month or so ago."

"At your convenience," Jim told him.

"How about the day after your retirement party?" Gene asked. "I just happen to be in Dallas that day."

"That'll work for me," Jim answered. "But we may need to do it later in the day. I plan on really enjoying my last day as a Marine."

"I understand," Gene told him. "Until then, Semper Fi"

CHAPTER 61

The day of Jim's retirement party started with Jennifer making her now famous Huevos Rancheros. After breakfast, Jim started clearing the table while Jennifer headed to the bathroom to get ready for her full day of hairdresser, nail salon, and whatever else she needed to do to prepare for the big night.

Jim finished the dishes and went into the bedroom to recheck his uniform for the evening. This'd probably be the last time he wore it, and he wanted to make sure everything was just right.

Jennifer left for her beauty appointments an hour later and left Jim sitting around the house. He'd just finished a BLT sandwich when the phone rang.

"Hello," Jim said as he sat the plate in the sink.

The caller from American Airlines asked if he'd be available to start training on the twenty-seventh. Thinking that was the day he was due to start, he told them that he'd planned on it as directed in the letter of acceptance he'd received earlier.

The caller then explained that the twenty-seventh date

was for this month, not over five months from now. There'd suddenly become an opening, and it was being offered to him.

Knowing how the seniority system worked with the airlines, a five-month head start could ensure a seniority number that was possibly four or five hundred ahead of where he would be if he didn't take the offered slot.

Telling the caller that he'd indeed make the training date, Jim hung up and looked at the calendar. That date was less than a week away. The tentative plans he'd made with Jennifer to go visit both his mother and her parents were now on hold.

Jim had taken the 727 engineer's written test months earlier in preparation for the interviews but remembered almost nothing about it. The only thing he did know was that the engineer had to know each system in depth. All the systems that he'd more or less taken for granted in the F-4 were now his responsibility.

When Jennifer came in several hours later with her hair styled, nails on fingers and toes painted to match, and a shopping bag full of who knew what, he told her the news.

Following her into the bedroom, he explained the advantages of starting early and how it might make the difference in later furloughs and advancement from the engineer's seat to First Officer and then Captain. She understood but was disappointed that she didn't get to go see her parents as they'd planned.

"That's no problem," Jim said as he watched her start arranging her clothes for the evening's party. "I'll be staying at the Howard Johnson's motel somewhere over by the airport for the training. You can go ahead and go see your parents whenever you want."

"Why do you have to stay in a motel?" Jennifer asked.

"Can't you stay home and drive to class?"

"I could," Jim answered, "but we go through the training as a class, and it helps to have other people studying with you. I couldn't do that at home. And sometimes the simulators are late at night, and it'd be easier if I were closer."

"How long will you be gone?" she asked.

"About three weeks," Jim said, "maybe longer if there are any problems." Jim added, "Another thing. The first year, I'm on probation. I wouldn't want to be late or miss a class because I got stuck in traffic or something. It just makes more sense for me to stay with the rest of my class."

"I understand," she said. "I knew that this airline thing was going to mean that you'd be gone a lot more time. I guess I just didn't think it'd happen this soon."

"It'll go fast," Jim assured her. "Plus, I'll probably have a day or two each week off, and I'll come home when I can. But my primary concern is learning the airplane so I can do my job."

Jim and Jennifer arrived at the party just a few minutes early and headed straight for the bar. The minute they walked in, Jim's Squadron mates began coming by congratulating him and trying to buy him a drink. Jennifer wound up with a group of wives or girlfriends while Jim mingled with the men.

It was almost an hour into the party when Lt. Col. Jerry "Bull" Winkle, the current Squadron Commander, began calling for everyone's attention. When the noise level dropped to where he could be heard, he began talking about how the Squadron and the Marines were going to miss Jim.

Then he allowed various members of the Squadron to come up and tell some story about what they'd seen Jim do, or something that'd happened to them on some deployment, or other humorous events.

After about fifteen or twenty men had told their tales, Bull Winkle came back up and told the crowd that there was a special guest at the party. As the crowd looked around to see who it might be, General Barker entered.

Stepping up beside Bull, Gene said, "Looks like I've found the place. I almost missed it because you Marines are so quiet and timid that I didn't hear a party going on."

After the laughter died, Gene continued. "I had a special reason for coming here tonight. Most of you don't know Jim the way I do. When I first met him, he was a member of a Marine Recon team that'd almost been annihilated. Matter of fact, he is the only surviving member of that team."

Gene said, smiling, "One of the very few benefits of being a General is that sometimes you get to influence the career of a good Marine. I saw in Jim the qualities that make Marine pilots the best in the world. So, with a little persuasion, I talked him into giving up the luxury of being an enlisted mud grunt Marine and joining the thankless job of driving jets around the world, destroying our enemies so the grunts won't have to leave the comfort of their luxurious field accommodations."

Again, after waiting for the clapping and laughter to die, he went on, "I must say that having followed Jim's career, I think I made at least one correct decision in the thirty-plus years I was with the Corps. Tonight proves me right. Lieutenant Colonel Lashley has made me proud of him, the units where he's been assigned, and the Corps."

Raising his drink, Gene concluded, "And I can announce tonight that Jim has been promoted to full Colonel. Congratulations, Colonel Lashley. I wish you the very best in your retirement. Semper Fi!"

CHAPTER 62

It was shortly after noon when Gene arrived at Jim's house. Sitting in the living room with fresh glasses of iced tea, Gene began telling Jim about the program known as Muddy Water.

"Are you aware that there are approximately seventy-five countries around the world with which we have diplomatic relations but no extradition agreements?" Gene asked.

"No, sir, I wasn't aware of that," Jim answered.

"In addition to those countries, there're five others with which we have no diplomatic relations, therefore, no extradition," Gene informed him.

"How does that matter?" Jim asked. "I understand that if we have a person in another country that's wanted for a crime here, we can't necessarily get him back for trial, but do we go there and take care of the problem?"

"Not necessarily," Gene continued. "Our biggest concern isn't with our people or their people that aren't in the States. Our concern is their people that are here."

"If a citizen of another country is here," Jim argued,

"we can still arrest them and take them to court, can't we?"

"Of course," Gene agreed. "The problem arises when they either can't be charged, we can't prove the charges, or they serve their sentence."

"There's lots of people roaming the streets that can't be charged due to lack of evidence or the method with which the evidence was gathered," Jim protested.

"That's also true," Gene said. "There'll always be those that slip through the cracks. That's just the way our justice system works."

"Why so much worry about the noncitizens?" Jim asked.

"First, let's have a quick history lesson," Gene said. "That may help you to understand part of the problem."

"After Castro took over, the first major influx of Cubans to come to the US were either middle- or upper-income class," he explained. "There was also a program in the early sixties called Operation Peter Pan that allowed thousands of children from Cuba to be brought in."

Gene added, "Then, in the eighties, another program called Mariel Boatlifts brought in thousands more. One problem that occurred simultaneously was that Castro slipped about twenty thousand men from Cuban prisons into the program."

Gene said, "Now, most of those were eventually returned over time due to some extensive negotiations, but not all. Then the issue of giving Cubans that arrive on our shores 'political asylum' has added more people that weren't exactly what we desired."

Gene asked, "Now the question becomes what to do about those 'repeat offenders' that we have in the system? Sometimes, there's no way to determine how the individual got here, and we can't send them back under the 'inadmissible' program we had for the prisoners we sent back."

He continued. "That leaves us with a problem. Assume that one of these people has been arrested several times. He serves his sentence and is set free. He continues his flaunting of our laws, knowing that most of the time, he won't be caught or escalate his activities."

Gene said, "We have to keep spending resources, tying up jail or prison assets, or dealing with the results of his activities. Our system of justice is handicapped for certain people like that."

"Can't the same be said for our citizens?" Jim asked.

"Certainly," Gene agreed. "The problem is more of a quantity of illegal activities that are attributed to any specific group. Certain communities are primarily composed of people of the same ethnic or geographic background."

He continued. "That's not necessarily a bad thing. There are communities of Italians, Greeks, Albanians, Russians, or any other ethnicity found around the world."

He explained. "The problem is really when an individual from a country where we can't deport him becomes too much of a pain. Within some of these communities, there's become a culture of lawlessness. Society can't afford the resources to solve the problem. That's where Muddy Water comes in."

"How do they 'solve' the problem?" Jim asked.

Gene smiled and said, "Pretty much the same way Dark Water operated."

"What you're implying is that we, the government, target individuals for termination outside of the justice system," Jim stated.

"Not necessarily," Gene said. "It may not be a 'termination.' But what we might do is guide the actions of one group against another."

Gene asked, "You remember the first operation that you performed for Dark Water?"

"Of course," Jim said.

"Our first attempt to resolve the issue wasn't termination. It was only after he failed to follow the agreement that other options were used," Gene said.

Gene continued. "Since he did that, the result was that the visit from another tribesman influenced his actions, and the fallout was against that tribe, not us. We always try to take the safest course of action. Very few investigations are done in cases of bribery or coercion. But assassination is dangerous. Society demands that the killer be caught.

"There are so many ways the assassin can be caught, and even with the remote possibility that it can be traced back to the organization, it's more of a last resort.

"As an example of a perfect operation, let's assume we have a drug problem in a certain area. We try to get the number one man of the drug ring but can never get enough evidence for a court of law. Possibly, the witness that would've proved our case disappears.

"Our first attempt to remove this person would be to use a rival organization that would benefit from his extinction. If we can orchestrate the scenario to let one bad guy eliminate another bad guy, we never have to get involved in the actual activity.

"One problem of doing that is the possibility of a large-scale turf war. We don't want that. Too many innocents suffer. So, what we attempt is more of a surgical means. We just want one specific individual removed. We want to do it in a way that either no one is ever caught, it looks like random violence, or, in some cases, the wrong person is caught and convicted. Sort of a two-birds-with-one-stone thing."

"How'd you do that?" Jim asked.

"Let's say a certain person is found dead," Gene told him. "Let's further say that there was known friction between that person and another. If we can orchestrate it right, the living person will be misidentified as the perpetrator."

He continued. "Evidence will be found at the scene that ties him to the murder. That person will have no provable alibi; there'll be enough cause for the police to investigate him, and with luck, he goes away."

"What if he doesn't?" Jim asked.

"Then we still took care of the first problem," Gene said. "But we may have to resolve the remaining issue at a later date."

"How do you expect an airline pilot to have the time and assets to do all this?" Jim asked. "Most layovers are barely long enough to get a quick meal, sleep, and be back at the airport."

"Again, going back to your first mission," Gene said, "everything was done before you arrived. Your only real reason for being there or here on a mission is to provide plausible denial for the team that sets it up. They load the gun. You pull the trigger while they are elsewhere."

"What if I come under suspicion?" Jim asked.

"That's where the preplanning is vital," Gene answered. "At the scene, if it's an assassination, there'll be evidence that leads to someone else."

"For argument's sake," Jim said, "let's say I fall under suspicion. It results in my arrest. What then?"

"First, if we do our jobs correctly, and we *always* do our jobs correctly, your name should never come up," Gene explained.

He continued. "You have a perfect explanation for being in every location. You're an airline pilot. The odds against any investigative branch tying your activities in several different locations to you are astronomical. Even should there be suspicion, trace DNA at the scene, hair samples, fibers that can't be traced to you will be discovered. Many methods of diversion exist.

Worst case, you fall under suspicion. You're arrested and charged. The organization takes care of any legal problems, and the attorneys they have are among the best at this sort of thing.

Should it ever get to trial, the company lawyers know exactly what evidence was left behind that may indicate your innocence. And if the prosecutor doesn't present it, it'll be brought out on defense. There'll be more than enough reasons for any jury or judge to dismiss the case or find you innocent due to reasonable doubt."

Gene concluded, "Again, that's the worst case. It's never happened, and there have been numerous missions. There's never been a hint of involvement by any of our personnel. Never."

"All right, I trust you," Jim finally said. "But I do have one question. Does the organization ever sanction someone for other than known or suspected criminal activity?"

Gene looked Jim in the eye and said, "There are other issues that involve national security that may need to be resolved. So, the truthful answer is yes."

CHAPTER 63

A month later, after Jim had finished the Flight Engineer course for the 727, he took his first flight. Everything he'd learned in the classroom and the simulator, except the emergency procedures, came into play over the course of the three days.

By the end of the third day and the sixth leg of the trip, Jim was becoming relaxed at his job and started watching the Captain and First Officer to see what their jobs entailed. Comparing it to his career of flying fighters in the Marines, their jobs seemed boring. It was not as boring as sitting at the Engineer's panel, but it was boring nonetheless.

For the next few months, Jim heard not a word from General Barker and was beginning to wonder if he'd ever be used for a mission here in the States. He still had some concerns about missions against citizens, or noncitizens, residing in the United States. But he also knew from watching the news or reading the papers that there were people out there who seemed immune to any type of justice.

Almost nine months after his first flight in the 727, an opening at DFW for an MD-80 pilot became available. Jim had put in his request for any First Officer slot at DFW the same day he graduated from the Flight Engineer's school.

Finally, the chance to be a pilot again had arrived. Granted, it wasn't a fighter, but it was still flying. He'd become so bored at the panel that he almost hated each trip. Preflight the airplane, maybe fifteen minutes before the flight, set systems up for the departure and adjust one or so after level off at cruise altitude and again during the descent. Maybe thirty minutes of actual activity during a two- or three-hour flight. It was boring beyond compare to a pilot who was used to having his hands on the controls every minute of a flight.

Finally finished with training at the Flight Academy, Jim was once again back on reserve. The major difference was that he actually enjoyed most aspects of his job now. He was still the junior crewmember, but the tradition of both pilots flying every other leg meant that he at least got to fly three times on each trip.

Six months later, Jim finally became senior enough again to hold a line bid and had a regular schedule. Not the most desirable one, of course, but still a known schedule for each month. The more senior First Officers all got their pick before Jim's choice of the few remaining lines of flying was assigned.

Now, almost a year since Jim had talked to Gene, he'd just gotten home from a three-day trip that had layovers in Chicago and Denver. He was emptying his suitcase and started repacking for the next trip four days from now when the phone rang.

"Hello," Jim answered, always expecting someone from the airlines to be calling about his upcoming trip or another pilot asking if he wanted to trade some future trip.

"How was the trip?" General Barker asked.

"Fine," Jim said. "There are places I'd rather have been for the night besides Chicago or Denver."

"The reason I called is that I happen to be in town and thought we'd have a little social visit if that's all right with you," Gene told him.

"Sure," Jim said. "Stop by anytime you'd like."

"How about in fifteen minutes?" Gene asked.

"Great. See you then," Jim said, hanging up.

Jim had just finished repacking his bag for his next trip when the doorbell rang. Opening the door, he said, "Hello, General. Please come in."

"So, how do you like your job?" Gene asked, walking into the living room. "Miss the Marines?"

Jim laughed and told him, "The job's all right, flying is boring, the Captain is occasionally an asshole, Flight Attendants are occasionally pretty, passengers are usually a pain in the ass, gate agents are unbearable, but overall, it's all right."

"Not as exciting as your former job?" Gene asked knowingly.

"No, but I have to admit that the accommodations are usually better," Jim answered. "And there's a toilet in the airplane, no more 'piddle packs,' meals are served, and we seldom sweat."

Jim added, "Oh yes, they pay better now that I'm finally off probation."

"At least you're still flying," Gene admitted. "Even if it is a bus with wings."

"So, I'm guessing that this is more than just a social visit," Jim told him.

"Yes, I think it's about time to get you back to work," Gene replied. "We have a slight problem in Atlanta that needs to be resolved. What are the odds of you getting a couple of Atlanta layovers next month?"

"I really don't know," Jim answered. "It just depends on how senior the trips go. All I can do is put it at the top of my bid list and wait to see if I get any."

"I understand," Gene said. "It'd help us if you'd do that. The situation isn't critical, and we have a couple of other options, but the situation needs to be resolved as soon as possible."

"I'll certainly try," Jim told him. "Can you discuss the problem?"

"A little," Gene said. "But it's still got some work to be done on our initial attempt at resolution."

"By initial attempt, I assume you mean something other than disposal of your problem?" Jim ventured.

"Exactly," Gene agreed. "Our first two tries didn't work too well. I think the individual believes that he can continue his 'operations' while he negotiates for a more favorable result."

"What sort of business is our problem in?" Jim asked.

"Corporate espionage," Gene answered. "And it involves some very high-tech issues."

"Can't the government shut him down?" Jim asked. "If he's selling classified information, there are lots of ways to stop that. There have been many instances where 'agents' of another country have persuaded our people to sell information, and we've managed to catch and incarcerate the offender."

"This is a very peculiar case," Gene explained. "The individual pieces of information are not classified. And it doesn't involve any government programs. The problem is when you take data from several sources and combine it, you have information that could possibly be used to harm our client."

"So this isn't a governmental problem," Jim deduced. "It's a private individual or corporation that's hired you to fix their problem."

"Yes," Gene said. "But there is also the possibility that if we don't resolve it now, it could impact a future contract that the military desperately needs."

"Can you be more specific about the problem?" Jim asked.

"Let's just say, for instance, the President of a large corporation that has had numerous contracts with the military comes under attack," Gene told him. "Let's just say that certain things in this President's background and/or current activities make him susceptible to blackmail."

He continued. "Now let's say that a group that's not sympathetic to the work of this company discovers things that, taken individually, mean nothing, maybe raise suspicion, but are hardly worth worrying about. However, if enough of these 'suspicious' acts were discovered and pieced together, it'd paint a picture that no one wants to see, especially since the whole picture is a falsehood, but it's hard to disprove."

"What's it going to take to eliminate these 'pieces'?" Jim asked.

"We've tried buying them," Gene answered. "The problem is that each time we make a purchase, more appear, not to mention that we've no assurances that each piece we buy hasn't been duplicated and can still be used."

Gene continued. "We're making one final, irrevocable offer. If it's successful, the only remaining issue is if there are duplicates. We have someone in place who will arrange the final bargaining meeting. He's in a position to demonstrate the folly of misrepresenting the facts if our person of interest fails in any regard to our arrangement.

Then, if necessary, we'll implement the final solution. Should we do that, it'll be done much as any other mission. Even if the people associated with our culprit can't prove our involvement, as they can't, or suspect some other organization or person, which we'll plan on, they'll certainly get the message."

"When do you expect this 'final offer'?" Jim asked.

"It'll take place within the next two or three weeks," Gene answered. "That means that sometime next month, we need to be prepared to respond as quickly as possible if the outcome isn't as we want. Delaying the final step reduces the impact of our actions on the others involved. We want that message to be loud and clear."

"Even if I don't get the Atlanta bids," Jim explained, "there are ways to trade trips with the pilot that is awarded those trips."

"Yes," Gene agreed. "I know about trip trades among both pilots and Flight Attendants. As soon as the bids are published, if you don't have an Atlanta layover, let me know. It may be possible to 'encourage' one of the trip holders to make the trade with you. I do know that occasionally, the Flight Attendants will offer a cash incentive for a trade. Maybe pilots do also.

But we'll look at that when the bids come out," Gene said as he stood. "Regardless of the bids, you'll be getting a call later this week."

Jim stood and followed Gene toward the door and asked, "The man calling wouldn't be named Rob, would he?"

Gene turned at the door, smiling, and answered, "Seems to be a lot of 'Robs' working for the company, doesn't there? Must be a coincidence."

"Right, sir," Jim said sarcastically. "It's amazing how

many coincidences there've been since I started working for the company."

"Sometimes things truly are as they seem," Gene said, walking toward his car. "I'll be in touch."

CHAPTER 64

Almost a week later, Jim received the call he'd been expecting for several days. "Can you meet me at the gas station on Main just west of Preston in fifteen minutes?" the caller asked.

"Sure," Jim answered. "How'll I recognize you?"

"I'll know you," the caller replied before hanging up.

Jim smiled as he stared at the phone. "Always the same," he said to the empty room. "Why do I keep asking?"

Jim hung up and checked his watch. Knowing he could make it in less than ten minutes, he debated getting there early and see if he could surprise the man he now thought of as Rob the one hundredth.

Pulling the 'Vette out of the garage, Jim half expected to see a surprise visitor sitting in the street. The handoff of the packages was not always as he was told, and he was no longer surprised when a mysterious car or person appeared.

Maneuvering through the almost empty streets and stop signs at nearly every corner, Jim pulled into the gas station a few minutes early. Parking beside the building, he looked around for other vehicles that might be the one bringing his assignment.

While he was sitting there, a couple of cars pulled in for gas, and the other cars parked there were finally driven away. Knowing he was at the right location, Jim wondered if something had happened that delayed the delivery. Just as he was about to get out of the car and go inside, a young man wearing a baseball cap and shirt with the station's logo came out and looked around.

Seeing Jim's 'Vette, he walked over, carrying a brown envelope. Stepping to the driver's window, the young man asked, "Are you Jim Lashley?"

"Yes," Jim replied.

"I was told to look for a 1962 Corvette and to give this to the driver," he said.

"Who gave you the package?" Jim asked, taking the large envelope from the man's hand.

"Some cute little redheaded lady," came the answer. "She said she was supposed to meet you here but couldn't stay. I told her I'd be glad to hold it until you got here."

"Okay, thanks," Jim told him. "Anything else?"

"No, sir," the kid answered. "She just gave me $20 and told me when you were supposed to be here. I saw you pull in and waited for you to come in, but when you didn't, I came out here."

"You did fine," Jim said, looking at the almost invisible but intact seal that would indicate the package had been opened. "Thanks again."

Jim laid the envelope in the passenger seat and pulled out to head home. As he turned right on Main Street, he saw a white Chevrolet sitting across the road with a woman behind the wheel. The glint on the car's windows made it impossible for him to see what she looked like, and her sunglasses made it even more difficult. But even so, she looked vaguely familiar.

As he passed the car, it started and headed in the opposite direction. Watching it in his rearview mirror, Jim thought, *At last, someone in the company that can't be a Rob. Maybe a Robin.*

Back at the house, Jim parked in the garage and carried the package into the house. Tossing it on the kitchen table, he made a glass of tea and sat down to see what information was in the envelope.

The first few sheets described the man who was obviously the target. It listed where he worked, his normal hours, where he lived, where he occasionally went if he didn't go straight home and other details about his life.

From the details about the number of times the man stopped by a bar before going home, where he usually stopped for gas, to where he ate breakfast, Jim knew that months of research and observation had gone into trying to predict this man's movements. There was even a summary of what the man drank and how many he usually had before leaving the bar.

Next, there were several pictures of him in various locations, including what appeared to be his house. Several were of him in either a bar or a restaurant in the company of other men or a lady Jim assumed to be his wife.

Following the pictures, there were several pages of information regarding the planning for Jim's assignment. There'd be a car, probably a rental, always at the hotel where American Airlines put the crews up for the night.

Inside the envelope, there was a set of keys that most likely belonged to the car. Details about what would be in the trunk varied with each night the car would be in the hotel's parking lot. Being a plain white Ford, it'd most likely go unnoticed among the other cars, but Jim figured it'd be removed except for when he was there.

That, of course, assumed that he was the only one assigned to this mission. He knew that there were other operatives because, in the past, he'd been canceled just prior to an assignment. Hearing that something had happened to his target just the day before and in exactly the same location and manner as his assignment made him realize that he wasn't the only one prepared to execute the mission.

That made perfect sense to Jim. Regardless of the planning, things could go wrong on his end. A flight got canceled, a sudden illness, or any number of things could prevent him from being able to fulfill the contract. With the expense and time involved in setting up the mission, the company would be foolish to depend solely on one operative. And as Jim had learned working with Dark Water for several years, this company wasn't foolish.

The final page detailed several options. These ranged from administering a drug that would induce almost immediate nausea and send him running for the restroom. Another that wouldn't take effect for hours, or one that would mimic a heart attack. Scenarios for differing periods and preferred approaches included time frames based on where the man was predicted to be almost every hour of every day.

These, along with more permanent solutions, were listed for informational purposes, and instructions for the exact method to be employed would be with the necessary equipment and materials in the trunk of the car on the night before the mission.

Almost an hour after Jim had finished studying the material and was preparing to burn it on the BBQ grill, the phone rang.

"Hello," Jim answered as he put the last of the pages

back into the envelope.

"Good afternoon," Gene told him. "How's it look for the Atlanta trip?"

"Not a problem," Jim answered. "I managed to get a vacation relief that has four nights in Atlanta. The First Officer that got the bid has vacation for the month, and I'll fly his trips."

"Great," Gene said. "I was hoping that you'd get to visit that lovely city. There's a lot of history there, and I know you'll enjoy any sightseeing you have time for."

"It looks like I'll have some time to visit some of the more interesting places," Jim said. "We don't get in until fairly late, but I'll have a couple of hours the next morning to do a little touring since we don't leave Atlanta until almost noon."

"That sounds reasonable," Gene told him. "Sometimes it's good to get up early and watch the sunrise. That way, you can get a lot done and still enjoy the rest of the day."

"Absolutely," Jim said. "My dad always said that sunrise is the best part of any day."

"How's the wife?" Gene asked.

"Jennifer's fine," Jim answered. "She likes her job, and her boss has been very good about letting her move her days off around to sort of match my flying schedule."

"That's good," Gene agreed. "As we've talked about before, one of the big problems of being married to someone in the airline business is that they're gone so much. If one of you is always working while the other is home and the other is working while you're home, it makes it tough on families."

"That's even more true of pilots that have Flight Attendants for wives," Jim said. "Unless they have matching schedules, they may never see each other more than two or three days a month."

"Well, there's no perfect job," Gene said. "There's always going to be periods of separation unless you're a farmer or rancher and your spouse stays home."

"Sometimes a little 'away' time is good for a relationship," Jim ventured. "But it can be carried too far. That's one of the reasons the divorce rate among airline pilots is so high."

"Of course, it has nothing to do with what those pilots are doing while they're away, does it?" Gene asked, laughing.

"Sometimes, maybe so," Jim acknowledged. "But the same thing was true in the military. Too much separation will exacerbate any problems that exist."

"Well, I've got to get back to work," Gene said, now knowing that Jim would be available for the Atlanta operation. "I'll let you know if I remember some of the places I used to enjoy visiting in Atlanta."

"I'd appreciate that," Jim told him. "It's always good to know a good place to go instead of wasting time wandering around, especially in a city as large as Atlanta."

CHAPTER 65

The next month, Jim started flying the trips he'd received as a result of the vacation relief line. The first day, they departed DFW and went to Mexico City (MEX). From there, they returned to DFW and cleared customs before continuing to La Guardia Airport (LGA) in New York.

Around noon the next day, they flew from LGA to ORD (Chicago) and sat for almost three hours before taking off for ATL (Atlanta). The last day of the trip was a single leg back to DFW, leaving ATL at one o'clock in the afternoon.

Jim had never met Capt. Randy Johnson before and didn't even know what he looked like. When Jim signed in for the flight on the first day, he saw that Captain Johnson had already signed in as well. Glancing around the room full of computer screens, Jim saw only one man with the four silver stripes denoting a Captain.

Walking over to where he was busy making computer entries, Jim asked, "Captain Johnson?"

"Yes, I'm Randy. You must be Jim Lashley," Randy said, sticking out his hand.

"Yes, sir, I'm Jim," Jim replied. "Good to meet you, sir."

Randy laughed quietly and said, "You must be military. None of the First Officers I've ever flown with have put so many 'sirs' in a single sentence unless they're military. Just call me Randy, please."

"Yes, sir," Jim said. "Is there anything special I need to know about this trip?"

"Not really," Randy told him. "Weather looks good all across our routes for the next three days. What branch of the service were you in?"

"Marines, sir," Jim answered.

"What'd you fly?" Randy asked as he pulled a length of paper from the printer. Tearing one section off, he signed it and tossed it in the basket beside the computer.

"F-4s, sir," Jim responded.

"Did you retire? You look old enough to have put in twenty years," Randy remarked.

"Reserves, sir," Jim told him. "I've got the twenty years, but don't draw retirement pay until I'm sixty."

Randy looked at him and asked, "Why didn't you join the airlines earlier? We have several pilots that still fly in the Reserves."

"When I was first eligible to get out after my commitment, I was just past the cutoff age for pilots," Jim explained.

"Ahhh, yes," Randy acknowledged. "That was thirty. How old were you?"

"Thirty-one, sir," Jim said.

"Too bad," Randy told him. "You'd be a Captain now if you'd joined American back then."

"That's all right," Jim said. "I enjoyed my time with the Reserves and have no regrets about the years I flew the

F-4."

"Vietnam?" Randy asked as he folded the sheets that he had ripped from the printer.

"Yes, sir. Three tours," Jim answered.

"All in the F-4?" Randy said as he cut one end of the computer paper off.

"No, sir. Two as an enlisted man and one as a pilot," Jim told him.

"That's rather rare, isn't it? Going from an enlisted man to being a pilot?" Randy asked as he took his hat from the counter.

Following Randy toward the door, Jim said, "Yes, sir, it is. But it's a rather long story, and I'd like to get out to the airplane a little early to do my preflight if that's all right with you."

"Sure," Randy said. "I'm going down to the gate to see if the Flight Attendants are already there. I'll meet you at the plane."

Jim turned and walked into the storage area, where all the pilots kept their kit bags filled with manuals, approach plates for every airport they used in the United States, Canada, and Mexico, and any personal items they needed to fly.

Taking his bag from the slot and his suitcase, Jim hurried toward the door that opened into the terminal. The gate for their departure was a short walk down the wide aisle, but it was congested with people coming or going to the gates located in the terminal. Dodging them and the courtesy carts carrying people, Jim managed to get to the gate just a few minutes behind Randy.

Nodding to the agent at the podium, Jim headed down the jet bridge and onto the airplane. Randy was standing in the aisle in the first-class section, talking to the three Flight

Attendants, as Jim put his suitcase in the forward closet. Tossing his kit bag and hat onto the right-hand seat, Jim sat in the Captain's seat and began checking all the circuit breakers and switches on the overhead panel.

After ensuring each system was operating normally and each switch was in the correct position, Jim stood and put his hat back on. Taking his checklist and a flashlight, he left the cockpit.

Exiting the jet bridge door, he climbed down the stairs and began his walk-around to examine the exterior of the plane. Inspecting all the items on his checklist, Jim went forward, around the nose, back down to the right-wing, around it back to the tail, and then back up the left side.

Having made sure everything was as it should be, he climbed back up the stairs and into the jet bridge. Taking off his cap as he entered, he looked at the Flight Attendant standing in the forward galley and said, "Hi, I'm Jim Lashley."

"Hi, Jim," she replied. "I'm Amber Bell. Would you like something to drink?"

"Dr Pepper, please," Jim said, stepping into the cockpit.

Hanging his hat on the wall beside the cockpit door, Jim stuck his flashlight back in the kit bag and moved it into the space between his seat and the side of the airplane.

"Everything all right?" Randy asked as he was setting all his instruments for the takeoff and departure.

"Yes, sir," Jim said as he pulled his earpiece and microphone from the plastic soap holder he used to carry it.

"Dr Pepper?" Amber said, stepping into the cockpit.

"Thank you," Jim said, turning to his left and taking the can and glass of ice.

"Anything for you, Randy?" she asked before leaving.

"Not unless you happen to have a couple of those Jack Daniel's minis handy," Randy joked.

"Later," Amber laughed as she returned to the galley.

Randy turned in his seat and asked, "How long have you been on the 80?"

"Almost a year," Jim answered.

"Here's my only brief, and you only get it once," Randy told him. "When it's your leg to fly, you make any decisions necessary. If you want my opinion, ask for it. I'd appreciate it if you'd tell me what you're about to do ahead of time, such as changing altitudes, directions around a buildup, or anything like that."

Randy continued. "If I disagree, we'll talk about it. The bottom line is I'm the Captain, and I get the final decision. Now, with your military experience, I don't expect to have many issues with your flying, and I expect you to voice any concerns over something I may be deciding to do."

Randy concluded, "Also, I'm just like any other airline Captain. I may be distracted by talking to the passengers, on the intercom with the Flight Attendants, or bored numb. If you see something I need to be aware of, let me know, even if it means waking me."

"Yes, sir," Jim said.

"One final thing," Randy said, smiling. "If there's a meal on your leg, you get the first choice of the chicken or the cow. But regardless of whose leg it is, I get the first choice of the Flight Attendants on the layover."

"That's not a problem, sir," Jim said. "I'm married, and you can have all the Flight Attendants if you want."

"How long have you been married?" Randy asked.

"About thirteen years," Jim told him.

"And how long have you been with American?" Randy asked, grinning.

"Almost two years," Jim said.

"Wait 'til you've been with American for ten years or so," Randy advised. "If you've still got the same wife you came with, you're the rare one."

When the agent finally stuck her head into the cockpit and told Randy that all the passengers were on board, he thanked her and listened to the ground man on the interphone clear them for engine start.

Shutting the cockpit door, Randy told Jim, "Let's start number one."

After both engines were running, Jim called for power back clearance and watched the guide man in front of the airplane give the hand signals. Once they had gone back several feet, the guide man saluted and gave them directions for their turn as Jim requested clearance from ramp control to leave the area.

Nearing the taxiway, Jim heard ground control give them clearance to taxi to the west side of the airport and began running the takeoff checklist as Randy followed the taxiway to the assigned runway.

After takeoff, Jim ran the radios while Randy flew south toward Mexico City. With the plane on autopilot, he and Randy finished the conversation about Jim's time in Vietnam, and each gave a brief recount of their flying careers.

For the next two days, the scene repeated itself at each airport as they took off and landed each leg of the trip. The second day ended at ATL, and Jim knew that he needed to check the car that should be waiting for him in the hotel parking lot.

After making sure the rest of the crew was in their rooms, Jim pulled on a pair of Levi's, a black T-shirt, and a pair of dark tennis shoes. Taking the key to the car from his suitcase, he went downstairs and out to the parking lot. After a couple of minutes of looking around, he spotted the white Ford parked at the end of the first row.

Seeing no one around, Jim opened the trunk and saw nothing but a letter-sized envelope. Opening it, Jim saw that the operation had been postponed for now. Shutting the trunk, Jim carried the letter back to his room and tore it into small pieces before flushing it down the toilet.

Well, I'll at least get a good night's sleep tonight, Jim thought as he undressed. *Maybe next week.*

CHAPTER 66

Jim had four days off after returning home. Although he wondered what had happened to postpone his assignment, he didn't expect to hear anything from the company. Since his first assignment in Syria, he'd been provided with scant information regarding the outcome of any of his missions.

Occasionally, like the TV news story, he'd learn what had been the result. Other times, he knew the result because he'd left the target dead. Why the company needed the permanent solution in certain cases was never divulged, and he knew better than to raise any questions.

In the rare instance when the company needed a debrief, he'd flown to Quantico and discussed his mission. This was generally because of his making a "field decision" that varied substantially from the original plan. Even then, he was never informed as to why certain things had been done.

The only time he came under criticism was when he terminated a target that was scheduled for mere incapacitation. When he explained that it became necessary to eliminate the target because there'd been an unknown weapon hidden in the man's clothing and he felt his own life threatened, the company acknowledged that the threat had made the actions necessary.

When Jim returned to DFW to begin his second three-day trip, he saw Randy in Operations as he arrived. "Hey, Randy," Jim said as he set his suitcase on the floor. "How was your time off?"

Randy looked up from the computer printout and said, "Pretty much the usual. Do a little lawn work, laundry, grocery shopping, try to find my next future ex-wife, you know, standard days off."

"Any luck in the 'future ex' department?" Jim asked as he looked at the signed copy of the flight plan.

"Nope," Randy admitted. "I think my interview process eliminates the majority of them before it gets too serious."

Jim smiled and asked, "What's your interview process?"

"It's rather detailed," Randy said as he trimmed the remaining printout. "I'll tell you about it on the way to Mexico City."

"Sounds interesting," Jim said as he walked toward the kit bag storage area. "Are you heading to the gate now?"

"Yeah," Randy answered as he followed Jim into the storage area to get his bag and suitcase. "Might as well."

Going back to the same gate as the previous trip, Jim and Randy tread their way through the crowd until Randy spotted another Captain talking to one of the gate agents.

"I gotta go talk to that guy," Randy said, indicating the other Captain. "I'll see you at the plane."

Jim continued down to the departure gate and opened the door to the jet bridge. Just as he was about to close it, he heard Amber call out, asking him to hold the door.

As she approached, Jim smiled and said, "Good morning, Amber."

"Good morning, Jim," she said, walking onto the jet bridge. "Thanks for holding the door."

"No problem," Jim said, following her down to the plane.

"Want me to make some coffee?" Amber asked as she stepped onto the airplane.

"Not for me," Jim said as he put his suitcase in the closet. "But a Dr Pepper would be great."

"Coming right up," Amber told him as she put her suitcase away.

Jim put his kit bag in the right seat and began his preflight of the cockpit. The logbook had no entries that concerned him, and all the systems checked out normally.

Grabbing his hat and flashlight, he was just leaving the plane when he saw Randy coming down the jet bridge.

"How about I do the walk-around this morning?" Randy said as he approached and handed Jim the paperwork for the flight. "It's been a while since I've done one, and since it isn't raining, too hot, or too cold, I need to refresh my memory of what the outside of the plane looks like."

"Fine with me," Jim said as he handed Randy his flashlight and returned to the plane. "I'll get the cockpit set up while you're doing my job."

For the next two days, each flight went smoothly as Jim and Randy had developed a high level of trust in each other's knowledge and skills. The easy rapport made flying together enjoyable.

Arriving in ATL at the end of the second day, they said their good nights and headed for their rooms, the same ones that they had used last week. Jim hung up his uniform and put on his jeans and a black T-shirt to go down and check the trunk of the car.

Parked one row further back, Jim spotted it quickly and opened the trunk. Inside was a walking cane, an Atlanta Braves ball cap, a pair of horn-rimmed glasses, and a large manila envelope. Taking them with him, he headed back to his room to see what the company had planned for him.

In his room, Jim tossed the cane, ball cap, and glasses on the bed and then opened the envelope. The first sheet he removed described where and when he was to make contact with the target.

Jim was to be in front of the restaurant where the target occasionally had breakfast at seven thirty the next morning. A meeting between a member of the negotiating team and the target had been arranged, and Jim was to wait until the meeting was over before taking any action.

If the two men left the restaurant together, Jim was to return to the hotel and put the cane, glasses, and cap back in the car.

If the man left the restaurant alone, Jim was to follow him to the corner of the block and step close enough to touch him with the cane while waiting for the "walk" signal at the crosswalk or, if not stopped, to use the cane as the man stepped off the curb.

Reading the instructions for the cane, Jim picked it up and noticed a strip of clear tape at the end where the tip was affixed to the wooden shaft. The instructions stated that the tape was to be left in place until getting out of the car at the restaurant.

Further instructions for the operation of the cane described how the small trigger in the cane's handle would retract the metal tip and expose a small needle once the tape was removed. Jim was to walk with the cane until ready to use it, lift it slightly off the ground, pull the trigger, exposing the needle, and poke the back of the target's calf.

Jim didn't know what was going to be injected but remembered the old story about the assassination of Georgi Markov using an umbrella containing a ricin pellet. According to the story, the poison was injected into the back of Georgi's leg, and he died three days later.

Jim cautiously removed the tape and slowly pulled the trigger to see how much pressure would be required. Only a slight pull was needed, and Jim looked at the one-half-inch long needle slide through the tiny hole in the metal tip as it slid up the wooden shaft.

Relaxing the trigger, the tip went back down to hide the needle and lock it in place so that any pressure exerted on the cane wouldn't damage the hidden needle. Replacing the tape around the tip, Jim tried to pull the trigger again, but the tape prevented the tip from retracting.

Walking around the room with the cane for assistance a few times, Jim got comfortable with matching the cane touching the ground as his right foot came down. Satisfied that it would appear normal, he put the cane back on the bed and put on the ball cap and glasses.

The large black rims of the glasses and the thickness of the lens made Jim's eyes almost invisible except from straight on. With the ball cap on his head and the glasses on, he would be hard to identify unless someone spent several seconds studying his face.

Knowing that anyone who happened to see him wouldn't pay enough attention to really get a good look at him, Jim wasn't too worried about either the target or some bystander remembering his description.

Setting everything aside, Jim set his alarm for five the next morning, took a quick shower, and went to bed. Lying there, he tried to envision just how the mission would go.

Assuming that whatever was being injected wouldn't cause an immediate reaction, Jim only worried about the man's behavior from the small sting the needle would undoubtedly induce.

Up before the alarm went off, Jim put on his jeans and the white T-shirt he'd worn the previous day under his white uniform shirt. Combined with the sneakers, ball cap, and glasses, he shouldn't stand out from the people on the street.

As Jim left the room, he made sure the "Do Not Disturb" sign was on the knob. Taking the stairs to avoid any chance of meeting in the elevator, Jim hurried to the car.

The short drive to the restaurant got him there almost fifteen minutes early. Jim pulled the brim of the cap low, put the glasses on, stepped from the car, and pulled the tape from the cane. Walking past the restaurant, he looked in and saw his target sitting at a table with another man. Positively identifying him, Jim went on to the corner and turned back.

Not sure which way the man would go, Jim walked back to a closed store adjacent to the restaurant and pretended to be looking at the clothing inside. The few pedestrians on the street paid no attention to him, and Jim began to feel comfortable with the plan.

With only a couple of minutes to go, Jim eased his way toward the restaurant door. As he looked in the window, he saw his target stand and head for the cashier. As the tension mounted in anticipation, Jim glanced both ways along the sidewalk to see if anything might cause him a problem.

Standing to where he could watch the man, Jim barely noticed when the man's breakfast companion joined him at the cashier. As the two headed for the door together, Jim turned away and walked slowly toward the corner. Glancing in the darkened window of the store where he'd previously stood, he saw that they weren't behind him.

Turning back toward the restaurant and where he'd parked the car, Jim saw them walking away together. Pausing for a few more seconds, Jim waited until they were well past his car before he followed them.

Jim drove back to the hotel, parked the car, and put the cane, glasses, and ball cap back in the trunk before heading up to his room. The adrenaline that had built up in his system was now leaving. All of a sudden, he just wanted to shower and try to get a couple more hours of sleep.

CHAPTER 67

Jim had been home for two days when the phone rang just before noon. Answering it, Jim was mildly surprised to hear Gene's voice.

"Doing anything this afternoon?" Gene asked.

"Not much, nothing that can't be put off until tomorrow," Jim answered. "What can I do for you?"

"Just thought I'd stop by and chat," Gene told him.

"Sure," Jim replied. "What time?"

"How about in thirty minutes?" Gene asked.

"That'd be fine," Jim told him. "I'll be here."

Jim hung up the phone and wondered what General Barker wanted to talk about. Hoping that Gene would shed some light on the Atlanta operation, Jim walked around the house, making sure it was relatively clean and presentable.

Answering the doorbell, Jim invited Gene in and followed him into the living room.

After they both sat down, Gene asked, "Are you a little curious about the Atlanta thing?"

"Of course," Jim told him. "But like you've told me before, it's not necessary for me to know the details of any assignment."

"That's true," Gene said. "But in this case, I think you should know why things are going as they are, especially since we've postponed once and aborted the other time."

"That's really none of my concern," Jim argued. "I just follow orders, same as in the Marines."

"I understand," Gene countered. "That's one of the reasons we usually select former military men and women for our programs. With very few exceptions, they all follow orders without questioning why."

"That's what we're trained to do," Jim agreed.

"But in certain circumstances, I believe it's important to provide additional information to the people sent into the field," Gene explained. "That's especially true in this case."

Gene continued. "The first time, we needed to postpone because the person we were using to contact our target was unable to complete the assignment. The target failed to make it to the meeting site. We later determined that the 'no show' had been unavoidable, and another meeting was arranged.

"The second time, our negotiator decided that sufficient progress was being made to abort your part in the operation. It was his call as to whether or not to try again at a less dramatic solution or to let you continue. I'm always in favor of the peaceful solution, as is the entire company, in situations here in the States."

"I agree," Jim said, "especially since this seems to be more or less a civil issue."

"Yes, to an extent," Gene said. "But as I told you before, it potentially has disastrous consequences affecting military contracts. It's only after attempting to resolve it by less dramatic means, evaluating what the real potential for damages to our customer is, and how the possible fallout from the operation will affect the overall situation that we resort to the most dramatic solution.

I believe you're scheduled to be back in Atlanta four days from now. With luck, the situation will be resolved, and no further actions on your part will be required," Gene then informed him, "In case you're wondering, your compensation package is credited with each assignment regardless of the actions directed. You completed each assignment as directed, and that's the basis of the pay. If it takes all four trips to resolve the problem, you'll be credited with four missions. If this next trip solves the problem, you'll have three completed assignments.

However, if you receive notification that a solution's been reached before you get directions in Atlanta, you're no longer on assignment for the company. At that point, you're just flying your normal line as you had bid."

"I understand, sir," Jim told him. "If a solution's reached after I leave here or after I've taken off, how'll I know if the mission's been terminated?"

Gene smiled and answered, "That's not a problem. We can make contact anywhere or anytime during your flights, sort of like when we contacted you after the Syrian operation."

Gene continued. "If I were you, I wouldn't even be surprised if the company has the capability to contact you while you're in the air."

The conversation turned from operations to family issues and normal topics regarding the news, the economy, and the weather.

After almost an hour of talking, Gene rose and shook Jim's hand, saying, "It's always a pleasure visiting with you, Jim. I've enjoyed knowing you these past years and hope we can always stay in touch."

"I hope so also," Jim told him.

Thinking about what Gene had just said, Jim paused and asked, "Are you implying that you may be leaving the company?"

Gene laughed and said, "No, I'm not quite ready to buy my rocking chair. I know I will someday. I was just saying that even after I do retire from this job, I hope we can still visit on a purely social basis."

Jim relaxed and told him, "Of course, you're always welcome here, official or not."

Two days later, Jim was back at DFW for the trip to start. After Gene's discussion about how the company could abort the mission at any point, Jim watched for anyone who might be bringing him a message. After looking around at all the possibilities for any passenger, crew member, or even someone behind the counter at any of the many kiosks in the airport, he realized that he'd probably never spot the messenger.

The trip to MEX and back to DFW went without incident, and the only delay was getting through customs. When Jim presented his passport, the customs agent spent several minutes on the computer while Jim stood watching.

About to decide that the agent was the messenger, Jim was mildly surprised when his passport was returned.

"What was the problem?" Jim asked as he put his stamped passport in his jacket pocket.

"Your name, sir," the agent said. "It matches one that's on our watch list."

"Is that a common occurrence?" Jim asked.

"More than you'd think," the agent said, "especially if it's a common name, like Brown, Smith, or Jones."

"How do you determine if you've got one of those wanted people or just a coincidence?" Jim asked.

"Sometimes it's quick," the agent explained. "Maybe a middle name, obvious age differences, gender, or in your case, the man we're watching for is black."

"Okay, thanks," Jim said as he picked up his suitcase and kit bag. "I appreciate the information. Maybe they'll take my name off the list before I come back through here next week."

Jim met Randy and the Flight Attendants at the gate for their flight to LGA. "Problems?" Randy asked as Jim walked up.

"Not really," Jim answered. "It seems that there's someone out there with my name that the customs people would like to talk to."

"You'd think that the airlines would provide customs with a list of all their employees to make things like that unnecessary," Randy remarked as they watched the last passenger from the inbound flight leave the jet bridge.

Heading down to the airplane, Randy stopped and talked to the Captain who had brought the flight in. Hearing that there were no write-ups in the book, Randy thanked him and came to the cockpit.

After putting his kit bag in its holder, Randy told Jim he was going back up to get the paperwork. Nodding, Jim finished his preflight of the cockpit and headed out to do the exterior walk-around.

By now, he had quit looking for or expecting someone to approach him about canceling the operation in Atlanta. Back in the plane, Jim took the Dr Pepper Amber offered and sat in one of the first-class seats to wait for Randy to return.

After spending the night in New York, they headed to ORD and their sit time before heading to ATL.

"You remember telling me about your interview

process for whom you date?" Jim asked as they sat in the crew room in Chicago.

"Oh yes," Randy answered. "I forgot that I was going to tell you about that."

"We've got almost three hours. Think that's enough time?" Jim asked.

"Plenty," Randy told him. "It's structured sort of like the interview process for the airlines. Phase 1 is that they have to come home with me, enjoy the night, and be gone when I get up in the morning."

He continued. "Phase 2, assuming they've passed phase 1, is basically the same except that when I get up, they're gone, and there's a fresh pot of coffee made."

Jim sat shaking his head and smiling as Randy went on, "Phase 3 is they spend the night, have coffee and breakfast ready for me when I get up, and then when I leave after eating, they clean the house and be gone when I get home."

"How many have ever passed phase 2?" Jim asked, laughing.

"None," Randy admitted.

They had just gotten their bags and walked to the gate for the flight to Atlanta when Jim saw Jewell talking to the gate agent. When she saw Jim approach, she nodded to the agent and walked up to Jim.

"Hey, Gyrene," she said, smiling.

"Hi, Jewell," Jim said. "Long time no see."

"I know," she replied. "It's a crazy business. You may fly with someone for a month, see them all the time, and not see them again for several years. I noticed your name on the crew list and wondered if it was you or another Jim Lashley."

"It's been a couple of years," Jim acknowledged. "Are you going with us to Atlanta?"

"Yep," she said. "I've got to go down there and work a flight back here tomorrow. Sitting reserve sucks, but at least that'll be two easy days."

"Before I forget," Jewell said, reaching into her purse, "a man named Rob gave me this to give to you."

Taking the envelope from Jewell, Jim looked at her, wondering if she was part of the organization or just someone the company knew would be on the flight.

"Thanks," Jim said. "Guess I'll see you on board."

Jim stuck the envelope in his jacket pocket and headed down the jet bridge. After putting everything away, he slipped into the forward lavatory and opened the envelope.

"Mission postponed" was the only information. Jim tore it up and watched it disappear in the swirling blue water of the toilet.

CHAPTER 68

The flight to Atlanta and then to DFW the next day went as scheduled. Jim still wondered if Jewell's sudden appearance had been a mere coincidence. They hadn't had a chance to talk during the flight since she'd been given a seat back in coach for the deadhead flight from ORD to ATL, and Jim didn't want to ask any questions about "Rob" anyway.

There was no contact with Gene or any other member of the organization during the four days Jim had off. Again, he worked around the house, washed and waxed the cars, and went out to dinner with Jennifer a couple of times.

The day Jim was due to start the last trip of the month, he stayed in the house, anticipating a call regarding the Atlanta assignment, but it never came. Driving to the airport, he still wondered about what would be awaiting him when they got to Atlanta.

The first day was routine, with clear skies and smooth air on each flight. After arriving in New York, the crew went to the hotel for the night. Jim and Randy met in the lobby and had a couple of beers and a sandwich at an Irish pub just a few blocks from where they were staying.

The rules regarding drinking on layover were well-known and well-disregarded. There was to be absolutely no drinking from sign-in until the trip was over; however, most crews would wait for the Captain to make the call about evening alcohol.

If he suggested a "debrief" or "afternoon tea," the rest of the crew knew that it would be all right to have a beverage or two. The main concern was to find a bar or pub away from the hotel since a lot of airline crews stayed there. No one wanted to be seen in the hotel bar.

There'd been rumors of disgruntled crewmembers reporting drinking of other crewmembers, especially when there was a grudge between them because of love gone wrong or learning that their current romantic interest was sharing his or her interest with another.

The safest thing to do was to get away from the hotel and use discretion when breaking one of American Airline's rules. Of all the infractions that could lead to termination, this one was near the top. Drinking on the job or being drunk on duty was, of course, much more serious.

The next morning, when they arrived back at LGA, Jim headed for the airplane to do the preflight while Randy pulled the paperwork. When Jim got to the airplane, he noticed a man wearing a mechanic's uniform but an unusual ball cap going out of the door on the jet bridge.

This wasn't abnormal since a mechanic would meet the airplane if the previous Captain had made a logbook entry or checked the book before the first day's flight to ensure it was ready to go.

After completing the cockpit check, Jim started to head outside when he noticed an envelope bearing his name lying on the panel to the right of his seat. Glancing at the back of the plane, he made sure there was no one around.

Jim quickly slipped into the lavatory and checked the seal of the envelope before opening it. The single sheet inside merely said that the Atlanta mission was on, but there may be an additional agent. The agent, should one be involved, would be identified by a distinctive shoulder bag. The bag would be carried on the left shoulder and have a lightning bolt embroidered on the side.

Everything else would be as previously instructed, but this agent was there as a distraction if necessary. He wasn't to make contact with the agent but to make sure he or she was aware of when he was about to execute his assignment.

Jim tore everything into small pieces and flushed it down the toilet as before. Throughout his exterior inspection, he wondered just what this additional agent would do as a distraction on the mission.

An hour later, when all the passengers had been boarded, and the gate agent had informed them that she was closing the forward door, Randy told Jim to start the "before engine start" checklist.

With the crew chief on the intercom, Randy started the first engine. Amber stuck her head into the door and said the cabin was ready. After the second engine was running, Jim called for power back clearance and glanced out of his side window. A man with the standard mechanic's uniform was standing just beneath the window, wearing an Atlanta Braves ball cap. Looking directly at Jim, the man nodded and turned away while removing the ball cap. Jim couldn't be positive, but he was pretty sure it was the mechanic he'd seen leaving the plane as he'd walked down the jet bridge.

Arriving at ORD, Jim and Randy sat in the crew room as before, waiting for the leg to ATL. The three hours passed slowly for Jim as he anticipated getting to ATL and checking what his instructions would be. The note he'd gotten back in

LGA had said everything would be as previously instructed, but the possibility of another person's involvement made him consider how he'd incorporate them into his plan.

That evening in Atlanta, Jim quickly changed into his jeans and T-shirt to get whatever information would be in the trunk of the car. Noting the cane, ball cap, and glasses as before, he took the manila envelope up to his room.

The repeat of the instructions regarding the use of the cane and other details held nothing new. The major change was the time. It'd changed from seven-thirty to seven o'clock, and the target was to be approached as he entered the restaurant. Having seen the direction the man had taken on the last mission, Jim assumed that he would be arriving from that direction toward the restaurant.

The sidewalks hadn't been crowded the last time, and thirty minutes earlier would probably mean fewer pedestrians; Jim decided that to be seen looking in the window as he'd done before would be too obvious. The thought of being in the restaurant when the target entered was quickly dismissed. The best option appeared to be parking where he had previously but waiting in the car until he saw the target approaching.

The next morning, Jim was awake almost an hour before he needed to leave for the restaurant. The adrenaline was starting to build, and he knew he couldn't sleep anymore.

Using the small coffee maker in the room, Jim started it and stepped into the shower. After drying off, he poured a cup and sat down to watch the news until it was time to go. He didn't want to get there too early. A lone man sitting in a car more than a few minutes would most certainly draw unnecessary attention.

Dressed in his Levi's and white T-shirt, Jim left the

room. As before, he checked to make sure the door was locked, and the "Do Not Disturb" sign was hung on the knob. Seeing no one in the corridor, he went down the stairs and out through the lobby. The only one there was the clerk at the desk, and she wasn't paying attention as he walked by.

Opening the trunk, Jim put the ball cap on, picked up the cane and glasses, and unlocked the driver's door. Laying the cane and glasses on the seat, he started the car and headed for the restaurant. With any luck regarding traffic, he figured he'd have no more than three minutes to wait in the car after he arrived.

This time, as he neared the spot where he wanted to be parked, Jim noticed a black sedan parked on the street that intersected the street he was on. Being around the corner from where he'd be, Jim knew that he wouldn't be visible to whoever was in the car until they turned the corner and headed toward him.

He wasn't sure, but there appeared to have been only one person in the car. There hadn't been enough light, and the glimpse had been too short to know if that'd been his target or someone else.

Jim parked halfway between the corner and the restaurant to wait the few minutes left. Checking his watch, Jim constantly watched the rearview mirror to see if his man was arriving. Just as he saw someone round the corner, the streetlight provided enough illumination for him to positively identify the man as the one he was waiting for.

Jim put on the glasses and was about to open the car door when another car slid past and parked two spaces down. The target was now only a few yards from where Jim was parked, and Jim wanted to be behind him as they got to the door.

Getting out of the car, Jim pulled the tape from the tip

and stepped onto the sidewalk a few steps behind the target. Just as they neared the restaurant door, the door to the car that'd just parked opened, and a woman with a bag on her left shoulder got out.

She stepped onto the sidewalk between Jim and his target only a few feet before they reached the restaurant door. Seeing the lightning bolt on the bag, Jim kept his distance and waited for her to distract the target. Being the only people on the street this time, Jim had wondered how he'd approach his man and not be noticed.

As the man reached the door, the lady coughed slightly to get his attention. Seeing her, he opened the door and held it for her to go in. As she passed him, she nodded her thanks and started in. Just as she was beside him, she stumbled slightly and bumped against him, causing him to reach out to take her arm.

Seeing the target's distraction from helping the woman, Jim quickly closed the short distance and raised the tip of the cane off the sidewalk. Pulling the trigger to expose the needle, he pushed it against the back of the man's right leg as he walked on past the restaurant.

Releasing the trigger, Jim continued down the side-walk, limping slightly and using the cane. Hearing a slight yelp, he turned his head just enough to see the lady disappearing into the restaurant and the man reaching around his leg to rub the spot where Jim had stuck the needle.

Jim continued down the street and turned the corner to the right. Looking back as he made the turn, he couldn't see either the man or the woman. He followed the sidewalk around the block until he was back on the street where he'd seen the black sedan.

There was no one in it as he passed and headed for his car; however, the car that'd parked in front of him was now gone. Jim opened the door and got in, wondering if the man was still in the restaurant and what the injection was going to do to him.

Later that day, the crew met in the lobby for their ride back to the airport and the flight to DFW. There'd been nothing on the news at the hotel and nothing in the paper Jim had seen driving from the hotel. It wasn't until the plane was almost full and Amber stepped into the cockpit that Jim learned the results of his mission, or at least what he thought it was.

"I just overheard two of the first-class passengers talking about someone that was supposed to have been on the flight with them," she told Randy. "He was some well-known attorney with one of the big companies here."

"What were they saying?" Randy asked, turning in his seat.

"They said that the man had a heart attack this morning," Amber answered. "Apparently, they were to meet him for breakfast, and just after they got there, the man fell over, dead."

"Well," Randy said, "I guess that just goes to prove that it can happen at any time. But at least now there's an open seat for any nonrev trying to get back to DFW."

Jim just nodded. Turning to look out the window, he started thinking about how vaguely familiar the woman at the restaurant had looked, took a sip of his Dr Pepper, and silently toasted the apparent success of his first mission for Muddy Water.